P9-CEA-779

PRAISE FOR
THE WESTCOTT SERIES

Someone to Remember

"Wistful yet hopeful, the story is a needed addition to a genre that usually celebrates the romances of younger protagonists." —*Kirkus Reviews*

"A charming novel, slowly paced and sweet, perfectly reflecting the gentle middle-aged woman at its center."
—Shelf Awareness

Someone to Honor

"A strong, compassionate heroine and a hero who learns to appreciate his worth discover the true meaning of love in this tender, perceptive, and infinitely entertaining romance that delightfully continues the saga of the unconventional Westcotts." —*Library Journal* (starred review)

"Poignant, heartrending, hopeful, and quietly profound, the latest exquisitely written installment in Balogh's Regency Westcott series is another sure bet for the author's legion of fans as well as an excellent introduction for new readers to Balogh's effortlessly elegant and superbly romantic brand of literary magic." —*Booklist* (starred review)

"This warmhearted addition to the Westcott series adds depth to a complex, congenial family." —*Publishers Weekly*

"*Someone to Honor* is classic Mary Balogh—the exquisite character development, the slow romantic angst, the clever plot, the myriad of interesting characters."

—All About Romance

"*Someone to Honor* has top-notch characters with a deeply moving story about love and family. This type of storytelling with characters whose stories suck you in is what makes a Mary Balogh novel so addictive." —Fresh Fiction

MORE PRAISE FOR AWARD-WINNING
AUTHOR MARY BALOGH

"The sheer perfection of Balogh's prose in the fifth superbly written installment in the Westcott series marries her rare gift for crafting realistically nuanced characters to produce another radiant Regency historical romance by one of the genre's most resplendent writers."

—*Booklist* (starred review)

"A story that is searing in its insight, as comforting as a hug, and a brilliant addition to this series. Another gem from a master of the art." —*Library Journal* (starred review)

"One of the best!"

—*New York Times* bestselling author Julia Quinn

"Today's superstar heir to the marvelous legacy of Georgette Heyer (except a lot steamier)."

—*New York Times* bestselling author
Susan Elizabeth Phillips

"A romance writer of mesmerizing intensity."
    —*New York Times* bestselling author Mary Jo Putney

"Winning, witty, and engaging."
    —*New York Times* bestselling author Teresa Medeiros

"A superb author whose narrative voice comments on the characters and events of her novel in an ironic tone reminiscent of Jane Austen."   —*Milwaukee Journal Sentinel*

"I loved this book. I read it in one sitting and it made me smile a lot and cry a little."   —Smart Bitches Trashy Books

Also by Mary Balogh

Someone to Cherish

A Westcott Novel

MARY BALOGH

JOVE
New York

A JOVE BOOK
Published by Berkley
An imprint of Penguin Random House LLC
penguinrandomhouse.com

Copyright © 2021 by Mary Balogh
Excerpt from *Someone to Love* copyright © 2016 by Mary Balogh
Excerpt from *Someone Perfect* copyright © 2021 by Mary Balogh
Penguin Random House supports copyright. Copyright fuels creativity, encourages
diverse voices, promotes free speech, and creates a vibrant culture. Thank you for buying
an authorized edition of this book and for complying with copyright laws by not
reproducing, scanning, or distributing any part of it in any form without permission.
You are supporting writers and allowing Penguin Random House to continue to
publish books for every reader.

A JOVE BOOK, BERKLEY, and the BERKLEY & B colophon
are registered trademarks of Penguin Random House LLC.

ISBN: 9781984802415

Printed in the United States of America
1   3   5   7   9   10   8   6   4   2

This is a work of fiction. Names, characters, places, and incidents either are the product
of the author's imagination or are used fictitiously, and any resemblance to actual persons,
living or dead, business establishments, events, or locales is entirely coincidental.

If you purchased this book without a cover, you should be aware that this book is stolen
property. It was reported as "unsold and destroyed" to the publisher, and neither the author
nor the publisher has received any payment for this "stripped book."

Someone to Cherish

The Westcott Family

Stephen Westcott m. Eleanor Coke
Earl of Riverdale (1704–1759)
(1698–1761)

Andrew Westcott m. Bertha Ames
(1726–1796) (1736–1807)

David Westcott m. Althea Radley
(1756–1806) (b. 1762)

George Westcott m. Eugenia Madson
Earl of Riverdale (b. 1742)
(1724–1790)

Mildred m. Thomas Wayne
Westcott Baron Molenor
(1773) (b. 1769)

Boris Wayne (b. 1796) Peter Wayne (b. 1798) Ivan Wayne (b. 1799)

Louise m. John Archer
Westcott Duke of Netherby
(b. 1770) (1755–1809)

m. Ava Cobham
(1760–1790)

Jessica Archer (b. 1795)

m. Gabriel Thorne
Earl of Lyndale
(b. 1787)

Evan Thorne (b. 1820)

Matilda m. Charles
Westcott Sawyer
(b. 1761) Viscount
Dirkson
(b. 1761)

Humphrey Westcott m. Alice Snow
Earl of Riverdale (1768–1789)
(1762–1811)

m. Viola Kingsley
(b. 1772)

m. Marcel Lamarr
Marquess of Dorchester
(b. 1773)

Camille Westcott (b. 1790)

Harry Westcott (b. 1752)

Abigail Westcott (b. 1794)

Anastasia Westcott (Anna Snow) (b. 1787)
m. Avery Archer Duke of Netherby (b. 1781)

Elizabeth Westcott (b. 1779) m. Sir Desmond Overfield (1774–1809)

Alexander Westcott Earl of Riverdale (b. 1783)
m. Wren Heyden (b. 1784)

Colin Handrich Baron Hodges (b. 1788)
m.

George Handrich (b. 1815)

Eve Handrich (b. 1817)

Nathan Westcott (b. 1814)

Richard Westcott (b. 1816)

Rosalie Westcott (b. 1818)

Josephine Archer (b. 1813)

Rebecca Archer (b. 1815)

Jonah Archer (b. 1816)

Beatrice Archer (b. 1818)

m. Gil Bennington (b. 1783)

m. Joel Cunningham (b. 1785)

Katy Bennington (b. 1815)

Seth Bennington (b. 1819)

Ben Bennington (b. 1820)

Winifred Cunningham (adopted) (b. 1803)

Robbie Cunningham (adopted) (b. 1810)

Sarah Cunningham (adopted) (b. 1812)

Andrew Cunningham (adopted) (b. 1812)

Jacob Cunningham (b. 1813)

Alice Cunningham (b. 1815)

Samuel Cunningham (b. 1817)

Emma Cunningham (adopted) (b. 1820)

Susan Cunningham (adopted) (b. 1820)

One

When he was twenty years old, Harry Westcott succeeded to the title Earl of Riverdale upon the sudden death of his father. With the title he inherited several properties, including Brambledean Court in Wiltshire, and a vast fortune his father had accumulated through a combination of prudent and reckless investments. Harry became head of the Westcott family, though he also acquired a guardian to manage his affairs until he reached his twenty-first birthday—Avery Archer, Duke of Netherby.

None of these new acquisitions remained his for long, however. A private investigation launched by his mother to find and pay off the bastard daughter her husband had supported all their married life, supposedly without her knowledge, resulted in what she and Harry and her two daughters came to think of ever after as the Great Disaster—they always spoke of it as though those two words would be capitalized if written down. For Anna Snow, the secret daughter, then twenty-five years old and teaching at the orphanage in

Bath where she had grown up, knowing nothing of her true identity, was *not*, as it turned out, illegitimate. The late Earl of Riverdale had been married to her mother before he wed Harry's, the present countess—and he had *still* been married to his first wife when he wed the second. The abandoned first wife had died of consumption shortly afterward, but the damage had been done for all time.

The late earl's marriage to his supposed countess of twenty-three years had been bigamous, and the offspring of that marriage had no legal legitimacy. Harry was stripped of title, properties, and fortune, his headship of the family, and his very identity. So were his sisters, the former Lady Camille and Lady Abigail Westcott. His mother resumed her maiden name of Kingsley and fled to Dorsetshire to live with her brother, who was a clergyman there. Camille and Abigail went to live with their maternal grandmother in Bath.

Harry, after getting very drunk the day he learned the news, took the king's shilling from a recruiting sergeant and prepared to join the ranks of a foot regiment about to be shipped off to the Peninsula to face the vast armies of Napoleon Bonaparte. He was rescued from such a fate, much against his will, by his guardian and sent to the same regiment—and the same destination—as a commissioned officer.

It was a tumultuous time, to say the least.

All that turmoil was so much water under the bridge by now, however, for it had happened almost ten years ago. Somehow everyone who had been caught up in those events had moved onward with their life. Most of them had prospered. Some had settled down happily to lives that were very different from anything they could have expected. But how could one reasonably expect anything of the future when even at the best and most tranquil of times it was a vast unknown? It was nothing short of amazing, in fact, how the human spirit could be rocked to its core by the most catastrophic events life could throw its way and yet steady itself and recover—and then thrive.

The title had passed to Alexander Westcott, Harry's second cousin, though he had been very unhappy about it. He had worked conscientiously in the intervening years to bring Brambledean Court back to prosperity after decades of neglect. Several years ago he and Wren, his wife and countess, had begun a new tradition of welcoming the whole family there for Christmas. Everyone loved it. This year, however, the family was not complete, for the illegitimate branch of it—which the legitimate branch vociferously refused to acknowledge as any less a part of the family than it had ever been—was absent. Viola, the former countess, with the Marquess of Dorchester, her present husband, went instead to spend the holiday in Bath with her daughter Camille and her husband, Joel Cunningham, and their nine children. Yes, the number had increased from seven during the past summer with the adoption of twin girls. Viola's second daughter, Abigail, and her husband, Gil Bennington, and their three children went there too.

So did Harry.

It was perfectly understandable, the rest of the family agreed, swallowing their disappointment. It would not have been easy, after all, for Camille and Joel to pack up nine children and an entourage of accompanying nurses and baggage for the journey to Wiltshire, especially in winter, when one could not be sure of either the weather or the roads. The Westcotts enjoyed their Christmas at Brambledean anyway, though they frequently talked about the absentees and wished they were there too.

In particular, they talked about Harry.

They were worried about him.

Major Harry Westcott had survived the Napoleonic Wars—barely. He had been severely wounded a number of times, but at the Battle of Waterloo he had come as close to death as it was possible to get without actually crossing over to the other side. His life had teetered on the brink for two whole years after that brutal, bloody day before finally Alexander and Avery had taken matters into their own hands. They had brought him back from the convalescent home for British officers in Paris, where he had been languishing, and settled him at Hinsford Manor, his childhood home in Hampshire. He had lived there ever since and had gradually recovered his health and strength. All had ended well, one might say.

His Westcott relatives would not say any such thing, however.

For Harry, the always cheerful, sunny-natured, lighthearted, beloved boy they remembered, had become a recluse. He almost never left Hinsford. It was amazing he had even gone as far as Bath this year for Christmas. He did not always come to Brambledean, and when he did, he was usually the last to arrive and the first to leave. He showed no interest in reclaiming whatever could be reclaimed of his position in society. He showed no interest in marrying and setting up his nursery and living happily ever after. It was all nothing short of heartbreaking. It was as though in ten years he had done nothing more than survive.

Most alarming of all to the family was the fact that Harry was approaching thirty. That was still young, of course, as the senior members of the family were swift to point out, but it was nevertheless a significant barrier. Thirty was a precarious age for a man who was still single and living alone and uninterested in changing either condition.

The family was worried. While Harry, blissfully unaware of clouds looming upon the horizon, celebrated Christmas with his mother and sisters in Bath, he became the focus of a number of lengthy conversations at Brambledean. Inevitably, an unofficial sort of family committee formed to *do something about it.* Equally inevitably, that committee was composed entirely of females and headed, as usual, by Matilda, Viscountess Dirkson, the late earl's eldest sister.

The men stayed above the fray. Or perhaps they merely held their peace and hoped their wives and sisters would not notice them. Avery, Duke of Netherby, maintained an almost total silence, as he usually did during family conferences, and looked bored. Lord Molenor looked amused. Viscount Dirkson patted his wife's hand whenever she looked to him as though for an opinion and smiled fondly at her. The Earl of Lyndale raised his eyebrows whenever he caught his wife's eye, but refrained from offering any opinion, at least in public. Adrian Sawyer, Dirkson's son, but not by birth or marriage a Westcott, was rash enough to comment upon one occasion that whenever he saw Harry Westcott, which was not often, admittedly, Harry always looked perfectly cheerful and contented. He said no more after intercepting grins from both Colin, Lord Hodges, and Alexander and receiving no encouragement from the ladies to enlarge upon his opinion.

The basic questions to be decided upon, the ladies soon unanimously agreed, were two. First, what were they going to do to celebrate Harry's birthday, which occurred in April, after Easter, when the Season would be just swinging into action in London? Second, what were they going to do about his single state and the sad lethargy into which his life had sunk?

But what they needed to discover first, Mildred, Lady Molenor, Matilda's youngest sister, pointed out, was whether Harry could be lured to London for the Season or even a small part of it. If he *could* be, they would be able to plan a grand party there for him. It would be relatively easy to accomplish once they had decided upon a time and place, for they would have no trouble whatsoever persuading guests to come. Harry, though illegitimate, had after all been brought up in the earl's household as his son and educated accordingly. Besides, almost all his relatives on the Westcott side were both titled and influential. And, besides again, he was a handsome young man and personable when he chose to be.

"But he always is, Aunt Mildred," Jessica, Countess of Lyndale, protested. She was the daughter of Louise, Dowager Duchess of Netherby, Mildred's elder sister. "Harry may be a near recluse, but he is never morose or bad-tempered. He is always quite jolly, in fact."

"Such a party would, of course, be held at our house," Anna, Avery's wife and the Duchess of Netherby, said. "Harry is my brother—my *half* brother, anyway—and Avery was once his guardian."

No one was about to argue.

"There could be no better setting than Archer House to make a firm statement to the *ton*," Louise, Avery's stepmother and Dowager Duchess of Netherby, agreed. "Everyone will come. And among us all we can surely compile a list of eligible young ladies for Harry to consider. He will, in fact, be spoiled for choices. Perhaps we ought to pick out three or four to bring particularly to his attention."

"But for this option to work, Louise, Harry must come

up to town," Elizabeth, Lady Hodges, Alexander's sister, pointed out. "That is by no means assured."

"Far from it," Jessica agreed. "He will never consent to come, especially if he gets a whiff of a birthday party."

"We will have to see to it that he does not suspect, then," Althea Westcott, Alexander and Elizabeth's mother, said. "But what can we say to lure him?"

"I fear there is nothing," Anna said with a sigh, breaking a short silence. "I believe my dream of hosting a party for him at Archer House will be dashed after all. If anyone knows any other man as stubborn as Harry, I would be surprised." For ten years Anna had been trying to persuade her half brother to accept his share of the vast fortune she, as the lone legitimate child of the late Earl of Riverdale, had inherited from their father. For the past four of those years she had also been trying to persuade him to take ownership of Hinsford Manor, which was legally hers, though he had lived there most of his life and lived there now. It was his *home*, for goodness' sake.

"I agree with you, Anna, much as I wish I did not," said the Dowager Countess of Riverdale, her grandmother and matriarch of the family. "Harry is very like his grandfather in that way. It is pride more than stubbornness in his case, however."

"I do know that, Grandmama," Anna said. "Unfortunately, pride and stubbornness have the same symptoms. Sometimes I could cheerfully shake him."

"What we need, then," Matilda said briskly as the committee showed signs of sinking into despondency, "is a plan B to fall back upon if plan A cannot be made to work. What are we going to do if Harry cannot be persuaded to come to London? The answer is obvious in one sense, of course. *We* will have to go to *him*. But it would all need very careful organizing. We are going to have to make *two* complete sets of plans, in fact, since we will not have the luxury of sitting together like this after we all return home next week."

"Viola will surely wish to be involved," Wren, Alexander's wife and the Countess of Riverdale, said. "She is worried about Harry too. She is his mother, after all. So are Camille and Abigail, I expect. And Viola is more familiar with Mrs. Sullivan than we are."

"The housekeeper at Hinsford Manor?" Mildred said. "Yes, she will certainly need to know our plan B. We do not want to give the poor woman an apoplexy by turning up on Harry's doorstep en masse and unannounced."

"But Harry must not know," Jessica said. "If he even suspects what may be in store for him, we will arrive to find that he has already left on a six-month walking tour of the Scottish highlands."

"Poor Harry," Elizabeth said, laughing.

"Right," Matilda said, drawing paper and ink toward her and testing the nib of a quill pen. "Plan A first. London. Grand party. Archer House." She wrote the words down and looked up, pen poised, for details to add.

Harry Westcott, all unbeknownst to him, was about to fall victim to the loving determination of his female relatives to see to it that he enjoyed his thirtieth birthday as he had never enjoyed any birthday before it, and that during those happy celebrations he met enough eligible females that he could not help but fall in love with one of them and proceed to make his offer and set his wedding date. He was going to find his happily-ever-after whether he knew he wanted it or not.

The only faint ray of hope for him, Colin, Elizabeth's husband, observed to a group of men who had retreated to the billiard room one afternoon, was that the Westcott women did not actually have a stellar record as match-makers.

"Most of us have ended up in marriages of our own choosing via weddings of our own fashioning despite rather than because of their efforts," he said fondly.

"Quite so," Avery agreed as he chalked the end of his cue and surveyed the mess of balls on the table with a keen eye. "But our women can be formidable when they grab hold of a cause. On the whole it is wiser—and ultimately quite harmless—to hold one's peace while they scheme and plan and think they have the world and its turning under their control."

Harry meanwhile spent Christmas at the big house in the hills above Bath where his elder sister, Camille, lived with Joel Cunningham, her husband, and their large family. He enjoyed their company and that of all the rest of his family on his mother's side—it included Mrs. Kingsley, his maternal grandmother, and the Reverend Michael Kingsley, his mother's brother, with his wife, Mary.

Truth to tell, Harry was glad of an excuse not to spend any part of Christmas at Brambledean with the Westcott side of the family. It was not that he was not fond of them all. He was. It was more that their obvious concern for him always made him decidedly uncomfortable. The guilt of what his father had done was something they had taken upon their own shoulders, especially his grandmother and the aunts, his father's sisters—Matilda, Louise, and Mildred. They felt somehow responsible for seeing to it that all turned out well for Harry, their brother's only son. They worried about him. He always felt compelled to be openly jolly in their company. But he could not live happily ever after just to please them. *Contentedly ever after* was not good enough for them, it seemed.

It was quite good enough for him.

He had lived alone at Hinsford Manor for four years now, at first recovering his health and strength—a frustratingly slow process—and then settling in to a life of quiet contentment as a country gentleman with a large home and farms to oversee and neighbors with whom to socialize. He really was quite contented there even though there were people, most notably his family, who could not believe it of a man who was still in his twenties. If restlessness crept in under his guard now and then, he simply ignored it until it went away, for he could think of no other way of life that would suit him better or even as well.

He enjoyed Christmas even more than he had expected to, considering the fact that it was busy and noisy with so many children. Abby and Gil had a new baby since last year, and Camille and Joel's family had expanded during the past summer to include the twin baby girls they had adopted because no one else would take them together.

Only three of their children were their own. The other six were adopted. It was a distinction that blurred into insignificance within the family, however. They were all equally Camille and Joel's children.

It ought to have been an impossibly chaotic Christmas. And in a sense it was, since Camille and Joel ran a rather informal household in which the children were rarely confined to the nursery with their nurse unless they were eating or sleeping or at their lessons—which they were not over the holiday. It did not help that both twin babies were teething and being a bit cross about it, or that Abby and Gil's Ben had recently learned to crawl and used his new mobility to disappear from everyone's sight and cause mass panic while he embarked upon unceasing explorations of his world, especially dark corners and narrow gaps between furniture. And the two dogs of the family were irrepressibly excited by the arrival of a third, Beauty, Gil's great lump of a canine, and chased and followed her wherever she went—when various children were not hanging all over her instead, that was, or sleeping with their heads pillowed on her back.

But it was also an unexpectedly good time for all of them, Harry included. An unencumbered uncle was communal property, he soon discovered, to be climbed upon without a by-your-leave and talked at and quarreled over and slept upon and, once, vomited over. He enjoyed himself so much, in fact, that he stayed to see in the New Year and then, in the middle of January, went to Gloucestershire with Abby and Gil and stayed with them a month.

He had not been away from Hinsford for so long at a stretch since before his return there from Paris. He would not have thought it possible. He would have expected to feel some panic. But he stayed away by choice and enjoyed every moment. Well, perhaps not the vomit moment.

When he set about analyzing what it was about this Christmas that had so warmed his heart, he realized that it was mainly the evidence all about him that life had worked out well for his mother and sisters. One could not know, of course, how it would have turned out for them if the Great Disaster had not happened. But Harry found it difficult to imagine that they would all be as happy as they actually were.

It was a strange realization. Did disasters sometimes happen to turn one away from a wrong course into the right one, the one that would bring the most happiness and the greatest fulfillment? Were some catastrophes not really catastrophic at all when one could look back and see the whole picture?

His mother had married Marcel a few years ago and seemed younger now than Harry could ever recall her being. He remembered her as a quiet lady of unshakable dignity and marble demeanor. Life with his father, he had realized even at the time, could not have been easy, though she had certainly been unaware that it was not a legal marriage. Now she was warm, vibrant, ready with smiles for everyone and open arms for her many grandchildren—and she was never far away from Marcel, who did nothing much to hide the fact that he adored her.

Camille had been the biggest surprise. She had been a stern, rather sour young woman—or so she had appeared to her younger brother—always very moral and upright and judgmental, and she had been betrothed to a viscount who was very much like her. Happiness and Camille could never realistically be mentioned in the same breath back in those days. Now she was vigorous and cheerful, always slightly disheveled though never downright untidy, almost always with a small child balanced on one hip or a baby, sometimes two, cradled in her arms while other children hung about her, tugging at her skirt for attention or simply enjoying being close to her. Joel, though he led a busy life as a portrait artist of growing renown and as a teacher in the orphanage school where both he and Anna had grown up and where he had met Camille, usually had a child on his lap too or perched on an arm of his chair or hovering about his easel when he painted, as likely as not washing out brushes for him that did not need washing. Yet they enjoyed an unusually close personal relationship too, those two. Not that Harry was ever able to observe them in their private apartments, of course. Heaven forbid! The happiness they shared was obvious anyway. And when had Camille become beautiful, even to a brother's eyes?

And then there was Abby, who had been about to make her debut into society when the ghastly discovery was made. She had been looking forward to a Season in London, with its dizzying number of balls and other entertainments and the prospect of meeting an array of eligible gentlemen and making a brilliant marriage. She had fled to Bath instead to live with their grandmother and had been sweet and quiet and placid and apparently resigned to her lot in life for several years after. But then, after Gil had helped bring Harry home to England and stayed with him at Hinsford for a while, the two of them had met and married. *Not* for love, it might be added. Gil had needed a wife so that he could persuade a judge to return his young daughter to him from his late wife's parents, who considered him an unfit father. It had not taken long for the marriage to turn into a love match, however. They lived now in a modest manor within a big idyllic garden close to an equally idyllic village. Gil farmed and Abby tended her garden and visited her friends and involved herself in village affairs and looked after the three children. Their happiness with each other was a palpable thing.

Harry was head of his immediate family, for what that was worth now that he was no longer head of the whole Westcott family. He had suffered after the Great Disaster as much on behalf of his mother and sisters as on his own account. He had felt so very helpless to shield them from the pain and the ruin and the bleak prospects the future had seemed to offer. He had been a mere twenty years old, for the love of God.

He need worry about them no longer. Life had been very good to all three of them.

They worried about him, though.

His mother took him aside a couple of days after Christmas, having invited him to take coffee with her in the small sitting room attached to her bedchamber. Marcel was downstairs somewhere, probably putting into practice some of the ingenious hand signals seventeen-year-old Winifred, Camille and Joel's eldest daughter, had devised to communicate with Andrew, who was deaf and mute and liked to follow his grandpapa everywhere.

Harry knew he had become the despair of his whole family because they no longer understood him. They worried because they feared he was turning into a hermit, though in fact he was *not*, and because they were still not convinced he had fully recovered from his war wounds. He had, though he still grappled with nightmares and no doubt always would. They worried because he was approaching his thirtieth birthday yet showed no apparent interest in *settling down*. Good Lord, how much further down could he settle?

"I love my grandchildren so much my heart sometimes seems fit to burst," his mother said as she set down his cup before him. "But occasionally, for sheer sanity's sake, I need to withdraw to a quiet room and shut the door behind me. I do not know how Camille and Joel do it. Or Abigail and Gil, for that matter. I daresay that is why parenting is done by young people."

"If I had been asked ten years ago what would be the perfect life for Cam," he said, "I would never, given a million tries, have described this one. It suits her to perfection, though, does it not?"

"It does," she agreed. "And Abigail. I was so very worried when she married Gil without a word to any of us except you. It seemed impossible to me that she could ever be happy with him. Sometimes I simply love being proved wrong."

"Gil is a good man," he said. Gil had grown up in the gutter, to quote his own words, the bastard son of a village washerwoman and Viscount Dirkson, who was allowed no part in his upbringing and who was now connected to the Westcott family through his marriage to Harry's aunt Matilda Westcott a few years ago—but that was another story. Gil had risen through the ranks in the army until he jumped the almost insurmountable barrier to officer status, courtesy of his father after his mother's death. He had ended up as a lieutenant colonel, one rank superior to Harry's. "I knew he and Abby loved each other, Mama, when I encouraged them to marry, though *they* did not yet know it themselves."

She took a sip of her coffee, set down her cup, and sighed audibly. "And then there is you, Harry."

He answered her merely with an interrogative lifting of his eyebrows. *Here we go,* he thought.

"It hurts my heart to see you forever placid and cheerful," she continued. "Will I never get my boy back? I begin to despair of it. When will I see you eager and vibrant and exuberant again and enjoying life to the full?"

He thought he *had* been eager and vibrant and all the rest of it, besieged by nephews and nieces and dogs as he had been for the past week, and actually enjoying himself without having to be deliberately jolly.

"If you are referring to the time before the Great Disaster, Mama," he said, "then I would remind you that I really was just a boy then. I was twenty. Do you truly want to see me conducting myself with bouncing high spirits, spouting superlatives and hyperbole with every utterance? I hope I have grown up a bit since those days. I am contented with my life as it is."

She shook her head, obviously unconvinced, and regarded him for a while with a disconcertingly steady gaze. "But I want to see you *happy*, Harry," she protested.

He grinned despite himself as a shriek of childish laughter and an excited woofing wafted in from somewhere beyond the shut door. "With a wife and six children, I suppose," he said.

"I am not sure about *six*," she protested, grimacing and then chuckling. "But yes, I would love to see you with a woman who can make you happy. With a woman whom you can make happy. With someone or something to make your life . . . oh, *vivid*. Do not shake your head like that, Harry, and don that amused, knowing expression. Love, happiness, vividness of life, *do* exist, and I am proof of it. I am living all my dearest dreams with Marcel."

His smile softened as he looked back at her. "Yes, I know, Mama," he said. "And I could not be happier about it."

"Harry." She leaned forward and took one of his hands in both of her own. "I want to see you happy with someone you . . . Oh, with someone you can *cherish*."

He cringed inwardly though he did not stop smiling. "Time to change the subject," he said, turning his hand to squeeze one of hers before taking up his cup again, draining his coffee, and getting to his feet. "Better yet, it is time to take myself off. I seem to remember challenging Robbie to a game of billiards this morning. He will accuse me of cowardice if I fail to show up." Robbie was Camille and Joel's eleven-year-old.

"Forgive me, Harry." His mother got to her feet too and hugged him warmly. "Your life is yours to live your way, as Marcel is forever reminding me when I worry about you. Let us go and enjoy the rest of Christmas."

Which they did.

Two

Much as he had enjoyed Christmas in Bath and the month in Gloucestershire, Harry was very happy to return home in February with signs of early spring all around him in the form of greening grass and budding trees and catkins and snowdrops, primroses and crocuses. For the past week or so he had begun to crave his own home and the quiet serenity of his life there.

For the ensuing week he enjoyed his aloneness, though admittedly it was not complete solitude. He spent time on the home farm, delighting particularly in watching the new lambs frolic on spindly legs about their mothers. And his two particular friends, Lawrence Hill, son of Sir Maynard Hill, a neighbor whose land adjoined Hinsford, and Tom Corning, the village schoolmaster, each came and spent time with him. Both were friends he had had since boyhood. Lawrence brought an invitation from his mother to take his potluck with them for dinner. Tom invited him to an evening of cards with some neighbors that his wife was organizing. Harry was soon feeling that he would never want to leave again, in fact. This was where he belonged and where he was most contented.

Except . . .

Well. Dash it all. Annoyingly, he appeared to have brought a certain restlessness home with him, and it could not be as easily ignored as it always had been. He kept thinking—with great satisfaction, it might be added—about how happy his mother was. And how happy Camille and Abigail were. They had each found what Harry considered among the rarest and most precious of graces: love and companionship with the men they had married. But then his thoughts would shift to himself. Would there ever be someone like that for him? That one woman in the whole wide world made just for him? How had his mother phrased it?

Someone to cherish.

He could start looking anytime he wished, of course. If he did not seek, he could not expect to find, after all. He was reluctant to go on a search, however. What were the chances he would find unhappiness instead—to be discovered only after he was married, when it would be too late to bow out and regain his freedom? Did everyone fear that sort of disaster? Of marrying the wrong person? Hadn't his mother's first marriage, to his father, proven how unhappily it could turn out?

But if he *did* want to start looking, he would almost certainly have to leave Hinsford to do it. There were a few eligible ladies within his circle of friends and acquaintances here, it was true—Rosanne and Mirabel Hill, for example, Lawrence's sisters, and Theresa Raymore, daughter of the local magistrate. Harry liked all three and believed they liked him. They were all pretty girls and doubtless on the lookout for husbands. Harry might stand a chance with any of the three if he really pushed it. He did not believe his illegitimacy would be any great hindrance. However, he felt no noticeable tendre for any of them and detected none in them toward him. Certainly it was impossible to think of any of the three as *someone to cherish.*

Sometimes he wished he had never heard that phrase. But—could he ever settle for anything less?

So any courtship here was out of the question. For there was absolutely no one else. Yet he did not want to leave home. He certainly did not want to descend upon London in the middle of a Season. But where else would he look? And when else?

He did not really want to get married anyway. Not yet. Did he?

Why could he not just forget the whole thing, then, and return to normal? But he knew why. His thirtieth birthday was approaching. Why there should seem to be such a difference between twenty-nine and thirty he did not know. But there was. A man ought to know his own mind by the time he reached his thirties instead of floating along like a piece of driftwood on a river. A man ought to be settling down by the time he reached thirty.

He was not ready to settle down.

He was contented as he was, and what was wrong with contentment, after all? He felt aggrieved at the question, though there was no one asking it except himself.

Yes, he was contented. Was he *happy*, though? As his mother was happy? As Camille and Abby were? Three out of the four of them finding happiness with the perfect life partner was not bad, was it? Did not the common experience suggest, though, that it was too much to expect that the fourth would find a similar sort of happiness?

And there he went with the pessimism again.

Harry had still not recovered from his annoying restlessness when he read a letter from his mother at the breakfast table one morning a week or so after his return. She and Marcel had just arrived home too after spending a few weeks with Estelle and Bertrand, Marcel's adult twins. They had spent Christmas with the aunt and uncle who had raised them after the accidental death of their mother when they were babies. Harry had the vague idea that their father had been largely absent during their growing years, driven by his grief to riotous living. Harry did not know the details or particularly want to. But whatever he had been in the past, Marcel was clearly a changed man now. He was, as far as Harry could see, an excellent husband and an attentive father. And a happy man, damn it.

Was the whole world happy except Harry Westcott?

But he was *contented*.

His mother's letter was full of cheerful news—until it arrived at what had surely been her principal purpose in writing. She wanted to know if Harry was planning to go to London for part of the Season, as she and Marcel were— and as Estelle and Bertrand were for the first time in a couple of years. It would be quite perfect if Harry were to come too. *Would* he?

He would not. He cringed at the very idea.

He did go up to London now and then, if there was a good enough reason—a specific family event, for example, or the necessity to be fitted for a new coat or new boots. It did not happen often and he never stayed for more than a few days, a week at the longest. He could never leave soon enough, to be quite honest. Once upon a long time ago, immediately after his father's death, when he had become the Earl of Riverdale and the instant darling of the *ton*, especially the younger element of it, he had basked in the glory of his new social prominence and had set about sowing some pretty wild oats despite the fact that he was officially in mourning. Then the Great Disaster had struck as from nowhere and the whole big party had come to an abrupt end. It was a memory he did *not* care to dwell upon.

Now, ten years later, he had no desire to go back to London or to try to recapture some of that faded glory. He probably could do it if he wished. Despite his illegitimacy, he would still be received by most if not all of the *ton*. He was just not going to do it.

But why did his life here suddenly seem so damnably dull? For four years it had been his haven. Almost his heaven.

Harry flung his napkin down beside his plate, got determinedly to his feet, and strode off to the library to reply to his mother's letter without delay and make clear to her that he had no intention whatsoever of going to London this year. He was *not* going to have her and his Westcott relatives planning some grand surprise birthday party for him, which was probably why his mother wanted to know his intentions for the spring. Nor—ghastly thought!—was he going to have them playing matchmaker for him.

If and when he decided to marry, he would find his own bride, thank you very much.

He would get this letter written and sealed, and then he would go out and find something to keep him busy and use up some energy. There was never any lack of work to be done on his farm, and he was always willing, even eager, to participate in it. There was that card party to look forward to this evening at Tom and Hannah Corning's house in the village. He would enjoy that.

But first . . .

He dipped his quill pen into the ink and attacked the letter to his mother.

Lydia Tavernor was seated in one corner of Hannah and Tom Corning's parlor, listening to the conversation of the people around her but not, at the moment at least, participating in it. She was conscious of an inner welling of contentment as she looked about at the familiar faces of her fellow villagers and of a few people from somewhat farther afield. It was not exactly a party, and was not a particularly large gathering. Lydia was even more pleased, therefore, to have been included on the guest list for what Hannah had described as "an evening of cards and conversation with tea and cake." The card games were over, and the guests were enjoying cake and pastries and tea while exchanging news and opinions and even a bit of good-natured gossip.

Sometimes Lydia felt a bit guilty about her contentment, even when it did not well up quite as abundantly as it did this evening, for she had been widowed only fifteen months ago and perhaps ought to be still prostrate with grief. It was what some of her neighbors might expect.

Her husband, the Reverend Isaiah Tavernor, had been the vicar here for only three years before his sudden death, but he had made a lasting impression upon the community both by his life and by the manner of his dying. He had been a young man—only thirty-three years old when he died—and handsome, vigorous, and charismatic. His eyes had burned with zeal in the service of his Lord and in his duty to the sheep of his flock. Apparently he had been a great contrast to the quiet elderly vicar who had preceded him, though Lydia had never known the Reverend Jenkins.

Many people had considered Isaiah a welcome change. Some, it had seemed to Lydia, had even come close to worshiping him, almost as though they had put him in place of the very God he preached about. He had worked indefatigably for his church and his people. He had died by drowning while rescuing young Jeremy Piper from a river swollen and flowing fast and furious after several days of torrential rain.

The general opinion in the days of bitter shock and grief that had followed the tragedy was that Jeremy was a bad, useless boy who had defied strict orders to stay away from the water and would surely come to no good for the rest of his miserable life. Meanwhile, he had caused the death of a man who was goodness through and through but had now been cut off from doing the work the Lord had appointed him to do. No one had thought to suggest that perhaps the Lord had appointed him to save the child's life, even at the sacrifice of his own.

Lydia's shock and grief had been absolute. She had not collapsed or taken to her bed, but she had turned totally . . . blank for days afterward, moving about as though in a dream. Or nightmare, rather. For her whole life had revolved about Isaiah's. He had always called her his helpmeet—almost never his wife—and that was exactly what she had been. His work had been her work. His beliefs and opinions had been hers. She had not known for days on end how she could continue without him.

Yet here she was now, continuing on. She was invited almost everywhere now that her official year of mourning was at an end. Most of the time, she supposed, she was invited for Isaiah's sake rather than her own, for she could not be described as the life and soul of any gathering and never had been. She far preferred to listen rather than to talk.

Though every conversation needed listeners, did it not? And in her experience far too many people preferred to talk, pausing only long enough during a conversation to be polite while someone else spoke before launching back into speech.

Not that Lydia was overcritical of talkers, especially those who just needed a sympathetic ear into which to pour their concerns, their aches and pains, or their loneliness. She was particularly kind toward and patient with those people whom others habitually avoided if they could do so without being too obvious about it—the long-winded bores and those, usually the elderly, who liked to tell the same stories they had been telling to the same audience for many years past. Lydia could always be relied upon to listen attentively and to respond as though she were hearing the stories for the first time.

No one was talking specifically to her at present. She was at leisure to listen to everyone and to look about and conclude that contentment was actually more desirable than active happiness. For where there was happiness, there was almost invariably unhappiness awaiting its turn. Extremes tended to be like that. They had a way of attracting their opposites, as though some cosmic balance needed to be restored. It was better and safer to settle for some position in the middle. Not that one could always choose, of course. Life was never that neat, nor its ups and downs that much within one's control. But . . . Well, tonight she felt as though her life had turned out well for her.

She had chosen to remain in this place after her husband's death because she liked the village of Fairfield and had grown fond of the people who lived here. She could have gone back home to her father's house. He and her brothers had certainly assumed that she would. When Papa and James, her eldest brother, had come for Isaiah's funeral and then accompanied her to his brother's home for his burial in the family plot, they had expected to take her directly home with them afterward. It was their very assertiveness, perhaps, that had pulled her out of her dreadful lethargy. It would have been so easy to allow them to take charge—of her situation, of her life, of *her*. They had been astonished—not to mention alarmed—when she had announced her intention of returning to the village and staying.

"Alone?" Papa had said. "Lydie! It is out of the question. You are not thinking straight—as how could you be? I cannot think of anything worse that could have happened to my dearest girl. Go get the bag you brought with you and come immediately, while you have James and me to give you our company and support and to protect you on the journey. The rest of your things can be sent for. James will see to everything. You must not addle your mind over it. You know this is what Isaiah would want."

Oh yes, she had known that. And perhaps for the first time it had really struck her that Isaiah was no longer with her and never would be again. She had dug in her heels and insisted upon going home. Home being *here*.

She could have stayed where she was with Isaiah's brother, Bruce Tavernor, Earl of Tilden, and his wife. They had been civil enough after the burial to offer her a home with them, even to urge her to stay, since she was their last surviving link with Isaiah. She had not been ungrateful.

"Though you will no doubt be going home with your father, Lydia," her brother-in-law had said. "If, however, you would prefer to remain here to live with Ellen and me, even if just for a while, you would be very welcome. For Isaiah's sake. It is what he would expect of us, and not without reason. We must all be proud of him, you know, even though it is difficult to feel anything but raw grief at present. He died a hero."

His own grief had been profound, and Lydia had hugged him tightly and clung while Ellen wept into her handkerchief.

Both Lydia's father and Bruce lived in mansions set in large private parks and run by a host of servants, both indoor and out. Both had offered her a life of ease and security, a balm to the great bruise that was her life. She had chosen instead to come back to Fairfield, though she had moved out of the vicarage a week after her return, of course, to make room for the Reverend Bailey, the new vicar, and his wife, who had both been unfailingly kind to her ever since. She had been fortunate enough to have been left enough money to purchase a small cottage on the edge of the village and have enough remaining with which to live modestly for the rest of her life.

Her father had declared himself lost for words, though he had somehow found plenty anyway in the letter that had arrived after she announced the purchase. How could she possibly prefer to live in a house that would surely fit into a mere corner of his own? How could she possibly choose to live *alone*? But to Lydia her cottage soon became as precious as a palace. It was *hers*, and there she was answerable to no one but herself. That fact, totally unexpected in her life, was a luxury surpassing all others.

Her neighbors had doubtless been as surprised as her relatives when she decided to stay and live all alone among them. She would not even consider hiring someone to be her companion, though her father—when he had understood that she was not to be budged, at least at present, when she was still clearly out of her mind with grief—had suggested an indigent female relative who would be only too happy to come and lend her some respectability. Lydia had said thank you but no, thank you. She did not invite Mrs. Elsinore, the cook and housekeeper Isaiah had hired to run the vicarage, to move with her. While Isaiah had lived, Mrs. Elsinore had prefaced most of what she said in answer to Lydia's directions with, *"But the reverend says . . ."* After his death she had changed that habitual response to, *"But the reverend would say . . ."*

Lydia hired no one to replace her. The house was not so large that she could not keep it clean and tidy herself. She did not possess so strong a personal vanity that she could not groom herself to look decent in company. She did not have a stomach so large that she could not feed herself, though she had never in her life had to do so until then. She discovered that she actually enjoyed cooking and baking, once she had gathered some recipes from her neighbors and done some experimenting and made a few adjustments until she was able to produce edible and eventually appetizing meals. Even dusting and polishing could be satisfying when she looked upon the results. For jobs like scything the grass and cleaning the outsides of the windows and running certain heavy errands, there was the blacksmith's middle son, a lad who was happy enough to earn a little pocket money.

Lydia was living the life she had hardly dared to dream about before fifteen months ago. She had relatives and in-laws of whom she was dearly fond and with whom she corresponded regularly, but she was not answerable to any of them. She had neighbors who were amiable and fussed over her in quiet, sympathetic ways while she was still in mourning, forever bringing her flowers and baked goods and produce from their gardens. Mrs. Piper, the saved boy

Jeremy's mother, was particularly attentive in these ways, almost to the point of being intrusive, since she always brought her offerings right inside the house without waiting to be invited and looked around with avid curiosity as she talked.

The neighbors now included Lydia in the social life of the community, both simple gatherings like this one tonight and more elaborate events, like dinners at Sir Maynard Hill's and the assemblies above the village inn, where there was music and dancing. But from her neighbors—*most* of them, anyway—as much as she valued their kindness, Lydia could withdraw to the privacy of her own home whenever she wished.

She had even acquired a few real friends over the last year or so, women like Lady Hill and Hannah Corning and Denise Franks, with whom she could visit and sit and talk and laugh. Women she could welcome into her own cottage. She had never been able to enjoy that luxury at the vicarage, where people were invited only on formal church business, organized and conducted by Isaiah and catered to by Mrs. Elsinore. Lydia had never had women friends until recently, in fact. She liked it.

There was only one thing she needed now to make her life perfect. Oh, it was not a man. Well, not exactly, anyway. She had had a man. Indeed, she had had nothing but men all her life, it seemed, ever since she was eight, when her mother died a few weeks after giving birth to Anthony, the youngest of her three brothers. She had no sisters and no grandmothers. Her only aunt, her father's sister, was estranged from him since she had insisted upon marrying a man he had considered less than respectable. Then, at the age of twenty, Lydia had married Isaiah, who had one brother but no sisters and no living mother. Lydia had not had even a sister-in-law until three years ago, when she was twenty-five and first Isaiah's brother and then her own had married. She had been married to Isaiah for a little over six years before his death.

There had been nothing but men in her life since she was eight—*twenty years ago*—until recently. She had decided during the past fifteen months that she had had enough of them, though none of them had ever been openly cruel to her. But there would be no more men—not, at least, men who would own her and have charge of her life and her very mind and person. Freedom was a wonderful thing, she had discovered. It was far too precious to give up. Ever.

Mrs. Bailey, the vicar's wife, was arranging her considerable bulk on the pianoforte bench, having been invited to play by Tom Corning himself. She was by far the most accomplished pianist in the community. Unfortunately, the instrument was slightly out of tune, as it had been for as long as Lydia had been at Fairfield, and the key of high C stuck whenever it was depressed with any degree of pressure and had to be manually restored to its position before the music could continue. Everyone listened indulgently anyway while Mrs. Bailey played and Major Westcott stood at her shoulder to turn the pages of the music and lend his assistance with the sticky key.

"Tom," he called across the room when the first piece came to an end and the smattering of applause had died down, "if you do not hire someone within the next week to overhaul this instrument and repair that key, I swear I will undertake the task myself and you will be sorry."

"He will probably saw off the key altogether, Tom, and leave a gaping hole in its place for Mrs. Bailey and others to break a finger through," Dr. Powis warned. "I would not chance it if I were you, though the broken finger would be business for me. Get the dratted piano tuner here."

"You have been threatening to have the thing tuned for at least the last four years, since I came home," Major Westcott said. "Hannah must have the patience of Job to put up with it."

"I am not such a saint, Harry," Hannah said. "I have been threatening to tune *Tom* over it for at least that long."

There was general laughter. Tom Corning and the major had apparently been close friends since childhood and were grinning at each other as they bickered.

Lydia laughed with everyone else.

No, it was not a man that was missing from her life.

It was a lover.

They were one and the same thing, of course, some might argue. But those people would be wrong. A man in her life, whether father, brother, brother-in-law, or husband, would want to own her—he *would* own her. He would also want to dominate her. She would not allow herself to be owned or dominated ever again. A lover, on the other hand, could be enjoyed and sent on his way when his presence became bothersome.

Mr. Carver, one of Major Westcott's tenant farmers, who lived a mile or so beyond the village, had come to sit beside Lydia before the music began. As soon as Tom and Major Westcott had finished calling across the room to each other, he launched into an account of the sudden and mysterious lameness of one of his horses in the right foreleg, just when there was a great deal of farm work to be done. Lydia turned her attention to him, though at least part of her mind was imagining how very deeply shocked he and all her neighbors and friends would be if they were aware of her deepest musings.

A lover could be enjoyed and sent on his way . . .

She had been the Reverend Isaiah Tavernor's wife and *helpmeet*. That was the word he had liked to use to describe her. It was as though she had had no identity of her own. She was only his *helpmeet*. For more than six years, first as a curate's wife, then as a vicar's, she had cultivated modesty and invisibility because it was what he had expected of her. Not literal invisibility, of course. Everyone had seen her, welcomed her, apparently liked and approved of her. She had forever been busy about parish business and the performance of good works, as befitted the wife of a vicar. But nobody, it seemed to Lydia, not even her closest acquaintances, had really *known* her. She had had no close friends while her husband lived. She had been too busy, all her time and attention devoted to furthering the work that was his passion. Sometimes she had had the rather dizzying suspicion that she did not know herself. Was there even a self to know? Someone quite separate and distinct from her energetic, zealous, charismatic husband?

Since Isaiah's death she had chosen to remain more or less invisible. It had been better thus while she was still in her blacks, and it was easier now so she could guard her fragile, hard-won freedom. She was known, she supposed, as the amiable, placid, even bland Mrs. Tavernor, the brave, tragic widow and helpmeet of their much-revered deceased vicar. She did not mind. At least for the present she did not.

Yet here she was, seated in the midst of a number of her fellow villagers, dreaming of a lover.

Specifically, of Major Harry Westcott.

Who very probably scarcely knew she existed.

She had never flirted with him or tried in any way to engage his interest. She would not even know how to go about either one anyway if she wished to try. She had no

serious designs on him. The chance that she would find a
lover, any lover, here in this small village was slim to none.
Actually, slimmer even than that.

But a woman could dream, could she not? Dreams were
often ideal pleasures because one could make of them
whatever one wished. And if they never came true, as most
did not and this one certainly never would, then what did it
matter? Her real life was very nearly perfect as it was. Her
dreams merely brightened it a little more.

Major Westcott was a young man, probably about her
own age. He was tall and lean—*not* thin. That was too
negative a word. Besides, his arms and shoulders and chest
looked strongly muscled beneath the well-tailored coats
and waistcoats he always wore. And his legs were long and
shapely and powerful-looking beneath his pantaloons. They
looked even more so beneath riding breeches and boots,
she had noticed on other occasions. He was fair-haired and
good-looking even if not outstandingly handsome. He had
a good-humored face, with blue eyes that almost always
smiled. She was not deceived by either his face or his eyes,
however. What had always fascinated her most about him
was the suggestion of darkness that he kept very well hidden.

Perhaps it did not even exist. His mask—if it *was* a
mask—never slipped in public, or never had when she had
been present to witness it, anyway. And he was generally
known as an even-tempered, sunny-natured man without a
trouble in the world now that he was back home after the
Napoleonic Wars in which he had fought. Lydia did not
believe it. She knew very little of his past, but she knew
enough to understand that there had been much suffering
in his life, and that it was unlikely he had either dealt with
it all or otherwise put it behind him. It was far more likely

that he had pushed most of it deep. Lydia knew all about that.

Once, very briefly, after the death of his father, he had been the Earl of Riverdale, with properties and fortune that had made him a very wealthy and socially prominent young man. He had been brought up and educated for just that life. But he had lost everything after the bigamous nature of his father's marriage to his mother had been discovered. It all must have been absolutely devastating to his family. And to him. Oh, he was treated here with great deference despite that huge change in his life. Most people here had known him since he was a child and had always liked him. He was still treated as lord of the manor, somewhat above all of them in rank. He could no longer be called *my lord* or *Lord Riverdale*, of course, but he could be and was called *Major Westcott* as a mark of their respect, even though he was no longer a military officer.

He had been severely wounded at the Battle of Waterloo and had spent years recovering, first in France and then here at Hinsford Manor. He seemed perfectly fit now and had no visible scars, but Lydia doubted his recovery was complete or ever would be. Perhaps there were wounds of war that were not entirely physical. She had no evidence of that, but she had always thought it. How could one fight other human beings to the death, witness the slaughter of dozens, watch one's friends and comrades dying, be wounded almost to the point of death oneself, and come away from it unscathed?

How did one live with memories of hell?

Why did people speak of battlefields as fields of glory? They must be as close to hell as it was possible to get in this life.

Oh, there was surely darkness in Major Westcott. Lydia could sense it. But it served only to make him more impossibly attractive to her than his appearance and outer manner already made him.

Could something be *more* impossible than impossible?

Lydia smiled to herself, gave herself a mental shake, and focused more of her attention upon Mr. Carver, who was still speaking even though Mrs. Bailey was playing again.

"Perhaps," he was saying, "he has just grown too old and is ready to be put out to pasture. Do you think that might be it, Mrs. Tavernor?"

"Perhaps he just needs to rest for a while until his leg is better," Lydia suggested.

As soon as the music had finished, Mrs. Bartlett, Lydia's next-door neighbor, approached her and smiled apologetically down at her.

"Mrs. Tavernor," she said. "I am sorry to interrupt your conversation. My daughter-in-law has persuaded me to go out to the farm with her and my son to stay for a few days. There is room in the carriage for me to go with them tonight. I have things out there and will not need to go back home first. I always welcome the chance to spend some time with my grandchildren. I will not need you to walk home with me after all, then. I know you are not afraid of the dark, but I do hope you will not mind going alone."

"But we can squeeze Mrs. Tavernor into the carriage too, Mother, and give her a ride home," her daughter-in-law protested, appearing at her side. She smiled at Lydia. "It will be no trouble at all."

"There really is no need for you to go out of your way," Lydia assured her as she got to her feet. It was indeed growing late. "I will enjoy the exercise and the fresh air after all the excellent cake I have eaten. And I really do not have far to go."

"But—" the younger Mrs. Bartlett began, while all about them other guests were also getting to their feet and preparing to leave.

"Mrs. Tavernor will not have to walk alone, Mrs. Bartlett," Tom Corning called across the room. "I'll run upstairs and fetch a coat and come with you, ma'am. I doubtless need the exercise, and you really ought not to walk on your own at night."

Lydia opened her mouth to protest. The main street of the village was not terribly long, after all, even though the Cornings lived at one end of it and she lived a little beyond the other end. A number of people between here and there would be at home with lamps or candles illumining their windows. There was absolutely nothing of which to be afraid. And then another voice spoke up, from the direction of the pianoforte, where Mrs. Bailey was gathering up the music and Major Westcott was putting it away neatly inside the bench.

"I am going in that direction anyway, Tom," he called, "and would be happy to escort Mrs. Tavernor home. You will be perfectly safe with me, ma'am. I can fight off wild bears and wolves with my bare hands."

"That would be a sight to behold," Tom said derisively, grinning as he spoke. "Do you wish to take the risk that he is merely boasting, Mrs. Tavernor?"

"Since I have never in my life seen a wolf or a bear, stray or otherwise, in this neighborhood," Lydia said, "I believe it is safe to take the chance. Though I hope I am not dragging you away earlier than you intended to leave, Major Westcott."

"Not at all, ma'am," he assured her. "Tom and Hannah

will probably be glad to see the back of me. And it will be my pleasure to walk with you."

He smiled at her. A sweet, quite impersonal, devastatingly attractive smile.

"Then thank you," she said.

Oh goodness.

Three

❧

Harry had grown up at Hinsford Manor, knowing almost everyone in the vicinity for most of his life. The arrival of new residents was rare. It had happened four years ago, however, not long after he returned from France and only a month or so after the wedding here of his sister Abigail to Lieutenant Colonel Gil Bennington. Mrs. Jenkins, the old vicar's wife, who had been a witness at that wedding, had died suddenly, and the vicar, brokenhearted and lost without her, had decided it was time to retire and go to live with his son and daughter-in-law. His son, also a clergyman, was vicar of a church fifty miles or so away. The day of Mrs. Jenkins's funeral had been a sad one for the community. That of the vicar's departure had been equally affecting, for he had been here more years than most people remembered and was much beloved.

His replacement, the Reverend Isaiah Tavernor, could hardly have presented a greater contrast. He had been a young, vigorous, handsome man, eager to serve his God and his flock with every ounce of his being. He had been a charismatic man, a burning-eyed zealot who had held his congregation in the palm of his hand as he preached, often at considerable length, the gospel of moral rectitude, sober living, and devotion to duty and service. He had lived what he preached. There had been no hypocrisy in the Reverend Tavernor.

It had not taken long for many of his parishioners to become utterly devoted to him. It was *not* that they had thought any the less of the Reverend Jenkins, some had been at pains to explain when the topic arose in conversation, as it often did. It was just that this new man was a welcome change. He stirred things up. There were those, however, like Harry himself, who had never quite been able to warm to the new vicar, even though they had been equally unable to find any fault in him. It was because they missed Mr. Jenkins, Harry had supposed. What was new was often resented. Quite unreasonably so, but sometimes one's deepest feelings were hard to shift.

No one had expected that the new vicar would stay longer than a few years, for he was the second son of an earl and had no doubt been intended for the church from the moment of his birth. He had served as a curate for a while before being appointed to his present living. But it had been very clear to all that he was destined for higher things, for a bishopric at least, perhaps even an archbishopric before his time was done. Alas, his time was done all too soon in the performance of an act of suicidal heroism when he rescued a young boy from a fast-flowing river swollen by two weeks of heavy rain. He had tossed the boy unharmed onto the bank, not counting a few scrapes and bruises and a great deal of fright, but he himself had been swept away by the current and drowned. It had taken a full day to recover his lifeless body and carry him home.

He had left behind a young widow, who had surprised everyone after his death by purchasing a cottage that had sat empty for a year on the outskirts of the village and moving in soon after the funeral. Mrs. Tavernor had been a diligent and loyal helpmeet to her husband. She had always been seated quietly in the front pew of the church at Sunday services, had busied herself with church and community duties, had led a number of women's committees, and had worked tirelessly at visiting the sick and the elderly. It was said that she had never turned a vagrant from her door without first feeding him and pressing a coin into his hand, though those poor beggars more often than not had to endure the frowns of her housekeeper and a lecture upon the temptations of sloth and shiftlessness from her husband while they consumed their soup and bread.

She had lived a life of near solitude during the year of her mourning but had gradually rejoined the social life of the community during the past few months.

Yet despite Mrs. Tavernor's four-year residence in the village and her involvement in its affairs and her indefatigable devotion to good works, it struck Harry as he walked away from Tom and Hannah's house, her hand tucked lightly through his arm, that if he were to encounter her on a street in London or some other bustling town, he might well pass her by without recognizing her. It was a startling admission. He might also not recognize her voice if he heard it without also seeing her. He had not been sure how tall she was until now, when she was walking along at his side—the top of her head reached halfway up his ear—or what exact shade her hair was or how she dressed it. Did

she wear a cap? He could not for the life of him remember.
And what color were her eyes? He could recall hearing that
she was the daughter of a well-to-do gentleman, though he
did not know who the man was or where he lived. The father had come for her husband's funeral, but Harry had
been away from home himself at the time. He knew virtually nothing about her, in fact, and had never been curious
enough to find out. While her husband lived, it had been
easy to dismiss her as a mere shadowy appendage of him
rather than accept her as a person in her own right. Since
his death she had been virtually invisible.

Harry was not proud of his lack of awareness. No one
deserved to be totally disregarded, as though their very existence was of no significance. Everyone deserved to be
noticed. To be treated with respect. To be listened to. To be
recognized as a fellow human being. During his military
years he had always made a point of knowing each of the
men under his command, down to the lowliest recruit.

For a few moments he felt a familiar clutch of panic in
the region of his stomach as his thoughts shifted to all those
faceless multitudes of men who in his nightmares marched
inexorably toward him and their deaths. Scores of them,
even hundreds, coming to be slaughtered by his own hand
or by his command to his men to fire their muskets and ri-
fles. Anonymous beings whom he had never dared think of
as people. Whom in his nightmares he could think of as
nothing *but* people—for whose deaths he was guilty, for
the suffering of whose mothers and wives and sisters he
was responsible. Yet he could not put a name or even a face
to any of them.

He turned his head to see Mrs. Tavernor's face, to im-
press it upon his conscious mind at last—and perhaps to
assure himself that yes, of course he knew what she looked

like and would recognize her anywhere. But her face was hidden by the brim of her bonnet and would not have been easily visible anyway in the darkness.

"It was a pleasant evening, was it not?" he said, aware of the silence now that they had walked away from the other departing guests. "I won three shillings at cards."

"I lost sixpence, alas," she said. "What a good thing it was—for me—that large wagers were forbidden. I shall think for days of how I might have spent those six pennies."

Her tone was serious. Yet—there surely was a glimmering of humor in her words. That was a surprise, though why it should be he did not know. But yes, he did. Humor had seemed to be totally lacking in her husband. It was perhaps one reason Harry had never quite warmed to him.

"It was, however," she added, "a pleasant evening. It was kind of the Cornings to invite me."

"Let us walk down the center of the road," he suggested. "It is smoother there. The outsides are rather badly rutted after all that rain we had a few days ago. Feel free to hold my arm more tightly, Mrs. Tavernor. I would hate for you to step awkwardly and turn an ankle. Tom would blame me, as well he might, and remind me of it for the next decade at the very least. Sometimes lanterns seem to cast more shadow than light, do they not?" He hoisted the one he held a little higher. It had been necessary to bring it from home, as he had a winding, tree-shadowed drive to negotiate after turning off the village street.

"Thank you," she said. "I appreciate your offer to accompany me, Major Westcott, though it was unnecessary. There are enough houses along here that I always feel perfectly safe walking home alone, even at night."

Harry was no longer a major. He had sold his commission a few years ago. However, most of his acquaintances, those who were not on a first-name basis with him, that was, still addressed him by that title. Perhaps doing so saved them the embarrassment of having to call him *Mister* Westcott when they had once addressed him as *my lord*.

Mrs. Tavernor had a low, rather pleasant voice. Harry deliberately took notice of it, though he could surely forgive himself for not having known what it sounded like. He did not believe he had heard her speak so many words all together before tonight. "Your cottage is a little beyond the end of the street, though," he said, nodding ahead. It was almost exactly opposite the gateway to the manor drive, separated from the string of houses along the main street and hidden from them by a thick copse of trees and a slight bend in the road. "You are not nervous about living there alone?"

"I am not," she assured him. "Who would come and bother me there? Bears? Wolves? Ghosts?"

"You have no servants?" he asked, though he was almost sure she did not.

"The housekeeper we had became quite insubordinate after my husband died," she told him. "She resented taking orders from me when she had always taken them exclusively from him. I decided I could do very well without her and left her at the vicarage for the new vicar and his wife to inherit. It was a bit spiteful of me, perhaps, but I understand Mrs. Bailey quickly established command over her own domain. Mrs. Elsinore is still there. I do not miss her services, however. I have found myself quite capable of looking after my cottage and my needs with only a little help from one of the blacksmith's sons. Reginald—Reggie. Do you know him?"

"The lad with the turned-up nose and all the freckles?" he asked. "The first lad one would suspect if there had been some mischief afoot?"

"The very one," she said. "For some peculiar reason he likes to regale me with tales of some of his more daring exploits. He has something of a storyteller's gift. He does some outdoor jobs for me. Otherwise, I manage very well alone. I am actually proud of my independence."

"I sometimes find myself claiming that I live alone," he told her. "And then I look about me and notice that I am waited upon by a butler, a valet, and a small army of other servants, both indoors and out. You put me to shame."

"Well," she said. "I cannot quite picture you bustling from room to room at Hinsford Manor, a duster in one hand, a mop in the other."

"Can you not?" He looked at her, but again all he saw was the brim of her bonnet. "Or cooking my lone lamb chop and single potato in the Hinsford kitchen?"

"When I do try to picture it," she said after a pause, "my mind presents me with a great big empty blank."

She definitely had a sense of humor. It was a pleasant discovery. Had he expected, then, that she would be no more than a leftover shade of the Reverend Isaiah Tavernor in every way? That she had no identity apart from his?

"I cannot blame you," he said. "How does one heat up an oven anyway?"

She recognized the question as rhetorical and did not attempt an answer. "You must console yourself for your helplessness with the knowledge that you are the biggest employer in the neighborhood," she said. "And not just on your farms. The whole economy here would collapse without a trace if you decided to assert your independence and do everything for yourself."

"I think I would probably collapse before the economy did," he said. "Besides, I believe I would feel very alone indeed if I had to rattle about Hinsford without even my valet for company."

"I have my dog," she told him.

That little ball of yappy white fluff he sometimes saw behind the fence of her front garden when he came down the drive, he supposed. From any distance it was difficult to tell the front end of the creature from the back or one side from the other. Only the high-pitched yips and barks with which it objected to his approach identified it as canine in nature.

"Can you get a word in edgewise, though?" he asked. "My valet does pause for breath occasionally. I am not sure your dog does."

"She does like to bark at strangers," she admitted. "She is guarding her territory, which for her encompasses my house and my garden and the road beyond the fence. She barks at me too when I have been gone for a while and she is excited to see me back. Otherwise she is a very good listener. She never answers back or scolds or lectures. She listens attentively and simply falls asleep if I become tedious."

"And do you often become tedious, Mrs. Tavernor?" he asked.

"Do not we all?" she asked him in return. "When we become too engrossed in ourselves? When complaint and self-pity creep into our discourse?"

"And what is it you have to pity yourself over?" he asked her. "The loss of your husband?" He could have bitten his tongue as soon as the words were out of his mouth, for they had been talking with a surprisingly light sort of banter. Her husband had been dead only a bit longer than a year. A little self-pity, even a lot of it, would be perfectly natural.

"I did not mean that," she said. "I was speaking in hypotheticals, Major. Isaiah died in a manner befitting his life and his faith, and a young boy lives who would otherwise be dead. It would be wrong to mourn his death by pitying myself."

They were passing Mrs. Bartlett's house and then rounding the bend past the grove of trees. Mrs. Tavernor's cottage was tucked away just beyond them within its neat garden.

They stopped outside her garden gate, and she withdrew her hand from his arm and turned to him.

"Thank you, Major Westcott," she said. "It was kind of you to walk me all the way home. I did not once look nervously about me for bears and wolves."

"You might have been very nervous indeed if one or both had put in an appearance," he said. "I would probably run in the opposite direction as fast as my legs would carry me."

She did not laugh. But in the dim light shed by his lantern he could see the way her eyes crinkled at the outer corners and somehow smiled. She *was* wearing a cap. He could see the frilly border of it forming a frame about the inside brim of her bonnet. She had a face that of course he recognized, he saw in some relief. A face that was neither pretty nor ugly. Nor even plain for that matter. It was a pleasant face. In the uncertain light he could not decide what color her eyes were—or the little he could see of her hair.

"Good night, Major Westcott," she said, and turned to open the gate.

"But," he said, "I must now prove to you, ma'am, that I am not a coward after all. I will accompany you to your door and offer my protection if any burglar or monster should leap out to frighten you."

"Oh," she said. "I believe Snowball would make short work of anyone who was not me trying to get into the house. But thank you. Maybe you will hold your lantern aloft until I light the candle inside the door."

Snowball? Well, it was an appropriate name for the dog, anyway.

Harry followed her along the path to the front door and, sure enough, the dog set up a frenzied yapping from within and came bouncing outside as soon as Mrs. Tavernor had turned her key in the lock and opened the door. It did not know whether to greet its mistress first or attack Harry, and ended up dashing hither and yon, getting beneath both their feet.

"Yes, yes, I hear you," Harry told the dog. "You are very brave to think yourself capable of saving your mistress from any villainous designs I may have upon her."

"No one has told her she is not a mighty warrior, you see," Mrs. Tavernor said.

"And no one ever should," he said. "No one should ever diminish her spirit with even the slightest dose of reality, even though, to my shame, I just tried it."

"And does that apply to all females, Major Westcott?" Mrs. Tavernor asked as she busied herself lighting the tall candle that stood on a table just inside the door, a tinderbox beside it.

"That is far too deep a question to be asking me at this time of night," he said, grinning at her back. "But yes, it does. And to all males too. We ought not to try imposing limits upon one another even when we mean well."

She turned back to him. There was light in the cottage now. It looked cozy and safe in there.

"Good night, then, Mrs. Tavernor," he said.

"Good night. And thank you once more," she said. But

as he turned away she spoke again, her voice hurried and a bit breathless. "Major Westcott?"

He turned to look back at her, his eyebrows raised.

"Are you ever lonely?" she asked him.

He stared at her, transfixed. For a moment he did not know how to answer. She was standing very still, one arm reaching slightly forward, palm out, as though she had wanted to stop him and had got frozen in the gesture. Her face registered dismay.

Was *she* lonely, then? But why else would she have asked the question?

"I suppose everyone feels loneliness from time to time," he said. "It even happens sometimes when one is in company with other people. Have you noticed? It is the price one must pay, perhaps, for keeping oneself intact. Whatever that means."

"Oh, I know what you mean," she said. "Some people thrive upon company, upon drawing everyone's attention and holding it, often by the power of their will or by doing more talking than anyone else. It is as though they derive their sense of self from crowds. Then there are the people who need to keep a greater distance from others, even if they are not quite hermits. They draw their sense of self from . . . themselves. They . . ." She paused and bit her lip for a moment. "But they are sometimes lonely as a result. *The price they pay,* as you put it."

Had she been describing the relationship between her husband and herself, however unconsciously? Whenever the Reverend Tavernor had been in a room, all attention had somehow been riveted upon him without any apparent effort on his part. He had had that effect upon people even though he had not habitually tried to dominate a gathering. If anyone else started a conversation, all eyes would turn his way to see what *he* would say in return. It would not be surprising if his wife was lonely now. She must miss him dreadfully. She was very young to be a widow. She was probably no older than he, Harry thought, perhaps even younger.

"You are still very young," he said, his voice sounding a bit stilted and awkward. What could he say to comfort her, after all? He was embarrassed. "You will surely marry again and your loneliness will go away."

She returned her arm to her side at last while her dog settled at her feet. "Ah," she said. "But I would have to give up my freedom for the dubious pleasure of gaining a husband and losing a bit of the loneliness I sometimes feel. Would it be worth it?"

Dubious pleasure?

He did not believe she expected an answer. But what did her words suggest about her marriage to the Reverend Tavernor? That it had been so perfect that it could never be replicated? Or that it had been quite the opposite and was never to be repeated? It was really *none of his business*, Harry decided. But she had aroused his curiosity.

"Is a woman quite unfree when she marries, then?" he asked. "I have two sisters who would take issue with that notion. And a mother."

"They are fortunate," she said, suggesting an answer to his unspoken questions. "But you have not married."

"No, ma'am," he agreed in a tone that he hoped would discourage her from continuing. "I have not."

"I will never marry again," she said, folding her arms beneath her bosom and hunching her shoulders as though against the chill of the night. "I value my freedom and independence too well. But they do come at a cost, Major Westcott. I sometimes wish . . . With someone who feels as

I do about marriage, that is, but nevertheless is sometimes lonely . . . I . . ." Her words were spilling out quickly and breathlessly and a bit incoherently. "Oh, goodness, I do not know what I am trying to say. Nothing of any sense or significance, I daresay. Ignore me, please. It is late."

What the devil?

What the devil?

Harry stood where he was on the path just below her doorstep as she gazed at him for a moment, stepped backward into the house, raised a hand in farewell at the same moment as she gave him the ghost of a smile, said good night again though not much sound escaped her lips, and closed the door.

What the devil? Harry thought again.

She had not been flirting with him. One could not imagine Mrs. Tavernor flirting with any man. And she was not in search of another husband. She had said so, and in no uncertain terms.

But she wanted *something*.

Had she been making him a proposition? Was it even remotely possible? *Mrs. Tavernor?* The bland, pious, almost silent widow of the zealously puritanical Reverend Isaiah Tavernor?

She wanted a *lover*?

Specifically *him*?

I sometimes wish . . . With someone who feels as I do about marriage, that is, but nevertheless is sometimes lonely . . .

By God, she *had* made him a proposition. Or started to, anyway. Until her impulsive words—for they surely *had been* impulsive—had shocked her and she had tried her best to unsay what had already been spoken and could never be recalled.

Good God!

Yes, he was sometimes lonely. Of course he was. He had admitted it to himself just lately. But was it not true of everyone? As he had said to her? He just never knew quite what to do about his own loneliness when it hit him—which was not by any means all the time or even very often.

Harry wondered suddenly if she was peering out through the curtains drawn over her front window and feeling a bit uneasy about seeing him still standing here like a statue on her garden path. He turned to leave, stopping only briefly after passing through the gate to shut it behind him.

He was not ready for marriage yet. But . . . an affair? With a willing partner? A social equal? Someone who clearly understood—and would make him clearly understand—that it was *not* a courtship and never would be? Someone close to home? At the end of his own drive, in fact?

Mrs. Tavernor?

The Reverend Isaiah Tavernor's widow?

Harry strode along the drive with incautious haste, given that it was pitch-dark and his lantern was not as effective as it might have been.

The very idea ought to be laughable. Or horrifying. Bizarre. Beyond the realm of reality. He was pretty sure, however, that she had been serious, though she had not come out and said specifically that that was what she wanted. She had stopped herself in time. There was nothing else she could have meant, though, was there?

One thing was beyond question. After a number of years during which he had been almost completely unaware of her existence, Mrs. Tavernor had suddenly become a very real person to him in the past hour—not even that long—and quite distinct from her late husband. She had come alive as a woman who valued freedom and independence, even though the price she had to pay was some loneliness and—presumably—an occasional craving for sex.

Devil take it, it really *was* bizarre. Mrs. Tavernor and sex just did not go together in his head.

But she wanted a lover.

Him.

Are you ever lonely?

Four

༄

Lydia kept herself determinedly busy throughout the following week, bustling about as though she had a mansion to run instead of a cottage. She cleaned and cooked and baked and cleaned again. She weeded the flower beds behind the house and chopped wood and took Snowball for walks in the early morning, along country lanes no one frequented at that time of day. Even so, every time she left the house, always by the back way, or came to a new turn, she peered in every direction first like a child playing hide-and-seek, to make sure there was no one in sight.

Specifically Major Harry Westcott.

The only person she ever did see was Jeremy Piper, the boy her husband had saved, who liked to slink around at all hours, often carrying what looked like a slingshot. Fortunately, he always seemed intent upon avoiding Lydia. Perhaps she reminded him of an episode in his life he would rather forget.

Lydia could not *believe* what she had said. She had actually enjoyed the walk home from the Cornings' house with Major Westcott, though she had been a bit alarmed at first at the prospect of having to make conversation with him. It had proved surprisingly easy, however. They had even joked with each other, something she had not done with anyone besides her women friends for years. It had felt lovely. So had the firmness of his arm beneath her hand and the solidity of his chest and shoulders close to her, accentuated by the capes of his greatcoat. She had not wanted it to end—and it had not ended when they reached her gate. For he had insisted upon seeing her safely inside her house.

That had proved to be her undoing. *If only* when he had turned to leave she had kept her mouth shut. But no. After they had already said good night, it had occurred to her that this was her big opportunity, probably her only one. Ever. All she needed was the courage to seize the moment . . .

So she had opened her mouth and spoken. She, Lydia Tavernor, who never spoke without first weighing her words and being quite sure she had something of value to say. *Are you ever lonely?* she had asked—and had not had the sense to stop there, though even that would have been bad enough.

Her stomach had been a churning cauldron ever since. She had been unable to sleep properly, and when she *did* doze, she had bizarre dreams that were so much like reality that she jerked awake in a panic only to find that reality was worse. Her only faint hope—*very* faint—was that she had not said enough to make her meaning clear to him.

I value my freedom and independence too well. But they do come at a cost . . . I sometimes wish . . . With someone who feels as I do about marriage, that is, but nevertheless is sometimes lonely . . .

There was no way on this earth he could *possibly* have misunderstood.

What a colossal humiliation!

Two days after it happened, she had the opportunity to go into Eastleigh, a market town eight miles away, with the vicar and his wife, who often offered to take her when they were going themselves. Lydia suspected that the Reverend Bailey did not enjoy shopping and was quite happy for the chance to sit in the coffee room of a comfortable inn while his wife had the company of another female who enjoyed looking around the shops as much as she did. Lydia spent far more than she ought, with Mrs. Bailey's full encouragement. She purchased a new ready-made dress, plain of design but of such a pretty pink fabric that she could not resist it. Isaiah had always liked her to wear sober colors, and since his death, of course, she had worn almost exclusively black and gray.

She spent most of the rest of her disposable money at her favorite place, which was fortunately Mrs. Bailey's too—a needlework shop, where she bought a supply of bright yellow wool and a smaller amount of pink wool, several shades darker than her dress. It would make a very pretty shawl. It was an age since she had last knitted. She was going to start again. The vicar's wife meanwhile left the shop with a fat bundle of embroidery silks.

Back at home, Lydia knitted whenever she could not invent something else to do—she could not concentrate upon reading. But knitting, alas, occupied only the hands, not the mind too. She tried knitting and reading at the same time, but the rather intricate pattern she was working made it impossible.

Perhaps by the next time she saw Major Westcott he would have forgotten. Perhaps he had not paid much attention even at the time. Yet he had stood on her garden path, frowning at her door—not that she had been able to see his expression in the darkness around one lifted corner of her curtain, it was true, but she would have bet the sixpence she had already lost at cards that he was frowning. He had stood there for what had seemed like an eternity.

Denise Franks, one of the friends she had made during the past year, distracted her one afternoon by calling and staying to share a pot of tea. They exchanged news and recipes, and Denise admired her knitting, which was already a few inches long, and chuckled over the bright yellow color. She had come to invite Lydia to a surprise birthday party she and her sister had decided to give for her father's seventieth birthday. She was very grateful when Lydia offered to make a birthday cake, since she and her sister were swamped with all the other preparations.

"It was an impulsive decision," she explained. "It was only when Papa told us a couple of days ago that we must on no account make a fuss over his birthday that we realized that yes, really we ought and must. He clearly expects it."

"He will scold you and be delighted," Lydia said, laughing.

She baked the cake the next day and decorated it with marzipan and icing the day after. By the time she was finished with the decorating, Snowball was restless. She had had only a brief outing before breakfast and was hovering at the door, whining. The front door.

Lydia hesitated. She had been avoiding the front entrance all week like the coward she was. Her front garden was directly across the street from the entrance to Hinsford Manor. In the past she had often been outside when Major Westcott came down the drive. She had never felt any awkwardness about smiling at him, raising a hand in greeting, even exchanging a few meaningless pleasantries about the weather with him. The sight of him had always brightened her day, in fact, though she doubted he had ever really noticed her.

It would no longer brighten her day to see him for the very reason that now he would almost certainly notice her.

Why oh why oh why had she done it? And why was it impossible to recall words once they were out of one's mouth? If she could just hide away in a hole somewhere and stay there until he grew old and died or until *she* did, whichever came first, then . . . Well, then nothing. Sometimes one's mind churned out the silliest of absurdities.

All her spring flowers were blooming merrily out there, most notably the daffodils, her favorite flower in the world. But the weeds were thriving too. The poor flower beds had never been so neglected. And all because she was a coward and afraid to go out front. Yet she had to see him again *sometime*.

"Right, Snowball," she said as she went to get her gardening tools and gloves. "Out we go. You can run around while I tackle the wilderness."

Snowball rushed out as soon as Lydia opened the door. She dashed over to the fence that bordered the copse, did her business, and dashed back again, bringing with her a stick that looked incongruously big and heavy for her. She dropped it at Lydia's feet outside the door, wagged her stub of a tail, and gazed up hopefully.

Lydia glanced across at the empty drive. Nothing and no one. She looked at the gardening things in her hands, winced as she saw the flower bed beneath the front window—it seemed even weedier without the barrier of a pane of glass—glanced back at her dog, and laughed. Why not? Good heavens, *why not*?

Snowball woofed her agreement.

"Just for a few minutes, though," Lydia said. "I do have more important things to do, you know."

She was down at the bottom of the garden ten minutes later, her back to the fence, throwing the stick yet again in a game Snowball never seemed to tire of, when she heard the unmistakable sound of clopping hooves. She darted a dismayed glance over her shoulder at the drive and saw no one riding down it. Her relief was short-lived, however. Major Westcott must have ridden into the village earlier while she was busy in the kitchen. He was returning now along the street, his horse's head just coming into view around the bend.

Foolishly, Lydia turned sharply away and pretended she was so engrossed in the game that she had neither heard nor seen him. She willed him to sneak by without saying anything. He might be just as desirous of avoiding her as she was of avoiding him, after all.

Apparently he was not.

"Good morning, Mrs. Tavernor," he called, his voice pleasant and cheerful, as it always was. Lydia looked around in feigned surprise while her dog abandoned the stick game in favor of the greater excitement of charging toward the fence, growling and baring her teeth and then barking as though she considered herself the equal of man and horse combined.

"Good morning, Snowball."

"Oh," Lydia said, all bright with false amazement. "Good morning, Major Westcott. I did not hear you coming. It is a beautiful day, is it not?" It was actually blustery and chilly. Clouds hung low with the promise of rain at any moment.

"I find every morning beautiful when I wake to the realization that I am still alive to enjoy it," he said, touching the brim of his hat with his whip.

And it struck Lydia that she had done him an injustice by thinking of him as good-looking but not outstandingly handsome. Actually he looked nothing short of gorgeous astride his horse. And virile. And several times more powerful—and appealing—than he looked when he was not riding. Though even then . . . He sat there now with graceful ease, as though he and his horse were an indivisible unit.

Snowball was incensed by them.

"There is no doubting how you came by your name," the major said, addressing the dog.

"She was a gray, bedraggled puppy with ragged, matted fur when Mrs. Elsinore found her squeaking and crying on the back step of the vicarage," Lydia told him. "She was shooing the poor thing away when I happened to come into the kitchen. I believe a vagrant we had fed earlier must have abandoned her and left without her. She looked dreadful, but after I had fed her some milk and washed her and rubbed her dry with a towel, I discovered she was white and fluffy and eager to live and to wash my face with her little pink tongue. That was early spring two years ago, and the snowdrops in the garden were just coming into bloom. I thought she needed a pretty springlike name and called her Snowdrop for a day or two. But she looked far more like a snowball, so that is who she became."

Far too much information, Lydia, she told herself. She rarely spoke at such length to anyone except perhaps her new friends. Certainly not to any man. But she had talked more than usual last week too when he had walked her home, she remembered. And in the end she had spoken *far too much.*

Isaiah had wanted her to find another home for the dog. He had not been a hard-hearted man—far from it—but he did not believe animals belonged inside a house. Definitely not his own. Lydia had defied his wishes for surely the only time in their married life.

Major Westcott looked intently at her as she spoke, and it was obvious to Lydia that today he was really seeing her. It was not a reassuring thought. She would far prefer to be invisible again. She could feel herself flushing.

"She has appointed herself your guardian and defender, then," Major Westcott said, "out of gratitude for being taken in and loved."

And oh. He smiled. Really it was just with his eyes and a slight lifting of the corners of his mouth. Not a full-on, dazzling smile. It did not matter. Her knees trembled anyway. Idiot woman.

"I have just been invited to a party in honor of Mr. Solway's birthday tomorrow evening," he said. "He will have reached the grand age of seventy, and his daughters consider it an occasion for celebration. One can only hope he will agree, since it is to be a surprise. Will you be there?"

"I will," she told him. "I will be taking a cake I baked."

"I will be walking there," he said, "since Solway's house is even closer to home than Tom and Hannah's was last week. May I have the pleasure of escorting you home afterward, Mrs. Tavernor?"

Her first instinct was to refuse. Mr. Solway lived only a few houses along the street. Besides . . . It would be ungracious, though, to tell him his escort was unnecessary. He was looking steadily down at her, waiting for her answer, while his horse pawed the ground and snorted disdainfully at Snowball, who was still bouncing around on her side of the fence, defending her territory with the occasional warning growl. The horse did not otherwise move, however. Major Westcott had perfect control over it.

"Thank you," Lydia said. "That would be very kind of you."

He straightened in the saddle. "Until tomorrow evening, then," he said. But instead of riding away immediately, he continued to look steadily at her, that half smile still softening his eyes and curving his lips. "What kind of cake?"

"Fruit," she said. "With spices. And marzipan and icing."

"I wish now I had not asked," he said. "I may not be able to sleep tonight in anticipation."

Lydia laughed in surprise at his answer and bit her lip as she stared after him while he rode off up the driveway to Hinsford Manor.

Why on earth did he want to escort her home tomorrow evening when the distance was really quite insignificant? It did not have anything to do with what she had said to him last week, did it? He was not . . . Oh, surely he was not thinking of taking her up on the offer she had not really made. He could not possibly . . . *She* could not possibly . . .

But he had looked very intently at her while they spoke.

He had said—as a joke—that he would not be able to sleep tonight in anticipation. Of eating a slice of her cake tomorrow, he had meant. But what about *her*—in all earnestness?

How was *she* supposed to sleep tonight?

Whenever Harry dared to believe that perhaps he had fully recovered at last from his war experiences, something could be relied upon to reveal to him that he had not. That perhaps he never would.

The old, annoying nightmares had returned with a vengeance during the past week, and he knew why. He had felt guilty about being essentially unaware of Mrs. Tavernor's existence for the past four years although he had seen her at least once a week at church and had even spoken to her and exchanged pleasantries with her outside her cottage during the year or so she had been living there. She had been a nonentity to him. Yet he prided himself upon his courteous attention to other people—people of all social classes and both genders. Courtesy should involve more than just amiable nods and smiles and rote comments upon the weather—and an essential unawareness of the other's existence.

For years, however, he had deliberately and for his very sanity's sake looked upon the French armies as one impersonal entity, to be obliterated from existence at every opportunity. He had never looked into the faces of individual French soldiers, either during battle or afterward, when large numbers of them lay strewn, dead, upon the ground between the armies.

Had he saved his sanity? Or had something been pushed so deep inside him that it would forever torment him?

In his nightmares he saw them. Sometimes they were still frighteningly faceless. Sometimes, even more frighteningly, they had the faces of his friends and family. Occasionally they had the face he saw whenever he looked into a mirror. He could go for days or weeks without those nightmares. And then . . . not.

He had thought that at least he had learned something from the ghastly experiences of war and from his own loss of status and identity. Concern, compassion for all. A conscious awareness of the existence and precious individuality of everyone he met. Yet unconsciously he had dismissed Mrs. Tavernor as someone not worthy of recognition as a human being.

Maybe because she was a woman? But no. In that at least he was surely being unfair to himself.

He would not absolve himself with that assurance, however. The fact that he loved his mother and sisters and female relatives did not necessarily prove that he saw all women as deserving of the same attention as men. And the fact that he had never totally ignored Mrs. Tavernor did not prove that he had therefore treated her as he ought. No woman was a mere appendage of her husband. No widow belonged in a shadow world.

Harry rode home, aware that he had looked fully and consciously at Mrs. Tavernor for the first time today. He had deliberately stopped to speak with her, though he might easily have avoided talking at all. He was well aware that she had seen him coming but had pretended not to. She had appeared flustered when he spoke to her and forced her to turn to him in feigned surprise. The poor woman had no doubt been consumed with embarrassment over the memory of what she had said to him so impulsively last week.

But he had wanted to look at her, to speak to her, to listen to her, even if it had meant embarrassing her. For if he had ridden past without speaking this time, an awkwardness would have been imposed upon all their future encounters.

She had looked rather pretty, though it was perhaps a bit shallow and condescending of him to notice that about her before all else. Would he have been less surprised by his lack of awareness of her in the past if he had discovered her to be plain? She had been wearing a blue dress, neither dowdy nor in the height of fashion, with a matching shawl about her shoulders to protect her against the chill of the day. She was slim and rather shapely. Her hair was chestnut brown, though he had not been able to see much of it beneath the white cap that covered her head and was tied neatly beneath her chin with narrow ribbons. Her cheeks had been flushed, her nose too in the cold, her eyes large with that pretend surprise, and somewhere between blue and gray in color. She had a wide, generous mouth, which did not seem quite to fit the rest of her face but nevertheless made it more pleasing.

It was actually surprising that he had scarcely noticed her until a week ago. She was a young, good-looking woman. Attractive, one might say. Why, then, had he *not* noticed her? He was as red-blooded a male as the next man. He noticed pretty women. Why had he not noticed her? Because she had been a married woman until fairly recently, and her husband had been a man of exceptionally forceful character and piety? But he noticed other pretty wives. Had she perhaps not *wanted* to be noticed? Had she been content to be the Reverend Isaiah Tavernor's shadow? The vicar's wife. The vicar's helpmeet. He seemed to recall that Tavernor had always referred to her with that word, never as his wife. And never by name. Harry thought back to Mrs. Jenkins. She had perfectly fit her role as the vicar's wife. Yet she had been unmistakably a person in her own right. The same could be said now of Mrs. Bailey.

Well, even if Mrs. Tavernor had kept herself deliberately in the shadows, Harry was not excused for not seeing her there. Especially as he had not really liked Tavernor. He ought to have looked more closely at the wife.

She had made him a proposition last week. And the memory of doing so had caused her acute embarrassment today. It would be as well to let the matter rest there, Harry thought. She regretted her words, and he had decided during the intervening days that it would *not* be a good idea to begin either a flirtation or an affair with her—or with anyone else from the neighborhood when, no matter how discreet they both were, word would inevitably get out and complicate both their lives and even perhaps trap them into a marriage neither of them wanted. One could not get away with sneezing in a village this size without at least half a dozen people who were nowhere in sight blessing one's soul. To try engaging in a clandestine affair . . .

Well, it would be madness.

Why, then, had he asked if he might escort her home from Solway's house tomorrow evening? Why was he even going to a birthday celebration he would normally have avoided? He did not attend every social function to which he was invited, after all. He tended to socialize more with his own class for the simple reason that he had more in common with them and was more comfortable with them— and they with him. He had gone to Tom and Hannah's last week only because Tom had been his close friend for as far back as he could remember.

Had he accepted this invitation because it might give him an opportunity to see and talk to Mrs. Tavernor again? And good God, she did not need to be escorted home afterward. She lived only a stone's throw away. But he *had* agreed to attend the party, and she *was* going to be there too, and she *had* consented to his taking her home.

He was not behaving rationally, Harry thought. It must be because his mind was weary from lack of sleep. He had better do some clear thinking between now and tomorrow evening, though. Talk sense into himself.

Mr. Solway was certainly surprised when a large crowd of his neighbors, having gathered first at the church, appeared all at once on the threshold of his house, all yelling, *"Surprise!"* in unison when his daughters answered the knock upon his door. Those near the front saw him first recoil in alarm, then shake his head and wag an admonishing finger at his daughters, and then smile with what looked like genuine delight as he spread his arms and beckoned everyone inside.

"If it is an old man you have come to commiserate with on his birthday," he said, "you have come to the right place. I told my girls there was on no account to be any fuss made, but I might as well have saved what little breath is left me to blow on my tea. One's children don't pay any attention at all after one passes the age of seventy. Be warned. Come right on in so that those at the back don't have to spend the evening out in the garden. Have you come too, Major Westcott?" He held out his right hand and beamed his pleasure. "This is an honor indeed."

He shook Harry heartily by the hand, and Harry squeezed his shoulder with his free hand and wished him a happy birthday and hoped he would have many more. He was always touched when his neighbors treated him with the deference he might have expected if he had continued to be the Earl of Riverdale instead of being plain Harry Westcott, illegitimate son of the former earl.

It was a pleasant, merry evening. It began, after they were all inside and the older ones among them had been given chairs and the noisy greetings had subsided, with the Reverend Bailey offering a prayer of thanks for the seventy years upon this earth that Mr. Solway had enjoyed and asking a blessing upon the celebration and the years, however many of them the Lord had allotted, that lay ahead for each of them. Then a few of Solway's contemporaries got to their feet one at a time and recounted generally funny stories of their younger years together. The church choir led a round of hymn singing, which was a little ragged without the musical accompaniment Mrs. Bailey always provided at church but was nevertheless hearty. Solway's grandchildren, who were in attendance despite the fact that several of them would be up well past their bedtime, got under everyone's feet and upon more than one nerve. And finally everyone feasted upon the savories and dainties Solway's daughters had prepared in lavish abundance and kept hidden from their father until the party was no longer a secret and everything could be loaded upon the table after two extra leaves had been added.

The birthday cake, elaborately iced, took pride of place at the center of the table. Yet Mrs. Tavernor kept very quiet about it while the guests exclaimed upon how beautiful it looked and what a pity it was that it had to be cut, and then upon how delicious it tasted, so moist and fruit filled and richly spiced, and was it not a good thing it *had* been cut and not merely kept as a decoration? Harry noticed because he had been particularly watching her—and because he knew that it was she who had made the cake. Her demeanor of quiet modesty was deliberately assumed, he noticed. Even when Mrs. Franks, one of Solway's daughters, announced that it was Mrs. Tavernor who had baked and iced the cake and thanked her for it, she did no more than half smile before ducking out of sight. As a consequence, Mrs. Franks's announcement went largely unnoticed. Most would remember the cake tomorrow. How many would also remember that their former vicar's wife had made it?

Perhaps, then, Harry thought, it was not entirely his fault that he had never taken particular notice of her either until just over a week ago. It seemed that she really did not want to be noticed. That was strange. Most people surely wanted to be seen and recognized and acknowledged. Her late husband, the Reverend Isaiah Tavernor, had always been noticed wherever he went.

Had it been the attraction of opposites with those two?

"A penny for them, Harry, my lad?" Tom Corning slapped a hand on his shoulder. "You look as if your mind is a million miles away. Which may not be a bad thing. It may be less congested there than it is here. Can you imagine living for seventy years?"

"My grandmother will be eighty next year," Harry told him.

"No!" Tom said. "The dowager countess? Is she aiming for a hundred?"

"It would not surprise me," Harry said. "Every time death comes calling, she probably gives him the evil eye and he slinks back where he came from to wait awhile longer."

Tom laughed.

At a certain point in the evening, as usually happened at such gatherings, someone decided it was time to leave, and put the decision into effect without any fuss or fanfare, yet somehow set off everyone else too, with the result that everyone was suddenly standing and there was a flurry of voices calling for children and spouses and coats and shawls and gloves, while other voices were raised in goodnight greetings to one another and renewed birthday wishes to Mr. Solway and thanks to his daughters. A great deal of hand shaking and backslapping and cheek kissing and hugging proceeded in Mr. Solway's vicinity and then everyone was spilling outdoors more or less together and calling out to one another again with yet more farewells and last-minute messages and then dispersing to their various homes, most of them on foot, a few who lived beyond the village in gigs and chaises.

Solway looked sorry that it was over, Harry thought as he stepped outside, one of the last to leave, as the old man had wanted to wring his hand once more and thank him again for condescending to come and make his birthday party even more memorable than it would otherwise have been.

Harry half expected that Mrs. Tavernor would have set out for home alone, especially as her house was so close. But she was still outside the door, hugging each of Mrs. Franks's three children, who were about to be hauled unwillingly home by their father while their mother and their aunt remained behind to tidy the house.

Mrs. Tavernor waved the children on their way, turned to Harry, and fell into step beside him as they made their way along the street. No one seeing them would make anything of it, he thought. They were just two neighbors taking the same direction home for a few steps before their paths diverged.

He had better make sure there was no more to it than that.

Five

❧

"Mr. Solway enjoyed himself even though he told his daughters he wanted no fuss made of his birthday," Mrs. Tavernor said. She had clasped her hands behind her back beneath her cloak and thus discouraged Harry from offering his arm.

"He did," he agreed. "He likes to pretend to be a crotchety old man, and I daresay he will grumble to his long-suffering daughters, but he loved being the focus of everyone's attention. Your fruitcake, by the way, was fully appreciated. It was the best I have ever tasted."

"You are kind," she said. "But you flatter me. I have had very little experience as a baker. I do know, though, that a fruitcake ought to be baked considerably sooner than two days before it is consumed. The spices need time to blend together and pervade the whole, and the fruit needs time to moisten and enrich the cake. However, I had very little advance notice. I did the best I could under the circumstances."

"Your best was actually better than that," he said.

She turned her head to look at him. "My cake was better than the best?" she said. "How very reassuring. And how grammatically illogical."

He laughed. He liked her quiet flashes of humor. He had no doubt most of his neighbors had no idea she was capable of them.

Her cap this evening was trimmed with a double border of delicate lace. He had noticed every detail of her appearance tonight: the neat, modest dress—long sleeved and high waisted, with a plain round neck, lavender in color—her gray shawl, the cap. She wore it now beneath her bonnet, to very pretty effect, it might be added.

Now there was a decision to make. There really ought *not* to be. He had told himself that quite firmly just a few minutes ago.

They walked past the copse of trees and around the curve in the road to stop outside her gate. It was not too late simply to see her to her door as he had the last time, bid her good night as soon as she was safely inside with a candle lit, and continue on his way home. No harm would have been done. He would merely have shown her the sort of neighborly courtesy any other man would have. She surely had no real expectation of more. She had not been specific last week and had immediately wanted to take back what she *had* said. He had not been specific yesterday morning. She probably would be relieved if he took this unspoken thing between them no further, and he would be saved from doing something he would almost certainly regret.

Alas, good sense did not prevail.

"Will you invite me inside?" he asked even before they stepped beyond the gate. "For a cup of tea, perhaps?"

She turned to him and raised her eyebrows, though in the near darkness—he had not lit his lantern when he left

Solway's house, having planned to light it from her candle—it was impossible to read the expression on her face. There was a moment of silence before she answered.

"I did not bake today," she said.

Was that a no?

"I have already eaten far more than I ought," he said, "including a very generous slice of your birthday cake."

She turned back to the gate without another word, opened it, went through, and continued along the path to her door without shutting the gate behind her.

Was that a yes?

He stepped in after her and closed the gate. She had the door open by the time he caught up to her and she was bending to pat the dog, which had come dashing out to greet her with excited yips before turning its ire upon Harry.

"I know," he said. "You are a fierce guard dog even if you *do* look like a mere bit of fluff. I am in fear and trembling."

The dog barked again, decided that Harry was to be tolerated even if not welcomed, and turned to trot back into the house. Harry chuckled and stepped inside after Mrs. Tavernor, who was busy lighting the candle. He shut the door while she removed her bonnet and cloak, hung them up, and went to light two more candles on the mantelpiece in the living room. Then, still without looking at him, she disappeared through an archway into what he could see was the kitchen, where she poked the fire that had been banked in the range, built it up, and set the kettle over the heat to boil. Harry did not move from where he stood or offer to help.

Neither of them had spoken a word since they were outside the gate.

There seemed to be a bit of a shortage of air in the house.

Harry had never been gauche or uncomfortable with women. But then he could not remember a time when he had been completely alone in a house with a respectable female, especially late in the evening when both of them were aware that they were considering having an affair.

She was the first to break the silence. "The kettle will not take long," she called. "The water has been keeping warm while I have been away."

Harry had never seen the inside of the house before, though he must have passed it hundreds of times. The dressmaker who used to live here had retired when he was still a boy and become something of a recluse, though she had always nodded and smiled sweetly at him and his sisters when she saw them go past. She had died a couple of years or so ago.

It was a well-designed house, furnished for comfort as well as elegance. The living room looked inviting and cozy. There was a workbox on one side of the chair by the fireplace, a knitting bag on the other. Two needles poked out of the top of the latter, displaying something soft and warm-looking and sunshine yellow. There were three books rather haphazardly spread on one cushion of the sofa facing the fireplace. Two of them had well-worn leather covers. The third looked newer. Cheerfully bright and pleasingly mismatched cushions were strewn against the backs of the sofa and the two chairs. Those on the chair that was obviously her favorite had not been plumped when she last got up from it.

She was tidy, then, but not fanatical about it.

She came to stand in the archway, and Harry realized he was still just inside the door, wearing his coat, with his hat clutched in his hand. He would give anything, he thought at that moment, to be striding alone up the drive to his house.

It had been a cardinal rule of his mother's—one with which he had always concurred without question—that one did *not* become sexually or even romantically involved with anyone who lived within five miles of Hinsford Manor. *Not* unless she—or *he* in the case of his sisters—was being given serious consideration for matrimony. That, of course, had been in the days when his mother was the Countess of Riverdale and he was heir to the earl's title and his sisters were *Lady* Camille and *Lady* Abigail Westcott. His status had changed since then, but he had continued to observe the rule.

One's reputation was a precious commodity and virtually impossible to retrieve once it was lost. That would apply doubly to Mrs. Tavernor, of course. A man's reputation was usually more durable than a woman's. But not much more in a village like this.

Yet here he was.

They looked at each other, and he wondered if she was having similar thoughts. But how could she not be? She was not only a woman. She had been the vicar's wife. Briefly he considered flight.

"Major Westcott," she said, "will you have a seat?"

He did not move immediately. Then he took off his greatcoat and hung it, with his hat, on an empty hook beside her cloak and turned to look into the room. She had not told him *where* to sit. He considered one of the chairs, the one that was not hers, but then chose the sofa instead after first stacking the books on the table beside it.

The newer book was a Bible.

He waited to see where she would sit. But the kettle was beginning to hum and she returned to the kitchen.

"I do beg your pardon after just inviting you to be seated," she called a few moments later, "but would you be good enough to light the fire, Major Westcott? It is made up ready. All it needs is a spark."

All it needs is a spark. Unfortunate choice of words. And was it really cold enough in here to make a fire necessary? Harry felt quite warm enough. A bit *too* warm.

He got up to do her bidding. He remained on one knee to make sure the spark had caught the kindling and would spread to the wood. Soon he could feel a thread of warmth against his face. He could hear the clinking of china as she came back in from the kitchen, and he rose to his feet to take the tray from her hands. There was a teapot covered with a knitted cozy and two cups and saucers of fine bone china with a matching milk jug and sugar bowl and two silver spoons. He set the tray down on the low table before the sofa and resumed his seat while she poured their tea, standing on the other side of the table while she did so.

Neither of them spoke—again. Firelight and candlelight flickered behind her.

When she straightened up, she looked at him, her face in shadow, and he was aware that she was hesitating. Her chair was to one side of the hearth behind her. The sofa had only two cushions upon which to sit. It was actually more a love seat than a sofa. Then she came around the table and sat beside him, and half the remaining air went from the room, and that fire had surely warmed to an inferno. Their shoulders did not quite touch, but he felt her closeness as a physical thing. She smelled of a faintly floral soap or perfume. It was an enticing scent, whatever it was.

The dog, which had followed its mistress everywhere, stood in the narrow space between them and the table and eyed Harry through the white fluff that almost hid its eyes before yipping a halfhearted threat and plopping down across one of her slippers. It did so in such a way, however, that it could gaze up at Harry to make sure he behaved himself.

He felt a bit as though there were a chaperon in the house after all—and one who was not about to tolerate any nonsense.

"It is still a little chilly in the evenings without a fire," Mrs. Tavernor said, breaking the lengthy silence at last. Her voice was stilted and just a bit too loud.

"Yes," he agreed, his own voice far too hearty. "It is."

The conversation—*what* conversation?—threatened to die a well-deserved death.

"Major Westcott—" she began again, arranging her cup and saucer before her.

"It is Harry," he said.

"Oh." She turned her head to glance at him before biting her lip and looking away again. "I am Lydia."

It suited her, he thought. He did not know anyone else of that name.

"Harry," she said, "I do not know quite what this is about."

Neither, God help him, did he. Though they both knew only too well. Actually he had no idea why he was behaving so much like a gauche schoolboy.

"Perhaps," he said, "it would be as well if you were to think of me just as a neighbor whom you have been kind enough to invite inside for a cup of tea before he walks home along a dark, winding drive."

"Is that what it is?" she asked.

Yet even that would be improper.

"If you choose," he said. "It can be anything you wish it to be. It could be the beginning of a closer acquaintance than we have yet had. Even a friendship. Or it could be the beginning of something else. Whatever you wish."

"Something else," she said, and frowned down into her

cup. "What does that mean, Major Westcott?" But she held up a hand, palm out, before he could answer and turned to look fully at him, still frowning. "That was an unfair question. And a stupid one too, for after all I am the one who started all this last week. Whatever *all this* is. Oh dear, I—"

She stopped and drew a sharp breath.

It was time for some plain speaking.

"You made it clear on that occasion," he said, "that you do not wish for a second husband. Not yet, at least. You are happy here in this cottage in this village with your freedom and your independence, and I cannot blame you. Sometimes it must be hard to be a woman, or so I would imagine. But there are needs all of us share, men and women alike, cravings it is hard to deny and not so easy to satisfy—especially for an unmarried woman. Perhaps you believe you have detected a kindred spirit in me since I too live alone and am single. Perhaps finding yourself unexpectedly in company with me that night gave you the idea to broach the possibility of a mutual understanding, though you lost your courage before you could be fully specific. I do not believe I misunderstood your meaning, however, Lydia. You want a lover. Perhaps I do too. Perhaps that is why I asked to be invited in tonight and why you did invite me."

"Did I?" she asked him. But she answered her own question before he could. "Yes, of course I did, but I did not want the responsibility of having done so. I left the gate open."

Even in the flickering light of the fire and the candles he was aware that her cheeks had flamed red. But to her credit she had admitted the truth and she did not look away from him. Neither did she stop frowning.

"It seemed like such a splendid idea when I was simply dreaming it," she said. "But when I was presented with the unexpected opportunity to actually say it, I realized how totally outrageous and unthinkable it was. I hoped I had stopped before you understood, but of course I had not. I am mortified. Oh, what a colossal understatement. I am sorry."

"Sorry you made the suggestion?" he asked her. "Or sorry that I understood it and asked you to invite me in tonight?"

"I—Oh, I really do not know what to say," she protested—and smiled so unexpectedly that Harry moved his head back an inch. Good God, she looked suddenly vivid and very pretty, that prim, lacy cap notwithstanding. "I keep waiting and hoping to wake up, actually. I am so dreadfully embarrassed."

"You need not be," he said. "I am flattered that you focused your dream upon me."

She laughed and bit her lip again. That wide mouth, he thought, would be lovely to kiss. How the devil had she kept herself so virtually invisible all these years? That it had been at least partly deliberate he no longer doubted.

"I find that hard to believe," she said.

"Why?" he asked. "Lydia, you must not underestimate yourself. If we are to have an affair, it will be between equals. Neither of us will be condescending to the other. Neither of us will be inferior or beholden to the other. Or superior either and merely conferring a favor."

"An affair." She did what he had done a few moments ago. She jerked her head back a fraction and then looked down at the hands spread across her lap, her eyebrows raised. Her vivid smile was long gone. "That sounds awfully . . . wicked."

The dog had nodded off to sleep and was snoring slightly. It looked like a large white pompon on her slipper. Some chaperon.

"It is by no means inevitable," he told her. If he were to press matters now and they ended up in bed together, they might be forever sorry. They *would* be, surely. They would find it impossible to face each other tomorrow and forever after. They were just not ready, if they ever would be. "I can drink my tea and go on my way, and we can forget the whole thing."

She attempted to raise her cup from the saucer, but her hand was shaking. She set it back and put both cup and saucer on the table beside the tray.

Harry drew a slow breath. "We do not even know each other, do we?" he said. "Though we have been acquainted for several years. I suppose you know some basic facts about me. And I know that you were the wife of the Reverend Isaiah Tavernor and are now his widow. I have heard that you are the daughter of a gentleman of some substance. That is all I know, though. Perhaps before we make any decision neither of us seems quite ready to make we ought to learn more about each other and find out if we can be in any way comfortable together. If we can *like* each other at the very least. Tell me about yourself. Or is that too broad a request? Tell me who you were before your marriage."

She sat back against one of the bright cushions and spread her hands in her lap again. They were bare except for the narrow gold band of her wedding ring. Her fingernails were short and neatly kept.

"I was Lydia Winterbourne," she said. "My father is indeed a gentleman of property and fortune. He likes people to know that his grandfather was a viscount. I have three brothers, two older than I, one younger. The eldest was married two years ago. I have met my sister-in-law only once, at their wedding. Isaiah took me. My mother died when I was eight. She never fully recovered from giving birth to my youngest brother. My father has never remarried."

"It must have been hard," he said, "growing up as the only female in a house full of men. Or was it not hard at all? Were you the much adored treasure in their midst?"

She thought about it. "Both," she said. "I was loved, even adored, to use your word, and sheltered from all harm. From the wicked world of men, that is. My father and James and William, my elder brothers, were all united in agreeing that it was very wicked indeed. I loved them dearly in return—I still do—and appreciated both their undoubted affection and their determination to keep me from all harm. Sometimes, though, especially as I grew older, I found it all more than a bit irksome and longed to break free."

Hence the fact that she coveted her freedom now?

"You did not think of returning to your father's home after your husband's passing, then?" he asked her.

"Oh, they wanted me to go," she told him. "All of them. My father and James came here for the funeral, as did Isaiah's brother, and then accompanied me to his burial. Perhaps you remember?"

"I was away from home at the time, I regret to say," he told her. "I was visiting my grandmother and her sister, my great-aunt, who lives with her. She—my great-aunt, that is—was ailing at the time and my grandmother was very much afraid she would not recover. I stayed until she rallied and began to get better."

"They fussed and blustered and bullied, all three of them," she said. "Though the word *bullied* is a bit unfair, for they had my best interests at heart, or what they thought were my best interests. I could not go back to my father's house, though. I simply *could* not. And though my brother-in-law has always been kind, both he and his wife are nevertheless virtual strangers to me. It was good of them to offer me a home, but there was never any question of my accepting."

"You do not like being looked after?" he asked her.

She gave the question some thought, and it seemed to Harry that perhaps this was characteristic of her, not to chatter on about anything and everything but first to consider what she wished to say. Though she had spoken without due consideration just over a week ago, had she not?

"I do," she said. "Of course I do. Who does not like being cared for? But only if it is a reciprocal thing. Only if I can care for you as much as you care for me." She darted him a pained glance. "I ought to have used the pronoun *one* instead of *you* and *me*. I was not speaking specifically—"

"I understood your meaning." He reached out and covered one of her hands with his. His awareness of her became instantly more physical. It was a warm, soft, very feminine hand. "And I know how you feel. I can recall the time when I was brought home from the convalescent home in Paris—by my brother-in-law, my cousin, and my best friend, a fellow officer—still as weak as a newborn kitten and wholly unable to look after myself. My family descended upon me en masse and proceeded to *fuss*. You would not remember. It happened a short while before you came here with your husband. I appreciated their concern and also resented it—not, as I thought at the time, because I wanted to be left alone, but because they made me feel even more helpless than I already was. There was nothing I could do for *them*, you see."

"You must have been very badly wounded at the Battle of Waterloo," she said, "if you were still almost incapacitated two years later."

"I was," he said curtly. "There were times when I almost

wished I had been killed outright, but those times were rare. Life is always precious. And my mother and sisters, my grandmothers too, would have been devastated by grief if they had lost me."

"You were not intended for a military life, were you?" she asked.

"No," he said. "I was brought up to be the Earl of River-dale after my father. When I lost the title and all that went with it, I reacted with all the maturity of a bitterly disappointed twenty-year-old and got myself very drunk. I went and took the king's shilling from a recruiting sergeant and prepared to go to war as a private soldier. I was furiously annoyed when my guardian, now my brother-in-law, found me, persuaded the sergeant to take the shilling back—*not* an easy thing to do—and purchased a commission for me instead. When I did go off to war, it was as an infantry officer."

"Was it dreadful?" she asked.

"Yes," he said. "And no."

"You do not like to talk about it," she said.

His hand was still on top of hers in her lap. She was as aware of it as he was, he knew. Her own hand was very still and a bit stiff. He curled his fingers around it into her palm. He continued to look into her face but did not answer what had not really been a question.

"How did you come to marry your husband?" he asked. "Was he a clergyman at your church?"

"He was a curate at the time, though not at our church," she said. "But he was intended for far greater things. He had been groomed from birth for an ecclesiastical career and he gave himself to the life wholeheartedly. He was dedicated and ambitious. He was also full of genuine zeal and faith and energy. And terribly handsome. He was at university with my brother James. They remained friends afterward, and he came on a visit when I was twenty. I am not sure if he was brought there as a potential suitor for me. There had been a few others over the previous two or three years, all carefully selected. My father was a bit dubious about the lowliness of Isaiah's position at the time, but of course he was the son of an earl and actually the brother and heir of the current one, and it was clear he was destined eventually for a position in the upper echelons of the church hierarchy. It did not matter to me anyway. I fell headlong in love with him. We were married two months after we met."

"It must have been a terrible blow to you to lose him so young," he said. A master understatement. How could it not have been? *I fell headlong in love with him.*

She half smiled and changed the subject. "The tea has grown cold," she said.

She was as reluctant to talk about her marriage and its tragic ending as he was to talk about his military career, then. That was fair.

"Lydia." He lifted her hand to his lips and kissed the backs of her fingers. "Shall we take things slowly? Or even— Would you rather end it now? It is quite all right if you would."

"Is it what you wish?" she asked.

He ought to say yes and get out of here. But . . . He did not really want to. Not yet. He did not generally consider himself to be lonely—and quite possibly would not think so now if he had not recently spent a month and a half surrounded by family members who were anything but lonely, dash it all.

"I would suggest we get to know each other," he said, "and make decisions about our future relationship as they become necessary. *If* they become necessary."

Her cheeks flushed again as she gazed back at him. "I think," she said, "it would always be wrong."

"To be friends?" he asked her.

"No," she said. "To be . . . lovers."

"Shall we try friendship instead, then?" he asked. "There is no hurry to take it further than that, is there? Tell me, who chops your wood?"

She looked at him in blank mystification. "I do," she said.

"Let me come tomorrow," he said, "and chop a load for you."

"But that would lay an obligation upon me," she said.

Ah. Her need for independence.

"You may do something for me in return, then," he said, turning his head to look at the bag beside her chair. "I assume you are a knitter. You may knit me a scarf. The only one I own is very nearly threadbare."

Her eyes filled with sudden laughter. "When summer is coming?" she said.

"A British summer," he reminded her. "Will you? Or is that an unequal favor? Will it lay too heavy a returning obligation upon me? I would provide the wool, of course."

"Black?" she asked. "Gray? And *I* would supply the wool. I daresay you would not know what to choose that would not rub your neck raw."

"How about scarlet?" he suggested. "Or yellow?" He tipped his head toward the bag. "What *is* that, by the way?"

She laughed. A delightful sound that did something to his stomach. "It is Timmy's sunshine," she said.

"Of course it is," he said. "I am sorry I asked."

She laughed again. "Timothy Hack," she explained. "A little seven-year-old who has a weak chest and has been bedridden for almost two years now."

"Daniel Hack's child," he said. "Dan is one of my gardeners."

"I know," she said. "I know too that you brought a physician all the way from Eastleigh a while ago when Dr. Powis admitted he was baffled. And you paid for the medicine that was prescribed. These things do not go unnoticed in the village."

"What is Timmy's sunshine?" he asked.

"I took him some sweet biscuits in the shapes of various animals a month or so ago," she told him. "We had some fun while he tried to identify them. He did not have a great deal of success, which fact reflected more upon my artistic skills, alas, than it did upon him. He thought the horse was a fox. But he was dreadfully pale and listless most of the time I was there, and his room was dark with the curtains drawn across the window. And stuffy because the window was shut tight. Nothing in the room had any color. He told me that what he wants more than anything else when he gets better is the sunshine. I cannot take him that, alas, though I do hope that when the weather gets warmer he will be carried outside some days to feel the sun's rays on his skin. What I *can* do, though, is knit him some substitute sunshine. It is a blanket, small enough not to weigh him down, large enough to cover his legs and even be pulled up to his chin if he wants extra warmth without exposing his feet to the cold. When it is finished I am going to embroider his name across the top band in red, green, blue, orange, and purple letters. It is going to be downright *garish*. And I am going to buy him a book I saw the day I purchased the wool in town. It is full of adventure stories for children, and it has pictures."

"Dan cannot read," he said. "I doubt Mrs. Hack can either."

"But Timmy can," she said. "Isaiah taught him when he was just five. And he gave him a Bible and a book of moral tales for children to practice on."

Harry smiled at her. "I will find out from the physician if fresh air and sunshine—the real outdoor sunshine—will be good for Timmy," he said. "I cannot imagine they would not be, but who am I to claim to know for certain? If the doctor says yes, then I will have a word with Dan."

"Thank you," she said. "Come and chop my wood, then, if you must, but on one occasion only. You will not then have to make an exhibition of yourself by wearing a scarf of my making in July."

"Oh, but I must have the scarf. I will not chop your wood otherwise," he said, getting to his feet and grinning at her as she got to hers.

She laughed again, and he crossed the room and pulled on his greatcoat. He lit his lantern from the candle by the door, put on his hat and gloves, and turned to take his leave of her.

"Good night, Lydia," he said. "Thank you for the tea. Oh, we did not drink it, did we? Well, thank you for the conversation. Anything but pink for the scarf. Though preferably not black or gray either. Too . . . staid." He grinned at her again. "Why should Timmy have the sunshine while I have to make do with the rain clouds?"

"Good night, Harry," she said. "You really must not feel obliged to come here to chop wood tomorrow, you know. I am quite capable of doing it for myself."

"I do not doubt it," he said, and leaned forward to kiss her cheek before opening the door to let himself out. Her cheek was warm and smooth and smelled of that soap or perfume he had noticed earlier. Her dog, which had been pitched off her slipper, was yapping at him, since clearly it was his fault that its sleep had been disturbed.

Perhaps, he thought as he made his way home, Lydia Tavernor really did not want him to go back there. It was what he should want too—or *not* want. Something had started between them last week and continued into this evening, however, and neither of them seemed to know if it was something they should encourage or . . . not.

The biggest surprise for him was that he found her attractive. *Very* attractive, actually.

He had promised to return tomorrow morning.

To chop wood for her, for the love of God.

In return for a red or yellow scarf or some other color that was not black or gray or staid. Or pink.

Six

❧

Lydia was in the kitchen, baking ginger biscuits and hovering over the oven more than was necessary. She was also glancing through the window more than she ought, though she did stand a little to one side as she did so, half hidden behind the curtain, so she would not be spotted. Not that he was ever looking her way. He was too busy.

Major Harry Westcott was chopping wood. Really quite a vast pile of it. Not just a one-day supply, which was all she could seem to achieve for herself before running out of energy, but enough to last her a week at the very least. And he was showing no sign of being finished yet.

Lydia had tried to persuade herself that he would not come. So she would not be disappointed if he did not, perhaps? She had also tried to persuade herself that she did not *want* him to come. Last evening ought to have convinced her beyond any doubt that the whole idea of having an affair with him, or with anyone else, was out of the question, not to mention outrageous. She could not remember ever spending a more uncomfortable hour than the one she had spent seated beside him in her living room. Especially—*oh goodness*—when he had covered her hand with his own and then actually curled his fingers about it. And when he had kissed her fingers and then her cheek as he was leaving.

He was too much—vastly too much—for her to handle, she had thought as she had peeped about her curtain and watched him walk away, his lantern swaying from one raised hand. It would be like trying to contain a hurricane or a tornado.

Oh no, she had not wanted him to come back. He was threatening to make her life unbearably . . . what? Alive? And *carnal*. And dangerous. There were too many complexities to him. She *knew* there were. He was not as sunny natured and even tempered as he always appeared to be, or at least he was not either of those things through and through. She had sensed it before, but last evening she had *known* it. She had known it from his silences. And from his clipped answer when she had observed that his war experiences must have been dreadful. *Yes,* he had said. *And no.* And there had been something in his eyes, in his voice. Something she had shied away from. She had not wanted to know more. She had been afraid. Was that the right word—*afraid*? Her life had been too bland for too long a time, too structured, too predictable.

He was none of those things.

Then there was the fact that he was so *attractive*. So good-looking, so tall and broad shouldered. So . . . *masculine*.

She was just plain afraid to move out into the sun. Or, just as likely, into the storm. Ah, but she wanted sunlight in her life. And excitement. But did she dare? Would she ever dare? Such contradictory thoughts and emotions had teemed through her mind all night. She had woken from a troubled sleep, hoping he would not come—and dreading that he might not.

He *had* come. And how had she proved that she had hoped he would not? Well, when his knock had sounded upon her back door, she had dropped her knitting in the middle of a stitch, shot to her feet, and rushed to open it lest he think she was away from home and leave before she could get there. Yes, she really had behaved that way.

It was impossible now to keep her eyes off the window for longer than a minute or two at a time—or to move out of the kitchen at all. The weather had turned suddenly warm overnight, as sometimes happened in springtime. By now—it was ten o'clock, Lydia saw with a glance at the clock on the sideboard—the sky was clear, the sun was shining, and Major Westcott was in his shirtsleeves, having abandoned both his coat and his waistcoat. And his sleeves were rolled up to the elbow.

He was *suffocatingly* attractive. And overwhelmingly masculine. Her mind was beginning to repeat itself.

She turned from the window to take the biscuits out of the oven. She should go and do some more knitting, always soothing to the nerves. She really did need to rescue that stitch she had left stranded between two needles and in danger of becoming enlarged beyond repair. Instead, she glanced outside again. He was stretching, one hand spread over his lower back, the other clasped about the handle of the axe, the head of which was resting on the ground. His buff-colored breeches were skintight and showed off long, shapely, well-muscled legs. His black top boots were old and supple but obviously well cared for. His shirt had pulled partially free at the waist. Sometime since she last looked, a mere few minutes ago, he had discarded his neckcloth, and his shirt was open at the neck. His fair hair, which appeared almost golden in the sunshine, was disheveled. One lock of it had fallen over his forehead.

Snowball was outside with him. After taking noisy exception to his arrival earlier and his obvious intention of staying and taking possession of her back garden and her axe and her woodpile, the dog had capitulated without striking one blow in defense of female independence. She had patrolled the back fence and the trees of the copse a few times, yipping at any bird or squirrel that dared come too close, but she lay now in a fluffy ball of contentment a safe distance from the action to watch and yawn in the sun.

Lydia caught herself feeling envious. She distracted herself by brewing a pot of coffee.

Perhaps they could be friends if nothing else, he had suggested last evening. Was it possible? With a man? During the past year she had acquired a few women friends for the first time in her life. But even an innocent friendship with a man would surely be misconstrued if they spent time alone together. Someone would find out. How could it possibly *not* happen? Besides, how could one stop a friendship from developing into something else when one already found the other impossibly attractive?

She must thank him with all sincerity when he was finished, offer him refreshments, and then firmly send him on his way.

And then knit him a scarf.

Were ginger biscuits and coffee enough to offer a man who had been hard at work for well over an hour? Perhaps he would need something more substantial. Toast, perhaps? With eggs? She had never had to wonder about such things with Isaiah. Mrs. Elsinore had cooked for them, and Isaiah had always given her orders for the day before he went about his own work. Lydia had hated that arrangement, the way she had been cut out of what ought to have been one of her principal duties. But Isaiah had explained when she had broached the subject with him one day that she ought to be above such menial tasks as planning and preparing meals. She was far better employed doing the Lord's work as his helpmeet in the parish.

How she had come to hate that word—*helpmeet*. It was dehumanizing. No, maybe not that. Depersonalizing, then. That was more accurate. If one was a helpmeet, one was useful, perhaps. Busy and helpful, perhaps. Indispensable, maybe. Loyal and obedient, certainly. But one was nothing in oneself. One had no identity separate from the man for whom one was a help and a mate.

It felt undeniably good to be in charge of her own kitchen, wondering what she ought to put before Major Westcott when he had finished chopping her wood. She could feel domesticated to her heart's content, but she could also please herself, not be forever at the beck and call of some man who happened to be in charge of her life. She did not have to offer the major anything. She did not suppose he expected to be fed, and there was a pump outside from which he could drink water. She could enjoy doing it anyway because she did not have to.

When she left her kitchen, Lydia did *not* go into the living room to rescue her stretched stitch before knitting on. The blue sky and sunshine beckoned her, and if she remained inside it would be only because *he* was out there and she was too self-conscious to join him. This was *her* home, she reminded herself, and that was *her* wood he was chopping. At the rate he was going there would be enough to last a fortnight even if the weather turned cold again. She wrapped a shawl about her shoulders, opened the back door, and stepped resolutely outside into air that was even warmer than she had expected. It felt like early summer.

Snowball came dashing toward her on legs that were virtually invisible beneath all her white fur, and yapped excitedly about her ankles until Lydia stooped down and picked her up and cradled her in her arms, drawing back her head with a laugh to avoid the little pink tongue that would have lapped at her face. Major Westcott looked up from the chopping block.

"Harry," Lydia said. "Enough. Please. I will have to knit you a scarf ten feet long to make up for all this. And perhaps a hat too. Come inside. I have coffee on and biscuits fresh out of the oven. May I make you some toast and eggs too? You must be hungry."

He propped the axe against the block and turned toward her. "Yellow with red stripes?" he asked—and grinned. And oh dear, he was the one who ought to be breathless, not she. But he was lean and long legged and broad shouldered, with muscles in all the right places. And if he did not close his shirt, though it was only very partially open, she might never get her breath back.

"With orange dots?" she suggested. "*Would* you like toast and eggs?"

"Perhaps toast and cheese if you have some," he said. "And freshly baked biscuits, you said? If you feed me so lavishly, Lydia, I will release you from the obligation to knit the hat. It would probably look like a tea cozy on my head anyway and I would be a laughingstock."

She laughed as though to prove his point and went back inside to slice the bread and start toasting it on the end of the long toasting fork held to the fire. When had she last felt this lighthearted? she asked herself as one side browned and she turned it on the fork. Life had always been a serious business with Isaiah. Frivolity was sin, or at least opened the door to sin. But she *would* not think about the years of her marriage. Not in any negative way, at least. He had been a good and earnest man.

She had four thick slices of toast piled on a plate by the time Harry came inside. They were keeping warm by the hearth while the butter with which she had lavished them soaked in and she was slicing the cheese. The biscuits were heaped on a plate on the table. The coffee was ready to pour into the large, cheerful mugs she had bought on a whim the last time she had been shopping in Eastleigh with Mrs. Bailey—the same day she had bought her pink dress and the bright yellow wool.

He had washed his hands under the pump outside and was rolling down his shirtsleeves when he stepped into the kitchen. He had already closed his shirt and donned his cravat and his waistcoat.

"Are you willing to tolerate me without my coat, Lydia?" he asked. "I want to go back out after I have eaten to tidy up a bit before I leave."

"I did not expect you to chop the whole pile," she told him. "The least I can do is tidy up myself." Though she had not noticed much of a mess when she was out there.

"I will do it," he said. "You will be busy knitting."

"I have made the toast," she said. "I can make more if necessary. The cheese and the biscuits are on the table. So all I owe you is a scarf? No hat? How sad! Hats are my specialty. And no one has ever mistaken them for tea cozies."

"Toast and cheese at the expense of cold ears," he said. "It sounds a fair enough exchange to me. Especially if those biscuits are ginger ones. They smell as if they are. Are they?"

"They are," she told him as he sat down while she

poured their coffee. He stirred milk and a little sugar into his.

"This is a man-sized mug," he said, lifting it from the table to examine the design. "I approve."

He ate in silence for a minute or two while Lydia held her own mug between her hands, something she would never have done either as a girl or as a married lady. She even had her elbows on the table. It was quite ungenteel, but the mugs and the sunlight streaming through the window—and his lack of a coat—somehow invited informality. She gazed at him for a while, consciously enjoying the sight of him.

There was definitely darkness in him. But he had not allowed it to prevail in his life. He was habitually good-humored, as he was now. She could not remember seeing him in a somber mood or hearing him say anything that suggested irritability or anger. He was not a complainer. Even his criticism of the pianoforte at Tom and Hannah Corning's had been made in the form of a joke. She believed he was also a solitary man, though. Despite the friends and friendly acquaintances he had in the neighborhood, there was something suggestive of loneliness about him. He had even admitted it to her that night, though he had spoken of it as part of the general human condition.

She knew there were many facets to his character. The sadder ones he kept to himself while the world saw only the cheerful good nature. She wanted to know all of them, Lydia realized—a disturbing admission when she knew she must discourage any further acquaintance at all.

"Do you resent the man who became Earl of Riverdale in your place?" she asked him. His hand, carrying the last bite of toast to his mouth, paused halfway. He frowned in thought for a moment before returning the toast to his plate.

"It would be difficult to resent Alexander even if I felt so inclined," he said. "He really did not want the title or the responsibilities that went with it, you know, and his position was made very much more awkward by the fact that my father's fortune did not accompany the title and properties, since they were entailed and it was not. The fortune went to my father's only legitimate child—my half sister, Anna, now the Duchess of Netherby. Alex is hardworking and conscientious and has repaired the effects of years of neglect at Brambledean Court, the ancestral home of the earldom. He has done it with the help of Wren, his wife, who brought a fortune of her own to their marriage. He did not marry her just for her money, I must add. They are extremely fond of each other."

But it still must have been unbearably painful for Harry, Lydia thought, to see his cousin do what ought to have been his task.

"I put all the blame where it belongs," he continued. "I suppose you know the story. How my father could have done what he did to his first wife when she was dying of consumption and he married my mother for her dowry I do not know. It was a wickedness compounded by the fact that he hid Anna away in an orphanage even though she had maternal grandparents who adored her and would have been only too happy to raise her. And how he could have done what he did to my mother and ultimately to my sisters and me is beyond understanding—or forgiveness. Generally speaking, one is expected to give loyalty and affection to one's parents, but in the case of my father it has been impossible to do."

"I am sorry," she said. "It was an impertinent question." And what a dreadful burden to bear—the inability to love or respect one's father.

"Not so," he said. "Friends ought to be willing to share some personal details with each other."

He paused and hesitated a few moments, one hand turning his cup on the table. He looked up at her then, and there was something troubled and hard in his eyes, something Lydia had never seen there before. His voice, when he spoke again, was abrupt.

"But friends should also be honest with each other," he said. "*Of course* I resented Alex. I *hated* him. Suddenly he had *my* title and *my* properties and *my* responsibilities. He even had my *name*, for the love of God. And I hated Anna, who was *totally* innocent and had grown up in an orphanage not even knowing her true identity. But suddenly she had *my* birthright and *my* fortune. She was being welcomed with open arms into the bosom of *my* family—of which, by the way, I had so recently been the head—while my mother and my sisters were outcast and lost all the identity they had ever known. *And there was nothing I could do about it* even though I was the man of our own family. When Anna tried to insist that she share the fortune with us, her half siblings, I hated her even more. It seemed like such presumptuous condescension. I was consumed with hatred, Lydia. Perhaps I was fortunate to be able to turn it in a very physical form against the forces of Napoleon Bonaparte, whose ultimate ambition was to invade and take over *my country*."

Lydia no longer leaned slightly toward him, her elbows on the table. She sat back in her chair and stared intently across at him. He looked different. His usual expression of open good humor had vanished. Until it returned all in a rush.

"I do beg your pardon," he said. "That was all probably far more than you wanted to know."

"But I did ask," she said.

"You did." He smiled and then laughed and put the last bite of toast into his mouth with a hand that shook slightly.

"Do you still feel that way?" she asked. She had not seen him as a man who hated or bore grudges. Yet how could he not have done both?

"About Alex and Anna?" He frowned in thought again, his eyes on his mug as he turned it slowly between his hands. "No. And even at first, when everything was too raw for common sense to prevail, I knew that I was being unfair to hate them or even to resent them. Neither had done anything whatsoever to hurt either me or my family. That was all on my father. And Alex genuinely did not want what had been mine. He would have repudiated it if he could. Anna would too, I believe. At the time she was teaching at the orphanage in Bath where she had grown up, and she was contented there and attached to her pupils. It must have been more than bewildering for her suddenly to discover that she had a family—an aristocratic family, no less. And to learn that she was fabulously wealthy. She was pathetically delighted to find that she had a brother and sisters— us. Camille, Abby, and me. We shunned her, turned our backs on her, flatly and contemptuously refused her offer to share her fortune with us. We behaved despicably and shamefully."

"But very understandably," Lydia said.

"You are too kind," he said. "No, I do not still hate them. Or resent them. I can only hope they do not hate me. Or— worse—pity me. It certainly did not help that I was carried home here four years ago, more dead than alive after more than one encounter with an enemy bullet *and* an enemy blade at Waterloo. Or that Alexander and Avery—the Duke of Netherby, Anna's husband—helped do the carrying.

Hinsford Manor does not even belong to me, you know—or perhaps you did not know. It is Anna's, though she has tried several times to gift it to me. According to her, I have a moral right to it. And she has insisted upon willing it to me and my descendants. In the meantime we have agreed that I will live here on its income—and pay its expenses. They are good people, Alex and Anna. Better than I deserve."

Lydia had not heard any of this from anyone in the village, though a number of people understandably talked about him, wondered about him, and speculated. Most people here could remember him as a boy, son of the Earl of Riverdale, being brought up to take his father's place one day. People remembered his mother, the countess, with respect and affection. They remembered him and his sisters in the same way. And it had always seemed to Lydia that they held Major Westcott in the same high esteem now as they had always done in the past even though he had lost everything, even his legitimacy. But no one, she suspected, knew many inside details of his life now, even though they frequently met him at various social events.

She felt touched, privileged, at what he had told her. He must trust that she would not go about the village blabbing to their neighbors. For despite his friendliness with everyone, he kept himself very private and well hidden behind that mask of cheerful amiability. Though it was not really a mask. There was nothing false about it.

She knew all about masks from her own experience. Nobody here—or anywhere—really knew her. Even her new women friends. Even her father and her brothers. She knew what it was like to project an outer image—quiet, self-effacing modesty in her case—and keep almost everything that was her to herself.

"I beg your pardon," he said. "I must be sounding very

self-pitying. And very self-absorbed. It is your turn. One thing has been puzzling me since last evening. You told me how protective your father and your brothers were as you grew up. You told me how your late husband came to your house at the invitation of your older brother, and how he courted you and then married you. You mentioned that a few other potential suitors had come there before him. But why is it, since you are the daughter of a gentleman of property and fortune who is therefore, presumably, a member of the *ton*—why is it you were never taken to London for a come-out Season, Lydia? Or were you?"

"No," she said. "My father and brothers love nothing more than to reminisce about the bold exploits of their youth and the wild oats they sowed, though I suppose I only ever heard strictly expurgated versions of those stories. However, it was those very memories that worked to my disadvantage. They were united in their determination not to expose me to all the wickedness that existed in the world beyond our doors—and they knew all about that wickedness. It was all really quite funny and quite horrible for me. I must be kept away from London and the dangers of a Season there at all costs. One would have thought from listening to them that the balls and parties and masquerades and such for which the spring Season is known were absolute cesspools of vice. They were positively frightened for their dearest Lydie."

Harry laughed, but he tipped his head to one side and regarded her with what looked like sympathy too.

"They were terrified I would fall prey to rakes and scoundrels and fortune hunters," she said. "They were not even consoled when my aunt, my father's sister, offered to bring me out under her sponsorship and supervision. My father quarreled with her years ago when she made what he considered a rash marriage with an unworthy man. I daresay he was afraid she would encourage me to do the like, though on the only occasion when I met my uncle, I liked him considerably and it seemed to me that he and my aunt were happy together. In any case, I had no come-out Season."

He was leaning back in his chair, one hand playing idly with his cup. "Were you very disappointed?" he asked.

She hesitated. It seemed disloyal to complain, especially when she had never doubted her father's love for her or that of her brothers. But—he had been honest with her.

"Bitterly," she admitted, smiling ruefully. "I begged and wheedled. I wept and sulked. I may even have had a tantrum or two. I know I almost made myself ill. I hated them all heartily for a long while and told them so on more than one occasion. None of it did any good. There is no shifting my father when he has once made up his mind on a subject, and my brothers are not really any different. Sometimes, Harry, it is downright painful to be loved." She laughed softly, though the memories were not amusing ones.

"I know," he said. "But I am sorry you were deprived of the pleasures of a London Season. It happened to my younger sister too, though for a different reason. Our illegitimacy was discovered just as she was preparing to make her debut. I believe I might have coped with my own situation much better if my mother and my sisters had been saved from suffering. I wish you had not been made so unhappy, and all in the name of love. You must have been full of youthful hopes and dreams."

Oh, she liked him, Lydia thought suddenly. She had found him attractive for a long while, but she had not really known she would like him too. She *did*, though. He was a vulnerable man, a fact that made him seem more approachable. He was also a kind man. He seemed to care about other people's sufferings more than he did about his own. And if there had indeed been some self-pity in his reactions to his own sudden loss all those years ago, it was something he had quickly recognized and fought against. Now her long-ago disappointment over her lost Season saddened him even though it seemed trivial when compared with what had happened to him. *You must have been full of youthful hopes and dreams.* Ah, and so must he have been.

"It must be lovely to have sisters," she said, surprised by the wistfulness in her own voice. "Tell me about yours. But please do have some biscuits. I made them specially for you."

"Since they are ginger, my favorite, I will," he said, putting two on his plate. "Did you really make them just for me?"

"I did." Lydia fetched the coffeepot and filled his mug again. "Because you had come here to chop wood just for me."

Was that a fond look he just gave her? If it was, it passed too quickly for her to be sure. "Camille is older than I am," he told her when she sat back down. "She used to be the most stuffy, self-righteous, joyless person you could possibly imagine, and she was betrothed to a man who was all those things and more. He dropped her after what my family refers to as the Great Disaster—capital letters, I would have you know. She is now married to an artist and schoolteacher, and they live in a big house in the hills above Bath, running a sort of artists' school, live-in retreat from the world, performance center, party venue, name it what you will. They have nine children, six of them adopted, three of their own. Camille always looks ever so slightly disheveled and has a tendency to go about barefoot with a child astride one of her hips. The latest adoptees are twin baby girls whom no one else was willing to adopt together. She is as happy as it is possible to be. And more vividly beautiful than she ever was before, I might add. Joel, her husband, is equally happy. If what happened to us *was* a catastrophe, then it worked out remarkably well for my elder sister."

Lydia smiled. How wonderful Camille's life sounded. Chaotic, perhaps, but also wonderfully . . . *giving*. And it sounded as if she must have a close partnership with her husband.

"And the younger of your sisters?" she asked. "Is she younger than you?"

"Abigail. Yes," he said. "I am in the middle. Abby married my fellow officer and closest friend in the church here shortly before the old vicar retired and you came with your husband to take his place. It was a marriage of convenience made in haste to enable Gil to get his daughter back from her grandparents, who had taken her just before his first wife's death while he was away, fighting at the Battle of Waterloo. They were refusing to give her back. The marriage quickly turned into what is now very obviously a love match. They have two sons of their own in addition to Katy, the daughter for whose sake they married. They live in Gloucestershire, where Gil has turned, quite improbably, into a farmer. Abby informed me while I was visiting them after Christmas that she considers her life as close to perfect as it is possible to be. I believe her." He paused in thought for a moment. "I cannot say I have always considered it lovely to have sisters. I often thought them the world's worst pests when we were growing up. But I am extremely fond of them now."

He took another biscuit off the plate. "These are exceedingly good," he said. "You really need to hide the rest of them, Lydia, or at least move the plate out of my reach."

Instead she pushed it a little closer to him, and they both laughed.

"Temptress," he said, but he took yet another before he

got to his feet, scraping his chair back over the stone flags of the kitchen floor as he did so. "I must go outside and tidy up and then bring in some wood for your wood box. I see it is almost empty. I will need to get going then. I have promised to accompany my steward to the home farm this afternoon to adjudicate a dispute over whether we need an additional barn or a mere extension to the existing one. I have a hard life, Lydia."

"You do not need to do anything more here," she assured him. "You have already done a great deal."

But he smiled at her and did it anyway. By the time she had cleared the table and washed up their few dishes, all was neat and tidy beyond the window, and he was approaching the house with an armful of wood. She held the back door open as he carried it inside, and then she hovered in the kitchen while he washed up outside again, drew on his coat, and came back to take his leave.

"I do not know how to thank you," she told him.

"You already did," he said. "The toast and cheese were just what I needed, and your ginger biscuits are delicious. *And* you are going to knit me a scarf. But no hat. Please."

"I promise." She smiled back at him. "Thank you, Harry."

He stood just inside the back door, ready to take his leave. Snowball was sniffing his boots. There was a moment when he might have left without further ado, but he hesitated that moment too long and ended up setting his hands on her shoulders instead and brushing the sides of his thumbs along her jaw.

"Shall I return this evening?" he asked her, his voice suddenly low and husky, his eyes very direct on hers.

She felt her smile drain away as she swallowed and licked her lips. *Say no. This must not go any further. Say no.*

"If you wish," she said.

"I rather believe I do," he told her, and his eyes held hers before dipping to look at her lips. He tipped his head slightly sideways and drew her a little closer. Her heart felt as if it were about to beat right out of her chest—and her ears. He looked into her eyes again and then shut his own as he closed the distance between their mouths.

It was a soft, light kiss with closed mouths and no attempt to make anything more sensual of it. A kiss of friends? Lydia felt it all the way down through her insides to her toes as she set her hands on either side of his waist.

Then he was looking back into her eyes, his hands still lightly clasping her shoulders.

"Sometime soon," he said, "perhaps this evening, I will kiss you properly, Lydia. Or perhaps, in the spirit of independence, *you* will kiss *me*."

It seemed strange that last evening when he had asked her to invite him inside and she had tacitly agreed by leaving the gate open and not looking back, she had expected to go to bed with him. Yet now she felt everything was moving along much too fast. He was so much more . . . masculine than she had expected. So much more . . . real. And so much . . . lovelier. And oh goodness, what had happened to her vocabulary? He was so very . . . likable. What a very weak word.

But could she bear having this man as a lover? When she had conceived the idea, it had been entirely in the realm of dreams. She had wanted a balm to the ache of loneliness that seemed to be a part of her very being. She had wanted something to bring some vividness into her life. She had wanted to *live* at long last. Yet the dream had been essentially impersonal, perhaps because she had known it stood little to no chance of coming true. She had not known how, in the world of reality, she would feel in his company or when he spoke to her and smiled at her. And touched her and kissed her. It had not occurred to her that the reality would so far exceed the dream that she would be unable to cope with it. How could she have known? She had done so little living despite the fact that she was twenty-eight years old and a widow. Almost all her living so far had been done in the interior world of her dreams.

Could she bear to step beyond dreams into reality?

She was terribly afraid that something would be irrevocably lost if they did become lovers—not only this specific dream but her ability to dream at all. And the tentative friendship that seemed to be growing between them would be lost too, this mutual sympathy and understanding. This very precious something she had never known before with either a woman or a man.

Oh, she had opened some sort of Pandora's box a little over a week ago and had no idea what she had unleashed.

"Perhaps," she said. Perhaps she would let him kiss her tonight, she meant. Perhaps *she* would kiss *him*, though that at least seemed unlikely. She would not know how to go about it—strangely, when she had been married for six years.

She liked his grin. It came slowly now. It was so much more boyish than a simple smile. It set his eyes alight and showed just where laugh lines would settle into their outer corners as permanent wrinkles when he grew older.

"Until this evening, then," he said, releasing her and turning to the doorway. "Snowball, why are you growling now of all times? I am leaving."

"I think it must be for that very reason," Lydia said. "She is sorry to see you go."

"I have made a conquest of at least one of the ladies in

this house, then?" he said. "And, heaven help me, it is the dog."

Lydia laughed as he stepped outside and strode around the corner of the house on his way out. She hoped very much that no one would see him cross the road. Had anyone heard the axe all morning? It would surely have been very obvious to anyone who had that she was not the one doing all that chopping.

She wandered outside to eye the neat pile of chopped wood with satisfaction and stooped to pick up one small stick he had missed when tidying. It was as she was straightening up that Snowball began dashing along the line of the back fence again, yapping. Two hands clutched the top of it, and a head from the nose up appeared between them, peering over and down at the woodpile.

Both face and hands disappeared in a hurry. But they did not vanish before she had identified the intruder.

Jeremy Piper.

Annoyance at his cheekiness, however, was soon replaced by a feeling of enormous relief that he had not come slinking by any earlier. Five minutes ago, for example, when she had been standing just inside the open door being kissed by Harry Westcott.

Take warning, Lydia. Oh, take warning. You are playing with a terrible danger.

Seven

❧

By the time Harry returned from the farm late in the afternoon, having settled the dispute over the barn by suggesting that repairs be made to the loft to allow for more storage space and agreeing to an addition larger than originally suggested being added to the back of the building to make more room for the livestock, he felt both sticky and grimy and sent word to his valet to prepare a bath for him. While he waited for the water to be heated and carried up to his dressing room, he went into the library to look through the day's mail.

There were two personal letters, one from his cousin Jessica, whom he had not seen since her marriage two years ago to Gabriel, Earl of Lyndale. He had been present for their wedding when, quite coincidentally, he had been making one of his rare visits to London to be measured for a new coat and boots after his valet had warned him that the old ones would simply fall off from sheer old age one of these days. The other letter was from Aunt Matilda, Viscountess Dirkson, his father's eldest sister. He sat down behind his desk to read.

Jessica's letter was full of enthusiastic descriptions of her life in the north of England. She was a few years younger than Harry. She and Abigail had always been very close friends. As essentially an only child—Avery, Duke of Netherby, her half brother, was years older—Jessica had always adored all three of her cousins, and they had been dearly fond of her. One paragraph of her letter was devoted to details about Evan, her one-year-old son. They were going to London soon for the parliamentary session and the Season, she reported. Was Harry going to be there too? Jessica hoped so. She had missed seeing him at Christmas.

He had missed her too, Harry thought as he folded the letter and set it aside. And the rest of the Westcott family also, much as he had been relieved not to have to go to Brambledean for Christmas. But no, he was not going to London. Not this year. He knew what would almost surely be awaiting him there if he did—thirtieth birthday celebrations, for example. *No, thank you, Jessica,* he thought.

Aunt Matilda and Viscount Dirkson, her husband of four years, had just been on a visit to Gloucestershire to see three of their grandchildren, whom they had missed dreadfully over Christmas, though it was perfectly understandable that Abigail and Gil had wanted to spend the holiday in Bath. Gil Bennington was Viscount Dirkson's natural son. The two had been estranged through most of Gil's life until a few years ago but had edged warily about each other for a while after Abby and Gil's wedding and during the court case over the custody of Katy. Father and son seemed now to be cautiously fond of each other, due in large part to the influence of Abby on the one side and Aunt Matilda on the other, Harry suspected.

Everyone was well and thriving, his aunt reported, though of course Harry would know that since he had seen them all for himself very recently. Both fond grandparents—*and totally unbiased, of course, Harry*—were agreed that Ben was the most gorgeous baby ever, while Seth was the most gorgeous infant and Katy the loveliest little girl. Harry chuckled. Aunt Matilda had married late in life and was very obviously extremely happy. Even exuberant. Who could ever have predicted it?

Marital happiness really *was* possible, he thought. His mother had been quite right about that. The Westcotts seemed particularly good at it. Why, then, was he contemplating an affair that was not going to lead to marriage and would be risky besides, to say the least, given the size of the village and the fact that everyone in it and for miles around knew everyone else's business almost before the everyone else in question knew it themselves? Why was he going to see Lydia Tavernor tonight with a view, he supposed, to having an affair with her sometime in the foreseeable future, when he could simply go to London and find a wife? Surely if he set his mind to it he could find *someone* to suit him.

The inevitable question came in the next to final paragraph of his aunt's letter. Was Harry planning to spend at least a part of the Season in town this spring? Harry spread one hand over his eyes and laughed. For it was obvious now that this was a concerted family campaign. First his mother at Christmas, and Cam and Abby to a lesser degree. Then his mother again after his return home. And now his cousin and his aunt. It would be his grandmother next, he could confidently predict, and then his other aunts. Maybe Alexander or Wren. And Elizabeth, Alex's sister. Had he missed anyone? Ah. And possibly Anna, his own half sister.

Harry folded Aunt Matilda's letter and set it on top of

Jessica's. He was *not* going to London, no matter how often they asked. Sometimes being a Westcott was a massive pain. But he smiled even as he thought it. He would never forget how they had all rallied around, and continued to do so, after the Great Disaster, when they might just as easily have dropped his mother and Cam, Abby, and him as unworthy of their acquaintance.

And if he sat here any longer, he thought, getting resolutely to his feet, his bathwater would be cold or at least tepid, and he hated cool bathwater.

As he was climbing the stairs to his dressing room, he remembered that he had admitted this morning —to Lydia Tavernor of all people—what he had not confessed to another living soul in ten years. He had scarcely admitted it even to himself. He had resented and even hated Alexander when Alex became the Earl of Riverdale after he himself had been stripped of the title. He had resented and even hated Anna, who had stepped into the family as a full member, Harry's father's daughter and only legitimate child, at the very moment when Harry himself and his sisters had been bastardized. He had even hated Avery, his guardian at the time, for stopping him from enlisting as a private soldier and insisting upon purchasing a commission for him instead. He had seethed with hatred and impotent fury for a long time after he went to the Peninsula with his regiment even while he wrote cheerful letters home, claiming it was all a great lark and he was having the devil of a good time. He had poured out the whole shameful litany of his resentments to a woman he scarcely knew. One with whom he was contemplating having an affair.

What the devil must she think of him?

"You had better not come too close to me, Mark," he told his valet when he stepped into the dressing room. "I smell of barnyard and stale human sweat. I stink, in other words. You would be well advised to stand well back and hold your nose while I strip."

Mark Mitchell grinned and stepped forward to help him off with his coat. "One of these days when you tell me that," he said, "I will take you at your word. And then see how easily you can sack me for merely doing what I was told."

"Insubordination," Harry muttered.

Lydia also had a letter. After going outside to admire her woodpile and being a bit jolted by the sight of Jeremy Piper peeping over her back fence, she went to call upon Denise Franks to pick up her cake plate, and stayed to share a pot of tea. She called at the village shop on her way home to purchase a few items and was handed her letter. It was from William, her middle brother, she could see. She always loved having letters from home.

Back at her cottage, she waited a little impatiently in the doorway while Snowball dashed over to the trees, did what she needed to do there, and came meandering back, stopping to sniff the ground in a few places and then eyeing a bird that was pecking at a worm down by the fence before deciding that it was not worth laying chase to. She trotted back inside, drank noisily from her water bowl, and plopped herself down before the fireplace.

Oh lovely, Lydia thought as she broke the seal of her brother's letter, for there was another enclosed within it. Her name was written on it in the small, neat handwriting she recognized as Esther, her sister-in-law's. She read William's letter first.

Their father had taken a chill a couple of weeks ago after being out in a heavy rain while he was far from home. After a few days spent unwillingly in bed, however, he was recovering fast, though his temper had some catching up to do.

Lydia smiled. Her father had always despised any weakness in himself. He fretted whenever he was forced to be inactive. How on earth had James and William managed to keep him in bed for a few days? Had they tied him down?

Anthony, the youngest of the family, was almost finished with his studies at Oxford. He had abandoned his plans for an academic career, William reported, in favor of one with the diplomatic service. He had decided that he wanted to travel the world, preferably the hot, sunny parts of it. He was sick of the dismal weather that seemed always to settle over Britain to stay, summer and winter. He was convinced that it must be the most dismal country in the world.

I will give him a few years at the longest, William had written, *before he discovers himself only too happy to return to this dismal country. Can you seriously imagine anyone, Lydie, choosing to live anywhere else?*

No, Lydia thought, amused, she could not. But she had never tried living anywhere else. Or *been* anywhere else, for that matter. Neither had William. And perhaps all people considered their own country the best on earth in which to live. But she felt a surge of envy for her youngest brother nevertheless. At least he was free to dream large dreams and even to make plans for making them come true—because he was a man. So could she, of course—dream large dreams, that was. She could dream of living alone and having the means with which to sustain herself, for example. She *had* dreamed it, and now she was doing it. And she could dream of having a lover. She *had* dreamed it, and now . . .

But her stomach lurched uncomfortably, and she thought of what had happened, first out at the woodpile just after

Harry left, and then when she was at Denise's. They had been chatting upon various subjects when Denise had introduced a new one that had alarmed Lydia—if *alarmed* was not too strong a word.

"Did I see correctly last evening?" she had asked. "Did *Major Westcott* walk you home, Lydia?"

"We were going in the same direction for a short way," Lydia had said, hoping her face was not flushing. "It would have been silly to walk silently one behind the other."

"Oh, dash it," Denise had said. "What a very sensible and *dull* explanation. All night and all morning I have been busy conjuring a budding romance."

"Between me and Major Westcott?" Lydia had said, laughing. "How very absurd."

"But why?" her friend had asked. "You have been a widow for well over a year, Lydia. I daresay your grief is still quite acute, and I know you always say you could not possibly marry again. But you are not even thirty yet. One day you are going to look about you and change your mind. If your eyes should then happen to alight upon Major Westcott—"

"Denise," Lydia had said, cutting her off with a raised hand. She had still been laughing. "Really? *Major Westcott?*"

"Whyever not?" Denise had protested. "He is certainly attractive. And unattached. So are you—attractive *and* unattached, that is. And he walked you home from Hannah Corning's a week or so ago too."

"Because we were going the same way then too," Lydia had explained. "And he did it as a favor to Tom Corning, to save him from having to make a special journey out to escort me himself. Though it was all quite unnecessary. I am perfectly capable of taking myself the length of the village street, even in the dead of night. Men can be very foolish."

Lydia had taken her leave soon after that. But though Denise had raised the topic only to tease her and they had both laughed over it, Lydia had been alarmed. No, it was not too exaggerated a word. For if Denise had noticed, then other people would have noticed also. On two separate occasions Major Westcott had walked her home late in the evening. Those two incidents were nothing in themselves. But there was no room for any more.

And what if Jeremy had hoisted himself up and peered over that fence a few minutes sooner than he had?

It would be madness—absolute insanity—to continue what they had started. Even a friendship was forbidden a single man and a single woman—at least, any sort of friendship that could not be conducted in plain view and in a public place. And even then . . .

She must make this evening's visit as brief as possible, she had decided after leaving Denise's. She must make it clear to Major Westcott that there could be no more such private meetings. Surely he would recognize the wisdom of that decision. But even if he did not, she knew he would not argue. He was, she believed, an honorable man. Besides, the whole thing had been her idea in the first place.

She returned her attention to her brother's letter. How had she got distracted anyway?

We have been talking, it continued. *Papa and James and I.* And Lydia knew, even before she read further, that William was finally getting to the real point of his letter.

We understand perfectly well why you insisted after Isaiah's funeral and burial upon returning to your village. Papa and James regret the way they pressed you so adamantly on that occasion to return home with them. They did it out of love and concern for you, of course, as I am sure you must have been aware, Lydie. But they were wrong, and they are willing to admit it. It was right that you do your grieving where you had lived so happily and served so diligently with your husband. Leaving immediately after his death would have made you feel as though you were abandoning him. You must have felt that he was somehow still there in spirit. And you had neighbors and friends who loved you and grieved with you and no doubt needed your physical presence there with them. You did the right and the honorable thing in staying and the only thing that could have brought some healing to your broken heart. We know you loved Isaiah with unwavering devotion. I can still recall how exuberantly happy you were on your wedding day—the happiest I had ever seen you.

Lydia licked her lips, which had suddenly turned dry. Oh, she could recall it too, that deliriously happy day. That first day of what was to have been the sort of glorious happily-ever-after only the very young and the very naïve expect.

We have honored your decision and kept quiet on the subject for longer than a year. But, Lydie, you are a woman alone—a young woman. And unless something has changed, you do not even have a servant living with you. It is improper. You must realize that. It is unsafe. Now that your year of mourning is over and you have, presumably, left off your blacks, you are a prey to any and all impertinences from those men who can see that you are without male protec-

tion. Some will even choose to believe that your very decision to live alone is a deliberate invitation to their advances. We know that nothing could be further from the truth. But nothing could be more disastrous—for your reputation and for your safety.

Lydia's hands tingled with fury suddenly as they held the paper. Did William realize how insulting his words were? Yet she did not have full right to her anger, did she? Not after what she had started a little over a week ago. Not after she had invited Harry into her home last evening and allowed him to kiss her this morning. She read on.

I will come and fetch you as soon as we can be sure Papa's health is not going to suffer a relapse. We will see to the selling of your cottage and the removal of all your larger possessions. You must not worry your head over any of that. You must simply come and be at home again, where we can look after you. I daresay we will find someone else suitable for you to marry eventually too, though there is absolutely no hurry for that. Esther has written a note to enclose with this. She has some news that she hopes will entice you home if nothing else will.

Lydia folded the letter and shut her eyes. She might have known they would not take no for an answer. Not forever. Snowball was standing at her feet, her little stub of a tail waving, her eyes gazing mournfully upward, as if she sensed some emotional turmoil in her mistress. Lydia set the letter aside and lifted the dog onto her lap.

"They are not going to leave me alone after all, then," she said. "I know them, Snowball. Was a woman ever so besieged by men who love her? They are enough to give love a bad name."

Snowball turned twice on her lap before curling up and settling to sleep.

"So much for female sympathy and solidarity," Lydia said. "You know, Snowball, perhaps it would be easier just to give in and go home. To have Papa and my brothers for company—and my sister-in-law. There would be other people to run the house and clean and cook. And chop the wood. There would be familiar neighbors, familiar surroundings. There would always be someone or something to hold the loneliness at bay."

Perhaps it was as well she spoke aloud, for she heard her own words almost as though they were coming out of someone else's mouth. She heard the abjectness of them, the sound of defeat. She heard herself being Lydia as she always had been—until a little over fifteen months ago. And anger returned in full force, but directed at herself this time. Why *should* being a woman render one not only helpless but also spiritless?

Why had she not raged against Isaiah when it had become stunningly apparent to her *on her wedding day* that life with him was not going to be any different from the way it had been at home? Worse, in fact. Far worse, because he was her *husband* and she had just vowed obedience to him. Why had she never admitted even to herself in the six years following her wedding day that it was not a good marriage, that she had been cheated, that she was not happy—and was denying it every moment of every day? Oh, it was true that his had at least never been a physical tyranny. She had never been afraid of violence from him. He had never struck her or even spoken harshly or disrespectfully to her. But . . .

But it had been tyranny nevertheless. She had never let him know that she disagreed—vehemently disagreed—with his vision of their marriage. The power of his personality, his dazzling good looks, his all-consuming faith, his charismatic zeal as a servant of the Lord, had completely overwhelmed her and convinced her of her own worthlessness in contrast. When he had called her his helpmeet, she had meekly accepted that that was what she was. At first the word had suggested a shared closeness, a shared workload and mission. A togetherness. It was only as time went on that that one word—*helpmeet*—had begun to grate on her nerves, since really it labeled her subordinate position, her total lack of identity apart from Isaiah.

Yet she had never protested. Never raged. Never demanded to be seen as a person. She had never forced him to look at her, right into her eyes, to see her as . . . *herself*. As Lydia. She had even begun to doubt that there was any person to be seen. She had been Isaiah's helpmeet. It was how the parish had seen her—if and when they saw her at all. It was how they still saw her—though by her own choice now. For her invisibility since his death had somehow protected her identity, her personhood, her independence. Or perhaps just her fear.

She suddenly remembered her sister-in-law's note and picked it up and broke the seal. As she had half expected from the hint William had given, Esther was expecting a child at last, after two years of marriage. She was clearly excited about it. So was James, apparently.

Lydia had never been with child. And now she never would be, for her decision never to marry again, never again to surrender her freedom to a man, was a firm one and would not be shifted, as her friends believed and as her father and brothers believed it would be after she had recovered fully. But it was not a decision without disadvantages. She was a woman with a woman's needs. The need for a man, yes, or, rather, for a lover. But also the need—the yearning—for a child. She could not have it both ways, however. She must choose, and the choice had been made.

Esther knew that Lydia's father and brothers wanted her to come home. *She* wanted it too, she assured Lydia. They had met only once, when they had been too busy with the wedding to get to know each other as sisters ought. But like Lydia, Esther had no actual sisters and longed to have one with her now as she awaited the birth of her child and afterward, when she would need the close companionship of a woman. *Oh, Lydia, please, please come home,* she had pleaded just before ending the note. *My very dearest regards, Your sister, Esther.*

And Lydia had a sharp memory of her eight-year-old self begging and begging that the baby her mama had told her was coming to the house soon would be a girl so she would have a sister at last. Her mother had told her she could not guarantee it, as she did not get to choose the baby who would come. Lydia had hoped and prayed after that without openly begging. But then Anthony had arrived, and she had been bitterly disappointed. Very shortly afterward her mother had died, and she had had neither sister nor mother.

Now she had a sister.

And soon she would have a niece or nephew.

A baby in the family.

But not her own.

She would never go back home to stay, though there was a surprising and treacherous sort of temptation to do just that. To give up the fight and go back where she was loved, where she would have company. Where she would not have to see Harry almost everywhere she went. Where she could hide from the pain. And how silly that there *would be* pain and the sharpness of unhappiness after tonight. How *very* silly. She scarcely knew him. She could hardly claim to be in love with him. She was *not*. And she did not *want* to be.

No, she would not run away just because her childhood home and the people and the situation that awaited her there were familiar and safe. She would lose herself again if she went home.

She was too precious to lose.

She *was*.

If pain was the ultimate cost of freedom and independence and *being a person*, then so be it.

She was staying.

Eight

For someone who had made the very firm decision to put an end to a relationship that had actually scarcely even begun, Lydia took an inordinate amount of time deciding what to wear. She did not want to look overdressed—she rejected her new pink dress. But she did not want to look drab or dowdy either—definitely nothing black or gray or even lavender. The evenings were still too chilly for muslins or short sleeves, but long sleeves and high, round necks could look very matronly. And downright plain.

She was behaving, she thought as she finally donned a pale blue wool dress with long sleeves and a high, round neck, as though she had twenty wardrobes stuffed full of dresses in a wide variety of colors and styles. She did not. Isaiah had not encouraged either extravagance or vanity. No, correction. He had actively *dis*couraged both.

Then there was her hair. At first there seemed to be no real choices with that, at least. There was only one way to wear it that would fit neatly beneath a cap—in a simple coil pinned flat to the back of her head. But which cap should she choose? She had several, all white, all very similar. They were not worth dithering over, in fact.

But then a question asked itself in her head and threw her into total confusion. Did she *have* to wear a cap? She had started wearing one a few days after her wedding because Isaiah had thought the modesty of it befitted her status as a married lady and his helpmeet, and she had worn one ever since. She thought she might feel a bit naked without one now. Yet she was *only twenty-eight years old*. She was not a girl, it was true, and she was a widow. But she was not in her dotage.

Could she remember any other way to style her hair, though? Even if she could, could she do it without the help of a maid?

Did she dare try?

But why would she even want to? She was about to put a firm end to whatever it was that was developing between her and Harry Westcott. Since he was coming anyway, though . . . She had said he could come when he asked her this morning. It was only fair, then, to spend an hour with him, sitting and talking. Perhaps even joking and laughing a little. It was *not* sinful to do either. She had never believed it was, but it had been easier to behave for six years as though she did instead of trying to explain her opposing point of view.

She was not going to wear a cap.

It took her an hour to dress her hair in a style that looked, when it was finished, as though it had taken her five minutes, if that. She had to be content with hair brushed smooth over her head and above her ears and up off her neck and twisted into a knot high on the back of her head. By accident a few tendrils refused to stay with the rest and hung in waves over her temples and along her neck. She left them where they were. They did not look entirely bad. In fact, they looked almost deliberate, and thank goodness for that bit of a curl in her hair. The rest of it—the smooth, scraped back, utterly uninteresting bulk of it—at least shone in the candlelight.

She did indeed feel funny without her cap. But even as she might have dashed after all to find one there was a knock upon the front door and Snowball darted out of Lydia's bedchamber, yipping and barking.

He seemed almost sinister standing on her doorstep in the dusk of evening. He looked taller than usual in a long black evening cloak. But when he swept off his hat, he was instantly transformed by his fair hair and his smile. He stooped down to scratch Snowball under the chin, and her dog licked his hand and turned to trot back into the house, all ferocity forgotten. He looked up and smiled again at Lydia as he stepped inside and she closed the door. For a moment she stayed facing it, her hand still on the doorknob while she drew a breath and released it.

She was aware of him hanging his hat and cloak on an empty hook behind the door. His physical presence always had a more powerful impact upon her than merely thinking about him did—or dreaming about him. She should know that by now. She ought to have opened the door, smiled at him, apologized for bringing him all the way from the house at this hour, and explained that she could neither invite him inside nor see him privately ever again. It would be all over by now if she had done that. But of course she had not.

Let there be this present moment, then, she thought as she turned from the door. *Let there be this hour.*

He was turning at the same moment from hanging up his cloak, and they ended up gazing at each other, no more than a foot apart. Neither of them had spoken a word yet. He was no longer smiling, and his face looked less youthful than usual, less purely good-humored, more handsome. He had a far more powerful *presence* than he had ever had in the dreams she had dreamed of him.

He raised his hands and cupped them gently about her face before running his thumbs lightly along her lips, from the center to the outer corners. Lydia inhaled very slowly and licked her lips as she gazed into his eyes. Her stomach was unsteady. So were her knees.

He closed the gap between them and set his mouth to hers. Just as he had this morning. But there was a difference. His lips were slightly parted this time. So were hers. She spread her hands over his chest and felt the kiss as a raw ache in her mouth, down into her throat and her breasts and through her womb to settle between her thighs and even reach down to her toes, which curled into the soles of her slippers as though to anchor her to the floor.

And then his mouth was no longer touching hers, and his eyes were gazing back at her again, heavy lidded.

"Kiss me," he murmured.

At first the words puzzled her. Was not that what they had just been doing—kissing? But then she remembered what he had said this morning about *her* kissing *him*. She sank her teeth into her lower lip, and his eyes followed the gesture.

Oh, this was not what she had wanted of this hour—this standing here with him, just inside her front door, his hands cupping her cheeks, hers spread over his chest, her fingers nestled among the crisp folds of his neckcloth. Not touching him anywhere else, though she could feel the heat of him with every part of her body. She could smell the subtle musk of his shaving soap or cologne.

Kiss me.

She slid her hands upward to his shoulders, broad and firm beneath her grip, leaned closer, and kissed him. His lips were soft and warm, still slightly parted. Terribly masculine. So was the rest of him. For, in moving her hands and stepping closer, she had brought her bosom to his chest and the rest of her body against his. She could feel the muscled hardness of his body against the length of hers and the strength of his thighs through the light wool of her dress. A sharp stabbing of sheer raw desire sliced through her, and she pushed back from him, breathless and a bit panicked.

He looked back at her, his hands on either side of her waist, and said nothing.

"Harry," she said, and wished her voice were not quite so breathless. "I must apologize. For what I asked you when you walked me home from the Cornings' house, for what I then went on to say and imply, for inviting you in last evening, for letting you come to chop my wood this morning, for agreeing to your coming again this evening. It must end. Now. It cannot continue. We would only be courting disaster."

His eyes were smiling even if the rest of his face was not. He had removed his hands from her waist and clasped them at his back.

"You are right," he said. "I have been telling myself all day long—all *week* long—that it would be madness."

And how totally *illogical* of her to feel disappointed, to know that now, within the next minute or so, he would be gone and the loneliness that sometimes needled at her would come slamming back like a blow to the stomach.

She smiled back at him.

"You look very different without your cap," he said. "Very beautiful."

The compliment warmed her even though it was a gross exaggeration. Her cheeks were still hot. Her heart was still hammering. "Thank you," she said. "Harry, I am *so* sorry. But I *will* knit you your scarf."

His smile reached his lips. "You are upset," he said. "There is no need to be. You owe me nothing, not even a scarf. It was my idea and my pleasure to chop your wood. Sometimes one likes to feel manly, and what is more manly than hefting an axe, especially when one knows a woman is looking on?" His eyes were actually laughing now.

"Oh," she said, stung. "What makes you believe I was watching you? I was *baking*, if you will remember."

"My vanity made me think it," he said. "You will do horrible things to my conceit if you now tell me you did not look even once."

"Well," she said, "I would hate to deflate your image of yourself as a man. Maybe I peeped *once*."

"Thank you." He laughed softly. "Shall we agree to forget about the kisses and part friends?"

Ah, but how could one forget . . .

"There are some biscuits left from this morning," she said. "And the kettle is always close to boiling. Let me make some tea —"

"No tea. Or biscuits, even ginger ones. I came here straight from the dinner table," he said. "But I think it would be a good idea for us to sit down together for a while. For surely we *are* friends, Lydia, and ought to remain so. We will inevitably keep on running into each other, after all. Those meetings ought not to be embarrassing for us, ought they?"

She turned in to the living room and plumped up the cushions on the back of the sofa even though she had done it earlier.

He came and sat on the sofa, where he had sat last evening, and she took her place beside him again instead of going to sit on her chair, as she probably ought to have done. Snowball looked from one to the other of them before curling up on the hearth before the fire Lydia had lit earlier.

"Isaiah did not like me to be seen without a cap," she said for something to say. "He thought it unseemly for the vicar's wife to be bareheaded in public."

"But you are not the vicar's wife now," he said. "Nor are you in public."

"No." No, they were *not* in public and therefore ought not to be sitting here together. But it was such a *relief* that they were going to have this final hour after all. She liked talking with him. For he did not treat her merely as a listener to his monologues. He encouraged her to talk too, and he listened to her when she did. And looked at her.

"Lydia," he said, immediately proving her point, "tell me why you have hidden for so many years and still do hide outside your own home."

"Why I have hidden?" She frowned.

"When you asked me if I was ever lonely," he said, "I understood you to be admitting that you are. And I felt guilty over the fact that in all the time you have been in Fairfield, first with your husband as the vicar's wife and more recently as his widow, I had scarcely noticed you. I did not know you and had never made any effort to get to know you. I was deeply ashamed of myself. Until, that was, it occurred to me that perhaps you wanted it that way. It struck me that perhaps you deliberately hid yourself from notice even if you were not literally a hermit. I set out to watch for it at Mr. Solway's party last night, and it soon became clear to me that I was right. You constantly effaced yourself, even when you might have shone for a few moments as the maker of his birthday cake."

"That was really nothing to boast about," she said. "I enjoy baking, though I do not pretend to be an expert. Besides, it was a *birthday* cake. Everyone's attention needed to be upon Mr. Solway, not upon me."

"But you *constantly* efface yourself," he persisted. "Your husband shone wherever he went. He had an unusually charismatic . . . what is the word? *Presence?* It must have been difficult as his wife *not* to seem to be his mere shadow. Perhaps you did not do it deliberately then. But since then? You have remained a shadow. I might *never* have noticed you if you had not asked that question about loneliness. Why do you do it? Why do you hide? In plain sight, paradoxically. Why do you not want people to see you and know you?"

She did not answer for a while as she transferred her gaze from his face to the hands in her lap. It shook her a bit that he had realized all that about her. Well. He had been honest with her this morning about something that must have been painful and a bit shameful to admit. And they *were* friends. That was what she was going to miss more than anything.

"I fell very deeply in love with Isaiah," she told him. "I had been starting to fear that I would be a spinster all my life, for I was not going to have a come-out Season, and there was no one in our neighborhood. I did not like any of the suitors who were brought to the house on thinly veiled pretexts. And then Isaiah came. I had never met anyone so breathtakingly handsome, so firm of character, so full of purpose and energy. He talked of his beliefs and what he felt was his mission in life as though they really mattered. As of course they did. The church was not just a career to him. It was . . . oh, it was all in all. He was utterly sincere, wholly *genuine*."

"I believe everyone who met him felt that about him," Harry said.

"When I understood that he was singling me out for particular attention," she continued, "I could not believe my good fortune. When he asked me to marry him, I thought I had reached the pinnacle of happiness. All I wanted of my life was to please him, to help him with his work, to be a part of what he envisioned, and to make him comfortable and happy at the same time. In such ways I would make myself happy too. I did not doubt that for a moment. I had found all I had ever dreamed of."

She stopped there in order to draw a deep breath and release it slowly. She might not have continued if he had not sat silently waiting. The fire in the hearth crackled and shifted and sent sparks shooting up the chimney. Snowball, briefly disturbed, got to her feet, turned twice on the hearth rug, and settled for sleep again.

"He had very decided ideas about the role of a vicar's wife," Lydia said after a while. "As he did about everything. I was not to waste my time and energies on domestic duties. That was why there were servants—Mrs. Elsinore in particular. I had a more special role to play in his mission. I was his helpmeet. I must always be in the front pew at church services and by his side at church and community functions. I must serve on every women's church committee and be his voice there. When we were in company together, I must defer to his superior knowledge and judgment so his authority in the parish was never undermined. I must not speak unless I was addressed directly, and even then I must allow him to answer for me if the topic was a weighty one or a question of faith. One of my main duties was to visit the elderly and the sick and new mothers and their children. I was to take food with me, but only the baskets Mrs. Elsinore provided. I was to serve anyone who came to the vicarage door in need of help. It was not my task—or his—to question the depth of the need. I pleased him and so pleased myself. I *wanted* to please him. I *loved* him."

It was almost the truth. If there had been no more to their story it might have been the whole of it. She might so easily have been happy. And correspondingly heartbroken after his death. Heartbroken for herself too, that was, and not just for him. She really *had* mourned him.

She turned her head and raised her eyes to Harry's when he did not immediately break the silence.

"And after you were widowed?" he asked her. "Why did you choose to remain hidden, Lydia?"

"I was in mourning," she told him.

"Are you still?" he asked.

"No." She spread her fingers on her lap, pleating the skirt of her dress between them. "After he died, I chose to remain here in Fairfield rather than go home with my father and brother. I wanted to be free and independent, but I did not know quite how it was to be done. I had no experience. I did not want any sort of interference, however well-meaning. I wanted to find my own way."

"I understand," he said.

But how could he? How could he *possibly*?

"You cannot know what it is like to be a woman," she said, looking up at him again. "Always under the control of men, no matter how benevolent their rule. No matter how much appreciation and even love those men offer in exchange for the total hold they have over every facet of your life and even your mind."

He gazed back into her eyes, a slight frown between his own.

"I know women have few if any rights according to law and the church," he said. "It certainly is not fair and must be rectified in time. But life is not always lived strictly according to law. Custom can be just as strong a guide. Most of the women in my life, it seems to me, are strong, assertive persons, who hold their own against the men in their lives, usually resulting in a harmonious balance. Though I do have one cousin, it is true—Elizabeth—who was forced to flee her first, abusive marriage and stayed free of it only because Alexander, her brother, refused to give her up but confronted her husband instead and I believe knocked him flat and did some damage in the process. The law ought to have been on her side but was not. Brute force had to take its place to protect her."

"No man has ever used physical violence on me," she said. Though there were other kinds of violence.

"Alexander's wife, Wren, the Countess of Riverdale, was the owner of a prosperous glassmaking factory when she met him," he told her. "She was actively involved in the business and still is. I do not think Alex has ever tried to stop her or become involved himself. They are, I am certain, very happy. I can understand your craving for those twin dreams you speak of—freedom and independence. I can understand too your instinct to hide lest someone find you and spoil everything for you and put you back under the dominance of a man who will know better how to care for you than you know yourself. But life for women is not always as confining as it has been in your experience."

How envious she was of Wren, Countess of Riverdale.

"I have never known women, Harry," she said. "At least, not until very recently. I have a few friends here now and value them greatly. I enjoy their company. Until this past year all my living was done from within the world of men. Fortunately for me, none of them were violent men. I stay hidden now because I feel as though I am holding my breath and clinging on to my newfound freedom while I wait for someone to snatch it away. And while I try to discover if I really do have wings and can spread them and fly."

"You have wings, Lydia," he said. "And you will fly if you truly want to."

She felt tears spring to her eyes before she could look away. All the men in her life so far had been strong and assertive. Even now her father and brothers wanted to come and take her home with them so they could look after her. Harry had been a soldier, a military officer, and she did not doubt that he too was strong and firm of character and had been ruthless in the performance of his duty. But it was *kindness* that most characterized him now. It was kindness that made him smile almost constantly, that made him amiable to everyone, old and young alike, of the lower class and his own upper class alike, men and women alike. She had thought of his smile very recently as a kind of mask, and in a way it was, because she did not doubt there was the weight of darkness inside him. Not the darkness of evil, but that of suffering. It was kindness upon which he had chosen to base his daily life, however, and the willingness to listen and empathize and comfort. It had bothered him to know that he had dismissed her as a mere shadow until very recently.

It would be awfully easy, and a terrible mistake, to fall in love with Major Harry Westcott.

She swiped away her tears with two fingers.

"I have made you sad," he said. "Our conversation has turned somber, and the fault is entirely mine. Instead of asking why you have always chosen to hide, I ought to have told you how glad I am that you have gifted me with a glimpse of the real Lydia, even down to the absence of a cap this evening. Whenever I meet you from now on I will know you are someone whose friendship I would welcome."

"You are very kind," she said.

He got to his feet suddenly. "It is time I leave," he said. "I will take care not to be seen, Lydia, and you will have your quiet independence back, with not the slightest stain upon your reputation. Nor will I upon mine, for that matter. I wish we *could* be closer friends, though perhaps we can at least settle for being friendlier acquaintances in the future than we have been in the past?" He smiled down at her.

"Yes," she said. "Perhaps we can."

She stayed where she was as he crossed the room and donned his cloak and took his hat in one hand. He would not even have to light his lantern. There was still a grayness visible through the curtains. It was not quite dark. He had not been here long at all. Far less than an hour.

He turned toward her, presumably to say good night. He was no longer smiling. And he did not immediately say the words.

Neither did she.

They merely gazed at each other, half a room apart.

Lydia got to her feet but hesitated even as she considered going to hold the door open for him and watching him leave.

"Lydia," Harry said softly.

"Harry." Her voice sounded unnaturally high-pitched. And she took one hesitant step toward him.

He set his hat down on the table beside the door without watching what he did and took one step toward her.

And then somehow they were in each other's arms.

Nine

Harry closed his eyes and held her to him, breathing in the scent of her hair and her skin, feeling the slender, shapely lines of her body, warm and supple against his, allowing desire to wash over him, feeling an answering longing in her. And *longing* was just what it was. It was more than lust, more than simple desire.

He murmured her name against her ear, pressed his lips to her temple, and feathered kisses down her cheek until she tipped back her head and looked at him, her eyes huge with dreams and yearning. "Lydia?"

"Don't leave." Her arms were about him beneath his cloak. She was pressed to him from shoulders to knees. She would be able to feel the evidence of his desire. "Harry, don't leave. Stay."

He kissed her, parted her lips with his own, pressed his tongue deep into her mouth, drew the tip across the roof of her mouth, urged on by the shudder that ran through her and the sound she made deep in her throat. He was not totally mindless, however. He could still wonder if she was going to regret this. If he was. He looked into her eyes again, their faces mere inches apart.

"Will you regret this?" he asked her.

She shook her head. "But I must let you know," she said, "that I have never done this—"

He stopped her words with his mouth. "I know," he said. "I know you are not a woman of loose morals, Lydia. It does not need to be said."

She gazed at him for a few moments longer, drew breath as though to say more, but then shook her head slowly. "I do not want you to go."

And so he stayed. He unbuttoned his cloak, flung it over the back of the sofa, noticed that the fire, though it had burned low, was not out, and went to set the fireguard about the hearth. The dog had got up and trotted into the kitchen to lap water from her bowl. He took up one of the candles from the mantel and turned back to Lydia. She was standing where he had left her, but she turned without a word and led the way into her bedchamber. He followed her, shut the door, and set the candlestick down on the dressing table.

It was not a large room. There was just space enough for the bed and dressing table, and a small chest of drawers on one side of the bed. Another door probably led to a dressing room. It was a feminine chamber, though not frilly. It suited her. The cotton curtains had a cheerful floral design, and the bedspread looked as if it had been hand embroidered with flowers to match the curtains.

Lydia turned in to his arms, and he knew as soon as she kissed him again that she had not changed her mind, that her eagerness for this had not waned but rather intensified. She was hot and yielding. And it was evident that her slim shapeliness owed everything to nature and nothing to stays.

She wore none. He unfastened the two buttons at the back of her dress, high enough that she would be able to reach them herself without the services of a maid, and eased the dress down over her shoulders and down her arms and body. She allowed it to drop to the floor.

His fingers dispensed with the pins that held the bulk of her hair in a knot on the back of her head, and it came cascading about her shoulders and down her back, a dark cloud of unruly glory. He combed his fingers through it, held her head cupped between his hands, gazed into her eyes, and kissed her again, both of them openmouthed now.

Both hot.

"Harry."

Her hands were unbuttoning his coat and then his waistcoat and pushing them off his shoulders so when he straightened his arms they landed on the floor behind him. He dispensed with his neckcloth, dragged his shirt free of his waistband, pulled it off over his head, and sent it to join his coat. He heard her inhale slowly as he set his hands at her waist and held her at arm's length while he gazed at her, wearing only a cotton shift now, which ended just above her knees, and her stockings and slippers.

How had it ever been possible for her to render herself invisible?

She was nothing short of gorgeous.

He went down on one knee, rolled down her stockings one at a time, and drew each off her foot after first removing the slipper. Then he stood, slid the straps of her shift off her shoulders, and let it slide down her body to pool about her bare feet. He stood back again to look at her. And she gazed steadily back at him, though the flickering light of the candle from the dressing table showed him that her cheeks were rosy with color.

"You are so very beautiful," he told her.

She spread her fingers briefly in front of herself before curling them into her palms. She had been going to unbutton him at the waist but had lost the courage. He removed the rest of his clothes himself while she sank her teeth into her lower lip.

"Harry," she said, and reached out a hand to touch the seam of the worst of his old saber wounds, which slashed across his left hip. His body looked very much like an old battleground. "I came so close to never knowing you at all, did I not?"

She came into his arms again, all soft, hot, naked perfection.

He hoped he was going to be able to impose some control, some discipline, upon himself. It had been a long time. He wanted to make it perfect. For both of them. She had been a long time without too. But this was not just the lust of a long hunger. He could not recall ever wanting a woman as he wanted Lydia at this moment. She had crept up on him in her quiet, near-invisible way like all the dreams of love and perfection he had ever dreamed rolled into one. Yet she was no dream. *This* was no dream.

He drew back the bedcovers and she lay down and reached for him. It was only after he followed her that he thought of the candle, its flame multiplied several times in the wings of the mirror over the dressing table. He had not asked if she would prefer darkness. He did not ask now. He wanted to see her, and her eyes were feasting upon him, scars and all.

His control was put to the test. She was all panting need as she pressed herself to him, moved against him, and kissed him, murmuring his name. Her skin was warm and smooth, her breasts small and firm, her nipples hard, her waist narrow, her hips flaring, her legs smooth, the place between her thighs hot and moist. He felt them all with his palms, his fingers, his lips, his tongue. But there was little or no rousing to be done. She was ready for him, open to him, eager, reaching, hot, and repeating his name.

He moved on top of her, spread her legs with his knees, slid his hands beneath her to lift her and hold her steady, positioned himself, and entered her. Slowly. She was tight, and he remembered again that it had been a long time for her. But *so* tight. And then almost impossible. Until she flinched slightly and he slid with sudden ease to his full length deep inside her.

He lay still on her for a moment, savoring the tight, soft heat that encased him, and wondering, a bit startled, if . . . Considering an impossibility, shaking it off as absurd, but holding back the urge to begin moving so she could adjust to the feel of him. Then he slid his hands free, took some of his weight onto his forearms, withdrew, and pressed inward, once, twice, and again and again in the rhythm of sex. Slowly, while he watched her face so close to his own, her eyes shut tight, her teeth biting her lip. Her body was tense. She opened her eyes after a while and gazed into his, and he could feel her body relax even as her inner muscles tightened and then let go and tightened again as she learned his rhythm and matched it. She had stopped biting her lip. He kissed her.

Oh, God, this was . . . But there were no words. This was sex as it was meant to be. For she was not just a woman. She was Lydia. She was *his* woman. Though not that either, for it suggested ownership, a one-sided thing. She was not his anything, just as he was not her anything. She was the completion of him, just as he hoped he was the completion of her. They were *they*. But he was not thinking these things in sentences or even words.

There *were* no words.

He took her hands in his, palm to palm, raised them to her pillow, on either side of her head, laced their fingers, and lowered his weight onto her again before increasing the rhythm and the depth of his strokes until the need to spill into her roared like a torrent in his ears and set his heart pounding and his loins flaming. He waited for her, waited . . . But then could wait no longer.

He released deep into her, and heard her sigh against his ear. A warm, satisfied sigh. Surely, even though he had not felt an answering release. She whispered his name.

After a minute or two he moved off her to lie at her side. He slid an arm beneath her neck and she turned to him, nestling her head on his shoulder. She smiled and closed her eyes.

And he was left wondering. Not knowing for sure. And hesitant to ask. What an idiot he would make of himself if she looked at him in amazed incredulity. It was impossible anyway. Surely. Of course it was. She had been married for *six years*. To a young, vigorous, handsome man with whom she had fallen headlong in love and married two months after she met him. Unless Tavernor had been impotent. Or preferred men. Both of which seemed highly unlikely.

No, it was stupid even to be wondering. It was impossible that she had been a virgin until a few minutes ago.

He ran his fingertips lightly along her arm to where it bent at the elbow and then down over her hip. He was warm and satiated. He could easily fall asleep—and perhaps sleep through until morning. That would not be wise. Although the candle was behind her and threw her face into shadow, he could see that her eyes were open again. When he kissed her, her lips were soft and relaxed.

"When dreams come true . . . ," she murmured. But she left it at that. She did not make a complete sentence out of it. She had dreamed of a lover. Of *him*. And she had just had him.

He kissed her, their lips lingering on each other's, soft and warm. She sighed.

He would not let himself get hard again. Just in case . . . Even though it was impossible. And he must not let himself fall asleep.

He sighed too and kissed the top of her head. "I had better go," he said. "It would not do for me to spend the whole night here."

"No, it would not." But she sounded regretful. "Thank you for staying, Harry. I am terribly weak willed. I was determined to turn you away, but I could not do it. You must not blame yourself, as I daresay you will try to do tomorrow. I asked—no, I begged—and you stayed. Thank you."

He slid his arm free and got out of bed. He got dressed as she watched, leaned over the bed to kiss her good night, sliding his arms beneath her while she wrapped her own about his neck, and then left the bedchamber.

He lit the candle by the door after donning his cloak and then lit his lantern from it. He took up his hat while Snowball came to be petted. When he straightened up after scratching her back, he realized Lydia was standing behind the sofa. She was barefoot, though she was wearing a dressing gown, which she held across herself with both arms. She had hooked her hair back behind her ears. She was not smiling.

"Good night, Lydia," he said.

"Good night," she said, then drew an audible breath.

"This cannot continue now, Harry. You must not come again. I am sorry. I really am. I am *not* sorry you stayed, but . . ." She shrugged. "I *am* sorry I have sent such muddled and mixed messages tonight. I—" She stopped and shrugged again, and he realized she was on the verge of tears.

He was not surprised. And he was not going to argue. For he knew now he was not in the market for an affair. And *she* was not in the market for a husband. So this must be the end, whether he was happy about it or not. He must see her again, however. In private. For he had thought of something he had assumed he did not have to worry about.

"I *will* call tomorrow," he said. "Not to stay long, though. I must ask you something." Now, tonight, was not the right time.

"I am going to Eastleigh tomorrow with the Reverend and Mrs. Bailey," she told him.

"The day after tomorrow, then," he said.

"Perhaps." She looked very unhappy. She was biting her lip again, and blinking rather a lot.

"Good night, then," he said again, and let himself out of the house. He closed the door quietly behind him, looked cautiously both ways when he reached the gate, and hurried across the road onto his own drive. Yet he felt as though eyes were upon him, now when all was over between them and it would be particularly disastrous to be seen slinking away in the dark. He felt prickles across his shoulder blades and all down his spine. The consequences of guilt. For of course this really must be the end. He must honor her decision to be free. He must do nothing further to endanger her reputation in the eyes of her friends and neighbors.

All his previous lovers had been experienced women. All of them during his military years, without exception, had been widows from among the camp followers, a few of them widows several times over. All of them had known a thing or two about keeping themselves unencumbered while they followed the armies about under all conditions, making themselves useful, doing what they could to make life possible for a vast army on the move in a country not their own. They had all known how to keep themselves clean and free of disease. They had all known how to prevent conception.

Because Lydia Tavernor had been married for a number of years, and because she was childless, he had assumed without—admittedly—giving the matter much thought, that she knew how to stop herself from getting with child. But what if she really had been a virgin until tonight? What if she knew nothing? What if she had not even considered the possibility that a real lover as opposed to a dream one might get her with child?

But no. He had to have been mistaken. It would be just too bizarre . . .

But what if . . . ?

He sighed as he climbed the steps to his front door. If only when Tom had offered to walk her home that night, *he* had kept his mouth firmly shut. And if only after she had said good night to him on that occasion, he had not insisted upon following her through the gate and all the way to her door. If only his heart were not feeling a bit bruised tonight. More than a bit, actually.

If only, if only, and if only . . .

Lydia washed herself with shaking hands. She pulled on a flannel nightgown and then her dressing gown over it. She went back into the living room, took the guard away from the fire, and saw that it was out with not an ember still glowing. She did not bother to build a new one. She sat on her chair, her bare feet and legs curled up beneath her, pulled the cushion from behind her, and clasped it to her bosom with both arms. She slid her hands under the loose sleeves of her dressing gown to warm them.

She could not stop shaking even though it was not a cold night. She had to clamp her teeth together to keep them from chattering. Snowball was sitting before her chair, gazing mournfully up at her, but she had no attention to spare her dog.

What had she done?

And if there was ever a more rhetorical question than that one, she did not know what it could be.

She had given up willpower, common sense, sanity. She had done him a terrible wrong—telling him this morning he might come this evening, telling him as soon as he arrived that he must go, inviting him to stay awhile anyway, sending him away again, calling him back, *sleeping with him*, sending him away yet again, telling him never to return. It was a relentless list of weakness and contradiction and self-indulgence.

Harry.

What had she done to him? She was not so vain that she imagined she had broken his heart. But she had . . . *used* him. And then discarded him.

It had been nothing like . . . Oh, it had been *nothing* like anything she had expected. Sweet kisses, sweet romance, sweet bodily pleasure, and sweet memories to wrap about herself. That was what she had dreamed of. Not hot, mindless passion and raw sensation that was pain and fierce pleasure all inextricably bound together, and naked beauty and the overpowering sensation of being possessed body, mind, and soul. Suffocated by it. Though no. No! That was unfair. And wrong. If she had felt possessed and suffo-cated, it was by her own desire, her own passion to love and be loved. Though that was not the right word either. Some-thing more raw than love. More physical. If there was a word, she did not know it.

She shivered still in the aftermath of what had not been love, though she did not know what it had been. She was sore and throbbing. And yet longing at the same time. Yearning and longing. She tightened her arms about the cushion and lowered her head so her forehead rested on the top of it. She closed her eyes.

She had hated Isaiah.

What a wonderfully freeing admission, even if she *was* just thinking it and not shouting it from the rooftop. She had never admitted it even to herself before now.

She had hated him.

And it was not even past tense. She hated him still.

From her wedding day on she had tried and tried to please him, to make his vision and his mission her own. He must be right, she had always told herself. He was a *man of God*, and many of his parishioners here worshiped him as much as they did the God whose word he preached. She had made herself be one of them. For she had to be wrong in any rebellious thought that tried to invade her mind. There would be something bad about her if she did not love him. And so she did. By sheer willpower. She had had no real problem with willpower in those days. Perhaps if he had lived she would have kept on loving him and convinc-ing herself that it was not in reality hatred that she felt. And perhaps all that was herself would have disappeared more and more into him as time went on until she vanished alto-gether. She almost had. Perhaps it would have been as well if she had.

But what had made her think about Isaiah now of all times? Guilt? She laughed into the cushion, and Snowball whined. Lydia looked up.

"Guilt, Snowball?" she said. *"Guilt?"*

She laughed again, and Snowball tipped her head to one side and looked inquiringly at her.

"I lost my virginity tonight," Lydia told her dog. "And I am supposed to feel *guilt*? I am supposed to grovel before the sacred memory of my husband who was husband only in name?"

Snowball did not think so. She whined again and bounced before the chair. Lydia uncurled herself and set aside the cushion in order to lean down and scoop the dog up onto her lap.

She *did* feel guilt. Toward Harry. Who was beautiful. Inside and out.

How was she ever going to face him again? He wanted to call on her once more to say something. Briefly, he had said. He did not plan to apologize to her, did he? She would not be able to bear that. He was coming the day after tomorrow. Tomorrow she was going to Eastleigh with the Baileys, though she could not bear the thought of that either. How could she share a carriage with those good people and spend a day shopping with them?

But then an idea caught at her mind. A temptation, perhaps? To run away? To escape reality? To return to what was most familiar to her? Or perhaps merely a withdrawal, a chance to give herself space to sort herself out, to put herself back together so she could move forward again with the life she had set up so happily for herself during the past year?

She would not have to stay forever. It could be just a visit, to last as long as she chose. Maybe a week, maybe two. She had the perfect excuse. Her sister-in-law had just let her know that she was with child. She was excited about it and wanted Lydia to come home. She meant, of course, that she wanted Lydia to *move* home and stay. But a visit would be in order. Her father had been ill. They would all be happy to see her.

And she had the perfect opportunity. She would not have to wait until she wrote to Papa and he sent the carriage for her, as of course he would wish to do and insist upon doing. That would all take a week, probably longer. She could travel post from Eastleigh or even hire a private chaise. The Reverend Bailey would surely advise her upon which would be best. Papa would not like it, but he would be delighted to see her anyway.

Lydia sat for a few minutes longer, thinking. She had developed an alarming tendency lately to say and do impulsive things she later regretted. Was going away so abruptly something she would regret doing? Specifically, running away home to her father and her brothers—and her sister-in-law? Running away from Harry? Would coming back in a few weeks' time be even harder than staying now and facing him the day after tomorrow? Would she find it impossible to come back and so slip into the old life again, her lovely freedom and independence here merely a fading memory?

Lydia sighed after a while and ran a finger between Snowball's ears and along her spine. "You and I are going on a journey tomorrow," she said. "Will you like that?"

Snowball waved her stub of a tail and nudged her nose at Lydia's hand to encourage more petting.

Ten

❧

"He was quite adamant at Christmastime," Viola, Marchioness of Dorchester, said, "and he had not changed his mind when he wrote in February. He does not like being in town, especially during the Season, and he has no plans to come here this year."

"I daresay," Jessica, Countess of Lyndale, said, "he knows very well that if he comes here we are bound to arrange something for his birthday. He would hate it. Poor Harry."

She laughed, and Elizabeth, Lady Hodges, laughed with her.

"Poor Harry, indeed," she said.

"He wrote the same thing to me, Aunt Viola," Jessica added.

"And to me," Matilda, Viscountess Dirkson, said. "What a provoking boy he is, for sure. Though Charles keeps reminding me that he is no longer a boy."

"He is a provoking *man*," Mildred, Lady Molenor, said.

The five ladies, as well as Anna, Duchess of Netherby, and Louise, the dowager duchess, were gathered in the dining room at Archer House on Hanover Square, the Duke of Netherby's London home, to discuss the matter of Harry.

"Plan B it is to be, then?" Anna said. "We will go to him since he will not come to us?"

"There was a wistfulness about him at Christmastime," Viola said, frowning. "Marcel says I was merely imagining that Harry is not happy living all alone at Hinsford, like a hermit. He points out that it is the life Harry has chosen quite freely. But Camille agreed with me, and so did Abigail. Even Mary did. My sister-in-law," she added in case any of her Westcott relatives had forgotten.

"Wistfulness?" Elizabeth asked.

"Oh, he enjoyed himself," Viola said. "He did not even mind being mauled and pestered by all the children. He joined in every activity with enthusiasm. He scarcely stopped smiling. He seemed more reluctant than usual to go back home and even went with Abigail and Gil to Gloucestershire for a few weeks. I believe he felt his aloneness."

"It is possible to feel more alone in a crowd than in solitude," Matilda said. "No, Mildred, that is *not* nonsense, though you roll your eyes. Harry is lonely."

"It is also possible to be alone yet not lonely," Elizabeth said.

"But Aunt Viola says Harry looked *wistful*," Jessica reminded her.

"He also enjoyed Christmas," Louise said, "even though the house must have been very crowded and very noisy. He will enjoy a birthday party to cheer him up."

"I *hope* he will enjoy it," Viola said. "He will at least see that we all *care*."

Mildred patted her shoulder, for she was desperately try-ing to hold back tears.

"I will never forget," Anna said, "how gravely ill he looked when he arrived back from Paris and we all went down to Hinsford to see him."

Matilda blinked her eyes, cleared her throat, and took charge—something at which she excelled. Their meetings, when they had a particular object in mind, did have a ten-dency to lose focus as various tangents were followed and one led to another.

"We need to divide up the list of letters that need to be written," Matilda said.

Seven blotters had been spread around the table, with a neat pile of paper and an ink bottle and a quill pen above each.

"The letters do not have to be long," Matilda continued. "We sent a copy of both plans to everyone concerned after Christmas—and *that* took us a long time. Now all we need do is instruct everyone to ignore plan A and familiarize themselves with plan B. Dates and times and important de-tails are clearly stated there, and we must emphasize that everyone should follow those details to the letter. It is very important in particular that we all arrive on the same day. Better yet, we should all aim to arrive during the afternoon, within three or four hours of one another. We wish to sur-prise Harry, and we can do that most effectively if we all descend upon him at as close to the same time as possible."

"Poor Harry," Jessica and Anna said in unison, and they all laughed—even Matilda.

"Louise," Matilda said, "write to Mother and Aunt Edith, if you will. They are coming to town soon, of course, but it is important that they arrive in time to rest for a day or two before going down to Hinsford."

"Ought I also to mention Aunt Edith's niece and nephew?" Louise asked. Miranda Monteith, Aunt Edith's niece on her late husband's side, was one of the three young ladies chosen for Harry's perusal, though no one in the family except Aunt Edith herself knew the young woman, and even she had not seen her since she was a girl of fourteen.

"Yes, do," Matilda said.

Viola would write to her brother, the Reverend Michael Kingsley, and his wife, Mary; Matilda to Mrs. Kingsley, Viola's mother; Anna to Camille and Joel; Jessica to Abigail and Gil; Elizabeth to Alexander, her brother, and Wren; and Mildred to Cousin Althea, Elizabeth's mother.

Estelle and Bertrand Lamarr, the Marquess of Dorchester's adult twins, were not yet in London, but they were expected within the next day or two. Viola undertook to make sure they were ready to follow plan B.

Mildred took it upon herself to speak with Mrs. Leeson, mother of her eldest son's new fiancée. Miss Leeson had a younger sister, another of the chosen three possible brides for Harry.

"Since Boris's betrothal was announced on Valentine's Day, when none of us were in town, Aunt Mildred," Anna said, "we really ought to celebrate it as a family while we are all together at Hinsford. Especially if Miss Leeson's mother and sister are to be there too."

"That is a brilliant idea, Anna," Elizabeth said, beaming at her.

"Splendid." Matilda added it to the bottom of her copy of plan B. "And I will let Sally's mama know that we will definitely be going to Hinsford."

Sally Underwood was the third prospective bride. She was a niece of Viscount Dirkson's first wife, a pretty, vivacious girl, though Matilda admitted she did not know her well.

There were other details to be discussed, including exactly what information they must send to Mrs. Sullivan, Hinsford's housekeeper. But for now they all applied themselves to the task of letter writing. For the next half hour all that could be heard in the dining room was the scratching of pens and the occasional exclamation from Louise, who declared crossly at one point that her pen must have been made specifically to produce one ink blot for every ten words.

Harry did not even know that Lydia had left until after she returned.

He called on her twice on the day he had told her he would. The first time, late in the morning, when she did not answer his knock on the door, he assumed she was out. But when she did not answer during the afternoon either, he guessed that she was deliberately avoiding him. She had, after all, begged him not to return, and she was doubtless reluctant to come face-to-face with him just yet. But it must happen *sometime*. He had spent a couple of almost sleepless nights wondering if he had impregnated her.

She would not know yet, of course. His questions could therefore wait. If she was inside there now, holding her breath, hoping he would go away without making a fuss, he would not make things worse for her by knocking again. If she was *not* inside—and actually it was likely she was not, since there was no sound from the dog either—then he would be wasting his time trying to force an empty house to answer his summons. She had probably made good and sure to be away from her house all day.

He would give her a week and then try again.

But one week stretched into two.

During that time he avoided the village as much as he could, since he did not want to encounter her anywhere else but the cottage. He even missed church two weeks in a row though it was Easter. When he did socialize, it was mostly with neighbors outside the village. He dined with the Raymores one evening and went riding with Lawrence Hill and his sisters a couple of times. Lawrence rode over to Hinsford late one afternoon and stayed for dinner. Harry did walk into the village by the back way one day to spend an evening with Tom and Hannah, but there were no other guests. Just two men reminiscing about their boyhood and one long-suffering woman sewing quietly and smiling a few times and shaking her head a lot. Actually Hannah could reminisce with them over several memories, as she too had grown up at Fairfield.

Harry and Lawrence went to Eastleigh one day as escorts for Rosanne Hill and Theresa Raymore. While the ladies shopped and Lawrence looked at horses, Harry called upon the physician whom he had brought to Hinsford a while ago to have a look at Timmy Hack, and persuaded him to pay a second visit. Harry had called at the Hack cottage after his conversation with Lydia and found the situation just as she had described it. Timmy was indeed pale and listless and not recovering as well as he ought. Harry had been startlingly reminded of himself as he had been for almost two years in the hospital and convalescent home in Paris, the helpless victim of those who would have killed him with good intentions if he had not finally put his foot down and insisted upon returning to England and then upon being left alone at Hinsford to manage his own recovery. That was something Timmy could not do. He was still a child.

Harry spent most of those two weeks alone, however, reading inside the house on wet days, wandering about the park, admiring the spring flowers and the new foliage on the trees when the sun shone, or out on the home farm helping wherever he could, especially on the renovations to the old barn. He was, if the truth must be admitted, more than slightly depressed, and he did not like the feeling one little bit. He had fought suffocating, debilitating depression during the years that followed the Battle of Waterloo, first overseas in Paris and then here at Hinsford when it had seemed to him that he would never recover his full health and strength, that he would never be *himself* again. He had fought and won the battle. He resented the fact that it needed to be fought all over again now.

He ought not to have gone to Bath for Christmas. Or, if he had, he ought to have come back home immediately after, as he had originally planned. And he ought not—*damn it*—to have gone to bed with Lydia Tavernor. Against all his better judgment. Against the principles of a lifetime. Against what he knew were *her* principles. But like a couple of brainless idiots, with no control whatsoever over their lusts and passions, they had gone and hopelessly complicated their lives.

Someone needed to take a horse whip to him.

The solitude and contentment he had so coveted and so enjoyed for four years were suddenly feeling like something far worse, and he did not appreciate it.

Late one morning he was sitting on a stone slab beside the lake, a picturesque spot beneath a weeping willow tree, warming himself in the dappled sunlight and trying to convince himself that this was very idyllic and peaceful and all was right with the world. Instead he was feeling neglected. By his family.

It was the ultimate idiocy on his part.

Those letters from his mother, Jessica, and Aunt Matilda, all of which had touched upon the question of whether he intended to spend any time in London during the upcoming Season, had not fooled him for a moment. For their motive had been glaringly obvious. They wanted to lure him to town so they could put on some sort of grand party in celebration of his thirtieth birthday. And they very probably wanted to do some aggressive matchmaking at the same time. He knew the Westcott family as of old—or so he had thought. He had fully expected to hear from a few more of them soon after with the same question buried amid other news, or perhaps even with some definite reason why he *ought* to come or really *must* come.

He had indeed received more letters—one from his grandmother, and one from Anna. Neither one had made even a whisper of a mention of his going to London. Or of his birthday. Or, for that matter, of his very single state.

Had they forgotten that he had a birthday coming up? His *thirtieth*? Had they given up on him? Did they not *care*?

He was laughing out loud suddenly. Poor little spoiled boy!

He picked up a couple of loose stones from the flat rock upon which he sat to pitch one at a time at the lake. But the angle was wrong for them to skip. He was too far above the water. They all sank without a trace.

Now that he was not being pressed to go to London, he was very tempted to go after all. To get away from here for a few weeks. To kick up his heels a bit. To air out his head, whatever the devil he meant by that. But it would be madness. Easter was over and done with and the Season would be just swinging into full life. And his sudden appearance might cause someone with the last name of Westcott to recall that he had a landmark birthday soon.

He did not belong to that world any longer, and in all truth he did not want to belong. The Harry Westcott he had been at the age of twenty was not the Harry Westcott who was sitting here now, attempting the impossible by pitching stones from well above the level of the water and expecting them to skip.

He got up and went down closer to the lake to find more stones. He managed to skip the second one four times, gave himself a congratulatory pat on the shoulder, and turned to make his way back to the house.

He could not go to London.

Lydia was here. And Lydia might be with child. By him. Unless good fortune was on their side. Or unless all his instincts had been wrong on that night and she was after all the experienced widow he had thought her to be, and knew how to avoid pregnancy. Had her childlessness been a deliberate choice, by the way? Or was she barren? Or had she indeed been a virgin when he took her to bed? He could not shake off the horrible suspicion that she had been. There had been that tightness as he pressed into her, that slight flinch.

Dash it all, he could not go to London. He must find out if their . . . encounter had had consequences. At the very least it was surely the decent thing to go and check on her, to make sure she was all right. Her life of quiet independence was precious to her. He had put that at risk. He owed her an apology if nothing else.

It was two weeks to the day since he had called last at her cottage. Two weeks since he had gone down his own drive. He had gone out by other routes whenever he had left home during those weeks. It was time to put things to rights.

He walked down the drive the next morning under skies that threatened rain later and could see even before he reached the bottom of it that she was in her garden, kneeling down by the flower bed beneath her front window. The grass was looking a bit long, Harry noticed.

Snowball came bouncing and yipping up to the fence to greet him. Lydia looked sharply his way.

He crossed the road to the fence.

"Lydia," he said.

She turned her face away and set down her gardening tools unhurriedly and removed her gloves. She got to her feet and rubbed her hands together before turning and looking at him again. She had not said a word.

Ah, good God. Lydia.

Lydia had stayed away for a little less than two weeks. She had had a wonderful time. Her father and brothers had admonished her, of course, when she had appeared at their door without warning in the modest private chaise the Reverend Bailey had helped her hire. They had all also hugged her tightly enough to crush bones, she had feared, and certainly to endanger her ability to breathe. Esther had hugged her and clung to her and wept over her while declaring that she had never been happier in her life.

Papa had appointed a maid to her exclusive service almost before she had set foot inside the house. And from that moment on she had not unpacked a box or lifted a water jug or a brush or any piece of clothing. She had been waited upon literally hand and foot.

She had been wined and dined and taken to call upon

neighbors and had neighbors invited to come and visit her. She had been fussed and coddled and entertained and talked with from morning until night. She had been gently scolded for getting up too early in the morning and for going to bed too late at night. She had been taken to church on Palm Sunday and Easter Sunday mornings and proudly displayed in the place of honor next to her father in the padded front pew that was his. She had been introduced to the vicar, *"who is a single man, Lydie,"* she had been told afterward. She had been introduced to Mr. Johnson, a new neighbor who was reputed to have inherited a modest fortune a year or two ago—*"and is a single man, Lydie."* He had been promptly invited with a small party of other neighbors to dine a few evenings later and had been conspicuously seated beside her at the dining table.

Snowball had been treated with amusement and affection and gross indulgence. She was going to look even more like a ball if they stayed much longer, Lydia had thought a few times.

They had all assumed, of course, that she had come to stay. Or at least that she was persuadable. And perhaps for the first few days she had been. It had been so lovely to *relax*, to lower all her defenses. It had been a huge relief to discover after she had been there a mere two days that her night with Harry had not had consequences. During the first week she had been able to forget about that night. Or, if that was impossible, as of course it was, at least to look back on it as though it were something that had happened a long time ago to someone else.

She had not stayed, however. It had not taken long for her to feel a bit stifled by all the attention and overwhelmed by the never-ending company and talk and laughter. She had never been alone, except at night. Even when she had

tried a few times to withdraw to her room for a bit of solitude, someone had been sure to tap on her door and poke a
head around it to ask if there was anything wrong, if perhaps she had a headache and needed a draft of something
to ease the pain. If she had tried to take a solitary walk in
the park to enjoy the peace of nature, her father or one of
her brothers or even Esther, who was not supposed to exert
herself, had soon fallen into step beside her—*"to keep you
company, Lydie."* And if it was one of the men—or more
than one, as it often was—he had been sure to remind her
that she must never wander out of sight of the house if she
was alone. *"A woman can never be too careful, Lydie."*
Familiar words she remembered from her youth.

James clearly adored Esther, as she did him. But he
fussed over her constantly and hovered. He stopped her
from doing a thousand things—the number was probably
exaggerated, Lydia admitted to herself—she wanted to do.
Those things were either unwise or unsafe, or they would
tire her or threaten her delicate health or bore her or give
the wrong impression to other people. Or—and this one
Lydia had found most irksome—she must not worry her
pretty little head over them. If Esther expressed an opinion
on any subject, though she did not often do so, James would
be sure to admonish her, gently and affectionately, for
speaking on a topic she could not possibly comprehend or
for taxing her brain more than was good for her or for worrying over something the men would take care of.

"Esther," Lydia had said one day when they were alone,
"do you not want to scream sometimes when Papa or James
fuss over you and want to do everything for you but breathe?
Even *think?*" She had laughed to soften the harshness of
her words.

But Esther had looked at her as though she had sprouted

an extra head. "Oh, but Lydia," she had said, "they are *wonderful*. That I love James to distraction goes without saying, of course. But that when I married him I should also have gained such a father and such brothers makes me wonder sometimes what I ever did to deserve such rich blessings. They *care* for me and protect me. I . . . Well, I really ought not to say anything about my own papa and my brother. But I will say this much. They were never *anything* like yours, Lydia. How fortunate you have been. And to have married the Reverend Tavernor, who was *wonderful*, though I only met him that once, when he brought you here for my wedding."

Lydia had grown very fond of Esther during those two weeks. She was unfailingly sweet and affectionate. But Lydia doubted they could ever be close friends. They were too different in temperament and perspective.

So she had known by the end of the first week that she could not stay indefinitely. During the second week she had still enjoyed being there. And she had consciously loved her family and appreciated who they were as persons. But she had begun to long for her little cottage and her kitchen and her flower beds. She had begun to miss her neighbors and friends. And she had begun to long to see Harry again, to try to apologize to him if she could, to see if she had hurt him in any way, though it was far more likely he had shrugged off *that incident* as relatively unimportant. Men were like that, were they not? Their emotions did not get all tangled up with their pleasures.

Ah, but she was surely being unfair. She did not believe he had just been grabbing an opportunity for casual gratification that night.

Papa had not liked her decision to return home, and he had been very vocal about telling her so. James did not like it either. Nor did William. Anthony, who had come home from university for Easter, had already returned to Oxford for his final term and so had no chance to voice an opinion. Esther wept.

But home Lydia had come, with far more pomp and bluster than when she arrived. For Papa, of course, had insisted upon sending her in his own carriage with a coachman and a footman up on the box and a maid inside with her, as well as two outriders to deter any would-be highwaymen. He would have accompanied her himself, as would either James or William, but she had put her foot down and insisted that she would not so inconvenience any of them. Esther had looked frightened over her insubordination, but she had won the day after making a nasty threat.

"If you try to insist," she had warned the three men, "then I shall simply walk away in the middle of the night, taking only Snowball with me for protection."

"Ah, Lydie," her father had said reproachfully, and for a moment she had thought she detected tears in his eyes.

There had certainly been tears in hers when she left, hugged boneless and breathless again before she climbed into the carriage, and then waved after until the carriage turned a corner and they were lost to view. Then she had wept some more. For of course she knew—she had always known—why her father was so protective of her, his only daughter. He had adored her mother, set her up on a pedestal, felt unworthy of her, since he had been a wild man about town when he fell in love with her. He blamed himself for her death so soon after giving birth to his fourth child and the fact that Lydia had been deprived of her mother at such a young age. Oh, he had never spoken these things aloud, but Lydia knew. She had been eight years old. She had understood far more than her father and brothers probably realized. She could no longer allow him to dominate and protect her, but she loved him enough to hurt at times. Oh, love was *not* just a soft, feel-good emotion. Sometimes it tore painfully at the heart.

But now she was home. And happy. So was Snowball. Mrs. Bartlett had seen the bustle of her arrival yesterday and had brought over a bowl of soup and two freshly baked bread buns for her evening meal and welcomed her home but would not stay because she could see that Mrs. Tavernor was pale with fatigue and then stayed for a full hour anyway, telling her every tidbit of news and gossip from the past two weeks.

This morning Lydia was tackling the mess of her front garden. For of course grass and weeds—and even flowers, to a lesser degree—did not stop growing just because one was away from home. She was kneeling on the overlong grass beneath the front window, waging war upon weeds in the flower bed and planning to call at the smithy later to see if Reggie would come and scythe her grass soon, when Snowball started to yip and bark and bounce enough that Lydia knew someone must be coming along the street— or down the drive. She turned her head to see.

Ah, the moment had come. And she was not sure her knees would support her if she tried to stand.

Perhaps, she thought, he would merely nod and go on his way. But he crossed the road and came right up to her garden fence.

"Lydia," he said.

And she wanted to weep. For no reason whatsoever that she would have been able to explain to herself. She set down her gardening tools, pulled off her gloves, and rubbed her hands to rid them of the grains of soil that had got underneath the gloves—all with slow deliberation so she could collect herself before standing and turning toward him and looking fully at him.

"I got home yesterday," she said. "And the garden is a mess."

And so was she. A mess, that was. She had forgotten just how overwhelmingly gorgeous he was.

"Got home?" he said, frowning. "Have you been away?"

He did not know? Oh.

Oh.

"I went to spend Easter with my father and brothers," she told him. "And my sister-in-law. She is in a . . . delicate way."

"I did not know you were gone." He rested one hand on top of the fence and looked down. "Be quiet, Snowball. I see you."

Snowball settled on the grass, gazing upward.

"That was why I got no answer when I called here twice on the same day," Harry said, looking back at her. "I thought you were avoiding me. But I suppose you were."

"It was Easter," she said lamely.

"Lydia." He looked at her for long moments before continuing. "Are you with child?"

Oh goodness. She felt color flood her cheeks. "No," she said. "Oh, no, I am not."

His hand was gripping the fence, she noticed. But he only nodded briefly and said nothing more. He had come that day, then—twice? But not since then? He had not known she was away. Yet it felt as if she had been gone forever.

"Harry," she said. "I am sorry—"

"Please do not be," he said, cutting her off before she could finish. "I am sorry too. But it would be better, perhaps, if we did not belabor the point. You found your family well? Your sister-in-law too?"

"Yes," she said. "My father had a nasty chill a month or so ago, but he is quite better now."

"I am glad," he said.

They were talking like polite strangers, making stilted conversation. It was almost impossible, as she looked at him now, simply but elegantly dressed like a country gentleman, to believe that they had actually made love in the house behind her. That they had been naked together . . .

"The weeds did not stop growing while I was gone," she said.

"Why should they?" he asked. "They are as eager to survive as any other living thing."

"I suppose," she said.

He dropped his hand from the fence and took one step back. "Are you planning to attend the assembly at the inn on Thursday evening?" he asked her.

Ah, the spring assembly that always happened soon after Easter. She had always attended while Isaiah was alive. He had disapproved of the frivolity of dancing and would never dance himself—nor, consequently, had she—but he had not considered it actually sinful. And he had judged his presence to be necessary, as it was at all village events, so that he could open it with a prayer of blessing and thanks. She had always found that prayer a little embarrassing.

"I will be going," Harry said.

So would almost everyone else. It was a much-anticipated event. Each family took food, so the tables positively groaned with it. The music was always lively, the dancing vigorous, the conversation loud and merry. She had always behaved with quiet decorum while her heart danced to the music and her toes tapped, even if only imperceptibly inside her slippers. She had not attended last year, as she had been in mourning.

"So will I," she said. "Probably."

He nodded. "I will see you there, then," he said. And he turned and walked away. But not along the street into the village, as she had expected, but back up the drive in the direction of home. He had come specifically to call upon her, then, had he? After two weeks of not even knowing that she was gone?

Snowball scrambled to her feet and protested his leaving, but he did not look back.

"I will probably go," Lydia said softly.

Eleven

Probably turned into a definite commitment as the week went by, for the assembly was at the forefront of everyone's mind and it was hard to resist a communal lifting of the spirits. Each of Lydia's particular friends—Hannah Corning, Denise Franks, and Mrs. Bailey—asked her about her visit to her father in the days following her return and then wanted to know if she intended to go to the assembly.

Lady Hill, who together with Sir Maynard, her husband—they owned an estate that bordered Hinsford land—had met and liked Lydia's father when he came for Isaiah's funeral and had exchanged a few friendly letters with him since then, had been attentive to Lydia ever since she moved into her cottage and sometimes invited her to afternoon tea. Now, though, she invited Lydia to dinner on the evening before the assembly. When Lydia arrived, Lady Hill introduced her to her sister and her niece, Mrs. Ardreigh and Miss Vivian Ardreigh, who had come to stay for a couple of weeks. The only other guest was Theresa Raymore, the magistrate's daughter and a friend of the two Misses Hill.

Sir Maynard, Lady Hill explained, had gone with Lawrence and Mr. Ardreigh and his son, Vivian's brother, to dine with Harry Westcott, who had taken pity on them after Lawrence had complained to him that they were to be turned out of the house.

"Which was gross slander, Lydia, if not an open untruth," Lady Hill protested, "when all I had said in a passing remark was how lovely it would be just occasionally to have a ladies-only dinner and evening, like the ones men so often enjoy at their clubs in London."

"But you did particularly mention this evening and sighed mournfully, Aunt," Vivian Ardreigh pointed out with a smile.

"I did." Lady Hill laughed. "And it worked like a charm. I hope you do not mind there being no gentlemen present, Lydia and Theresa, but sometimes it is very relaxing to enjoy exclusively female company. We can gossip to our hearts' content and talk about bonnets and fans and beaux all evening without stopping to draw breath if we choose. Who is to accuse us of being frivolous and empty-headed?"

They all laughed. It was something they continued to do through much of the evening. And how lovely it was, Lydia thought as she was taken home in the Hill carriage at well past ten o'clock, to have been included in the gathering. She had enjoyed herself enormously even though the conversation had indeed been trivial—quite deliberately so on all their parts. Lady Hill had made only the briefest of inquiries after the health of Lydia's family. She had been more interested in knowing whether Lydia intended on going to the assembly.

"For it is always good to know once Easter is behind us

that we can look forward to kicking up our heels at a village dance and blow away all the cobwebs of winter," she said.

"I will be going," Lydia said, laughing. "But I do not dance, you know."

"Oh, we will see about that." Lady Hill tapped her hand sharply. "It was one point on which, if you will forgive me for saying so, I disagreed with the Reverend Tavernor."

The following morning, Lydia went to call upon Mrs. Hack and Timmy. She had had a few hours to spare in Eastleigh the day she went to visit her father. She had made two purchases to add to the bags she was already taking with her. One of them had been wool for a scarf. She had dithered over four different colors but had finally settled on what she could describe only as a brownish sort of burnt orange—an autumnal hue that was neither dazzlingly bright nor dowdy. Mrs. Bailey had approved when she knew the scarf was to be for a man. She had assumed it was for Lydia's father, and Lydia had not corrected her. The other purchase had been the book for Timmy she had seen on a previous occasion. The stories in it were *not* labeled moral tales, she had been happy to note, and the pictures were a delight in themselves. It had been expensive and a bit of a strain upon Lydia's purse when she had the additional expense of hiring a chaise. But she had compensated for the purchase by *not* buying the silk stockings she needed but could do without until next month.

Lydia took the book now with the finished yellow blanket. It was a bright, sunny morning and really quite warm. She was surprised to see as she approached the house, one of a row of identical thatched cottages with freshly whitewashed walls just beyond the village at the edge of Hinsford land, that the bundle of linen outside and to one side of the door, in full sunshine, was in fact a chair with Timmy sitting on it. He was so wrapped up in blankets and shawls that only his face was showing. But that face was beaming with pleasure even before he caught sight of Lydia. His mother was hovering beside him, adjusting his coverings, looking anxious.

"Timmy," Lydia cried. "Your wish has come true, and here you are in the sunshine."

Mrs. Hack was not at all sure it was a good thing and told Lydia so. She was terribly afraid Timmy was going to take his death of cold. But the major had called on the physician from Eastleigh again, and the physician had come and declared that fresh air and sunshine would do Timmy a world of good. He had prescribed half an hour a day whenever it was not raining, and one hour after the first week, two hours after the second. And the major was going to come and take Timmy for drives in the gig and for rides on his horse after a month or so and—

"And I am to go to *school*, Mrs. Tavernor," Timmy cried from within his cocoon of blankets, "as soon as I am able to be up and about. I am to learn all about the world from Mr. Corning's big globe that spins and how to do long multiplication. And I am to play with the other boys at playtime. And—"

"And if you get yourself overexcited, my boy," his mother warned, "it will be back into your bed with you, and your pa will not be pleased with any of us."

Timmy loved his yellow blanket and laughed with glee when he saw that his name had been embroidered across the top of it. It had to be added to the pile that covered him. His eyes lit up and his jaw dropped when he saw the book and learned that it was all his, to keep and read as often as he chose.

"I have *three* books now," he said in awe. "*Three*, Ma. And this one has *pictures*."

"You are the luckiest boy alive," his mother said. "But what is the first question your pa will ask when you tell him?"

"Did I thank Mrs. Tavernor," Timmy said sheepishly before proceeding to do just that.

Lydia walked back home a short while later with a light heart. It was so lovely to see the child animated and happy and bathed in sunshine, shawls and blankets notwithstanding. It was even lovelier to know that after listening to her story, Harry had intervened on Timmy's behalf, not by ordering the parents to take the child outside but by summoning the physician again—no doubt at considerable expense to himself—to give his professional opinion.

She had not seen Harry since the morning after her return home. She would see him tonight. He had said he was going to the assembly. He had always attended them—after he had recovered his health, anyway. For the first two years she had spent here she had scarcely seen him except at church on Sundays. It was only after seeing him at one of the dances that she had begun to dream about him. He had been even leaner in those days—*thin* might have been a better word then. But he had been vital and smiling and obviously enjoying himself. He had talked with everyone—even her and Isaiah on occasion, though of course he had never really seen her except to nod politely and smile. He had danced with all the women, regardless of age or social class or appearance. He had been . . .

Oh, he had been *golden*.

Lydia sighed as she opened her door and Snowball came bounding outside and greeted her with woofs and tail waves and hand licks before dashing off on more important business.

She would see him again tonight.

Lydia was wearing her pink dress.

It was of very simple design—high-waisted, short-sleeved, low-necked, though not *very* low. Well, really not low at all. It was just not tight to the neck. And though the skirt fell in soft, narrow folds from beneath her bosom, it was quite unadorned. There was no sash and no embroidery or scalloping at the hem. But it fit her, she felt, perfectly and made her look slimmer than she usually did, unless that was merely wishful thinking on her part. The color seemed more vivid now that she was wearing the dress. It was, she thought, quite the most gorgeous garment she had ever possessed. It was so gorgeous, in fact, that she almost took fright and peeled it off to replace it with something gray or lavender, something inconspicuous and more suitable for the wife of a vicar. She had to remind herself quite firmly that she was *not* the vicar's wife. Not any longer. That was Mrs. Bailey. She, Lydia Tavernor, was the widow of the former vicar. She was answerable to no one but herself.

She was going to wear the pink.

And she was going to wear it without a cap. She had pondered the matter, having resumed wearing one after that lone evening with Harry, but really it was high time she stepped away from the old life and into the new, no matter how frightening the prospect was. And she would do it boldly and all at once tonight. She had made the decision this afternoon while icing cakes to take with her.

The spring assembly was the perfect occasion upon which to unveil the new Lydia. And the pink gown was the perfect garment. It was a shame she had no maid to style her hair a little more elaborately than she could herself, but she was quite pleased nevertheless with the result of her efforts. And she was very glad the vicar and his wife had insisted upon fetching her in their carriage, though the inn was not far away—nothing was in this village. It had turned suddenly windy and cloudy during the afternoon and was actually raining in squalls now. Her poor apology for an elegant hairstyle would be ruined if she had to walk.

At least, she thought, Harry would not feel obliged to offer to walk her home tonight.

The carriage came early. Mrs. Bailey moved over on the seat facing the horses to make room for Lydia as the coachman handed her in. The vicar smiled from the seat opposite and wished her a good evening.

"And an ugly evening it is to have to go out in," Mrs. Bailey said. "But I do love the village assemblies, Lydia. They are so much jollier than the more formal dances to which we have been invited occasionally at Sir Maynard Hill's, with only the gentry folk in attendance. I love to dance. Much to the dear vicar's dismay, I might add."

"Isaiah disapproved of dancing too," Lydia said.

"Oh, I do not disapprove, Mrs. Tavernor," the Reverend Bailey assured her. "I like to see my parishioners trip the light fantastic, so to speak, and enjoy themselves. It is just that when the good Lord was handing out body parts around the time I was lining up to be born, he discovered that somehow he had more left feet than right and gave me two of them. Or perhaps he had an even number but was not paying careful enough attention at the time and someone about my age has been shuffling about for the past fifty years or so on two right feet."

He laughed heartily at his own joke while Mrs. Bailey

clucked her tongue, told him that Lydia would think he was a heathen, and laughed too.

"Though I daresay your dear husband enjoyed a good joke every bit as much as mine does, Lydia," she said.

Lydia smiled but did not offer an answer.

They were among the first to set foot in the assembly rooms.

"You may be sure, Lydia," Mrs. Bailey explained to her, as she had done on numerous occasions before, "that if we are supposed to be somewhere at a certain time, we will actually arrive at least a quarter of an hour before that time. It would be half an hour if I had not learned to ignore the vicar standing at the door, hand on the knob to open it, shifting his weight restlessly from foot to foot, and gazing reproachfully at me while I deliberately go about my business and wait until I can stand his silent impatience no longer."

Lydia laughed, thankful for the distraction of Mrs. Bailey's chatter. She felt very self-conscious indeed as she removed her cloak and hung it in the cloakroom and then entered the assembly rooms to take her plate of iced cakes over to the refreshment table. She glanced longingly at one grouping of chairs in the corner farthest from the door but would not go and sit quietly there, as she would normally have done. She had become an expert at going virtually unnoticed in company. But her decision tonight to wear her new pink dress and to leave off her cap was only a part of the larger plan she had decided upon this afternoon.

She was going to hide no longer.

She had been a dutiful wife. She had observed a quiet and decorous period of mourning. She had eased herself quietly out of that period. She was free now, with the means to remain free and independent. She had a home here and neighbors who respected her for Isaiah's sake and probably her own too. She had a few newly made friends. She was invited everywhere. There was *no need* to hide any longer. No one was about to come along to snatch everything away from her.

She was strong. It was a novel idea, but she had thought it through this afternoon and decided that it was true. She had always been controlled by men and conditioned to think of herself as a fragile, timid creature who could not possibly exist without their support and protection and direction. Well, she *could* exist alone. She was doing it. She had been doing it for more than a year.

She did not need to hide and hope no one noticed that she had escaped. Let them notice if they wished. There was nothing anyone could do about it.

She was free. And she was strong.

It was one thing to think it. It was quite another, of course, to live it.

She felt horribly nervous and exposed to view. For as she walked about the room, forcing herself to stop and talk with each group of new arrivals before moving on to the next, she would not allow herself even the limited protection of lowering her eyes and her chin. And the reaction of her neighbors to the sight of her was not reassuring. Most of them seemed to look at her twice in quick succession, first with only a passing glance and then with a more pointed awareness—taking in her pink dress, she supposed, and her bare head and smiling face. They looked surprised. And scandalized? She saw no evidence of the latter. Appreciative? Yes, in several cases. And it was not her imagination. A number of people of both genders commented upon how lovely she looked. That was surely an exaggeration, but at least it assured her that she was not looking as inappropriately clad as she had feared she might be.

Yet when no fewer than three men, including Mr. Roger
Ardreigh, Lady Hill's nephew, who had just been introduced to her, asked her for the opening set of dances, she
refused them all on the grounds that she did not dance. Old
habits died hard. But though she was determined to fight
those habits, there were limits upon what she was willing
to do. She would not make an utter spectacle of herself by
trying to dance in full sight of her neighbors and friends. It
had been a long time . . .

But from the moment she arrived, while she mingled
and talked and listened and looked about at her fellow villagers, at the food tables, at the orchestra tuning their instruments, she was really waiting for *his* arrival and trying
to convince herself that she hoped he would not come. And
telling herself that it would really make no difference to her
if he did or did not. For no matter what, they were in all
probability going to be neighbors for the rest of their lives
and must grow accustomed to seeing each other and even
to being in company together. And she had seen him once
since her return and even spoken with him and somehow
survived the ordeal.

Then suddenly he was here.

He was standing inside the door, talking with Hannah
and Tom Corning, laughing over something that had been
said, looking handsome and elegant despite—or perhaps
because of—the simplicity of his evening clothes. They
were, of course, expertly tailored. His clothes always were.
He wore silver knee breeches with a black evening coat and
silver waistcoat. Knee breeches for evening wear were old-
fashioned in town, Lydia had been told, except at Almack's
and at court, but they were what the other men here in the
country always wore for evening. His stockings and linen

were very white. His neckcloth, though neatly tied, was not an elaborate creation.

Lydia's heart turned over. Or her stomach. Or perhaps nothing turned at all but she was just reacting as any other woman would to the sight of a handsome man. Who also happened to have been naked in her bed with her not so long ago. Yes, it was definitely her stomach.

He looked about the room as he talked and laughed. Lydia could have stepped sideways and been hidden beyond Denise Franks and her husband and Lawrence Hill and Vivian Ardreigh, with whom she was conversing at the moment. She did not do so. She did not even pretend not to have seen him.

He reacted as a number of others had done. His eyes alit upon her, moved onward, and then came back to rest on her. He paused in his conversation and smiled and said something. Both Hannah and her husband turned to glance her way, Hannah smiling too as she answered him. And he moved away from them and came in her direction.

She needed a fan, Lydia thought. And it struck her that she no longer possessed one. Why until this moment had she been unaware of her hands and what she ought to do with them? Let them hang at her sides? Clasp them at her waist? Saw the air with them as she talked? But she was not talking at present.

"Mrs. Tavernor?" He made his bow and smiled at her, but with no suggestion that they had ever been more to each other than neighbors. "Mrs. Franks? Franks? Lawrence? And— ?" He smiled at Vivian and looked at his friend with raised eyebrows.

"My cousin Vivian Ardreigh," Mr. Hill said. "Major Westcott, Viv."

"I feared I was going to be late and would miss the opening set," Harry said after making his bow. "It seems I have arrived just in time, however."

The orchestra had fallen silent. All their instruments had been tuned and they were ready for the dancing to begin.

"Some lady is going to be glad you did arrive in time," Mr. Franks said, grinning. "And some ladies are going to be sorry they have already promised the dance to someone else." He half glanced at Vivian.

"Lydia has not promised it to anyone," Denise said. "She still insists that she will not dance at all. I have never heard such nonsense in my life." Her smile, directed at Lydia, could be described only as mischievous.

"But true," Lydia assured her.

"Tell me, Mrs. Tavernor," Harry said, "is it that you *will* not dance or that you *cannot*? Like the Reverend Bailey with the two left feet he likes to boast of?"

"Will not, certainly," she said. "And cannot, probably. I have not danced since I was a girl."

"And how many decades ago was that?" he asked.

Mr. Franks chuckled.

"It was enough years ago," Lydia told him, "that I have forgotten everything I ever learned and practiced."

"One does not forget how to dance," Denise said. "And it is not as though you have not watched any dancing in the intervening years, Lydia. You used to watch avidly before the Reverend Tavernor died. You may think I did not notice, but I did. You used to look positively wistful."

"Oh, I did not. You have a vivid imagination, Denise," Lydia told her.

Mr. Raymore, who was doing duty as the master of ceremonies tonight, was calling upon the gentlemen to lead their partners onto the floor to form lines for the opening set of country dances. Lawrence Hill extended a hand for his cousin's.

"Mrs. Tavernor," Harry said, "let me persuade you to put the matter to the test. Come and dance with me."

"I have already refused three partners," she told him. "It would be very bad-mannered to accept a fourth."

But just at that moment, one of those rejected partners, on his way out with Dr. Powis's eldest daughter to join the lines, decided to intervene.

"Talk her into it, Major," he called out cheerfully. "It's about time Mrs. Tavernor danced. A person cannot mourn forever."

"Yes, do it, Major," someone else agreed.

An anonymous someone whistled.

"Come on, Lydia dear," Mrs. Bailey coaxed from nearby, "If I can dance, anyone can."

It was time to be firm, Lydia thought. Time to assert herself.

Harry was smiling at her, one hand extended for hers.

Time to be decisive.

Time to be the new Lydia.

"You will be sorry," she warned him, setting her hand in his. "I will surely make a spectacle of you."

Someone actually cheered, and there was a smattering of applause.

Lydia could not have felt more on public display if she had tried.

Twelve

And there went one resolution, broken before the dancing had even begun, Harry thought.

He had come here with the full intention of nodding amiably to Lydia, exchanging a few friendly words in passing if he came face-to-face with her, and keeping his distance the rest of the evening without being too obvious about it. He would treat her as he did everyone else and as he had done for most of the past four years, for he had never deliberately ignored or avoided her then. He simply had not noticed her. He could not go back to those days, of course, but he could set the tone for the future.

Yet here he was about to dance with her, even over her own protests and her very reasonable argument that since she had refused three other partners it would be poor manners to accept him. He had persisted, with the encouragement of a few of his neighbors, who seemed to agree that it was high time she danced.

He escorted her to the line of ladies, bowed over her

hand, and took his place in the line of men. He hoped she
was *not* about to make a spectacle of herself and go pranc-
ing off to her left while everyone else glided gracefully to
their right, for example. She would be horribly embarrassed
and would almost certainly never dance again. And he
would be left knowing that it was all his fault.

There was something different about her tonight. Well,
yes, of course there was. One would have to be blind not to
notice. She was looking slender and dainty and pretty in
her rose pink gown. Her chestnut hair glowed in the candlelight. How clever of her to wear it in a simple style so that
the smooth sheen of it would not be lost in curls and ring-
lets. Or was it only that she did not have a maid? She wore
no jewelry. Because she did not have any to wear? Or because she had aimed for simplicity and got it perfect? Her
cheeks were slightly flushed, her face bright with animation
though not openly smiling.

But there was something else over and above the obvious differences—which were startling enough in themselves.

It was partly her eyes, he decided at last. They were
wide and unguarded and looked about the room with frank
interest. Including at him. She was looking at him now and
did not glance away when she saw him gazing back. Or
lower her eyes. And yes, *that* was what it was. She was not
in hiding tonight. She had worn that particular dress to be
noticed. She had left off her cap to be noticed. And there
was her chin as well as her eyes. It was raised. Not defiantly
or belligerently but . . . proudly? Was that the right word?

It struck Harry that she was neither the Reverend Isaiah
Tavernor's wife tonight nor his widow. She was herself.
Lydia Tavernor. Perhaps the Lydia Winterbourne she had
once been.

The orchestra struck a chord, the ladies curtsied, the men bowed, and the dancing began.

She did not make a spectacle of herself.

She danced with deliberate care, he noticed, each step and gesture one fraction of a second behind those of her nearest neighbors as though she wanted to be quite sure before she committed herself that she was getting it right. Her movements were deliberate and slightly wooden for the first little while, until they had performed all the figures once and she was confident that she could do them again without committing some ghastly faux pas. She smiled at him as they met between the lines with another couple and all four clasped hands above their heads and danced a full circle before returning to their places.

And good God, she was beautiful.

When they reached the head of the lines and their turn came to twirl alone down the middle while the other dancers clapped and tapped their feet to the rhythm, she looked at him with sparkling eyes and actually laughed. The woodenness was long gone from her movements, as well as the concentration upon getting the steps right, and what was left was pure, light-footed grace. There was music and rhythm and color and light, and there was Lydia to embody them all.

Harry laughed too.

He was in a bit of danger here, he thought. He might even be in a lot of danger.

"Thank you," she said when the set came to an end far too soon, and perhaps just as far too late. "I am relieved that I did not disgrace you after all. Denise was right. One does not forget how to dance. I must go and speak with Mrs. Bartlett. She was still not sure when I talked to her yesterday that she would come tonight. I am glad she did."

He escorted her to her next-door neighbor's side, stayed to chat for a minute or two, and then strolled away to have a few words with Mr. and Mrs. Raymore and solicit Theresa's hand for the next set. He danced after that with Mirabel Hill, Miss Ardreigh, Hannah Corning, and Mrs. Bailey. He drank a glass of wine with Lawrence and his uncle and ate a plate of food while the orchestra was taking a break. He was enjoying himself as he always did at the village assemblies. There was something so relaxed and merry about them.

And he was constantly aware of Lydia. He supposed it was inevitable. It would surely fade with time. He would simply have to be patient with himself. She danced every set and mingled between sets, smiling and conversing and generally being everything she had never been before to his knowledge. She positively *glowed*. She looked vividly lovely. She did not attempt even once to hide in any corner or disappear inside herself.

He found himself wondering if this transformation had anything to do with him. She would not marry again. She had been quite adamant about that from the start. But she had also learned from her experience with him that having a lover was an impossible thing when one lived in a village the size of Fairfield. Had she decided as a result of that realization to reach out to friends and friendly acquaintances for happiness? To do it in an active way, not as an observer from a shadowy corner but as a full participant?

Perhaps after all he had done her some good.

Harry was standing close to the doors of the assembly rooms late in the evening with the Reverend Bailey and his wife, when they were interrupted by the sudden appearance of a young man Harry believed was one of Sir Maynard Hill's farm laborers. He was not dressed for the occasion and in fact seemed to have come in from outside. He was very wet—and frowning and breathless as he caught the vicar by the arm.

"It's my gran, Reverend," he said. "She has taken a turn for the worse and Ma thinks she is going fast. I came for the doctor and for you too if you will."

"Ah, it is time, then, is it, John?" the vicar said in his calm, kindly manner, patting the young man's hand before raising his arm and beckoning Dr. Powis, who left his wife's side and came striding toward them. "Mrs. Wickend is coming to the end, Powis, and we are needed, you and I. You came on horseback, John?"

"I did," the young man said.

"The doctor and I will take my carriage, then," the Reverend Bailey said. "It is still raining, is it? Foolish question. You are soaked."

"It's coming down like cats and dogs out there, Reverend," John Wickend said.

"My dear—" Bailey began, turning to his wife.

"You must not worry about me, Stanley," she said, interrupting him. "Someone will give me a ride home. You go."

"It will be my pleasure to convey Mrs. Bailey home," Harry said as Sir Maynard approached to find out why one of his laborers had arrived in the rooms looking like a drowned rat, as he put it.

"Gran is on the way out, sir," the young man explained. "Ma sent me for the doctor and the reverend."

"Off you go," Mrs. Bailey said briskly. "Both of you."

They left within the minute, with very little fuss. It was doubtful many people had even noticed the little drama being enacted over by the doors, since the volume of general conversation was nearly deafening and the musicians were tuning their instruments again before the next set formed.

"It is very kind of you to be willing to take me home in your carriage, Major Westcott," Mrs. Bailey said. "I would happily walk on any other night, but I must confess I would not fancy it tonight, what with the rain and the wind."

"I would not hear of your walking anyway, ma'am," Harry said, "even if it were a balmy summer evening. My carriage is at your disposal whenever you are ready to leave."

"And whenever Lydia is ready," Mrs. Bailey said. "She came with us. You will not mind taking her too, I am sure. You will not even have to go out of your way. She lives at the end of your drive."

Ah.

"Absolutely not, ma'am," he assured her.

But he did mind.

And so, surely, would Lydia.

The final set of the evening finished well before midnight. People who lived and worked in the country did not, generally speaking, dance until dawn. Many of those who attended the assembly would not be able to sleep until noon tomorrow.

Even so, people were reluctant to leave. The women had to sort out the leftover food and claim their own plates and dishes, talking animatedly with one another as they did so, just as though there had been no other opportunity all evening for conversation. But the men were not hurrying them along or showing any particular signs of impatience to be gone. Most of them were downing one more pint of ale or glass of wine as they finished off their own conversations.

There would be no point in rushing outside anyway. Coachmen had to be rounded up from the taproom below and then had to collect their horses and hitch them to their carriages before they could drive up to the doors of the inn. Cloaks and hats and gloves and umbrellas had to be identified and claimed. Last-minute greetings and hugs and handshakes had to be exchanged.

It all took a good half hour.

Lydia was feeling both sad and relieved that it was all over and that soon she would be saying good night to the Baileys and closing her cottage door behind her, back in her own quiet, safe haven. She had enjoyed herself enormously and was immensely proud of herself. She had felt for most of the evening almost as though she were at a masquerade ball, safely hidden behind a disguise and able to behave out of character, secure in the knowledge that no one would ever know that she had been herself. *Almost* as though . . . What she had been doing in reality, of course, was just the opposite. She had thrown off her mask in order to be herself. As she had never had a chance to do when she was a girl. As she had never been allowed to do while she was married. As she had never dared to do since.

Tonight she had dared.

And it had felt wonderful. And horribly frightening, for several times, quite without warning, she had felt herself close to panic, as though were she to look down she would discover that she had forgotten to put her dress on before leaving the house.

Yet even as she had been enjoying herself she had longed for the evening to be over so she would not see Harry wherever she looked—dancing, smiling, talking, laughing, as she was doing herself. Unaware of her very existence, as he had been for most of the four years of his acquaintance with her.

Now, soon, she would be going home. Like Cinderella at

midnight. But with no glass slipper to leave behind her. With no prince to retrieve it and search for her even if she did.

She was also exhausted, not just with physical tiredness from all the dancing and conversing, but with the emotional exertion of having behaved so differently from usual—and of pretending indifference to Harry.

She had no plate to take with her. She had offered her leftover iced cakes to Mrs. Piper to take home for her children, and since Mrs. Piper's own plate had little room left on it, Lydia had told her to take the plate too. She would not miss it for a few days. She looked around, waved to Mrs. Bailey, and made her way toward her.

"Major Westcott has gone for the carriage," Mrs. Bailey said. "I daresay he may be waiting for us by now. I believe the heavens have opened out there, Lydia. We *are* having a wet spring."

"Major Westcott?" Lydia looked at her in incomprehension.

"It was kind of him to offer us a ride home, was it not?" Mrs. Bailey said. "Oh. Have you not heard, Lydia? The vicar and Dr. Powis were called away. Poor John Wickend came here, very agitated. He was convinced his grandmama is on her last—again. She does seem to have at least nine lives, just like a cat, though I mean no disrespect by the comparison. The men went anyway, of course. The vicar took the carriage. Major Westcott assured him that he would take us home. We would be *drowned* if we had to walk."

Had he known when he offered, Lydia wondered, that he would be taking her home as well as Mrs. Bailey? What a ghastly way for the evening to end. And this would make three times in a row after they had been at the same evening event. Twice he had walked her home. Now he was to take her in his carriage. She just hoped Denise would not find out and start teasing and speculating again. Lydia hoped no one else would find out either. But there was nothing to be done about it now, was there? It really was raining heavily out there, and it would be foolish to try to insist upon walking home. Besides, he was to take Mrs. Bailey home too. Thank heaven for that at least.

There was an unruly jumble of carriages outside, all of them pulled as close as possible to the inn doors instead of ranging themselves in an orderly line as they normally would. People were making a dash for them, laughing, shrieking, calling out to one another, generally getting soaked and mud spattered.

Harry's carriage must have been one of the first to arrive. It was standing almost directly across from the doors, and he was hurrying down the steps to hand them in as they came out. They were all seated inside within moments, and his coachman was about to put up the steps and shut the door when Mrs. Bailey threw up her hands.

"Oh, wait!" she cried. "The vicar's muffler. I would be willing to wager upon it that he left it behind when he went off with Dr. Powis. He is always doing it. I shall go back and fetch it now and save him from having to come back here tomorrow. No, no, Major. I will get it. I know what it looks like. You wait here in the dry."

And she was gone, down the carriage steps with the assistance of the coachman's hand, and across the pavement and back inside the inn before Harry could do anything to stop her or even insist upon accompanying her.

Lydia felt suddenly very alone in the carriage with him.

"I am so sorry about this, Harry," she said. They were sitting on opposite seats, their knees almost touching. "I could have walked."

"In the rain," he said. It was not a question, but his tone told her what he thought of that idea.

"I suppose," she said, "it would have been a bit foolish."

"More than a bit," he said. "If I allowed it, the Reverend and Mrs. Bailey would look reproachfully at me for the next year at the very least every time I stepped inside the church. And the whole of Fairfield and its surrounds would wonder what on earth I had done or said to you that you preferred to get soaked to the skin rather than ride home in my carriage. Everyone would talk of nothing else for a month."

"If you *allowed* it," she said.

"Poor wording," he admitted.

And for some reason they both laughed.

"Am I permitted," he asked her, "to tell you how lovely you look tonight and how well you dance?"

"Yes, you are," she said. "Which is just as well since you have told me anyway."

He laughed softly again.

"I suppose Mrs. Bailey has searched every room in the inn for a muffler that is snugly about the vicar's neck at this very moment," he said.

"Probably," she agreed. "She is very precious. They both are. They are warm and human."

Mrs. Bailey came back after several minutes without the muffler. She hurried into the carriage with the assistance of the coachman and a hand Harry offered from inside.

"It was not in the cloakroom," she explained as she settled beside Lydia. "I looked in the assembly rooms too and even the taproom, though it was unlikely to be in there. It is as well to be thorough, however. One never knows. You must take me home first, Major Westcott. It would make no sense to go to Lydia's and then have to turn back to the vicarage with me, would it? And she is no girl to need a chaperon over such a short distance."

"The vicarage first, then," Harry told his coachman.

Lydia was relieved to find that Mrs. Bailey seemed to fill the carriage with her cheerful presence and her chatter about all the pleasures of the assembly even though it was sad to think that while they had danced and enjoyed themselves poor Mrs. Wickend senior not so far away was perhaps really dying this time after suffering increasingly failing health over the past few months. But such was life, and she had lived to a good old age.

"None of us can live forever," she concluded as the carriage drew to a halt outside the vicarage. "Which is a very good thing, as the vicar always points out, as our poor world would get so full of people we would all have to stand upright on it with our arms pressed to our sides."

Harry drew a large umbrella from a holder beside his seat and escorted Mrs. Bailey up the garden path to her door.

And then he was back inside the carriage while the rain beat down on the roof and against the windows and the wind rocked it on its springs. The interior suddenly seemed more crowded than it had when Mrs. Bailey was still inside with them and very quiet despite the almost deafening noises of weather and horses and carriage wheels.

"I have finished knitting your scarf," Lydia said as the carriage moved away from the vicarage. "I knitted it while I was away."

"Oh," he said. "You did not need to do that, Lydia."

"And you did not need to chop my wood," she said. "I have been wondering how I would get it to you. I will give it to you tonight."

"Thank you." He was gazing across at her, though there was very little light by which to see.

She could not think of anything else to say, and he remained silent. But she felt sadness welling for a reason she could not quite understand. It was over between them because it could not possibly work. She had her life to live, the life of freedom she had never expected, the life with which she had been gifted anyway. It was a way of life that brought her great contentment. And it was a life into which she had moved fully tonight, out of the shadows cast by her marriage. She was no longer anyone's helpmeet. She was herself, Lydia Tavernor.

But for a brief moment there had been Harry.

And he had left behind in her a trace of sadness.

He took up the umbrella again as the carriage drew to a halt outside her gate. He raised it as soon as he was outside and held it aloft as he helped her descend the steps—carefully, for they were slippery with rain. He tipped it slightly against the wind as he opened the gate, and then drew her to his side with an arm about her waist as he hurried up the path with her. He kept her dry while she fumbled with her key in the lock and opened the door before bending over Snowball, who had come dashing and yapping to greet her and reproach him for keeping her out so long.

She lit the candle and turned toward him, pushing back the hood of her cloak as she did so.

"Step inside out of the rain," she said. "I will fetch your scarf."

He did as she suggested and lowered the umbrella, shook some of the wetness from it, and stood it against the doorframe. He half closed the door, presumably so that the wind would not blow out the candle.

Lydia got his scarf from her bedchamber, folded into a neat oblong. "I should find something to wrap it in," she said. She was feeling a bit suffocated by the sight of him inside her house again, though he was only just inside.

"There is no need," he said, reaching out and taking it from her. Their hands brushed. "Thank you, Lydia. It is a lovely bright color. It will mean a great deal to me. I will think of you whenever I wear it."

"As I think of you whenever I sit before a fire," she said. "I still have a pile of your wood left."

He smiled at her, and she smiled at him. And the sadness was a dull ache about her heart.

"Good night, Harry," she said. "And thank you for the ride."

"Good night, Lydia." He raised one hand to hook behind her ear a lock of her hair that had come loose when she lowered her hood. He kissed her forehead.

But the wind blew the door open again as he did so, and he turned, tucked the scarf beneath one arm, raised his umbrella, ducked beneath it, and hurried back to his carriage.

Lydia shut the door, leaned back against it, closed her eyes, and touched the fingers of one hand to her forehead.

Thirteen

The first sign of trouble came the following morning when Mrs. Piper arrived on Lydia's doorstep. She had brought Lydia's plate.

"How good of you to return it so promptly," Lydia said with a warm smile after she had opened the door. "I did not expect it so soon. And I daresay the road is very muddy after all that rain. Was it not torrential? But do come inside. The kettle is close to boiling. I'll make a pot of tea."

She was actually not sorry for the distraction. She had been feeling melancholy all morning despite all her efforts to concentrate upon the happy memories she had of the assembly.

Mrs. Piper was not responding either to her smile or to her invitation to step inside out of the damp, chilly air that had succeeded the overnight rain, however. She held Lydia's plate against her bosom. Her lips were drawn into a thin, hard line. Her eyes were expressionless.

"I put your cakes on the plate with my own last night and called after you to take your plate," she said, thrusting it suddenly at Lydia, who took it from her. "You did not hear me because you were too eager to go off with Major Westcott. Jeremy was waiting outside to walk me home and offered to run over to your house with the plate right then even though it was pelting with rain. I have a good boy there, always eager to do things for his mother and his neighbors. He ran all the way, but when he got here he was too shocked to bring you the plate. You were standing in your doorway kissing the major while his coachman had his back turned, pretending not to notice."

"Oh." Lydia was too startled for the moment to say anything else. "Major Westcott was kind enough to give Mrs. Bailey and me a ride home in his carriage after the Reverend Bailey was called away with Dr. Powis to old Mrs. Wickend's sickbed. He insisted upon escorting each of us all the way to our door because the rain was heavy and he had an umbrella in the carriage. I am so sorry to have embarrassed Jeremy after he had come all this way in the rain. But he did misunderstand what he saw, poor boy."

Good heavens. Oh, gracious heavens.

Mrs. Piper's expression had not changed. "The reverend gave his life for my son," she said, her voice trembling with some emotion that might well be rage. "The Reverend Tavernor, that is. A heavenly martyr he was. I will never forget him as long as there is life in my body. He was one of God's holy angels come down to earth. The last thing I expected—the last thing *anyone* expected—was that his wife would turn out to be a woman of loose morals."

"Mrs. Piper!" Lydia stared at her, aghast, and now she was the one clutching the plate to her bosom. "Jeremy misinterpreted what he saw. But even if he had not, even if I really had been *kissing* Major Westcott, would that be such offensive behavior that it must reflect badly upon my morals? I am a widow, not a wife. I was unwaveringly loyal to my husband while he lived. That must have been evident to everyone here. I am *sorry* Jeremy saw what he did and was embarrassed and drew the wrong conclusion. But I must admit to resenting the hasty judgment *you* have passed upon me based solely upon what he reported to you. If you care to listen to my explanation, I will give it, though I do not recognize any obligation to do so."

Mrs. Piper clearly did not care to listen to anything. She took a step back, though she did not immediately turn away. "Oh, it is not just that one thing," she said. "You had him chopping wood here for you all one morning, and then you had him inside your house for more than an hour afterward—with the door shut. And you had him back again that same night for more of what he got in the morning. I suppose it all got started when you talked him into walking you home from Tom Corning's one night—yes, I heard all about it—and from Mr. Solway's the week after. And last night! That dress you were wearing, if you don't mind me saying so, was shameful for a woman who had the privilege of being the reverend's wife before he became a holy martyr and gave his life for my boy. You *danced* and you smiled and laughed and made an exhibition of yourself, though everyone knows the reverend believed dancing to be sinful and putting oneself forward in company to be immodest in a woman. If he could have seen you last night he would have turned over in his grave. He was the most upright and pious and godly man that ever walked this earth. And I never did think you were worthy of him. I always thought you were a sly one. I am sure a lot of people thought so too, though we have kept our mouths shut until now out of respect for him because he doted on you. *My helpmeet,* he always called you. Some helpmeet!"

Oh, gracious heaven! Lydia watched, half paralyzed, as Mrs. Piper turned and strode out of her garden, leaving the gate swinging behind her, and along the street until she was out of sight behind the copse. Snowball trotted along the path, though she stopped outside the gate and stood in the middle of the road looking after her before trotting back in, wet mud and all.

Lydia closed the door and stood with her back to it, her eyes squeezed shut, the plate hugged to her bosom with both arms. It took several minutes for the jumbled ball that was her mind to sort itself into coherent thought.

So that morning when she had seen Jeremy's head above her fence, it had not been the first time he had looked. He had seen Harry chopping her wood. He had seen him come inside for refreshments. He even knew the visit had lasted one hour, though it was very unlikely he possessed a pocket watch. He knew about the visit that evening. *Oh, dear God, he knew about that.* He knew she had walked home from Tom and Hannah's with Harry—Mrs. Piper had not been at that social gathering, but Jeremy must have seen her anyway. He had seen Harry kiss her forehead last night.

Had he been spying on her for some time, then? No, that was not a question. He had been spying.

But why?

Because Isaiah had saved his life and he had taken it upon himself to make sure she was safe? Quite frankly that did not sound convincing. Because he wanted to be a sort of watchdog, then, making sure that she was honoring Isaiah's memory with upright living? That would make sense surely only if he hoped she was not. He must know that his mother disliked and resented her—but *why?*—and would like nothing more than something specific with which to reproach her. Mrs. Piper had always been a bit of a gossip. A spiteful one, for the gossip she spread was never of the happy variety. *Viciously pious* was how Lydia had sometimes thought of her. She had loved nothing better than to bring to Isaiah's notice the perceived transgressions of her neighbors. To his credit, he had never encouraged her.

Other people *did*, however.

Most people, of course, if they were strictly honest with themselves, enjoyed a bit of gossip, especially if it was basically harmless. There were some, though, who thrived upon the sort of gossip that tore someone else's reputation to tatters. Such people generally showed little concern for facts, especially if the facts threatened to disprove what they wanted to believe.

Lydia drew a deep breath and released it slowly. It was too much to hope, she supposed, that Mrs. Piper would keep her moral outrage to herself. Or that she would keep to herself all the *facts* she had amassed, courtesy of Jeremy's spying, to prove that she, Lydia, was a woman of loose morals who had set out to get her hooks into Major Westcott. Of course it was too much to hope. And those bare facts, she did not doubt for a moment, would be fleshed out and embellished until they were quite unrecognizable as truth.

And the facts themselves? Well, she was not entitled to feel the full force of righteous indignation, was she? She had *lain* with Harry.

But yes, of course she was entitled to her fury. They were both adults, she and Harry. They had both passed the age of majority long ago. They were both unmarried and unattached. It was no one's business what they did together in private. Yet they had both been aware that in a place like

this people would make it their business. They had bowed
to that awareness and given each other up—as lovers and
even as friends.

They had given each other up precisely because of the
possibility of what was now happening anyway.

For there was no possible chance that Mrs. Piper would
keep her outrage and her *facts* to herself. Lydia was about
to become the victim of an explosion of salacious gossip.
Her life, her precious life of quiet freedom and independence, was about to change. Forever. She did not believe
she was overdramatizing.

"Oh, Snowball," she said with a sigh when she looked
down at the trail of muddy paw prints that stretched from
the door into the kitchen. "*Look* what you have done."

And look what I have done, she added silently.

The shreds of his contentment seemed to have deserted
him, Harry admitted to himself later that same afternoon,
and he despaired of getting them back. It had all started at
Christmas, of course. But then it had continued into this
thing with Lydia Tavernor, which had stumbled along from
its improbable beginnings until it flared into a brief, uncon-
trolled burst of passion. And last night had not helped, even
though he usually enjoyed the village assemblies.

What had happened, he supposed, was that during the
past few months he had come face-to-face with the essential emptiness of his existence. It had been bound to happen
sooner or later. He had this large house and park to enjoy,
but no one with whom to share them. He had a troubled
past, which was best left where it was, and a present that
was marginally satisfying—though *lonely*, damn it—but
no future to look forward to except more of the same.

Somehow *more of the same*, with which he had been perfectly content for four years, seemed like a dreary prospect.

There was no one special in his life.

No one to love or to *cherish*, to use his mother's word.

He had come to hate that word whenever it popped into his head.

And no sex.

There had been plenty of the latter during the years with his regiment, lusty and satisfying. There had been none during the years of his convalescence, very little since.

And then Lydia.

He had spent an hour or so of the morning in his steward's office, going over the account books, and then another hour or two out on the home farm, mostly admiring the new and not-so-new lambs. He had sat down to a cold luncheon, for the plainness of which his housekeeper, Mrs. Sullivan, had apologized with the peculiar excuse that she and the kitchen staff were more than usually busy taking inventory of their supplies. Afterward Harry had wandered out to the summerhouse among the trees east of the manor. He sat inside it now, out of the chilly wind, on the leather-upholstered seat that circled the interior wall of glass, gazing out over the park and across one corner of the village to the countryside beyond.

Perhaps this restlessness was a healthy sign. Perhaps it showed that he had finally and fully recovered his health and was ready to move on to a more active phase of his life. But what would that be? Or perhaps the restlessness had something—or even everything—to do with Lydia Tavernor. He frowned at the thought. For why should it? Whatever there had been between them was over, by mutual consent. She was not looking to marry again, and he was not ready for marriage yet—*was* he? She no longer wanted a lover, and he was not in search of a mistress. Not here, anyway. Not anywhere, actually.

Dash it all. He *wished* he could get his life back, the one he had lived with such contentment and with very little reflection just a few months ago. The maddening thing about life, though, was that it would never go backward. It would not stand still either. And it did not offer any clear image of what was ahead. Which was perhaps just as well.

Maybe he needed to get away for a while. But where? London, heaven help him?

His thoughts were interrupted at that moment by movement among the trees to his right. He brightened immediately when he saw Tom Corning striding in his direction. School must be finished for the day. Tom opened the door of the summerhouse unbidden and stepped inside.

"Ah, warmth," he said, closing the door quickly and rubbing his hands together.

"How did you find me?" Harry asked as he slid farther along the seat so Tom could sit beside him and enjoy the same view.

"Your butler thought you would be either at the lake or here," Tom said. "I tried here first. It would be madness to wander about the lake on a day like today. Why is he all dressed up so smartly?"

"Brown?" Harry said. "My butler? *Is* he? He looked his normal self when I saw him a short while ago. Not that I was paying particular attention. How was school today?"

"Fine." Tom leaned forward slightly and rested his forearms across his thighs with his hands dangling down between them. He was looking down at the floor instead of admiring the view Harry had made available to him. "Harry, old chap, I think you ought to be warned that you were seen last night."

"Seen." Harry frowned at the back of his friend's head. "Well, that is hardly surprising, since I do not have a magician's power to make myself invisible. Let me see. I was at the assembly rooms for three or four hours, mingling and talking with almost every adult from the village and the countryside around. I danced almost every set. No, *every* set. And I was *seen*, was I? How very shocking. Seen to be doing what exactly?"

"Kissing Mrs. Tavernor in the doorway of her cottage," Tom said. "I am not saying there is anything scandalous about that, especially when you must have had every reason to expect privacy from prying eyes. But the person who saw you was the lad who gives me the most trouble with truancy from school, the lad Tavernor saved from drowning. He is a sneak and a poacher as well as a truant and has apparently taken it upon himself to keep an eye on Tavernor's widow, with what motive one can only imagine. My guess would be that he does it so he can report back to his mother on anything Mrs. Tavernor does that might reflect badly upon the late vicar's memory. She was one of his more fanatical followers."

"The Piper lad?" Harry said. "He says he saw me kissing Lydia last night? Then he is a damned liar in addition to the other things you listed."

"*Lydia*, is it?" Tom asked, turning his head briefly to glance at his friend.

"I saw her to her door beneath an umbrella because it was *raining*," Harry said, "just as I did a few minutes before that with Mrs. Bailey. I stepped inside for perhaps thirty seconds while she went to fetch a scarf she had knitted for me. In return for a pile of wood I chopped for her a few weeks ago, before you ask," he added when Tom raised his eyebrows. "I said thank you and I said good night and—

ah, yes—I pecked her on the forehead. And left. A peck and a kiss are quite distinct things, Tom."

"I will take your word for it," his friend said, sounding uncomfortable. "It's none of my business anyway. But even if you *did* kiss her, I don't know why there should be such a big fuss about it."

"*Is* there a big fuss?" Harry's stomach was doing funny things.

"Afraid so," Tom said. "Or so Hannah says. I found her pacing when I got home from school. Jeremy ran home to his mother last night with his shocking report, and Mrs. Piper confronted Mrs. Tavernor at her house this morning. Mrs. Tavernor apparently told her she would entertain whatever man she wanted to entertain and however many she chose and that she would kiss whomever she wanted to kiss and Mrs. P could go to the devil with a flea in her ear. Though I cannot quite imagine the lady using those exact words or even saying some of the things she is reputed to have said. I daresay what she *did* say to Mrs. Piper had been reworded and exaggerated and embellished beyond all recognition by the time it got to Hannah's ears and then mine. But whatever the truth of it is, Harry, the whole silly episode has blown up into what seems like a grand scandal that will enliven everyone's dull lives for days or even weeks to come. Hannah was bursting with indignation when I got home and would not even let me sit down to enjoy a cup of tea before coming to warn you of what is in store for you. She fairly pushed me out the door."

"Good God." Harry gazed at him. "And devil take it and any other blasphemy you care to add." He jumped to his feet. "God damn it all, Tom, I'll throttle that boy. What the devil was he doing out on a night like last night anyway?"

"Spying upon Mrs. Tavernor, apparently," Tom said.

"Drumming up mischief," Harry said. "But what a storm in a teacup, Tom. What he saw was one innocent peck on the forehead, for the love of God. With the door open. In full sight of my coachman if he had cared to watch. A grand seduction scene indeed. Was ever anything more ridiculous?" He laughed, but his laughter somehow fell flat on its face.

Tom's discomfort seemed to have grown. He rubbed a finger along the side of his nose. "That is not the whole of it, Harry," he said. "Mrs. Piper has spent the day pulling a whole lot of other dirty laundry out of her bag and strewing it everywhere. That kiss last night was the mere culmination of other things she has been keeping to herself because she hates to gossip."

"What the devil?" Harry glared at his friend as though *he* were the one with the upturned laundry bag.

"In Mrs. Piper's mind," Tom explained, "the Reverend Tavernor is a saint and a martyr and an angel and perhaps even a little bit of the deity himself all rolled into one. She believes that in order to do justice to his memory, Mrs. Tavernor ought to be the Virgin Mary and all the female saints combined. You walked her home from our house one evening and from Solway's a week or so after that. You apparently spent a whole morning at her house chopping wood—you just admitted it to me—before going inside *and* shutting the door for what must have been considerably more than a glass of water since you remained there for a whole hour. You went back the same evening and stayed there for an indeterminate amount of time— I'll wager Jeremy cannot count high enough, more shame to his teacher. The Lord only knows what you were up to while you were there, but I daresay there is no shortage of speculation, especially as the curtains must have been drawn so Jeremy could not see inside."

"Damn their eyes," Harry said. "The whole lot of them."

"You danced with her last night when she had already told several other men that she would not dance at all," Tom continued. "You got her laughing and sparkling. And you gave her and Mrs. Bailey a ride home but dropped Mrs. Bailey off at the vicarage first before taking Mrs. Tavernor home and kissing her most scandalously. She has no one living at the cottage with her, not even a maid. That in itself is a shocking thing to someone like Mrs. Piper. She can have chosen to live quite alone—Mrs. Tavernor, I mean—for only one possible reason, and a lot of people are quite certain they know very well what that reason is. This is not me talking, Harry. It is not Hannah talking either or any number of other people with some sense between their ears. But it is what large segments of the village are buzzing about. It does not take determined gossips very long to weave a growing and pretty damning narrative out of the most threadbare of facts."

"It is all pure nonsense," Harry protested. *Except for one thing.* But that was no one's damned business except his and Lydia's. "Good God, Tom."

Tom looked up at him and shrugged. "*You* know it is all nonsense, Harry," he said. "*I* know. Hannah is getting together with Denise Franks. She was merely waiting for me to come home from school first. The two of them are going to the vicarage to talk with Mrs. Bailey and the vicar to discuss what they can do. *They* all know it is nonsense. But wildfire is pretty difficult to put out once it has got a hold. So is scandal."

"*Scandal,*" Harry said, pushing the fingers of one hand

impatiently through his hair. "That is a bit extreme, surely. But I do know gossip. And one can be sure it will focus almost exclusively upon Lydia. Very little of it, I suppose, will land upon me. Devil take it, Tom, I could commit murder. But throttling young Piper would be a bit like slamming the stable door shut after the horse has bolted—or some such nonsense. I had better go and have a word with Mrs. Piper. If she is at home, that is, and not still gallivanting about from house to house, spreading her laundry and her poison."

What he was also going to find himself doing, he thought, ridiculous as it seemed, was persuading Lydia Tavernor to marry him.

He jerked open the door of the summerhouse and strode out onto the path through the trees back to the house without waiting for Tom. Good God, he might have known something like this would happen. He *had* known, in fact. They had *both* known. It was why they had ended what was between them, even the possibility of a friendship that had shown some promise.

Harry had worked himself into a towering fury by the time he reached the terrace and approached the house. He was about to bark an order to his butler, who was conveniently standing just outside the open front doors, dressed indeed and rather bizarrely in what looked like his best uniform, to have his horse saddled and brought up to the door within the next ten minutes. But sound penetrated his consciousness and brought him to an abrupt halt as he swiveled about to look along the drive to see what it was.

Two carriages were approaching. Grand traveling carriages that did not belong to anyone local. The first one was already turning onto the terrace and rocking to a stop a few feet from Harry. He could see bonnets and feathers inside.

"Grandmama," he muttered. The Dowager Countess of

Riverdale was on the seat facing the horses with Great-aunt Edith Monteith, her sister, beside her. Opposite them sat a young man and woman Harry could not immediately identify.

He turned his head sharply to look, aghast, at the second carriage. A familiar ducal crest was emblazoned upon the door. Within it he could see his half sister, Anna, and Aunt Louise seated facing the horses, with Cousin Jessica squeezed between them. Opposite them sat Avery, Duke of Netherby, and Gabriel, Earl of Lyndale.

Brown, *whose best butler's uniform was now explained*, was opening the door of the first carriage and setting down the steps when Harry turned his attention back to it.

What a damnable time to discover that the whole of the Westcott family was in the process of descending upon him. For Harry did not doubt they were all coming. Already a third carriage was rolling into sight.

And a fourth.

Of course they were coming to him.

He had refused to go to them, after all.

Fourteen

L ydia closed all the curtains in her house, washed up
Snowball's paw prints as well as Snowball herself,
cleaned the house from top to bottom, and baked a batch of
biscuits for which she had no appetite whatsoever.

She cast on stitches for her pink shawl, knitted two rows,
and then lost all her stitches after they had stuck on the
needle and she jerked them toward the tip and they all came
rushing off. She had been knitting too tightly. She picked
up the stitches, knitted a row to make sure everything was
as it ought to be, and stuffed the work into her bag. She got
to her feet to poke the fire, saw there was no fire because
she had not lit one, and sat down on the sofa with a book
She read a whole paragraph before slamming the book shut
and tossing it aside. She let Snowball out into the back garden and stood just inside the doorway, glancing furtively
around to check for heads popping up above the fence and
listening for rustlings in the copse. She shut the door firmly
after Snowball came trotting back inside.

Perhaps after all Mrs. Piper had taken her indignation home with her to nurse in private. Perhaps she was even feeling remorseful about her hasty rush to judgment. Perhaps . . . Well, perhaps pigs would fly one of these days.

Confirmation of her worst fears came when she answered a knock upon her front door late in the afternoon and found Mrs. Bailey, Denise Franks, and Hannah Corning standing ranged across her doorstep, all wearing identical smiles while Snowball bounced along in front of them yapping until Hannah bent and scooped her up.

"Oh," Lydia said without returning the smile. "It is as bad as that, is it?" And she turned to walk back into the house, leaving the door open behind her. They could follow her in if they wished or go back home if they did not. It was up to them.

They followed her in.

"I do blame myself," Mrs. Bailey cried, "for not insisting that Major Westcott bring you home first before taking me to the vicarage. I ought to have taken upon myself the role of chaperon. But it is all absolute nonsense anyway, and the vicar agreed with me when he came out of his study to find out what all the fuss was about when Mrs. Franks and Mrs. Corning came to see me. The major is being maligned for being the perfect gentleman and seeing both of us to our doors beneath his umbrella. The vicar is blaming himself for going off with our carriage and leaving you and me to someone else's care. And Mrs. Wickend did not even die. One sometimes wonders if she ever will. But you, my dear Lydia, have taken the worst of it all."

"Lydia." Denise spread her arms, but Lydia did not step forward to be hugged. "If he *did* embrace you, even if it was a passionate, full-on-the-lips kiss, all I can say is good for him. And good for you for allowing it. I totally fail to see what is so scandalous about a man kissing a woman on her doorstep after he has escorted her home from an evening party. Mrs. Piper is a silly, hysterical, overly pious gossip. She seems to believe that you ought to have devoted the rest of your life to mourning your husband's passing. Eternal widowhood and celibacy. The woman is mad."

"It is like a tomb in here, Lydia." Hannah set Snowball down and threw the curtains back from the living room window. "My next-door neighbor, though she does not condemn you, has given it as her opinion that it was indiscreet of you to entertain Harry inside your own house, when you do not have even a servant living here with you. But really, where else could you be private in order to get to know each other properly? It is not as though you are a green young girl, after all, or he a notorious womanizer. Unfortunately, however, gossip does not thrive upon sound reason or common sense. People have too little to talk about that is of any real interest to them, and so they will grab at any gossip, the more salacious the better. But you are not going to have to face all this rubbish alone. We have decided that."

"We have indeed," Mrs. Bailey said firmly. She sniffed. "Lemon tarts? Is that what I smell?"

"Sugar biscuits with some lemon added," Lydia said.

"They smell delicious. I never could resist lemon in sweet things," Mrs. Bailey said. "Perhaps we can invite ourselves to sit down in your kitchen and be cozy for a little while. May we? And you must tell us if there is indeed anything of a courtship between you and the major. I must say you looked very good together last evening when you were dancing. I remarked upon it to the vicar after I had finished dancing myself. Perhaps this bit of bother will prod the major into coming to the point. Men can be very slow about such things. It took the vicar eight months to work up the courage to propose to me after *everyone* knew he would get there in the end. I was near to screaming with frustration. I dropped hints as heavy as bricks. But perhaps the major has already asked you?"

Lydia was plumping up the already plump cushions on the back of the sofa while her three friends were standing in a line with their backs to the window.

"I will go and make a pot of tea," she said. "I will be delighted to have you help me eat some of the biscuits. I made a double batch."

But before she could move away, they all heard the noisy clopping of hooves and rumbling of wheels and jingling of traces coming from outside, and all of them turned to look through the window. A grand traveling carriage was turning onto the drive to Hinsford Manor. Another carriage, even grander, with a bright crest emblazoned upon the door and a coachman and footman in colorful, smart livery up on the box, turned after it.

"Major Westcott has visitors," Mrs. Bailey said unnecessarily.

"I have seen that carriage before," Hannah said, wagging a finger at the second one. "It belongs to the Duke of Netherby. That is the ducal crest. The duchess is Major Westcott's sister. Half sister. The legitimate one."

"I wonder," Denise said, "if he is expecting them. Has he said anything to you, Lydia?"

Lydia did not answer.

"They must be coming for his birthday," Hannah said. "He is going to turn thirty next week, though he has not said a word to anyone. Tom knows, though. He has been talking about arranging some sort of party, perhaps even at the assembly rooms. It looks as if that is going to be unnecessary, however. Oh dear . . ."

A third carriage had come into sight and turned after the others onto the drive. And then a fourth.

The Westcotts were coming in force, Lydia thought. To shield him from any adverse effects of this stupid . . . *scandal* that was brewing and threatening to swallow her up. But they could not possibly know about that yet, could they? She did not doubt they soon would, however, and when they did they would close ranks about him and turn up their collective aristocratic nose at the very idea that he could be dragged into such trivial and sordid gossip, all over a mere nobody of a vicar's widow.

Her bitterness surprised her. She did not even know any of them. It was just that her emotions were a bit on the raw side today. Well, more than a bit, to be perfectly honest.

Her friends were unabashedly watching the show proceeding beyond her garden fence. Yet a fifth carriage was approaching. Snowball stood by the front door, barking.

Lydia went into the kitchen. Well, she thought, it was all her own fault that she was not able to enjoy the show with the others.

Are you ever lonely?

Never, *surely*, had an impulsively asked question brought such ghastly consequences in its wake.

This would all have been highly coordinated, of course, Harry realized within seconds of clapping eyes upon the first carriage, followed by a second. By the time the others hove into sight, one after another, like some grand parade, he was not even surprised. How very foolish of him to have assumed that his family had simply given up after he had assured a few of them that he was definitely not going to London this spring. This was the Westcott family, after all.

They never gave up on something once they had set their minds upon it. They just became more stubborn—and more creative.

And really the answer to this particular problem had not needed a great leap of imagination. If dear Harry would not go to them, then they would come to dear Harry. As clear as day. Yet Harry himself had not thought of it. *Even though they have done it before.* When Avery and Alexander had brought him home from Paris, they had expected to take him to London, where his mother and the whole family awaited him. He had insisted upon being brought here instead. *But . . .* the family had arrived within days.

They had all arrived now too. Every last one of them. Plus a few extras for good measure.

So Mrs. Sullivan and the cook had been too busy taking inventory earlier to serve him anything more elaborate than a cold luncheon, had they? For the first time in living memory, it might be added. And Brown had felt impelled for no apparent reason to change out of his everyday, perfectly respectable butler's attire into the smart uniform reserved for special occasions, of which there had been very few if any during the past four years, had he? And Mrs. Sullivan had been so intent upon getting the spring cleaning done as soon as possible this year that she had felt it necessary to hire all sorts of extra help during the past few weeks? And extra help in the kitchen in order to feed all the extra help?

No doubt his whole house had been cleaned and polished to within an inch of its life and every bed in every spare room made up while he had been almost wholly oblivious. Mrs. Sullivan would have counted upon his maleness making him quite unobservant about matters pertaining to the house. Clearly she knew her man well. Had his head gardener counted upon the same thing with regard to the park? It occurred to Harry now that he was looking for it that the lawns about the house were more than usually immaculate. And he would wager that if he were to wander from one flower bed to another, he would search in vain for either a weed or a drooping bloom.

His family all arrived within three hours of one another. It was a remarkable feat but not, obviously, above the organizing skills of the aunts—and probably his mother. And Wren and Anna and Elizabeth and all the rest of the women. It was no wonder he had not suspected a thing. The men of the family seemed singularly lacking in such devious organizational abilities. Though they were not necessarily an abject lot. There was the famous occasion, for example—Harry had been in the Peninsula at the time— when Avery had whisked Anna off one afternoon to marry her by special license at the very time when the usual committee was deep in the throes of organizing a grand *ton* wedding for them. It was one of Harry's favorite family stories. One thumb up for the men of the family.

The Dowager Countess of Riverdale, his paternal grandmother, came despite her advanced age, as did Great-aunt Edith, her sister. The aunts came, his father's sisters— Matilda, Louise, and Mildred, the eldest and youngest of them with their husbands. Then there were Avery and Anna; Alexander and Wren; Elizabeth and Colin; and Cousin Althea, Alex and Elizabeth's mother. They all brought their children, a few of whom were adults, most of whom were decidedly not. Viscount Dirkson and Aunt Matilda brought his son from his first marriage, Adrian Sawyer.

Aunts and cousins and assorted others shook Harry's hand, slapped his back, clasped his shoulder, hugged him, kissed him, laughed and squealed over him, scolded him,

and generally greeted him with hearty enthusiasm and un-
abashed affection. Children, released from long hours of
being cooped up inside stuffy carriages, roared and
shrieked over the terrace and the lawn and darted into the
house, where those who remembered being there before led
the way up to the nursery floor while parents largely ignored the mayhem and nurses clucked and fussed and
shooed and tried to bring order out of chaos.

Then there was Harry's immediate family. First to arrive of that group was his mother, with Marcel and Marcel's
two adult children from another marriage, the twins, Bertrand and Estelle Lamarr. Harry's stepsiblings.

"I suppose," his mother said after hugging him tightly,
"you were expecting us."

Harry felt like the village idiot because the answer was
no. He refrained from answering.

Truly remarkably, Camille and Joel had done what they
had avoided doing at Christmastime. They had left their
home in Bath and come all the way to Hinsford with their
whole brood.

"Because I could not possibly allow you to turn thirty
without being here to hold your hand, Harry," Camille remarked as she kissed his cheek.

Andrew, the deaf one of her children, plucked at Harry's
sleeve and then held up all ten fingers, closed his fists, held
up all ten again, and did it once more. *Thirty.*

Harry ruffled his nephew's hair. "Your uncle Harry is
getting to be an old man, alas," he said, making sure the
boy could read his lips, though he was not an expert at it.

Joel was carrying a sleeping twin on each arm and was
thus unable to shake his brother-in-law's hand. He winked
at him instead.

They had brought with them Mrs. Kingsley, Harry's maternal grandmother. His aunt and uncle, his mother's brother, had come from Dorsetshire, though somehow they arrived with everyone else.

Abigail and Gil were the last to arrive, with their three children.

"We have a bit of a soft spot for Hinsford, Harry," Gil said, wringing his friend's hand almost hard enough to break bones after Abigail had hugged him. "It was here that we met and married."

"The only reason you came, I suppose," Harry said, rescuing his hand.

"There should be another reason?" Gil grinned at him.

It said a great deal for Mrs. Sullivan's competence, Harry thought during those hours as he fought bewilderment over the invasion of his quiet, peaceful home and park, that she had a bed for everyone without exception in the house, though it was surely almost bursting at the seams. And presumably she had enough food and space for everyone in the dining room. Harry decided that he simply would not worry about any of it. The women's committee and Mrs. Sullivan between them would have thought of everything, down to the finest detail and beyond. He would only cause confusion if he tried issuing orders. But he felt a bit as he had when he was brought home from Paris—totally helpless, that was, and rather as if his presence in his own home was redundant despite the fact that he was the reason for everyone's being here, as he had been then.

Oh, and upon the theme of the house bursting at the seams—there were a few other guests, all strangers to Harry. They included Miss Leeson, who a month or so ago had become betrothed to Boris Wayne, Harry's cousin, eldest son of Aunt Mildred and Uncle Thomas. Miss Leeson's mother had come too, with another daughter, Miss

Fanny Leeson. Great-aunt Edith had brought her great-nephew and great-niece, Gordon and Miranda Monteith, who had come to London from the north of England with their parents for a month or two and had been persuaded to spend a week or so of that time here. And there was Miss Sally Underwood, a cousin of Adrian Sawyer's on his mother's side.

It did not take Harry long to detect a theme.

If they could not matchmake for him in London at the great marriage mart, his fond female relatives would do the best they could here. Each of the three unattached young ladies was pretty in her own way and refined in manner and doubtless of impeccable lineage and accomplished in all the arts in which young ladies were expected to be accomplished.

If someone would just be kind enough to shoot him now, Harry thought when he was finally alone and dressing for the evening with more than usual care, that someone would be doing him a great favor. He grinned rather grimly at his image in the glass.

"A rather elaborate creation, Mark, do you not think?" he asked his valet as he saw what had been done with his neckcloth.

"Any London valet would weep at the simplicity of it," Mark said.

The insubordination of valets! Harry viewed it with a jaundiced eye and turned away from the mirror.

Amid all the bewildering bustle of the past few hours, he had not for one moment forgotten about Lydia and what had happened to her today. There just had not been a single moment in which to do anything about it, however.

"We decided to surprise you for your birthday, Harry," Grandmama Westcott informed him unnecessarily when he weaved his way across his crowded drawing room to make his bow to her. Everyone else seemed to be enjoying predinner drinks without his having to do anything about offering them. "I hope you are happy." Her manner warned him that she expected an affirmative answer.

"Ecstatic. And certainly surprised, Grandmama," he said. "You could have knocked me down with one of the feathers from your bonnet."

He smiled at her when she looked at him suspiciously.

He had not asked yet what was planned for the actual day of his birthday, and no one had volunteered the information. Perhaps that was to be a surprise too. On the whole, he thought it best that it remain that way. It was going to be unavoidable anyway, whatever it was. Just as with a looming battle, all he could do was carry on with his life and face the ordeal with as much courage and fortitude as he could muster when the time came.

What the devil had happened to Tom Corning this afternoon? He had probably made his escape even before the first carriage rocked to a halt outside the doors of the house, and slunk home to his quiet tea with Hannah. Lucky devil.

And what was happening with Lydia? Perhaps nothing. Maybe by now the whole stupid storm had blown over for lack of fuel. Was there a mixing of metaphors there? Perhaps the procession of so many grand carriages through the village earlier had provided enough food for chatter and speculation to crowd out all else.

And just perhaps he was being very naïve.

Mrs. Piper had decided to whip up trouble—with some success, if Hannah had thought it necessary to send Tom here after school to warn him. Jeremy Piper was a notorious mischief maker, and it sounded very much as if he had been spying upon Lydia, no doubt in the hope of digging up some dirt to feed his mother's love of a good salacious story to carry to her neighbors. Most of the Reverend Tavernor's fervent women followers had been half in love with him, Harry had always thought. They were probably jealous of Lydia since she now had all the glory of being his widow.

Most people must realize what nonsense it all was, of course. What was so very scandalous, after all, about a single man kissing a single woman on her doorstep when he escorted her home in the rain—with his coachman as a witness? Or about his chopping wood for her? Or accepting refreshments from her afterward? But . . . Going to call upon her during an evening and staying a good long while when it was common knowledge that she lived alone? Dash it all, he had known there might be a problem if that ever became known. So had she. It was why she had ended the affair almost—though not quite—before it began.

Even if only a few people chose to be shocked and out-raged by Mrs. Piper's story, though—and actually there might be more than just a few who would be *disapproving*, even if not fully outraged—Lydia's life would be less than comfortable for a while. That realization gnawed at Harry all evening while he was besieged with news and chatter from his uninvited guests.

"Mama," he said quite late in the evening, when a num-ber of the guests, especially those who were not family, had retired after a long day, "may I have a word with you?"

"Of course, Harry." She looked up at him with an ex-pectant smile and raised eyebrows. Wren and Alexander and Bertrand Lamarr, with whom she was conversing, looked at him with interest.

"In private?" he said.

"But of course." She got to her feet.

He might as well have stood in the middle of the drawing room blowing a bugle, he thought ruefully as he opened the drawing room door to allow her to precede him out. A sort of hush had fallen upon the occupants, who had all been chattering merrily in their own groups a moment ago.

So much for quiet discretion.

Fifteen

L ydia was preparing to go out late the following morning. She was going to walk into the village to buy a few items she did not really need. She was not going to hide away at home, she had decided overnight. Nor was she going to hang her head and hurry along the street and hope no one noticed her. She had certainly had plenty of time to make her decision, for she had scarcely slept. If people had anything to say, they could say it *to* her rather than just *about* her. That would be a nice change for them. If people wished to shun her or give her the cut direct, then she would give them the opportunity to do it today. In the meanwhile she was going to carry on with her life as usual.

She had started the day by throwing wide every curtain in the house. And when she let Snowball outside, she went too and even played the stick game for ten minutes, though admittedly she did so in the back garden rather than the front.

She really had no idea just how bad it was going to be.

Denise had been a bit vague about it when she called earlier. She had fully supported Lydia's decision to go out and face the whole thing down, however, and had even offered her company. Lydia had said no. This was something she must do alone. There was going to be no more hiding behind or clinging to anyone, not even another woman. What she had begun doing on the evening of the assembly, despite the rather disastrous results, she was going to continue doing.

She would *not* retreat back into her shell.

Perhaps the village would be talking today about the new arrivals at Hinsford Manor. Lydia had not counted the number of carriages yesterday, but it had been considerable. Where had all the people been put? And all the horses and carriages? Had anyone been expecting them? Had Harry? Lydia's guess was that the whole of the Westcott family had come to stay, and they were an illustrious lot, to say the least. Surely it was not too much to hope that the pathetic gossip that had erupted yesterday into near scandal over the silly fact that Major Westcott had kissed her in her doorway would be superseded today by all the excitement of knowing that a good chunk of the English aristocracy was virtually on their doorstep?

There was a knock upon her front door just as she was getting up her courage to don her pelisse and bonnet. It would be Hannah this time or Mrs. Bailey, she supposed. But when she opened the door, she discovered that it was neither.

"Oh," she said while Snowball went into an ecstasy of yipping and bouncing and tail waving. Harry Westcott was removing his hat, his expression surely as grim as it must have been when he was facing a regiment of enemy soldiers charging into battle. He was not alone. There was an older lady of aristocratic bearing and elegant appearance with him. Her eyes, steady and grave, were leveled upon Lydia.

"Lydia," Harry said, "may I have the honor of presenting my mother, the Marchioness of Dorchester?"

"It is too late to ask permission, Harry," his mother said. "The deed has already been done. How do you do, Mrs. Tavernor? May we step inside? Or are we interrupting something?"

"I was about to go out," Lydia said none too graciously. "But it can wait."

She stood reluctantly to one side while the Marchioness of Dorchester stepped into her cottage, filling it, dwarfing it with her aristocratic presence and the faint smell of some expensive perfume. Lydia would have scooped up Snowball and held her out of the way, but Harry had already done it himself. The dog was trying to lick his face and was wriggling with what looked very like sheer joy.

Lydia had not felt kindly disposed toward Major Harry Westcott during the night, imagining as she had that he was reveling in the company of his family, untouched by scandal, contemptuous of gossip, and sparing not a single thought for what she might be enduring. She had known that she was being unfair, but sometimes it was hard to ward off self-pity and an accompanying irritability. Sometimes it was hard to admit that one was almost entirely and solely to blame for the ills that came into one's life. For he would not have kissed her forehead the night before last if she had not asked him some time ago if he was ever lonely. He would not have chopped her wood or any of the rest of it. By his own admission he had hardly known she existed.

The marchioness had moved right into the living room, but only, apparently, to make more room in the porch. She turned to look steadily at Lydia again.

"I believe I had an acquaintance with your mother," she said. "She was *Julia* Winterbourne? Your father is Mr. *Jason* Winterbourne?"

"Yes." Lydia raised her eyebrows. "You knew her well, ma'am?"

"Not very, I am afraid," the marchioness admitted. "But I do recall that she was quite pretty and seemed amiable and sweet-tempered. However, I believe she is about to become a very dear friend from my younger years. And I am about to be transported with delight at the discovery that her daughter is living in the very village where I spent so many years with my children during their growing years."

Lydia stared mutely at her. She was very aware of Harry standing silently just behind her. At the edge of her vision she could see his arm moving as he petted Snowball. "But I do not suppose," she said, "you can be feeling any great delight at the way my name has been coupled with your son's in local gossip since yesterday."

"Lydia—"

But his mother cut Harry off with a look and a lifting of her eyebrows. "It is being said, apparently, that you exchanged a good-night kiss with him on your doorstep a couple of evenings ago when you had every reason to believe yourself to be unobserved," she said. "Is that what happened, Mrs. Tavernor? Harry says not quite. He says he kissed your forehead, but you did not return the kiss in any way. I believe him, unless he is being chivalrous and is lying to shield your good name. But even if you contradict him and say it was a mutually shared, even passionate, embrace, it would seem hardly deserving of being spoken of as though there were something sordid about it. I do not remember Mrs. Piper, though I do recall her husband's family. Vaguely, however. They never worked on the Hinsford estate. I understand she feels a particular obligation to honor the memory of your late husband, who died saving her son's life. That is understandable, but it is no excuse for spreading unsubstantiated and doubtless exaggerated rumors in a deliberate attempt to cause embarrassment, even trouble, for his widow. According to Harry, her son appears to have been spying on you for some time."

"I will not apologize for what happens in my own home," Lydia said. "Or try to explain or justify. But to you, ma'am, since you are his mother and have been civil to me, I will say that I am not ashamed of anything that has happened between Major Westcott and me. And until the evening of the assembly there had not been any contact at all between us for a couple of weeks. I was away visiting my father and brothers and sister-in-law. Your son and I are not close friends. We are friendly acquaintances."

She heard Harry inhale sharply behind her as though he was about to say something, but his mother looked at him again and he held his peace.

"I believe you, Mrs. Tavernor," she said. "This is a particularly lovely morning after a bit of a dull start. There is not a cloud in the sky, and there is scarcely a breath of wind. Your front garden is a glory of spring color. Is your back garden just as pretty?"

"Not quite," Lydia said, frowning at the sudden change of subject. "The woodpile is back there, and there is a shed. They take up almost half the garden."

"I will take a look out there anyway, if I may," the marchioness said. "Perhaps your little dog would like to accompany me. I will find a back door in your kitchen, I presume?"

"Yes," Lydia said, taking a step toward the kitchen. "I will show you—"

"Oh, I think it very unlikely I will get lost," the marchioness said, taking Snowball from Harry's arms and laughing as the dog first yipped at her and then licked her hand and tried to do the same to her chin. "No, little dog. Manners, please. I like you well enough, but I do draw the line at having my face washed."

And she stepped past Lydia, made her way through the kitchen, and let herself out into the garden. She shut the door behind her with an audible click.

Lydia turned a frowning face upon Harry. "What—?"

"She has deliberately left us alone," he explained.

Her frown deepened.

"Lydia," Harry said, "this is all absurd and bizarre and a number of other things. But it has happened. I walked over to Tom Corning's earlier this morning, and he told me that Mrs. Piper has had some success in whipping up indignation in that segment of the population that believes you are not entitled to a life of your own but ought to commit the whole of it to grieving for your husband. They are the people who followed him with fervent devotion while he lived and have revered him as a martyr since his passing. They set you on a pedestal along with him when he was vicar here and elevated you even higher after he was gone. You became to them the model of the perfectly devout and virtuous widow. Your behavior in the year or so following his passing confirmed them in that opinion. They may not have appeared to pay you much attention, but your quiet modesty was a comfort to them, I suppose. They did not expect that the time would come when you would wish to start living again."

Lydia sighed and went to stand behind the sofa so she could cling to the back of it and put some distance between them. That was one way of explaining what was happening, she supposed. Her own interpretation was another. It all amounted to the same thing.

"I thought that by remaining invisible to all but a few close acquaintances, I would be shielded until I found myself," she said. "I made the conscious decision to become fully myself in time for the assembly. I wore a pink gown that I suppose some are now describing as garish, even vulgar. I danced and talked with almost everyone and smiled and laughed. I was proud of myself, and everyone seemed to be kind. And then the Wickends sent for the Reverend Bailey and you offered to take Mrs. Bailey and me home in your carriage. Jeremy Piper came after us with the plate I had left behind with cakes for Mrs. Piper to take home for her children. And finally—disaster. I invited you over the threshold out of the rain while I fetched your scarf, and you—" She stopped and sighed again. "As you just observed, it is all utterly absurd and bizarre and I intend simply to ignore it all. People will forget eventually. They always do. And I do not suppose *everyone* will treat me as a pariah."

"I think you had better marry me, Lydia," he said.

She laughed softly but entirely without humor as she turned her head to look into his face. He was still looking grim. Also very pale. He appeared as if he had slept as little as she had.

"That was not the best of proposals, was it?" he said, taking a step toward her. "And there is no excuse. I have been practicing a speech since last night. I cannot recall a single word of it. Though yes, I can. The word *ardent* was in there somewhere. Oh, and the phrase *the happiest of men*."

Incredibly, they both laughed. And seemingly with genuine amusement. But only for a moment.

"Lydia," he said. "It is the only thing that will silence the gossip. A man walks home with the woman he is courting. He chops wood for her. He can be excused for calling upon her in the evenings, even if it is not quite the thing if she lives all alone. He dances with her at a village assembly. He kisses her good night when he brings her home. The gossip will turn to understanding and congratulation from most people once our betrothal is announced."

"No, Harry." Lydia grabbed one of the cushions from the sofa and held it to her with both arms. "I will not be bullied—"

"I am very fond of you, Lydia," he said. "I understand your fear of giving up your freedom to yet another possessive man just when you have begun to enjoy it. But I beg you to believe that it would never occur to me to try to exert dominance over you based upon the single fact that I am a man and you are a woman. Or upon any other fact, for that matter. As my wife you would be my equal. I believe we would be able to offer each other companionship and affection. I would certainly offer them to you, and I am in hope that you would give them in return. You would always be free to be yourself just as I would be free to be myself. But there could be an added sense of togetherness that perhaps we both crave even though both of us have been a bit afraid to risk giving up our single state. Dash it—all this is mere verbiage. I am massively bungling the whole thing, am I not? I am not bullying you, but I really think you should marry me. Will you?"

It *was* a strange marriage proposal and obviously not the one he had rehearsed. That very fact touched her. She felt tears well in her eyes and blinked them determinedly away.

"I did not mean *you* were bullying me," she said. "I meant that if I were to agree to marry you, I would have been bullied into it by public opinion. Oh, Harry, you are very kind. Indeed you are. But, no. It would be wrong—for you, for me, for the situation in which we find ourselves. Why should we be forced into marriage simply because of a spying child, a hysterically pious mother, and a segment of the community, albeit a rather large and vocal one, that is all too ready to believe the worst of me? We should *not* give in to it. Does your mother know you are offering me marriage? But of course she must. Why else would she have decided that she wanted to see the back garden—alone?"

"She does know," he said. "Lydia, was it so very bad that night?"

"It?" She felt her cheeks heating even as she asked the question.

"You dreamed of a lover," he said. "Of me. You had both. Was it so very bad?"

"Oh, Harry." The tears sprang again, and his face blurred before her eyes. "You *know* it was not."

"Well, then?" he asked.

"I cannot marry you just for *that*," she said. "I cannot marry. I will not."

"But circumstances have changed," he said, "as we knew they would if word got out that we were seeing each other privately. Damage has been done to your reputation and your ability to go on living in peace here. You must allow me to make amends. No, scrap that, please. There is no *must* about it, of course. But . . ." He paused and sighed deeply. "Dash it all, Lydia. Please marry me."

Ah, did he not see that it was the very *last* thing she could do? Not because she did not like him. She did. Not because she did not *love* him. She did, God help her. *Certainly* not because she had not enjoyed making love with him. Not even entirely because of her coveted freedom and independence. She could not marry him just because a village was gossiping about her and making a loose woman out of her. She *would* not. It would be a terrible basis for a marriage.

"You do not trust me," he said.

She blinked back her tears so she could see him clearly.

It would be easy to voice an instant denial. But really that was at the root of everything upon which she had based her life and her plans for the past year and a half, was it not? She could trust herself. But could she trust someone—a man—to have legal ownership of her again, to do with her as he chose? For that was what being married meant. She had loved and trusted Isaiah with her whole heart. Who could have been more apparently trustworthy than he?

"You cannot answer," Harry said. "Because you do not want to lie, I suppose, and hurt me. Your life will be difficult from now on."

"Only if I allow it to be," she said.

He gazed at her in obvious exasperation before turning sharply away to look out through the window. "Do you regret that you remained here at Fairfield, knowing as you do now that the widow of the Reverend Tavernor would be held to a higher standard of behavior than anyone else?" he asked her.

She gazed at his back—tall, straight, *military*—and thought about it. "Regrets are pointless," she said. "They do not change whatever that thing is that one may regret if one allows oneself to do so. That one thing for me would be asking you if you are ever lonely. I ought never to have asked. But there have been positive results as well as negative. I had a lot of wood chopped for me all at once."

He looked at her over his shoulder and came very close to smiling before turning away again.

"I am still using the wood," she said. "I will be forgetting how to wield the axe myself. Has *all* your family come, Harry? Hannah says it is probably because you have an important birthday very soon. Your thirtieth. You must be enjoying their company."

"A pointed change of subject," he said, turning from the window and drawing breath to say more. But before he could do so the back door opened with more noise than was necessary. Snowball trotted into the room, hesitated, and went to sniff Harry's boots. The marchioness cleared her throat before coming to stand in the archway to the living room. She looked from one to the other of them.

"Well?" she asked, addressing Harry.

"She has said no," he replied curtly.

"I would have been surprised," she said, "if it had been otherwise. A bit of silly outrage over a kiss that was apparently hardly even worthy of the name is a poor reason for two people to marry if there is no other. You do not wish to marry my son, Mrs. Tavernor?"

"I do not," Lydia said. "Though it was exceedingly kind of him to offer."

"Then you must not be pressed further," the marchioness said. "You do indeed have a pretty back garden. Even the woodpile is picturesque—and very neat. It smells good too. You must spend a lot of time out there and at the front."

"Will you have a seat, ma'am?" Lydia asked, gesturing to one of the chairs. "May I make some tea?"

"Neither, thank you," the marchioness said. "You told us you were on your way out. My apologies for having delayed you. We have a few more calls of our own to make before returning to Hinsford. We will be issuing a few verbal invitations to my son's birthday party, though there will be more formal written ones to follow. Or rather *I* will be issuing invitations. I daresay Harry wishes us all in Jericho.

You must come to the party yourself, Mrs. Tavernor. It is to be in the form of a ball."

"Oh," Lydia said, glancing rather aghast at Harry. He had turned to look out the window again. "I think it would be altogether best if I did not go, ma'am."

"On the contrary," the marchioness said. "Why would you be excluded? Your late husband was a brother of the Earl of Tilden, was he not? And we have already established that you are the daughter of Mr. Jason Winterbourne and the late Mrs. Julia Winterbourne, a friend from my younger years."

"I—"

"You need not give an answer now," the marchioness said as she moved toward the front door. "You will receive your written invitation within the next day or two and can decide then how you wish to reply. In the meantime, we will walk with you, if we may, until our ways diverge. You are going to the village shop?"

"Yes," Lydia said. Harry had his hands clasped behind him. He was tapping them rhythmically against his back. "But—"

He turned. "Lydia," he said. "Word will spread around the village and the surrounding countryside faster than wildfire that you were seen today walking along the main street with me. *And with my mother, the Marchioness of Dorchester*—who was, by the way, held in the deepest affection and esteem when she lived here as the Countess of Riverdale. Everyone will understand that there is nothing clandestine about your acquaintance with me, and that it has my mother's approval. Allow us, please, to offer you this much countenance."

She raised her chin.

"Sometimes," he added, "when a person is fired upon,

the best possible way to respond is to line up *with one's comrades* and fire right back."

She pursed her lips.

"Put your bonnet on," he said.

"If you please, Mrs. Tavernor." The marchioness smiled, revealing herself to be a very pretty woman despite the fact that she was no longer in her youth. "I must be allowed to do all in my power to repair my son's reputation, you see."

Lydia sighed and moved toward the hooks behind the door.

And so it was that a few inhabitants of the village of Fairfield were treated to the unexpected spectacle of the newly notorious Mrs. Tavernor walking along the main village street with the Marchioness of Dorchester's arm drawn through hers, while Major Westcott, distinguished and elegant as always, walked on his mother's other side, nodding pleasantly to everyone they passed.

Sixteen

"Thank you," Harry said to his mother as they walked back home an hour or so later. "It would not, as you pointed out to me last night, have been appropriate for me to go there alone this morning."

"Tell me, Harry," his mother said. "Were you disappointed?"

"That she refused me?" he said after thinking about it for a moment. "No. As she herself pointed out, we would have been marrying for the wrong reason—because of some vicious gossip."

"Gossip can irreparably destroy reputations and lives, however," she said.

"She was on her way out as we got there, Mama," he said. "She was not cowering beneath her bedcovers or behind drawn curtains, or both, as I feared she might. She has backbone."

"When the two of you put an end to your . . . acquaintance a few weeks ago," his mother asked, "did you do so happily, Harry?"

"It was a relationship that was headed nowhere except possible disaster," he said. "She had made it clear from the start that there could be no courtship. She had a restrictive girlhood and what I understand was an unhappy marriage, though I know no details, and is enjoying her freedom. She is quite determined that she will never marry again. It did not take long to discover that it was impossible for us to have any other sort of relationship, even friendship. Not here, anyway. Present events have proved just how right we were."

"But were you *happy* that all ties were broken?" She was persisting with this line of questioning, it seemed.

"No, I was not," he admitted. "Perhaps you were right at Christmastime, Mama. Perhaps I have been a bit lonely. I have a few close friends here and a host of friendly acquaintances. Perhaps they are no longer quite enough. But I am *contented* here. This is where I belong and where I want to be. Forgive me, please. I am feeling a bit confused at the moment. I wish this had not happened at this precise time. It was very good of everyone to make the effort to come here. Even the grandmothers. Even *Camille and Joel.* I really was not—"

"Do you love her, Harry?" she asked softly, interrupting him.

"Lydia?" he said. "Good God, no. Pardon my language."

"That is what I thought," she said just as softly, though strangely he was not sure quite what she meant.

He had no chance to ask her. And she had no chance to explain. Three people were approaching down the drive, arm in arm—Winifred Cunningham, Camille and Joel's eldest; Ivan Wayne, Aunt Mildred and Uncle Thomas's youngest; and Gordon Monteith, Great-aunt Edith's great-nephew. Winifred was in the middle and laughing at something.

"I noticed at Christmas," Harry said, "how Winifred has suddenly grown up. She is no longer a girl, is she? She makes me feel like an elderly uncle. She has grown really rather pretty."

Winifred had been at the orphanage in Bath where both Anna and Joel Cunningham had grown up and where Camille had taught for a while after the Great Disaster. She had been very needy then. She had apparently tried to stand out by being almost ostentatiously well behaved and eager to draw attention to all the other children who were not. She had been more than a bit obnoxious, in fact—or so Harry had been told. Camille had seen something of herself in the girl, however, and when she and Joel married they had surprised everyone by adopting her.

"She is seventeen, Harry," his mother said. "And a real gem. She is not pretty. She never will be. But she has an inner beauty that transcends looks. Some man who is worthy of her is going to notice one of these days, though not just yet, I hope. She is *only* seventeen."

It was Winifred who had devised a sort of hand language to use with her deaf brother, who was not particularly good at reading lips.

"Well, Harry?" Ivan called, raising his voice when the two groups were within earshot of each other. "Will she have you?"

Harry winced inwardly. He had hoped yesterday to keep the situation with Lydia quiet, mainly in the hope that by today or tomorrow at the latest it would have died down, as gossip usually did. His mother had soon disabused him of that notion. Gossip that involved a respectable woman—"*and a vicar's widow, Harry!"*—could not be expected to die down quickly, she had warned, especially when the woman's name was being linked with Major Harry Westcott's. The arrival of the whole of the Westcott family on the scene just when the scandal was breaking, far from dousing the flames, would probably fan them. Everyone would be agog to find out what the Westcotts would do to squash Mrs. Tavernor beneath their collective heel. It was only fair to warn the family.

His mother, Harry had noticed, used the word *scandal* rather than just *gossip*. And Harry had realized, perhaps for the first time, just how bad this whole ridiculous situation might become. After he had talked with his mother in the privacy of the library last night, he had gone back to the drawing room, late as it had been by then, and told the whole story, barring only those details that were absolutely no one's business.

The family had, of course, stayed up very late in the hope of finding out why he had needed to take his mother away for some private consultation. He would be surprised if during his absence this morning the family had not been discussing how they were going to deal with the crisis.

Gossip. Scandal. *Crisis?*

Had the world gone mad? He had kissed Lydia's *forehead* on that fateful night. If it had lasted ten seconds he would be very surprised.

"She will not," he said curtly in answer to Ivan's question.

"I am so glad, Uncle Harry," Winifred said.

"What you don't have in your whole body, my girl," Ivan told her, "is a romantic bone."

"Nonsense," she said. "What woman would find it romantic to be forced into marriage by a little spiteful gossip?

And *stupid* gossip too. You agree with me, Grandmama, do you not?"

It occurred to Harry suddenly that not so long ago his mother had almost been forced into marrying Marcel for just such a reason. She had run off with him one day for a romantic fling without a word to anyone but had been tracked down by separate search parties sent out by the Westcotts and Marcel's family. She had resisted all pressure and married him later for her own reasons. Not that Harry had witnessed any of those sensational events except the actual wedding one Christmas Eve. He had been overseas with his regiment.

"I agree, Winifred," his mother said. "Men know *nothing* of romance, alas." She was laughing.

"But did you go down on one knee, Harry?" Gordon asked, grinning at him. "It is no wonder she said no if you did not."

Winifred tossed her glance at the branches over their heads. "If any man went down on one knee to me," she said, "I would laugh at him."

"You see?" Ivan said. "Not a romantic bone."

They all turned to walk back to the house together. Winifred took Harry's arm. "The great-aunts and great-grandmothers all have their heads together," she told him. "But Mama says there is nothing they can decide upon until they know if Mrs. Tavernor will have you or not. That is not stopping them, however, from discussing what is to be done if she will not."

"Personally, Winnie," he said, "I keep hoping I will wake up any moment now, I have never got tangled up in a more ridiculous dream in my life."

He kept thinking of Lydia walking into the village shop alone, with straight back and raised chin, after flatly refusing to allow them to accompany her inside. They had stood on the pavement outside for a few moments until it became apparent that she was not going to be tossed out.

Do you love her? his mother had asked a short while ago.

And God help him, he was beginning to ask himself the same question.

Lydia went to church the following day, as she always did on Sunday mornings. It was not easy this week, however. She had been served at the village shop yesterday, but with lowered eyes on the part of the shopkeeper and none of the usual bright chatter. On her way home someone had hastily crossed the street from her side to the other as though it had become suddenly imperative to be *there* rather than *here*. When she had passed her next-door neighbor's house, Mrs. Bartlett had been in the garden tending her flowers. But just as Lydia had been drawing breath to comment upon how lovely they were looking, Mrs. Bartlett had half turned her head, jerked it back again, and hurried into her house as though she had suddenly remembered something urgent she needed to do inside.

She sat in her usual pew toward the back of the church. There was a pool of emptiness all about her, but that was not unusual. Most people preferred to sit farther forward.

And then there was a buzz of sound and activity coming from the direction of the doorway behind her, and her neighbors came scurrying inside all at once, it seemed, and took their seats so they could enjoy the show of what could only be the Westcott family arriving for church. And still the pew beside her and the ones directly in front and behind remained empty.

Lydia did not know any of the Westcotts, except Harry

and his mother, but she distracted herself by trying to guess who some of them were. One of the three elderly ladies who came in together must be the Dowager Countess of Riverdale. Lydia guessed it was the one with the most plumes in her bonnet. One of the men must be the Earl of Riverdale, the one who had taken on the title when Harry was stripped of it. She guessed it was either the tall, dark-haired, very handsome man or the slight blond man of medium height who, despite his size disadvantage, fairly oozed aristocratic hauteur. One of them, the one who was not the earl, was perhaps the Duke of Netherby. One very distinguished-looking man of middle years was easy to identify. He had the Marchioness of Dorchester, Harry's mother, on his arm—she turned her head and nodded graciously to Lydia as she passed on her way to the front pews. He must be her husband, the marquess.

The front pews filled fast. One family group alone took up more than one pew, and Lydia guessed that the woman must be Camille Cunningham, Harry's elder sister. She and her husband were carrying seemingly identical babies, and they were trailed by a number of other children, varying in age, Lydia guessed, from three or four to sixteen or seventeen. It was pretty much impossible to identify any of the others.

Harry came with the last group, and Lydia clutched her prayer book and did not know whether to keep her eyes on it as he passed or to look across at him and nod pleasantly if *he* looked at *her*. She wished with all her heart that she could revert to the time when she had been virtually invisible. Oh no, she did not. She was not going to cower here. She turned her head to look very deliberately at him—and something inside her somersaulted, or felt very much as though it did. He had been inside her home, her very private

space. He had been inside *her.* They had talked—*really*
talked. He had admitted to her that he had had to struggle
with a wave of hatred for his cousin and half sister though
he had known he was being unjust. She had told him things
about herself that she had not told anyone else, even Denise
or Hannah.

He looked back at her. But instead of going on by, he
came along her pew toward her. The man and woman who
were with him came too, with a baby and a young child. A
third child, a little girl, looked ahead before following
them, just as the marchioness glanced over her shoulder
and then smiled and beckoned. The child ran ahead to
squeeze in between her and the man Lydia assumed was the
marquess.

But really she scarcely noticed. She looked inquiringly
at Harry and was aware that half the congregation must be
looking too even though she sat close to the back.

"Good morning," he murmured. "I have my sister and
brother-in-law with me. Abigail and Gil Bennington. Mrs.
Tavernor," he told them. "May we sit here?"

Abigail was fair-haired and pretty. Her husband had
very dark hair and a harsh, dark-complexioned, noticeably
scarred face. He was carrying the baby.

"I am pleased to meet you, Mrs. Tavernor," Mrs. Bennington said softly, and squeezed past her brother to sit beside Lydia. Her husband sat on his wife's other side and
Harry beyond him. Harry lifted the little boy onto his lap.

Had they all drawn straws to decide who would sit with
her? And had Harry's sister and brother-in-law drawn the
short one? Lydia clutched her prayer book more tightly,
murmured that she was delighted too, and was very thankful to see that the Reverend Bailey was coming from the
vestry and the service was about to begin.

She knew what they were up to—the marchioness inventing a friendship with Lydia's mother yesterday; her insistence that she and Harry walk along the village street with Lydia; Harry and some other designated member of the family sitting beside her at church this morning; the invitation, soon to be made official, to Harry's birthday party next Friday. They were trying to make it seem that Harry had a casual friendship with her and that they found nothing scandalous in it and were quite happy to pursue an acquaintance with her. They were doing it, of course, for Harry's sake, to protect him from any implication that there had been something improper in his behavior.

Lydia appreciated what they were doing anyway—and resented it. For they must, she realized, very deeply resent *her*.

She would not afterward have been able to recall anything of the service. She recited the prayers and sang the hymns without conscious thought, kneeled and stood and sat in all the appropriate places, responding entirely by rote. When Mrs. Bennington turned her head at one point to smile at her, she pretended not to notice. She was very aware of Harry three places away from her, bouncing the little boy on his knee once in a while, taking the child's hands in his at one point to clap them silently together and leaning his head forward to whisper something in his ear. The child tipped back his head and smiled up at his uncle and Harry kissed his cheek.

How could she possibly see all that without either turning her head or leaning forward? She did not know, but she did see.

He had asked her to marry him. In an abrupt, unprepared speech that had affected her far more deeply than a more polished proposal would have done. She bit hard on her upper lip at the memory and blinked her eyes fast.

At last the service came to an end and Lydia rose in the hope of slipping out before anyone else and hurrying home so she could shut the door behind her and be herself again. But Mrs. Bennington had turned toward her, and it was impossible to pretend again not to notice.

"I am indeed pleased to meet you, Mrs. Tavernor," she said. "Gil and I were married in this church four years ago. The Reverend Jenkins was the vicar then, and Mrs. Jenkins was still alive. She and my brother were the only witnesses. But I do believe it was the loveliest wedding ever. Not that I am biased or anything." She laughed. "You and your husband came here very soon after that—after Mrs. Jenkins died suddenly and the poor vicar decided to retire. I regret that I never met the Reverend Tavernor. And I do sympathize very deeply with your loss. It must have devastated you."

"Thank you," Lydia said, and she shook the hand that was being extended for hers. "It was a distressing time."

"My sister and I would like to call upon you within the next day or two," Mrs. Bennington continued. "If we may, that is. Will it inconvenience you?"

What could she say? And did she want to say it would? Why should she, after all? If nothing had ever happened between her and Harry—nothing outside her dreams, that was—she would surely be delighted to make the acquaintance of a few members of the Westcott family. She was, after all, the widow of the former vicar here. She was the social equal of any of them. There would be no condescension involved in their visiting her.

"Not at all," she said. "I will be delighted to see you."

The little boy was pulling Harry by the hand toward the other end of the pew to greet what must be some of his young cousins. The congregation were beginning to move from their pews. Some of them would hurry outside as quickly as possible to watch the exodus of the Westcotts. And her exit too. She was very far from being invisible this morning.

She smiled at Mrs. Bennington and made her escape while she still could without having to run the gauntlet of her neighbors outside.

Harry had realized two days ago that his family had arrived at quite the worst possible time. For of course they had come not just to celebrate his birthday but also to do some determined matchmaking. They had even brought three possible bridal candidates with them, though he was not sure if those three young ladies knew why they had been invited here. And now, of course, the family would see Lydia in one of two ways—as another possible candidate or as a threat, as someone who must be ousted from any pretension to Harry's hand with all the power of their influence. Not that the Westcotts always behaved as a cohesive unit, it was true. Opinion might well be divided.

A few of his male relatives had squeezed him reassuringly on the shoulder after he returned from the village with his mother on Saturday morning and reported on the failure of his marriage proposal. As far as they were concerned, that was the end of the matter, though it was possible more than a few of them knew their women well enough to suspect that the end was in fact nowhere in sight. The women seemed generally of the opinion that Mrs. Tavernor had behaved like a woman of principle. One could only admire her for saying no—and do all in one's power to offer her some support.

It was unclear, of course, in what exactly they intended to support her. In her decision not to have him? In being persuaded to change her mind? The Westcott women were really not to be trusted, and Harry did *not* trust them to leave well enough alone and mind their own business. In their minds Harry *was* their business, and since Mrs. Tavernor had got herself into a bit of bother over him, then she became their business too.

The mind boggled.

At dinner on Saturday night, Elizabeth, Lady Hodges, had announced her intention of calling upon Mrs. Tavernor the next morning. She knew from experience just what it felt like to be the target of unkind and unjust gossip, having once upon a time been the victim of a spectacular scene in which her then-fiancé had accused her in the middle of a crowded ballroom in London of flirting outrageously with Colin, the man who was now her husband. Wren, Countess of Riverdale, had promised to accompany her. So had Anna, Cousin Althea, Aunt Mary Kingsley, and Cousin Jessica before Gabriel, Jessica's husband, had reminded them that the next day was Sunday.

There had followed a discussion upon whether it was more likely that Mrs. Tavernor would go to church and brazen things out or remain at home to hide.

"From what I saw of Mrs. Tavernor earlier today," Harry's mother had said, "I would say she will most certainly go."

"And until fairly recently she was the wife of the vicar here," Uncle Michael—the *Reverend* Michael Kingsley—had reminded them. "Going to church is probably a matter of importance to her."

"Gil and I and the children will sit by her," Abigail had said with quiet determination. "If there is space beside her, that is."

Everyone had looked at her without commenting—a rare occurrence with this family.

"We will, my love," Gil had said.

"And so will I," Harry had added, trying to picture the scene and wondering if Lydia really would go to church, since she must realize that a large number of his family plus all the gossips and the curious certainly would. He had believed that she would go, however.

"But not right beside her, Harry," Aunt Louise had said.

"Close by but not next to," Aunt Mildred had added.

"Close by. Looking amiable." That contribution to the conversation, spoken with a great sigh of apparent boredom, had come from Avery.

"I cannot imagine Harry ever *not* looking amiable," Adrian Sawyer had commented.

"Tell that to a few thousand Frenchmen from Napoleon Bonaparte's armies," Gil—the former Lieutenant Colonel Gilbert Bennington, that was—had added. "The ones who are still living, anyway."

Through Saturday and Sunday, while the drama of Lydia was rumbling along in the family consciousness and in private family consultations, the matter of the three prospective brides somehow resolved itself quickly and painlessly and without embarrassment to any of those most nearly concerned. The Westcotts, in other words, were about as successful this time with their matchmaking schemes as they had ever been.

Sally Underwood was wide-eyed and pretty and shy and a bit blushy and giggly—and all of eighteen years and one month old, as she admitted to Harry when she walked beside him on the way home from church. He had the feeling the pairing had been maneuvered by Aunt Matilda, whose stepniece she was. She talked, after Harry had finally induced her to relax a little, about the balls and routs her mama planned for her to attend after she had returned to

London and her come-out Season was properly launched. And then, her tongue having been loosened by what she seemed to consider pleasant prospects, she talked about all the shopping and fittings and dancing lessons that must be got through first and about the beaux her mama had promised she would attract, what with all her new finery and the dowry her papa had to offer with her, which was more than respectable, for Papa was a wealthy man.

It had become apparent to Harry as they walked that she saw him as a sort of elderly uncle figure. All the time she was prattling—after she had recovered from her early awe of him, that was—she was eyeing Ivan Wayne and Gordon Monteith, the good-natured, freckled, slightly pimply, and very youthful nephew of Great-aunt Edith. If Aunt Matilda seriously expected that he and Miss Underwood would make a match of it, she must have windmills in her head. Or perhaps she had just not known the girl well when she chose her.

Miranda Monteith, Great-aunt Edith's niece on her late husband's side, had never lived in Scotland and appeared to have no connection to the country apart from her name and probably a few long-forgotten ancestors. She was, however, obsessed with all things Scottish, including its complex and gory history, as Harry discovered when he sat beside her at luncheon after church. She was serious-minded and intense and forthright in manner, and seemed quite unaware of him either as a man or as a prospective husband.

"I intend to stride about the park and countryside while I am here," she said. "With your permission, that is, Mr. Westcott. It is unfortunate that you do not have any of the mountains and rugged scenery around here that I most admire, but the landscape seems pretty enough. Mother insisted that I come to London this year, though I abhor cities and large towns. I was very happy to accompany Aunt Edith here for a week or so as soon as I knew that Hinsford Manor was in the country. Mother was not pleased, but she did agree to my coming with Gordon after Aunt Edith had had a private word with her, though I have no idea what she said."

If he should ever get into the business of predicting the future, Harry thought, he would say with some confidence that Miss Monteith was headed for the ranks of happily confirmed spinsters.

Miss Fanny Leeson might have been a bit of a problem, since it was obvious to Harry almost from the moment of her arrival that she was very well aware of why she had been brought to Hinsford. She had come with her mother and her sister, a vibrantly beautiful young lady who was happily engaged to an equally happy Boris Wayne. The younger sister was just as lovely, if a little less vibrant. She seemed to be a sensible young woman, however, who spoke little but usually had something decent to say when she did speak. It might be difficult, Harry thought with unkind feelings for the Westcott ladies who had trapped him in this situation, to depress her expectations without either hurting or humiliating her. However, it was to prove far easier than he feared.

She addressed the main issue with him after luncheon on Sunday when she approached him out on the terrace as he waited for several others to join him for a walk down to the lake he had suggested when they rose from the table.

"I think it only fair that you should know, Mr. Westcott," she said, keeping her voice low as she glanced over her shoulder to make sure no one had followed close behind her, "that my heart belongs to another."

Harry looked at her in some surprise. With almost any

other young lady, some of those words would have sounded as if they must be capitalized—*"My Heart Belongs to Another."* With Miss Fanny Leeson they sounded like simple fact. She was looking very pretty and very self-contained. Her cheeks were only slightly flushed.

"We are not betrothed," she went on to explain. "He has not yet spoken to Papa because I did not want to take attention away from Audrey, who has only very recently become betrothed to your cousin and is very happy about it. But we have a secret agreement."

"I must wish you every happiness, then," Harry said. He looked at her, a twinkle in his eye. "And I think it only fair that you know, Miss Leeson, that I am not really in search of a wife. I do believe, however, that my female relatives are in relentless search of one for me. They are very determined to force me into being happy."

"Oh," she said, smiling at last and looking even prettier than before, "I know what *that* feels like, Mr. Westcott. Are not relatives an abomination?"

They shared a private moment of guilty amusement before Bertrand and Elizabeth and Charles, Viscount Dirkson, stepped out onto the terrace.

Seventeen

꧁

Camille informed everyone at breakfast the following morning that she was going with Abby to deliver Mrs. Tavernor's written invitation to Harry's birthday ball.

"And Harry ought to go with you," Grandmama Kingsley suggested. "It would be very fitting, since the three of you practically grew up here at Hinsford and Mrs. Tavernor was once the vicar's wife."

"Of course," Harry said when all eyes turned his way.

Apparently Abigail had asked Lydia at church yesterday morning if she might call upon her today with Camille, and Lydia had given her permission. But how would she react when he turned up with them? It might seem like harassment since she had said a firm no to him just two days ago. But he wanted very badly to see her, to judge for himself whether she was coping with the disruption to her life.

She was at home when Harry arrived with his sisters. Not alone, however. Mrs. Bailey was with her, and the first few minutes were taken up with a flurry of introductions and hearty greetings and assurances by Lydia that no, their calling was not an inconvenience to her, and assurances by Camille that no, Mrs. Bailey must not feel obliged to leave on their account.

"We have come because I asked at church yesterday if we might," Abby explained after the ladies were all seated in the living room.

"Our mother has told us about her friendship with your mama when they were both young, Mrs. Tavernor," Camille said. "She was delighted to discover that her friend's daughter was living right here. Sometimes happy coincidences really do occur."

"Is this true?" Mrs. Bailey beamed her pleasure from one to the other of the ladies. "Do tell us more, Mrs. Cunningham."

Which Camille proceeded to do, with embellishments of the already embellished story their mother had told. The conversation moved by natural progression to London and Seasons past. Mrs. Bailey reminisced about her own courtship, which had come about because *her* mama had once enjoyed a friendship with *her husband's* mama.

"Not that he was my husband when we first met, of course," she added.

Harry was standing with his back to the room, looking through the window while Snowball, who appeared to have accepted him as a friend of long standing, settled across one of his boots. After a while, when it became apparent that Lydia was not participating in the conversation, he went to draw up a stool beside her chair, and she leaned down to lift the dog onto her lap.

"Is it very bad?" he asked, keeping his voice low.

"It will blow over as such things inevitably do," she told him. "I am grateful for what your mother did on Saturday and for what you and Mr. and Mrs. Bennington did at church yesterday. I am grateful too for this morning's call. I do not doubt they will all sway public opinion, if not quite in my favor, at least no further away from it. But this is enough now, Harry. I am quite capable of living my own life. I do not need any further assistance."

"I do not doubt it," he told her. "But Lydia, I—"

He got no further.

"We have brought your official invitation to Harry's birthday party, Mrs. Tavernor," Camille said, raising her voice. "It is to be a ball. I wish we had known we would meet you here, Mrs. Bailey. We would have brought yours too. I believe my mother intends to deliver it to the vicarage this morning. We want as many of Harry's neighbors as possible to help us celebrate. My brother will turn thirty only once."

"For which fact I am fervently thankful," he said.

Mrs. Bailey laughed heartily.

"Thank you," Lydia said, taking the card when Camille got to her feet to hand it to her. "I will consider it."

Abigail stood too and pulled on her gloves. "Wonderful," she said, smiling warmly. "We brought Mrs. Bartlett's invitation card with us too since she lives just next door. We must be on our way to deliver it."

"Lydia," Harry said, getting to his feet too and putting the stool back where he had found it, "after we have made that delivery—in about half an hour, I suppose—will you come with us and perhaps take a stroll in the park? With me? It is such a beautiful day."

He had not planned the invitation until the words were coming out of his mouth. And she was bound to say no. But dash it all, why should they deny themselves any sort of friendship when they had clearly grown to like each other?

And all because of the risk of the very stupidity that was now happening anyway? Why not be bold and open about it and to hell with anyone who wanted to make scandal of it? *Not* that she was going to see it that way, of course. And now he had probably embarrassed her in front of the vicar's wife and his sisters.

"That would be just the thing for you, dear," Mrs. Bailey said with a comfortable smile.

"Please do come," Abby said. "Your little dog looks eager for some exercise."

Snowball was standing on Lydia's lap, facing away from her, her fluff of a tail brushing across her bosom.

Lydia's chin had risen in a stubborn gesture Harry was beginning to recognize. "I shall be ready in half an hour," she surprised him by saying.

"Why not?" Lydia had thought when he asked. Why *not*? What had a more or less careful adherence to propriety and common sense achieved? And that was *not* a question that needed answering.

So here she was, doing what she had never done in four years of living in Fairfield and well over a year of being in her cottage right opposite the drive to the manor. She was on Hinsford property, walking through a park in which she had never before set foot toward a house she had never seen. The drive wound between large, ancient trees, giving the impression that one was moving into an enchanted place, a land apart.

She was with Major Harry Westcott, whom she had very sensibly and very firmly renounced—if that was not too strong a word—almost a month ago. She was not walking beside him, however. It was actually worse than that, for she was walking arm in arm with Mrs. Camille Cunningham, his elder sister. Just as she had walked a couple of days ago with his mother along the village street.

There was very little from the last few days that made any sense to her, either in what was happening beyond her doors or in what she herself was doing in reaction to it all.

What was it about Harry?

She was not in love with him, was she? Well, she supposed she was and had been for a long time, but in her dreams, not in reality. There was or ought to be a vast difference between the two—and it was entirely her own fault that there was not. She did not want to be in love with any man in this real world. She had made the deliberate choice to be alone and independent. And heart-whole.

She just wished someone would tell her heart that. It was not good when head and heart were divorced from each other and not on speaking terms. Of course, she had not done herself any favors by taking him as a lover one memorable night—and she tried very hard *not* to remember. An impossibility when he was within her sight, of course. Or when he was not, for that matter.

Snowball, on a long lead, was trotting happily at her side.

Mrs. Cunningham was telling her about the grand adventure of transporting herself and her husband with nine children, two dogs, and two nurses, plus her grandmother and her grandmother's personal maid—*"not to mention all our baggage, Mrs. Tavernor"*—from Bath to Hinsford while also preserving her sanity. Lydia surprised herself by becoming helpless with laughter more than once. Harry, meanwhile, was walking ahead of them with his younger sister. They were conversing quietly together, but both looked back more than once to smile at something their sister said.

No, there was absolutely no point in denying to herself that she was in love with him, Lydia thought when her eyes met his on one such occasion. He was smiling while she was laughing, and it seemed to her it was a shared moment of pure joy. Her stomach was even dancing, though not necessarily with joy.

However, one did not need to act upon one's feelings. One's actions ought rather to be based upon sober reason and common sense. With a little willpower, one could establish control over one's feelings and do what one knew one ought to do and what one really *wished* to do.

It all sounded so . . . reasonable.

So why was she here?

The trees were becoming less dense. There was more sky visible and more sunshine. There was more grass. There were flower beds. And the house.

It was not a vast mansion. But it was grand and attractive and well situated near the top of a very slight slope of land, with a wide lawn before it and trees surrounding it, but at a sufficient distance not to crowd or darken it, only to give an impression of rural seclusion.

It looked like a happy place in which to live, Lydia thought without stopping to ask herself what exactly she meant by that. Perhaps because it was *his* home. Or because a number of the people staying here were outdoors and there were shouts and shrieks and laughter coming from one group out on the lawn playing cricket, and chanting from a circle of very little children and their two adult supervisors at the top of the lawn. A group of riders was gathered over in front of the stables on the far side of the house. It looked as though they were about to go riding together. Three elderly ladies sat on the terrace, watching all the activity.

She should have expected this, Lydia thought with an

inward grimace. It was, after all, the sort of day that was made for outdoor activities. But surely Harry's intention was not to take her right into the midst of the throng and perhaps even introduce her to those ladies. He had asked her to walk in the park with him.

Even as she thought she might have been trapped into something quite different, however, Harry stopped and turned toward her.

"I do not suppose you are a star bowler or batter, by any chance, Lydia?" he asked.

"I am not," she said. Though her brothers had learned when she was still quite young not to lob easy balls at her just because she was a girl. She had punished a number of those balls with her cricket bat before they had taken her more seriously.

"It is just as well," he said. "The two team captains, whoever they are, would probably come to blows over you. Shall we stroll around behind the house? The kitchen gardens are back there and, beyond them, more trees and what as children we used to call the jungle walk. It was not designed or constructed by any landscape artist, alas, but the path is kept clear and it is quite pretty and not much frequented."

"I would like that," Lydia said.

"Watch out for snakes," Mrs. Bennington said, and all three of the siblings laughed. "Harry used to yell that as he was jumping out at us from behind a tree with a length of creeper dangling from one hand. After the first time or two we would just roll our eyes and walk on."

"You used to poke out your tongue and cross your eyes too, Abby," Mrs. Cunningham said. "I was more genteel. I merely stuck my nose in the air and made derogatory remarks about *boys*."

All three laughed again and Lydia smiled too. She had forgotten the days of tormenting brothers. After the disappointment over her come-out Season that never was and the terrible mistake of her marriage, she had allowed memories of her childhood and girlhood to turn sour.

Snowball began to bark suddenly and ferociously and pull on the lead as a great monster of a . . . creature came galloping toward them in pursuit of three shrieking little girls. Lydia stooped down and snatched up her dog. But who was going to snatch up *her*? And the others? She experienced a few moments of blind panic and horror before realizing that the creature was a large dog and that the little girls were not fleeing from him but rather being accompanied by him. They were shrieking with excitement at seeing Lydia's group. They all, the dog included, came to an abrupt halt when they were a few feet away.

"Mama," one of the little girls yelled, addressing Mrs. Bennington as though she were still half a mile away, "Rebecca has pulled out her tooth and Emma has cut one. *Both on the same day.* Can you believe it?"

"I was supposed to tell," one of the others complained loudly. "Because Emma is *my sister.*"

"Papa has my tooth," the third child cried. "He said he is going to have it set in gold and wear it on a chain about his neck for the rest of his life, but I think he was funning me. It would be . . . *disgusting* to wear my tooth, would it not, Uncle Harry?"

Snowball was yipping and wriggling, eager to get at the monster. The monster, meanwhile, was sitting on his giant haunches, looking ungainly and slightly lopsided. He—she? it?—was panting loudly and woofing a friendly greeting to its would-be assailant.

"Let me see that gap, Rebecca," Harry said, and took the

child's chin in his hand as she opened her mouth wide and pointed. "Hmm. No sign of a new tooth yet."

"*Has* Emma's tooth come through at last?" Mrs. Cunningham asked. "I have never known a more stubborn tooth. Or a crosser baby. Susan's pushed through last week."

"I believe," Mrs. Bennington said, "you girls left your manners back at the house. Make your curtsies to Mrs. Tavernor, if you please. This, Mrs. Tavernor, is my daughter, Katy." She indicated the child who had told the initial story. "This is Alice Cunningham, Emma's sister. And Susan's. They are twins. And the girl with the newly lost tooth is Rebecca Archer."

"*Lady* Rebecca Archer," Alice Cunningham said—and giggled. "Her papa is a *duke*. The Duke of Netherby."

"The dog is Beauty," Mrs. Cunningham added. "She was facetiously named by Abby's husband when she was a puppy, but she grew to fit the name."

There was a chorus of *"How do you do, Mrs. Tavernor?"* from the cousins, who looked to be all about the same age. They bobbed curtsies.

"I am very pleased to meet you all," Lydia said.

"Your dog looks like a ball of fluffy wool," Rebecca Archer said. "He is *sweet*. May I pet him? Will he bite?"

"She does not bite," Lydia said. "And she loves to be made a fuss of."

All three girls crowded around to pet her dog. They laughed with glee when Lydia told them her name.

"She *looks* like a snowball," Katy Bennington said. "How funny."

"She licked my hand," Alice Cunningham said, snatching it away with a squeal. "Come and see Emma's tooth, Mama. You can come too, Aunt Abby. And Uncle Harry. Would you like to see it, Mrs. Tavernor?"

"Mrs. Tavernor and I are going for a walk," Harry said. "I will come and admire the tooth later. Rebecca's too if she insists and if her papa has not already gilded it. Mrs. Tavernor?" He stepped forward to take Snowball from her. "Hush, dog. We know you are a mighty warrior, but you may frighten poor Beauty if you are set down." He offered Lydia his free arm.

"I scarcely recognize my home," he said as they walked away. "It has suffered an invasion. A surprise one, I might add. I did not have an inkling. Foolish of me."

"Do you mind?" she asked him.

He sighed and then chuckled. "I am extremely fond of them all," he said. "And I appreciate the fact that they made such a herculean effort to plan this surprise and come all the way here just to help me celebrate my birthday. Camille made their journey sound hilarious when she described it to you just now, but in reality it must have been . . . well. Nightmarish? Everyone has come. The whole family. Without exception. Even one grandmother who is almost eighty and the other who is not far behind. I am very grateful to them all."

"But?" she said. They had turned off the drive just when it had seemed inevitable that they would come close to more people. He was leading her along the east side of the house.

"There is no real *but*," he said. "This may all seem ridiculously extravagant for a mere thirtieth birthday. Everyone has one of those, after all, provided he or she lives long enough. It is more than that with my family, though. They all want desperately to make things up to me. They look upon me as being at the very heart of what happened ten years ago. I was the one who suffered most obviously. I lost everything—the title, the properties, the fortune, my legitimacy, any residual respect I had left for my father. I lost my position as head of the family. I lost my ability to protect and care for my mother and sisters. And then I went off to war and got myself horribly wounded a number of times. I was actually sent home to England to recover at one time and arrived with a high fever and pretty much off my head. I got myself very nearly killed at Waterloo and was eventually carried back here, ill, weak, and destitute except for what I could still expect from an officer's half-pay."

He paused to smile at Lydia.

"This family did not just feel sorry for me," he continued. "They did not even just feel that they must take me into their collective embrace and care for me. They felt *guilty*. As though everything that had happened was somehow their fault. My father was my grandmother's *son* and my aunts' *brother*. They blamed themselves for the way he turned out, though it seems extremely unlikely there was anything they could have done to stop him from being the rotten apple he was. Alexander blamed himself for inheriting what ought to have been mine, even though he made it obvious from the start that he did not *want* any of it. Anna blamed herself for being our father's only legitimate child—as though she could help *that*—and for inheriting everything that was not entailed. Even Hinsford."

"You told me before that it does not belong to you," Lydia said.

"She has tried a number of times to give it to me as well as what she insists is my quarter of the fortune," he said. "But I have steadfastly refused. Now that I think about it, though, perhaps my pride has made me unkind. It *is* unkind to rebuff a sincerely offered gift. My family's sensibilities have been soothed by the happy marriages of my mother and my sisters. But there is still me."

"And you are about to turn thirty," she said.

"Precisely." He stopped for a moment to set Snowball down to walk beside them.

"And you are still living here in the country," she said. "Unmarried and without children."

"And therefore in their estimation *not* living happily ever after," he said. "And they still cannot forgive themselves for offenses they did not commit. I cannot resent them, Lydia. They love me too dearly. And I love them."

"But," she said, and laughed.

"But," he agreed, and sighed—and then laughed too.

"Do you find all the children bothersome?" she asked.

"No." He looked at her in some surprise. "Why should I? I find them a delight most of the time, and when I do not, they are their parents' responsibility, not mine. I get the best of both worlds."

"Seeing those three little girls, cousins who look to be close to one another in age, reminded me of how much I longed for a sister when I was a girl," she said. "Though I would happily have settled for a cousin or two."

They had come to the back of the house by now and paused for a few moments to look at the long expanse of the kitchen garden. Spring flowers, presumably ones to be cut for the house, took up half of one side and were blooming in some profusion. Vegetables, many of them already pushing through the soil, stood in neat rows to fill the rest. Snowball, taking up the whole length of her lead, was sniffing along the roots of one row of crocuses.

Lydia felt herself begin to relax. Until Harry spoke again, that was.

"Lydia," he asked, "why did you not have children of your own?"

She froze. He *knew* the reason. Did he not? She had wondered, but . . . Oh, surely he had realized the truth.

"Sometimes one does not," she said.

"I beg your pardon," he said almost simultaneously. "I . . . had no right to ask."

They resumed walking and made their way beside the gardens toward the trees beyond them. Lydia was finding it a bit hard to breathe evenly.

"We decided not even to be friends," he said, apparently moving on to another subject.

"We did," she agreed. So why were they here?

"Which was utterly absurd of us," he continued. "I missed you while you were gone. Though I did not even realize you *were* gone. When I got no answer to my knock twice on that one day, I assumed you wished to avoid me and I respected your wish. I stayed away from the village. I did not even attend the Easter services at church. But I missed you, Lydia."

Perversely—*utterly* perversely—she was hurt by the fact that he had not even known she was gone.

"It is hardly surprising you did not know I was away," she said. "Just a few weeks before that you scarcely knew I existed."

Oh, petty words, Lydia.

"Because you deliberately hid," he told her. "Even though you went out and about, you made yourself virtually invisible. It was a remarkable performance."

"And obviously a necessary one," she said tartly. "As was my going away for a couple of weeks after . . . well, after we had agreed not to see each other again. You came anyway. *Twice.* My deliberate *hiding*, as you called it, and my going away to stay with my father for a few weeks stopped anything like *this* from happening."

"*This* being my calling on you again after you had been so unfairly singled out for gossip, I suppose," he said, "and offering you marriage to shield you from it, and sitting beside you with my sister and her husband at church yesterday to show that we are friendly acquaintances even if nothing more, and persuading you to come walking in the park with me today. All and everything that has happened to you during the past few days is *my fault*, I suppose. Yet as I remember it, Lydia, it was *you* who suggested that we become lovers."

"Oh," she cried, stung. "I did *not* suggest any such thing. All I did was ask you if you were ever lonely."

"You said a lot more than that, my girl," he told her, "even if you could not force yourself to the end of any sentence you started."

That was *it*. She was horribly mortified. And how dare he remind her? He was not a gentleman. She was sorry she had ever thought he was.

"I am not your girl or anyone else's, Major Westcott," she said. "I am not a *girl*. I am twenty-eight years old."

"And I am not a major," he said. "I am *Mr.* Westcott if you must be ridiculous enough to address me formally after what there has been between us."

There. See? Not a gentleman.

"I am not your girl, *Mr.* Westcott," she said. "And I would be obliged if you would turn around and take me back home. Better yet, I will take myself home. I do not expect I will get lost between here and my cottage."

He clamped her hand to his side as she tried to jerk it free of his arm. And he had the gall to . . . *laugh*.

"Our first quarrel," he said. "Wherever did that come from? I wonder. But do you think perhaps it means we are friends after all, Lydia?"

The man had windmills in his head. "Friends?" she said. "*Friends?* Harry, you are . . . You are . . . absurd."

"Yes, aren't I?" he said, grinning. "And I am *Harry* now, am I?"

"But I suppose I am still a *girl*," she said, refusing to be appeased. "May I please have my hand back?"

"Lydia," he said, keeping her hand, "you are very much a woman." And he spoke the words in a velvet voice, the provoking man. She felt it stroking down along her body, inside and out, until it reached her knees and turned them weak. How dared he? She glared indignantly at him.

"*Very* much," he said in the same voice. "Forgive me. You did not explicitly suggest that we be lovers."

"But you know very well that I did so *implicitly*," she said. "And it was not *explicit* only because I lost my courage. It does not matter. It happened anyway. But if you are a gentleman you will forget."

"The funny thing about memory, though," he said, "is that it cannot always or perhaps ever be commanded at will, can it? Perhaps you are right, though. Perhaps I am not a gentleman. If you wish to go home immediately, I will escort you. But please, will you consider strolling through the jungle walk with me instead? Let us change our minds and be friends after all, shall we? We do not also have to be lovers. Somehow that did not work out when we tried it, did it?"

She closed her eyes briefly and took a deep breath. Snowball was tugging on her lead, eager to move on, and Harry was *standing* here, invading her space and her consciousness, and she desperately wanted them to be friends again, as they had started to be before she recognized the hopeless danger of their seeing each other privately and tried to turn him away. Only to make love with him instead—and *then* turn him away.

Her mind was one churning jumble of confusion and contradiction—just as her actions had been a few weeks ago.

She released the breath. "Only if you can promise there will be no snakes," she said, opening her eyes.

"If I see one," he said, "I will pick it up and hold it a safe distance from you before warning you."

She laughed. Oh, how could she possibly *not* do so when his eyes smiled at her as they did now?

They walked onward, not talking. But it was a strangely companionable silence. The air was really quite warm. The sun was beaming down from a clear sky. There was a bit of a breeze. Perhaps it would blow away that stupid gossip. And it really was stupid. She did not understand now why she had not simply laughed at Mrs. Piper at the time and ignored all the rest of it during the past few days.

Perhaps, indeed, it was already blowing over. Mrs. Bartlett had appeared at her back door quite early this morning with two muffins fresh from her oven. They could have walked home together from church yesterday, she had told Lydia, but Mrs. Tavernor had already disappeared by the time she herself got outside. It was being said that Mrs. Tavernor's mother had once been a dear friend of Lady Riverdale, who was now Lady Dorchester, of course, though Mrs. Bartlett still thought of her as Lady Riverdale because that was what she had been when she lived here for so many years. But . . . was it true?

The warm muffins had been an olive branch, Lydia had understood. Owed entirely to the bogus story Lady Dorchester was spreading rather than to any faith in Lydia's good character. Even so . . . Well, an olive branch was an olive branch.

Snowball's lead had somehow got wrapped about her own legs, and Harry stopped walking to disentangle it. When he stood up again and they walked on, her hand was no longer drawn through his arm, Lydia noticed. It was in his ungloved hand, and their fingers were laced with each other's. She made no move to draw her hand free, and she said nothing. But this felt very . . . intimate. Almost affectionate.

They walked in silence again toward the trees and the path that led in among them.

Eighteen

❧

Harry had occasionally thought about having a proper wilderness walk back here, something with a grotto and follies, lookout points where there was something to look out upon, flowering shrubs, perhaps even a viewing tower, since the woods back here were not on enough of an elevation to provide any awe-inspiring vistas over the surrounding countryside.

But then he would come here and find that he liked the unspoiled beauty and seclusion of it all just as it was. The branches of the trees met overhead in places and bathed the rough path in a soft, verdant glow while not completely obliterating the sky. Sounds were muted here, except for birdsong, which seemed magnified. There was always a distinctive smell of greenery and soil. And while for most of the year the predominant color was green, at present there were carpets of bluebells among the trees. He always felt a million miles from civilization when he came here. Far from battle and slaughter and mayhem. And nightmares. And the annoying feeling that so often assailed him these days that he ought to *do* something with his life. He did not have to *do* anything here. He could just *be*.

Perhaps that was the best and most enduring of lessons one could learn from life.

The gardeners did a decent job of keeping the path clear of the inevitable debris caused by changing seasons, of removing large stones that popped to the surface from time to time as though from nowhere to trip the unwary, of clipping back low-hanging branches and undergrowth that forever tried to encroach upon the path.

Lydia's dog found a lot here to be sniffed at and yipped at. There were plants to be smelled and tree trunks to be marked and all sorts of rustlings and snapping of twigs as unseen wildlife went about its business. And since they were in no hurry, Harry stopped every time Snowball did. He was still holding Lydia's hand. He had taken it in his almost without thinking after he had disentangled the dog's lead a while ago. And she had not pulled it away. After a few moments he had laced his fingers with hers. It felt natural for her to be with him here, as though their friendship had somehow grown in the weeks since they had officially put an end to it.

They had not spoken for several minutes, another sign, surely, that they *were* friends at least. He felt no discomfort with the silence between them and could feel none in her. Only a heightened awareness.

Danger time, he warned himself. But perhaps it was already too late. No. It *was* already too late. But he did not have to act upon personal feelings, did he?

Snowball was yipping at a robin that had dared to land on a tree branch just overhead in order to sing a little song. It stopped and flew away, perhaps to find a more appreciative audience elsewhere. The dog gave the edge of the path a good sniff before moving on, her nose still to the ground. Not that her nose was ever far from the ground, of course, her legs being so short they were almost nonexistent. She looked for all the world like a snowball rolling along the path, attached bizarrely to a lead.

Harry turned his head to smile at Lydia and realized how close to each other the narrowness of the path had forced them. Their arms were straight at their sides, their fingers entwined. Their shoulders touched. Her face was partially shaded beneath the brim of her bonnet. But a shaft of sunlight slanted across her nose and mouth—that lovely wide, inviting mouth he had noticed as soon as he started to notice her at all. Her eyes were gazing directly into his own.

He kissed her.

And she kissed him back.

Both of them with closed mouths. As though they were nothing more than friends.

But did friends kiss each other on the mouth?

He glanced around before backing her against the trunk of a tree on her side of the path and looping the dog's lead over a low branch. He set his hands against the trunk on either side of Lydia's head and leaned his body against hers. She closed her eyes briefly, and he both saw and felt her inhale slowly. She made no attempt to push him away.

"Lydia," he murmured.

And he closed his eyes and found her mouth with his own—open this time. He slid one arm about her shoulders and the other around her waist, and moved his tongue over her lips until she parted them and he could touch the soft, moist flesh within and reach his tongue into her mouth when she opened it.

He had never been in love before. He had thought he was

a few times in the long-ago past. He had had women, especially during his military years. He had liked and respected them all, without exception. But it had never been love.

Not like this. At some time in the last month or so, when he was not paying attention, or perhaps on that one particular night when he *had been*, she had become all in all to him. The woman he wanted above all others. The reason for his restless depression during the past few weeks, when he had avoided passing her cottage and going to church or anywhere else she might be while all the time she had been gone.

"Lydia," he murmured again against her lips.

Her arms were about him. Her body was pressed to his, all the way down to their knees. She was slim, pliant, warm, lovely, and he throbbed and yearned for her. He moved one hand down behind her hips to press her more firmly against his erection.

He wanted her. As he had wanted her every day since the last time. As he would surely want her every day for the rest of his life. Not just with this urgent sexual need but in every way he could imagine. God, he wanted her.

"Harry," she murmured. A few moments later she said it again, but with more awareness. "Harry." She had got her hands between them and was exerting enough pressure against his chest to make him aware that she wanted him to step back. Yet she was not pushing hard or looking either upset or angry. Her eyes huge and dreamy, she gazed into his, surely with a longing to match his own.

He slid his hands to her hips, took a half step back, and forced himself to smile at her.

"You see," she said, "I thought we could be lovers and have some pleasure together. It was totally naïve of me. For when it happened there was far more than just simple pleasure. There was a whole explosion of physical sensations and powerful emotions. It was very foolish of me not to have understood that before it happened."

But how could she *not* have realized it? She had been married. For a number of years. To a man with whom she had admitted to having fallen headlong in love. Surely she had learned that any sexual relationship would bring with it more than just simple pleasure. Unless . . . He had been fishing earlier when he had asked why she had not had children. And for a moment, before giving him a noncommittal answer, she had frozen.

"There was all the terrible *carnality*," she added.

Terrible? Its literal meaning was *arousing terror.* Did she mean it literally? Had he brought her terror rather than pleasure that night? And *carnality*? She had not expected it? She had expected only a superficial sort of pleasure?

"I want to be free, Harry," she told him as he dropped his arms to his sides and took another half step back from her. "It is what I decided after Isaiah died, and I have not wavered in that decision since then." Her frown deepened. "It would be foolish to waver now just because of all this turmoil. I will not be forced into doing something I do not want to do."

He held out his arms to the sides. "You are free, Lydia," he said, though his heart—or something else inside him— was heavy as he spoke the words. "You do not have to let yourself be bullied by Mrs. Piper and her followers. And you certainly will not be bullied by me."

Snowball was yipping and bouncing and straining on the lead, frantic to give chase to whatever wild creature was cracking twigs somewhere among the trees on the other side of the path. Lydia turned away from him and unwound the dog's lead from the branch and continued along the path with her.

Harry fell into step on Lydia's other side, his hands clasped at his back. Love could not be either grasping or possessive if it was to be worthy of the name, he told himself. Yet it took every ounce of his willpower not to pour pleas and persuasion into her ears. She had chosen freedom and independence after her husband's death, and she had remained steadfast in that choice ever since, even though she had admitted to occasional loneliness and the dream of taking a lover—him. Even though she had actually done so. Once.

They walked in silence again. But a little farther along there was a wooden seat on one side of the path, the only one on the whole walk. The gardeners always did a good job of keeping it reasonably clean and free from both rot and moss. There was a gap in the trees ahead of it and something of a view diagonally across the eastern corner of the house to the summerhouse in the near distance and an edge of the village beyond it and a bit of countryside beyond that. It was a pleasant place to sit in the summer, either with a book or without.

Lydia stopped by it, though she did not move around it to sit down. Instead she grasped the back with both hands, the dog's lead still in one of them.

"You asked me why I do not have children," she said.

He ought not to have asked.

"You do not owe me an explanation," he said.

And suddenly he did not want to hear of disappointments stretching over months and years or of barrenness or—worse—of miscarriages. He was about to change the subject and point out his cousin Jessica, who was approaching the summerhouse with Gabriel and Abby and Gil. But she resumed speaking before he could do so.

"I did not have children," she said, "because there was never any possibility of its happening. Ever."

He closed his mouth. What the devil was that supposed to mean? *It means exactly what you think it means, Harry.* He had not been imagining things that night.

She was staring downward, her eyes directed at the ground in front of the seat. If she had noticed there was a view from here, she was showing no awareness of it.

"He told me he loved me," she said. "Before we were married, that is. And after too, a number of times. All the rest of his life, in fact. I believe he meant it. Isaiah did not tell lies. It was just not the sort of love I thought he meant. He explained to me on our . . . on our wedding day. Wedding night, actually. He wanted me to be more than a wife, he told me, that burning ardor in his eyes and his voice that had so attracted me. He wanted me to be his helpmeet. It was the word he always used of me after that. He wanted us to be servants of the Lord together. He wanted us to devote our time and energies, the pledge we had made to each other that morning, *our whole lives*, in service to the Lord. If there was one thing he admired about the Roman faith, he told me, it was the celibacy of its priesthood. But he believed that actually our priesthood could be even better than that because it could have both a man and a woman, both the male and female sensibility, in service together as a married couple."

Good God.

"He wanted us to dedicate ourselves to a celibate marriage," she said. "In fact, he had decided that we would."

There were a few moments of utter silence. Well, not quite. That robin, or perhaps one of its mates, was singing its heart out from somewhere among the trees not far off. A distant shriek of children at play rose from the front of the house.

"He did not discuss this with you before your marriage?" he asked. "Even though it was something that would drastically affect the whole of your life?"

"Isaiah never *discussed* anything," she said. "He decided and then he told. With all people and in all things. He spoke and acted out of . . . love and devotion to God. He spoke what he firmly and sincerely believed. But he would not brook opposition. He never had to. No one ever argued with him. It was because of his . . . charisma."

"*You* did not argue?" he asked.

"No, of course not," she said. "I was young and naïve. I had grown up under the benevolent despotism of my father and brothers. I had that very morning—on my wedding day, that is—vowed to honor and obey the man I had married. The man I *loved* with my whole heart. And I do not think I fully grasped at the time what it would mean. When I did, I . . . Well, one did not argue with Isaiah. I thought he must be right. I tried to make his vision of life and service my own. I thought my . . . longings were mere selfishness. Even sin."

She lowered her chin and wept.

Harry took the lead from her hand and wound it about the lower bar along the back of the seat. He took Lydia in his arms and pulled free the ribbons of her bonnet. He tossed the bonnet onto the seat and held her face against his shoulder.

Good God and good God, and were there no other words?

Good God!

He had not been mistaken. She had been a *virgin*.

He kissed the top of her head and turned his own to rest his cheek against her hair.

"Lydia," he murmured. "You are free now. You are free, my love."

Suddenly he could understand her absolute determination to remain that way, never again to surrender her freedom to a man, even one who professed to love her. Even to one she loved. *Especially* to one she loved.

She had thought it possible to take a lover and enjoy simple, uncomplicated pleasure with him. *It was totally naïve of me,* she had said.

Ah, Lydia.

He buried his face in her hair and had to swallow several times to prevent himself from weeping with her. She fell quiet after a while but made no immediate attempt to move away from him.

"I wanted a child more than anything else in the world," she said at last into his shoulder.

He rocked her in his arms.

"Or thought I did," she said. "But I have discovered that I want freedom more."

Pointless to tell her she could have both. With him. In order to discover that with him she could be as free as she was now—more so, as she would not be hemmed in by the rigid code of behavior imposed by society upon a widow who lived alone in an English village—she would need to take a colossal leap of trust.

In him.

But why should she trust him? He was a man.

"I am so sorry." She drew back from him at last and fumbled in a pocket for a handkerchief. She dried her eyes, blew her nose, and put the handkerchief away before looking up at him. "I must look a fright."

"Well, let me see." He tipped his head to one side and regarded her critically. "Red eyes. Red cheeks. Shiny red nose. Flattened hair. Yes, you do."

She smiled, and then laughed. "At least you are honest," she said.

"Always," he told her. "With you, always, Lydia. Your hair is flattened *and* untidy. You look beautiful."

"*Not* always honest," she protested, laughing again.

"Yes," he told her. "Always. I am sorry I pried. But I am not sorry I know." *I am glad he is dead.* He stopped himself from saying it aloud, but he thought it quite explicitly and without guilt. "There will be love for you. The sort of love you were denied when you were younger. There will be love, Lydia. And trust. And freedom. And surely children. But not yet. Not until you are ready."

He handed her her bonnet. He watched while she drew it on and tied the ribbons beneath her chin. The dog seemed to have fallen asleep in a slant of sunlight.

"You are a kind man, Harry," she said, looking at him again. "Have you always been?"

"Ask my sisters," he said. "The answer is no anyway. I was a very selfish young man. While my mother and my sisters donned black and dutifully curtailed all their social activities after my father died, unworthy as he was of even a day of mourning, I donned a token black armband and proceeded to sow some very wild oats. Every ne'er-do-well and sycophant in London was my best friend. I was the Earl of Riverdale and a very wealthy man. I often wonder how I would have turned out if the truth of my birth had not been discovered and I had not been suddenly stripped of everything. I believe I might have become a worthy successor to my father. Sometimes what seem to be the worst things that happen in our lives turn out actually to be the best."

"I think character runs deeper than circumstances, Harry," she said. "I think you must always have been a decent, caring man—and boy. I think kindness is something that is an inherent part of you. You were very young when it happened."

"Twenty," he said. "Is that an excuse?"

"Yes," she said. "It is. Forgive yourself."

"Your face is back to normal," he told her. "It is still beautiful, though, so you need not worry."

She laughed again. "You are also very absurd," she said.

"I like to see you laugh," he told her, and shrugged. "This is probably a stupid question. But would you like to come and meet my grandmothers? They may still be outside. If not, they will probably be in the drawing room, since neither likes to admit to the need of an afternoon sleep. Not during family gatherings anyway. And not when they have each other to compete against. They know what has happened to you. They know I offered for you and you refused. They did not turn their heads to stare at you when we passed earlier, but I am sure they were very well aware of you."

He was surprised to see that she was giving the question some consideration.

"Yes," she said. "I would like it. Thank you."

He ought not to have been surprised. Lydia had backbone, by Jove.

Nineteen

Her dark secret was out at last, Lydia thought as they continued walking along the path, which was sloping slightly downward now. Her dark, *bizarre* secret, which had always seemed a bit shameful to her. As though she must have been lacking somehow as a woman. And Harry had not known. It had not been obvious to him on the night they made love. Perhaps he had suspected, but he had not *known*.

He had not said a word in condemnation of Isaiah. Nor had he ridiculed her for so meekly accepting her lot during six years of marriage. He had held her instead. Yet rather than assuring her that he would shelter her in his strong, manly arms and protect and care for her for the rest of her life, he had reminded her that she was free now. Then, rather than assure her that she looked none the worse for her crying session, he had admitted she looked a mess and called her beautiful anyway. He had made her laugh. *Deliberately.*

He had mentioned trust.

There will be love, Lydia. And trust. And freedom.

He had talked more about the effect the discovery of his illegitimacy had had upon his twenty-year-old self. *Sometimes what seem to be the worst things that happen in our lives turn out actually to be the best.* He had shared something painful from his own life, she guessed, in order to distract her from her own. Or to remind her that everyone suffers in the course of a lifetime. No one is immune. And perhaps to remind her that there is an end to suffering.

There will be love, Lydia. And trust. And freedom. And surely children. But not yet. Not until you are ready.

She was terribly, terribly in love with him.

And trust.

It was the word that of all others had lodged in her mind. And she understood that it was what everything was all about for her. *Trust.* Or lack of trust. She had stopped trusting in love when it had prevented her from moving into adulthood as other girls of her social class did. It had wrapped her in a stifling cocoon of male protection instead. It had stopped her from developing any sort of discernment that might have saved her from the marriage she had made. For she could look back now and see that all of Isaiah's ardor, all the burning passion in his eyes, had been focused upon his faith. Yes, he had told her he loved her, but it was easy now to understand that there had been nothing personal in his protestations. He *had* loved her as a helpmeet, as a meek, biddable woman who would share his faith and his life of service.

What had been destroyed in her more than anything else was her ability to trust. And her ability to know *what* and *whom* she could trust. It had become safer to trust only herself.

She did trust herself. That was a start. She had not done so throughout her marriage. She had convinced herself that any disappointment she felt, any unhappiness, any stirring of rebellion, was wrong, even *sinful*, because Isaiah said so and he was both her husband and her pastor. She had put her trust in obedience, one of her marriage vows, and in her husband instead of in herself. She could trust in herself now, though. In her *real* self, that was, the self that was deep down inside her where she knew what was right for her and from which well of knowledge and strength she could withstand any outer force that might try to destroy her or make her doubt herself.

She was the social equal of anyone. She was the daughter of a gentleman of birth and property and means, and she was the sister-in-law of an earl. She was the widow of the late vicar of Fairfield. But over and above those connections, she was *herself* and did not need to hide or cower from anyone.

She did not want to go and meet any of Harry's family, especially the elders, the grandmothers, who would very probably look at her as though she were a scarlet woman who had seduced one of their own. She would much rather go home, preferably alone, shut her door, make herself a cup of tea, and give in to the exhaustion the last few days had loaded upon her like a leaden weight. But she would do it. She could not—would not—hide away. She was probably going to feel obliged to attend Harry's birthday party— a ball. She would be able to dance again if she wished. And she *would* wish it whether she wanted to or not—a mildly head-spinning thought. There was no point, then, in *not* going now to meet some members of the family. All the better that they were to be the two most intimidating ones: Harry's grandmothers.

Besides, he wanted her to go, and she owed him something. He had been kind to her. He had listened while she poured out her painful, embarrassing story and had not passed judgment. He had held her while she wept.

He was, perhaps, a man she could trust.

There. She had articulated the thought.

Perhaps she could trust Harry Westcott.

They came off the path to the east of the house, still among trees, though they were more widely spaced down here. There was a glass summerhouse off to their left—Lydia had seen it from that seat against which she had braced herself while she told Harry her story. Mrs. Bennington was sitting inside with her husband and another couple. Mr. Bennington turned his head, and then they all did and smiled and waved, though they did not come out and Harry did not turn in their direction.

"The couple you have not met are the Earl and Countess of Lyndale," he explained. "Gabriel and Jessica. She is our cousin, daughter of my aunt Louise, Dowager Duchess of Netherby, my father's middle sister. Avery, Duke of Netherby, is her stepson, but he is quite a bit older than Jess. He is married to Anna, my half sister. He was my guardian too after my father died. This is too much information, is it not?" He turned his head and grinned at her, and Lydia laughed.

"Is there to be a written test?" she asked.

"And the passing mark is one hundred percent. Ninety-nine will not do," he said.

"Ouch," she said. "I hope spelling does not count. So the little girl who has just lost one of her baby teeth—Rebecca?—

is your half sister and the Duke of Netherby's child? Your niece?"

"Well done," he said. "All three of them are my nieces. I have an army of them. Nephews too. All here. And all to be included on that written test. There are cousins and cousins' children. And spouses, with family names and title names."

"That really is too—" she began.

"Hush!"

He slowed their steps suddenly and clamped her hand more tightly to his side while Lydia stopped talking and looked at him in surprise. He had not stopped walking altogether, but he seemed to be listening intently. She listened too. She could hear the faint murmur of voices coming from the summerhouse, the distant crack of a cricket bat followed by a cheer, Snowball yipping at something in the trees that offended her.

Lydia drew breath to ask what he had heard.

"Shh."

And then he moved his head a little closer to hers. "You will like everyone, Lydia," he said in normal tones before jerking his arm free of hers, whirling about, and dashing off into the thicker trees from which they had just emerged. Almost before Lydia had stopped gaping, he came back out with Jeremy Piper almost literally dangling from his shirt collar, which was in Harry's firm grip.

"Ow!" the boy yelled, both hands clawing at his collar. "Put me down. I'm choking."

"Obviously not too badly if you can still talk," Harry said, jerking his hand higher until Jeremy was running along at his side on the toes of his boots.

Lydia held on to Snowball's lead. Her dog was barking and bouncing.

"I wasn't doing nothing. Put me down," Jeremy cried, his voice strained.

"Apart from trespassing?" Harry halted when they were several feet away from Lydia.

"I didn't mean nothing by it," the boy protested. "You're choking me. Let go."

Harry did let go suddenly, and the boy staggered and darted a look off toward the denser growth of trees.

"On your knees," Harry said.

"What?" Jeremy took one half step away.

Harry took a full step after him. And Lydia's eyes widened as he was transformed before her eyes into a very menacing military officer despite the absence of a uniform.

"On. Your. Knees," he repeated in a voice that turned Lydia's own knees a bit liquid.

Jeremy plopped down.

"Ow," he protested. "There's stones and roots digging in my knees. And what's this all about anyway? I didn't do nothing. I'll tell my—"

"Silence. Arms at your sides. *At. Your. Sides.*"

"There's a stone—"

"Silence."

Jeremy fell silent and held his arms to his sides. His eyes were still darting frantic glances at the trees.

"Straighten your back," Harry said. "Drop your shoulders. Raise your chin." All of which Jeremy did.

The occupants of the summerhouse were all standing and gazing this way, Lydia could see. Mr. Bennington was outside the door, one hand holding it open. And if that was not enough, there was a group of riders approaching from the east, weaving their way through the trees. They must have realized something untoward was happening ahead of them, however, and stopped when they were still some distance away.

"You have something to say to Mrs. Tavernor," Harry said.

"I don't have nothing—"

"*Silence,*" Harry said. "You will speak when you are told to speak. To Mrs. Tavernor. Whom you will address as *ma'am.* Do you understand that? You may answer."

"I don't have—"

"*Do. You. Understand?*"

"Yes."

"Yes, *what?*"

"Yes, I understand. But—"

"Yes, *what?*" Harry said again.

"Yes, sir," Jeremy said.

"You have something to say to Mrs. Tavernor, Jeremy," Harry said. "Say it. Address her as *ma'am. Raise. Your. Chin.* Look at her."

Jeremy looked, winced, and leaned down to adjust the position of his right knee.

"*Attention,*" Harry barked.

Jeremy, obviously close to tears, came up straight, and looked somewhere in the direction of Lydia's chin. "I am sorry," he said. "Ma'am," he added quickly, darting a glance at Harry, who was standing close beside him, his booted feet slightly apart, his hands clasped at his back.

Lydia drew breath to speak.

"And for *what* are you sorry?" Harry asked. "No, do not address me. Address Mrs. Tavernor."

"For telling on you," Jeremy said. "Ma'am."

"One *tells* on someone when that someone has done something wrong, Jeremy," Lydia said. "What was it, if you please, that I did wrong?"

"Back straight. Arms at your sides," Harry said.

Jeremy jerked to attention. "You was carrying on with 'im," he said, indicating Harry with a slight sideways motion of his head. "Ma'am. But I got nothing but grief when the reverend jumped in the river and killed 'imself thinking 'e was saving me. I was about to get out on my own when 'e jumped in and almost drowneded me. He just made an idiot of himself. And then everyone thought 'e was such a saint and you was such an angel."

Lydia held up a staying hand to stop Harry from speaking. "Destroying someone else's life, or at least her reputation, has soothed your feelings for what you perceive as an injustice to yourself, Jeremy?" she asked him. "You feel better about yourself now that you have toppled me from my pedestal in the eyes of your mother and other people in the village?"

"Mrs. Tavernor is awaiting your answer," Harry said when the boy did not immediately reply. "No. Stay as you are."

"Jeremy?" Lydia said as the boy snapped back to attention. "Do you feel better about yourself?"

"No," he said at last. "Ma'am."

"Are you happy," she asked him, "that you have made me the victim of malicious gossip?"

"You was kissing 'im," he said sullenly.

"Are you *happy*?" she asked again.

"No," he said.

"You have something more to say to Mrs. Tavernor, then," Harry said. "Do not forget how to address her."

"I'm *sorry, ma'am*," Jeremy cried. "I didn't ought to've done it, and I won't do it no more. I was just sick of everything, and I wished you would've left 'ere after 'e died so everyone would forget. My ma wished the same thing. But I shouldn't ought to've watched you till you done things I could tell 'er about. I'm sorry and I won't do it no more."

"Then I accept your apology," Lydia said.

"On your feet," Harry said. When the boy had scrambled up, wincing and staggering, Harry took one step closer to him so they were almost toe to toe. "Whatever you saw or heard here today, you have forgotten. Not one word of it will pass your lips. The penalty for trespass on my land is a thorough thrashing, the sort that makes it impossible for a boy to sit down for a week. It is normally administered by my head groom. With a whip he keeps especially for the purpose. I will waive that punishment for now. However, if I hear, or if Mrs. Tavernor hears, one whisper of your having been here today or one breath of a whisper of what you may have seen or heard here, then the punishment will be doubled, and it will be administered by me. Do you understand?"

"Yes." Jeremy's voice was close to a squeak.

"Yes, *what*?"

"Yes, *sir*."

"Starting tomorrow," Harry said, "you will attend school all day every day. If I hear from Mr. Corning that you have been absent *or late*, I will wish to know the reason why. Now go." He pointed in the direction of the back of the house. "I will give you five minutes to remove yourself from Hinsford property."

Jeremy took off at a run.

And Lydia and Harry were left staring at each other while the silent audience looked on from the summerhouse and the trees behind him. It was possible he did not even know the latter group was there and had forgotten the former group.

"I should have taken more notice of all the rustlings among the trees earlier and of Snowball's reaction to them," he said. "I assumed I was hearing rabbits or squirrels. I am sorry, Lydia."

"I do not believe he will spy on me again," she said. "You looked and sounded awfully ferocious."

And could she please, please, *please* wake up now, Lydia thought, and find that the whole of today—and the last three days too for good measure—were one hideous, bizarre dream?

"For a few moments," a new voice said, "I thought I was back with the regiment, Harry. I was in fear and trembling and about to snap to attention when I recalled that I was actually your superior officer. How do you do, Mrs. Tavernor? You handled that lad very well. My congratulations, ma'am."

Mr. Bennington was striding toward them from the summerhouse, looking more formidable than he had at church yesterday. He was frowning, and his facial scar was very noticeable. He was also quite tall and well built. She noticed again that his hair was almost black.

"If I had remembered I had an audience of more than Lydia," Harry said, looking over his shoulder toward the summerhouse and then spotting the riders, who were coming nearer, "I would have taken the boy over my knee and given him a good walloping. The humiliation would perhaps have done him some good."

"I remember Piper senior—probably this lad's father—as one of the crowd of regulars in the taproom at the inn when I lived here with you for a while, Harry," Mr. Bennington said. "I believe it may be time I renewed my acquaintance with him. You must come with me."

One of the riders spoke up, a dark-haired lady in a smart riding habit. "Since Harry has steadfastly refused to allow me to transfer ownership of Hinsford to him, Gil," she said, addressing Mr. Bennington, "I would feel quite justified in asserting my right of ownership. A slur has been cast upon my brother's good name and therefore, by association, upon mine. I shall go with you to make that call—though I would hope to speak to Mrs. Piper rather than her husband. I shall take Avery with us."

"*Shall* you, my love?" one of the other riders said—the slight, blond, very aristocratic man Lydia had noticed at church yesterday. He must be the Duke of Netherby. The woman must be Anna, Harry's half sister. "And shall I allow you to do all the talking?"

"Oh, Avery," the lady from the summerhouse whom Harry had identified as the Countess of Lyndale said. "You know your silence speaks volumes. You must let Anna talk while you look at Mrs. Piper through your quizzing glass. I just wish I could be there to see it."

"Quite so," he said. "Harry, you may wish to present the lady. Mrs. Tavernor, I presume?"

There followed a flurry of introductions while Lydia tried to memorize faces and names.

"If you please," she said, looking from Mr. Bennington to the duke and duchess, "I would rather you did not call upon the Pipers. What has happened is a matter that concerns Major Westcott very little if at all. *I* am the one who stands accused of being a woman of loose morals. I would prefer to handle the matter in my own way."

"Lydia values her independence," Harry explained.

"How admirable of you, Mrs. Tavernor," the Countess of Riverdale said.

She was the one, Lydia remembered, who ran a business of her own. She had purple marks—a birthmark?—all down one side of an otherwise beautiful face.

The duchess was smiling at Lydia. "It would have been such *fun*," she said. "But I agree with Wren. You are greatly to be admired, Mrs. Tavernor."

The summerhouse group was already retreating back inside, and the riders continued without further delay in the direction of the stables.

"Nicely done, Harry," His Grace said as he passed them. "And superbly done, Mrs. Tavernor."

"I think, Lydia," Harry said ruefully when they had all moved out of earshot, "you must be on the verge of collapse. Do you find yourself wondering, as I do, what on earth happened to your life of quiet, rather dull but perfectly happy routine? If the last few days have proved anything about life, it is that the only certainty upon which we can rely is its uncertainty."

Lydia bit down hard upon her upper lip. But she could not stop it, much as she tried because it seemed so inappropriate. Laughter bubbled up inside her and then spilled out. She spread her hands over her face and laughed until her sides hurt. When she looked up finally, it was to see Harry with his head tipped to one side, regarding her closely, his eyes smiling though he was not laughing.

"You are quite right," he said. "Sometimes the only answer to its uncertainty is laughter. I do *not* suppose you still want to meet my grandmothers, do you?"

"Oh," she said, and she could feel another gust of possibly hysterical laughter coming on. "Whyever not?"

"Lydia," he said, "I like you so much."

And this time he laughed with her.

Twenty

B y the time they came around the side of the house onto the terrace, the infants who had been playing circle games with Elizabeth and her mother had gone back indoors, probably for afternoon naps, and the cricket game had just finished. The teams were gathering up wickets and bats and arguing good-naturedly about something. Harry's grandmothers and great-aunt Edith were still outside. Aunts Matilda, Louise, and Mildred were with them. So were Lady Hill from the neighboring estate and Rosanne. Lawrence was down talking with the cricketers.

Poor Lydia was about to be exposed to more than she had bargained for. But it was too late to change direction now. They had been seen. He felt Lydia draw a deep breath and let it out slowly. Snowball, trotting along at her side, was straining at her lead and yipping in anticipation of confronting yet more strangers.

"Lydia, my dear." Lady Hill got to her feet and came a few steps toward them, both hands extended. "Maynard often tells me that I live with my head buried in the sand, which brings a rather horrid image to the mind. However, sometimes I think he must be right. We and our visitors all slept late the morning after the assembly even though it was over long before midnight, and we spent the rest of the day very quietly at home. On Saturday we went into Eastend to do some shopping. If you can believe it, we did not hear about all the bother here until after church on Sunday, by which time you had already walked home and we had a luncheon engagement to keep us away until the middle of the evening. When Rosanne and Lawrence and I called at the cottage today you were no longer there, and we discovered, just as you were coming around the corner now, in fact, that you were actually here at Hinsford."

She squeezed Lydia's hands, which were now in her own. "My dear!" she continued. "It is all such utter nonsense, as I have told everyone with whom I have spoken since Sunday morning, but distressing for you nonetheless. And embarrassing for Harry too, I do not doubt. But so many people are only too ready to listen to scandalous tidings, regardless of facts and common sense. How dared that horrid woman! It ought to have been obvious to everyone on Thursday evening that you and Harry are friends, as why on earth should you *not* be? Mrs. Monteith has just been telling us that your mama and Harry's mother were dear friends before your mother passed on. It is the most natural thing in the world, then, that their son and daughter should be friends too. But I am talking too much. How do you do, Harry? How does it feel to be almost thirty?"

She released Lydia's hands and resumed her seat while Rosanne smirked at Harry and gave him what looked suspiciously like a wink.

"May I have the pleasure of presenting Mrs. Lydia Tavernor?" Harry said, looking along the line of his relatives. "My paternal grandmother, the Dowager Countess of Riverdale, Lydia. My maternal grandmother, Mrs. Kingsley." He went on to introduce Great-aunt Edith and his aunts.

"I am pleased to make your acquaintance," Lydia said, including them all in her smile and inclination of the head. Snowball, on her best behavior, had flopped down beside her.

"How do you do, Mrs. Tavernor?" Grandmama Kingsley said. "You must have been just a child when my daughter and your mother were friends. And when your mama died."

"I was eight years old, ma'am," Lydia told her.

"That was very sad for you," his grandmother said. "Do you have sisters and brothers?"

"I have three brothers," Lydia told her. "Two older than me, one younger. My mother never recovered her health after the birth of my youngest brother."

"You were unfortunate not to have sisters," Aunt Matilda said. "I have always found mine to be a great blessing."

"So have I," Aunt Louise added. "Well, maybe not *always*." She smiled while the other two aunts chuckled. "I feel for you in the premature loss of your husband, Mrs. Tavernor. I lost mine far too early too."

"Thank you," Lydia said.

"You live alone, Mrs. Tavernor," Grandmama Westcott said. It was not posed as a question.

Lydia answered anyway. "Yes, quite alone, ma'am," she said. "My cottage is small and my needs are modest. I can clean and cook for myself and actually enjoy doing both. I also enjoy my own company."

"You were seen kissing Harry on the doorstep of your home a few evenings ago," his grandmother continued. "Living alone and allowing such intimate behavior to be witnessed by anyone who chances to be passing by is like an open invitation to unwelcome gossip and the necessity of a marriage proposal that the one party does not wish to make and the other does not wish to accept. That you did not accept is to your credit, at least. Perhaps you have learned something from the experience, Mrs. Tavernor?"

This time she *was* asking a question.

"Grandmama—"

"Mama—"

Harry and Aunt Mildred spoke at the same time, but his grandmother held up a staying hand, and Lydia answered.

"I have, ma'am," she said. "I have learned to look to my conscience for direction rather than to those people who observe my behavior or listen to an account of it and pass judgment. I have learned to respect myself and trust my own judgment."

Oh, well done, Lydia, Harry thought. She had spoken with quiet dignity. Not many people stood up to his grandmother.

"That sounds well and good," his grandmother said. "We can all admire someone who does not cringe in the face of adversity. Nevertheless, there is a certain code of behavior by which it behooves us all to live if society is not to fall into chaos."

Harry drew breath to intervene, but again Lydia forestalled him.

"I agree, ma'am," she said. "And if an acquaintance offers me a ride home in his carriage one evening because the clergyman who has promised to convey me has been called away to a sickbed, I would consider it ill-mannered to refuse. If he then escorts me to my door because it is dark and raining hard and he has an umbrella, I will be grateful. If he then, because he is something of a friend and not merely an acquaintance, chooses to kiss my forehead as he says good night to me, I am not going to slap his face or scold him for inappropriate behavior. When it happened, ma'am, I did not deem the kiss to my forehead in any way improper. I still do not, even though the gossips in the village have made me into something of a scarlet woman."

"Lydia knitted me a scarf as thanks for a pile of wood I chopped for her," Harry said. "She had just given me the finished scarf that night. Hence the infamous kiss—*on the forehead*. In the open doorway of her house with my coachman standing on the other side of her garden gate. If anyone is to blame for this whole stupid incident, it is I, not Lydia. I will not have her accused of impropriety."

"Mrs. Tavernor." Aunt Matilda had got to her feet. "Do come and sit down on my chair. We are having a tray of tea brought out. I shall go and make sure two more cups are added. And another chair. And I will have a bowl of water fetched for your dog, who is, by the way, adorable."

"Thank you, Lady Dirkson," Lydia said. "It is kind of you, but I will not stay. It has been a busy day and I am ready to go home."

"We will look forward to seeing you at Harry's birthday ball, then, Mrs. Tavernor," Aunt Louise said.

The cricketers, a mixture of adults and children and both genders, were making their noisy way up the lawn, still arguing about something and doing a great deal of laughing in the process. Lawrence Hill grinned at Harry and greeted Lydia.

"I'll escort you home, Lydia," Harry told her, offering his arm.

"Just look both ways first if you plan to kiss her on the doorstep," Lawrence advised him.

His sister was scolding him as they walked away.

"I am sorry, Lydia," Harry said.

"Why?" she asked. "You cannot be responsible for what other people say and do, Harry. Neither can I. I believe we have learned *that* in the past few days. And there is no need for you to accompany me, you know, especially as you have guests here to entertain. I believe I can make my way back down the drive without losing my way."

"Lydia! Have mercy on me," he said. "My grandmother Westcott—probably both grandmothers, in fact, *and* all the aunts—would scold me into next week if I did anything as improper as allow a lady to walk home alone."

She sighed.

"I believe," she said, "that was exactly how and why all this got started, Harry. First Tom Corning and then you would not hear of my walking home alone. Should I now proceed to ask you if you are ever lonely?"

Harry did not follow her beyond her gate. He did not turn away after she had stepped into her garden and shut the gate, however. He stood against the fence, his hands resting on top of it. She could sense him there and turned when she was halfway along the path, while Snowball curled up into a ball of fluff on the doorstep and waited to be let inside.

"Did I ever give you a definitive answer?" he asked her.

They had talked about a number of things on their way home, but Lydia knew to which question he alluded. It was the one that had come to define their whole relationship.

Are you ever lonely?

She gazed at him and waited.

"It is *yes*," he said. His eyes were softly smiling, yet he looked sad, Lydia thought. Just as she was feeling.

"Even now, with all your family surrounding you?" she asked.

He answered with a question of his own. "When you went home to your father's house," he said, "were you lonely? Perhaps more so than when you were here?"

"It would be illogical, would it not?" she said. "All those who are closest to me were there—my father, my brothers, my sister-in-law. I live alone here, apart from Snowball."

"As I do at Hinsford," he said. "Apart from an army of servants."

"Yes," she said after they had gazed at each other in silence for a few moments. "I was lonely."

"There needs to be a special someone, does there not?" he said. "Or rather . . . No. There does not *need* to be. One ought to be able to live alone. One ought to have all the inner resources to live contentedly with one's own company. We have to love ourselves, do we not? Or we are incapable of loving anyone else. I think we have both learned those lessons. And we have both been contented and perhaps will be again. But sometimes there is loneliness. And then— sometimes—there is a longing for someone special. Someone to move us from quiet contentment into a warmer happiness. Someone we do not *need*, but someone we *want* in order to fill in all the blanks in our lives. I am talking a pile of nonsense."

"No, you are not," she said, taking a step closer to the fence and then walking right up to it and grasping the top of it, her hands on the outsides of his. "There is a need . . . Ah, perhaps it is not actually a *need*. You are quite right about that. But there is a *craving* to trust. The loss of it, the loss of the ability to trust, is a terrible thing. It destroys so much. I have come to understand that my life is broken, and I have not been fully able to piece it back together. I dare not trust."

His eyes continued to smile. And they still looked unhappy. He nodded.

"Harry," she said. "Tell me I am wrong."

He shook his head slowly. "Only you can tell yourself that," he said. "When you are ready."

"Do you love me?" She gripped the fence more tightly. Oh, her impetuous tongue again. It happened when she was tired. And she was bone weary now. This day had seemed a week long.

"Yes." The word was so softly spoken that she read his lips more than she heard the sound.

"Am I your someone special?" she asked. "Am I someone you could . . . cherish?"

"Yes," he said again.

"I adore you." She blinked rapidly. She was *not* going to become a watering pot again. "And I *trust* you. I have thought about it from every possible angle during the past hour or so, but I cannot talk myself out of trusting you. The trouble with trust, of course, is that it is a future thing, and one can never be certain of anything in the future. One can only . . . trust. Or not."

"And you choose to trust me," he said.

"Yes." She had blinked back her own tears, but now there were tears swimming in his eyes. "And you are someone I could cherish, Harry. My someone special. Oh, I did not plan any of this. It is most brazen of me. I—"

His hands came down on top of hers and curled around them. "Lydia," he said. "I *still* cannot recall any of my pretty speech except the word *ardent* and the phrase *happiest of men*. But it was a grand piece of pomposity anyway, I daresay. *Will* you marry me?" He smiled at her suddenly, leftover tears and all. "*Will* you make me the happiest of men? I most ardently love you."

"Oh, Harry—"

"You were saying?" he said when she did not immediately continue, raising her hands to hold palm-in against his chest. Lydia had to take a step closer to the fence.

"*Will* I make you happy?" she asked him. And here she went having to blink her eyes again to rid them of tears. "Will *we* be happy? Harry, I do not have much experience with happiness."

"Neither do I," he said, holding her gaze. "We will seek it and find it together, Lydia. But I think happiness comes in moments, not in great swaths of time. I do not think it is a future thing at all but only a present something we can carry forward with us if we choose. I feel awfully happy at this precise moment because I believe you are saying yes, and I want you to say it more than I can remember wanting anything else in my life. Take a chance with me, Lydia. Trust me. Trust yourself. Trust the future. For though we cannot control it or have any real idea of what lies ahead, we are not entirely helpless. We can promise ourselves and promise each other that we will work on a marriage to each other every day for the rest of our lives. Both of us. As equals."

She gazed into his eyes—the loveliest eyes she had ever looked into, for there was kindness there as far back as she could see. As far back as the very essence of him, where darkness had led him to humility and empathy and kindness. And not just those things. There was love too. And right now it was focused entirely upon her—his someone special. She saw a little bit of uncertainty too and vulnerability because she had not yet actually spoken the word.

"Yes," she said, and smiled. "I *am* saying yes."

And nothing in her whole life, surely, had felt so right.

He gathered her against him, fence notwithstanding, but the brim of her bonnet got in the way as she tried to nestle her head beneath his chin, and they both laughed. And he kissed her.

Right out in the open, she in her front garden, he out on the road, the sun beaming down on them, for the whole world to see if the world chose to come and look.

"Soon," he said when he drew back his head a few inches.

"Yes.

"Very soon."

"Yes."

"Sooner than soon?"

"Absurd." She laughed, and he kissed her again.

"Lydia," he said, "I think you had better invite me to tea. We have some plans to make."

"Well," she said, "since I seem to have very little reputation left to lose, I think you might as well come in."

Lady Hill and her son and daughter did not remain long at Hinsford after Harry and Lydia left. They still had visitors at home, awaiting their return. A number of other members of the Westcott family had gathered on the terrace in the meanwhile—some of the cricketers, a couple of the returning riders, those who had been at the summerhouse, and a few from inside. The men among them wandered away soon after the visitors had left.

"So, Mama," Louise said, "you did not like the notorious Mrs. Tavernor?"

"Mama gave her a stinging setdown earlier, when Harry brought her here to introduce her," Matilda explained to those who had not been present to hear it.

"And she gave it right back to me," the dowager countess said. "The brazen minx."

"You liked her, then, Grandmama?" Jessica asked, smiling.

"She has backbone," the dowager admitted. "Which fact does not excuse the decision she made after her husband's death to live alone, without even a servant to add respectability, and then to entertain gentlemen at night."

"There is no evidence, is there, Grandmama," Abigail said in her quiet, gentle voice, "that Mrs. Tavernor has ever entertained gentle*men?* Harry is not plural."

"And there is a difference," Anna added, "between *evening* and *night*, Grandmama, when one is speaking of a gentleman calling upon a lady."

"Do I have any other granddaughters who wish to offer me some witticism or reproach?" the dowager asked, looking about the group. "Camille?"

"I think you like her, Grandmama," Camille said. "Because she stood up to you."

"Hmph," her grandmother said.

"Harry will be thirty years old before another week has passed, Eugenia," Mrs. Kingsley said. "My guess is that Mrs. Tavernor is close to him in age. Perhaps what they do in private together—or what they do *not* do, for that matter—is their business and not ours. Or that Mrs. Piper's."

"Quite right, Mother," Mary, her daughter-in-law, said.

"She handled herself admirably just a little while ago," Anna said. And she proceeded to describe what had happened with Jeremy Piper. "Harry was nothing short of magnificent."

"I do wish I had been there to witness it," Elizabeth said.

"But," Mildred said, "Mrs. Tavernor refused Harry's marriage offer just a couple of days ago."

"But of course she did," Viola said. "We would all like her considerably less if she had accepted it."

"You like her too, then, Viola?" Wren asked with a smile.

"Do not we all?" Viola asked.

"I have not met her," Elizabeth said. "Neither has Mama. Perhaps we will call on her tomorrow."

"I will come with you if I may," Mary said. "I have not met her either."

"She has been *indiscreet*," the dowager countess reminded them. "We ought not to forget that. But she does have backbone. And I never did say I did not like her, Louise, to get back to your original question."

"We are forgetting something, however," Louise said. "Three young ladies have come here to Hinsford in the hope that Harry will marry one of them. And we are responsible for bringing them and raising their hopes."

There was a pained silence for a moment.

"Fanny is both a pretty and a sensible girl," Mildred said, speaking of the sister of her son's betrothed. "I thought she might suit Harry admirably. But I did not give that as a specific reason when I invited her and her mother to join us here. I spoke more of celebrating the new betrothal."

"Besides, Aunt Mildred," Estelle Lamarr said, "her sister confided to me earlier today that she suspects Fanny of having not only an attachment to a neighbor of theirs but also a secret agreement with him."

"Gordon warned me," Edith Monteith said, "that Miranda is not interested in marriage even though she is twenty-two years of age. It is not what her mother told me or what I expected. But I have seen for myself now that she is not as other girls are. If she were a man, it would not surprise me at all if she were to disappear into the bowels of a university somewhere—no doubt in Scotland—and gather dust there as a professor or a don. But she is not, alas, a man."

"Poor lady," Wren said. "It is not easy to be an independent woman in a man's world."

"And then there is Sally," Matilda said with a rueful shake of the head. "She is a sweet child, and Charles and Adrian and his sisters all dote on her. Since she is now eighteen and making her come-out this year, it seemed to me that she would be a desirable match for Harry. However, she shows far more interest in Ivan and Gordon, who are closer to her in age. And really, I have found myself ever since we left London thinking of her as a *child* rather than as a young woman. She will not do, will she?"

"Fortunately, Matilda," Althea said, "she seems to have not one ounce of interest in Harry. There are, of course, the local girls for us to consider. Miss Hill and her younger sister, for example. Miss Ardreigh, their cousin, who is visiting them. The magistrate's daughter—Miss Raymore, I believe?"

Everyone gazed at her. No one took her up on her suggestion.

"As I thought," she said, nodding, and a few of them laughed.

"But she will not have Harry," Mildred said.

No one asked to whom she was referring.

"What does *that* have to say to anything?" her mother asked.

No one offered an answer.

"Mrs. Tavernor it is, then?" Louise said at last.

"What we need," Matilda said briskly, "is a *plan*."

Twenty-one

T hey did not have tea. Or go to bed. They were sitting
on the sofa in the living room, Harry slouched comfortably but rather inelegantly in its depths, Lydia across his
lap, her head on his shoulder, one arm about his waist.
Snowball was curled in her usual spot before the fireplace.

Harry kissed Lydia again, their lips lingering together.
They smiled lazily into each other's eyes when he drew
back his head.

I adore you. And I trust you. She had said both things
out by the fence. Infinitely precious gifts, both of them. But
it was the trust he most cherished. After all she had en-
dured, after all her determination to live independently and
trust only herself for the rest of her life, she had chosen to
trust *him*.

He ought to find it terrifying. He did not, for he trusted
himself. He would never let her down.

"So," he said, "sooner than soon. We could announce

our betrothal on Friday, Lydia, at this infernal birthday ball. That would make it seem altogether less infernal."

"So soon?" Her smile was still a bit lazy, but she did not immediately protest that Friday would be far *too* soon.

"Or," he said, twining the fingers of his free hand with hers, "we could announce our marriage at the ball."

Her smile was arrested. Her eyes narrowed. "What?" She frowned.

"We could get married," he said. "On Friday morning. And announce our marriage at the ball."

She sat up slowly on his lap and continued to gaze narrow-eyed at him. *"What?"* she said. "This is Monday. Friday is *four days* from now."

"I could shoot up to London tomorrow for a special license," he said, "and be back before Wednesday evening. I could have a word with the Reverend Bailey before I go. We could pick out two witnesses and ask them—Mrs. Bailey, perhaps. And maybe Gil—Gil Bennington, my brother-in-law."

"And no one else?" she said. "Harry, are you *mad*?"

He thought about it. "Possibly," he conceded. "It is just that I can remember Abby and Gil's wedding here, Lydia. Just the two of them and the vicar and two witnesses—I was one—and I have always considered it the perfect wedding. If we tell my family, there will be a fuss to end fusses. And we would not be able to do it on Friday because there would be all of them here but not a single person from your family. That would be unthinkable. I cannot bear to wait, though. For everyone would still *fuss*. And would they all stay here while plans were being made and your family was being summoned? Or would they all go home and plan from afar and try luring us to a different location for the wedding? I— Lydia, I just want to marry you. Now. Sooner. Even Friday seems too far off."

"Harry." She was *still* frowning. "Is this the protective male in you speaking? Are you intent upon protecting me from all this stupid gossip?"

"I have not given it a single thought since you said yes out there by the fence," he said quite truthfully. "No, my love. It is the deep-in-love and admittedly deep-in-lust male in me speaking. Lydia, I—"

But she had set her hands on his cheeks, cupping his face, and her eyes were suspiciously bright. "You *are* mad," she said. "This Friday? On your birthday? Just the two of us and the vicar and two witnesses? Oh, Harry . . ."

She kissed him.

"I'll go tomorrow," he said against her lips. "Early. I'll have a word with the Reverend Bailey now before I go home and with Gil this evening. And on Friday morning, while everyone is busy with preparations for the ball, we will go to church, you and I, and get married. Will we? Say yes again, Lydia. Say it. Please say yes."

"Yes, then," she said, breathing the words into his mouth. "If I am to have a mad husband, I might as well be mad too, I suppose."

"But a mad husband you *trust*," he said.

"Yes."

She settled her head on his shoulder again after kissing him and sighed. "We *are* mad." She laughed softly.

Good God, they were. He was *not* going to be popular with his family on Friday evening.

"Harry," she said after they had been quiet for a few minutes, "are your nightmares still bad?"

"Nightmares by very definition are bad," he said after thinking about it. "Mine come less frequently as time goes by unless something happens to provoke them. Then they come in clusters. I do not suppose they will ever go away entirely. And perhaps that is as it ought to be. I see endless lines of faceless soldiers coming at me—not to kill me so much as to be killed. *Cannon fodder*, they were sometimes called. It is how Wellington referred to our own side. Men. Human beings. As human as you or me. I am responsible for hundreds of their deaths." He was quiet for a minute. "There are all sorts of perfectly sound arguments, of course, to convince military men that they are not, in fact, murderers. Nevertheless, I am responsible. And if the only way I can pay homage to the humanness of those French soldiers, the vast majority of whom had no choice but to be there, is to have nightmares about them, then I will suffer them. Though *not* gladly."

She touched her fingertips to his cheek and kissed him. "Tell me," she said softly. "It took you two years of recovery after the Battle of Waterloo even before you came home, and then another year or more here. I can remember that when I first came here with Isaiah you were thin and pale."

He tried not even to think about it. It was in the past. Another lifetime. But his life belonged to her too now. All of it, even the past. Just as her life belonged to him—including the terrible pain of her first marriage, which she had confided to him earlier.

"Joining the military seemed to me the obvious thing to do after I lost everything that had given shape and meaning to my life," he said. "I hated it from the first moment—or perhaps my life was such at that time that anything would have seemed hateful. I wrote cheerful letters home from the Peninsula, telling everyone what a lark and a jolly good time it all was. It was death and blood and mud and mayhem, Lydia. It was dehumanizing. One had to fight constantly to retain one's humanity. Sometimes it was impossible. It would have been impossible to fight in any pitched battle if one did not allow the energy of the moment to convert one into a savage whose only instinct was to slaughter the enemy. I beg your pardon. This is not the sort of conversation—"

She set three fingers lightly across his lips. "I asked," she said. "Tell."

"I was wounded more times than I can recount," he said. "I suppose I ought not even to have been fighting at Waterloo. How I survived it the Lord only knows. I fell from my horse in the end, and the horse fell on me. I had numerous saber cuts and three bullet wounds—one bullet was lodged below my shoulder, close to my heart, and remained there for longer than a year before a surgeon dug it out. I had one broken leg and internal injuries that were probably never fully diagnosed or treated. I knocked myself senseless and had memory lapses for a few years. I had an almost constant fever. Perhaps what made everything worse than it might have been was the treatment. The favorite was bleeding to reduce the fever. Over the two years I spent in hospital I must have had enough blood removed to keep ten men alive. The other favorite was to keep me in bed in a darkened room, feeding on thin gruels and jellies. I would have died there in Paris if I had not eventually insisted upon coming home —and if Gil had not been there to insist for me, and if Avery and Alexander had not come to bring me."

One of her hands was smoothing back his hair. She was kissing the underside of his chin.

"The very worst of it, though," he said, "was the hopelessness, the lethargy, the conviction that I would never be myself again. The bone wearying depression. And the memories and the guilt. And the lingering resentment over all that had happened to expose me to the hell of those years. The lingering . . . hatred. Of my father. And of Alexander and Anna. Even sometimes of my mother. But then, after I had been here awhile, I somehow found the will to get better, to *make* myself better. And the time came, Lydia, when I understood the full miracle of what had happened to me. For somehow, without my even realizing it, Hinsford seeped into my bones. Not just as my home. But as . . . the peace that became the heart of me. The understanding that this—not just this place, but this . . . life—is who I am, who I was always supposed to be. It is hard to put into words. Nothing is static, of course. Lately I have known that peace and contentment, wondrous as they have been, are not sufficient. I have known that I needed something more vivid. *Someone.* You, in fact."

He turned his head to look into her face. She was gazing back.

"So you see," he said, "why the nightmares, horrible as they are, are somehow necessary. They are a reminder that I must not live in a cocoon of contentment without remembering the journey that has brought me here. Peace is hard won, and the effort to keep it is ongoing. We must never become complacent in life. We must never feel we have *arrived* and there is nothing left to do but enjoy."

"You have the Earl of Riverdale and the Duchess of Netherby here with you now," she said, her smile almost mischievous, "as a constant reminder of all you have gone through."

"Alexander has grown in dignity in the past ten years," he said. "He did not want the life he is now leading, but he has put everything that is himself into doing a conscientious job of it, both at Brambledean and in London during parliamentary sessions. He is very obviously happy with Wren and their children. He would not have met or married

her if he had not had the title foisted upon him. When I look
at him now, I see the Earl of Riverdale. And a cousin of
whom I am proud and very fond. The title does not seem
part of me any longer. I do not want it. I feel aghast when I
realize that if my father had only waited a month or two to
marry my mother, the title and all the rest of it would be
mine. I would *hate* the life I started to live after he died. Or
at least the man I have become would hate it. I would have
been a totally different person if my father *had* waited, of
course, because the past ten years would have unfolded differently and I would have been different as a result. So
many *differents*. Am I making any sense?"

"Yes, you are," she said.

"As for Anna, I have unfinished business with her," he
said. "It must *be* finished, though. Soon. I have not treated
her well. I have not been cruel, except perhaps at the start.
I have not been openly unkind either. I have not shunned
her or treated her with less civility than I have shown other
members of the family."

"But . . . ?" she said when he did not proceed.

"But I have not treated her as I treat Cam and Abby," he
said. "I have not fully accepted her as my sister. Yet I believe it is what she needed and craved more than anything
else when she learned of our existence and our relationship
to her. I have to put that right."

"You said *soon*," she said. "Before you leave tomorrow?"

He gazed at her. "Yes," he said. "Before I go."

She smiled and burrowed her head more comfortably
between his shoulder and his neck

"Your father may disapprove of me," he said.

"Because you are illegitimate?" she asked. "You are

also a Westcott, son of the late Earl of Riverdale and of the present Marchioness of Dorchester. You have a ridiculous number of titled relatives."

"Ridiculous?" he asked. "You had better not let any of them hear you call them that, Lydia, or you will find yourself cast into outer darkness."

"Oh." She laughed softly. "I took the measure of the Dowager Countess of Riverdale almost the moment I met her. She wants to be seen as the crusty matriarch at the head of the family. In reality she loves you dearly and wants desperately for you to be happy, not to become the victim of a woman who might bring you shame. I suspect she feels the same of all her family."

He grinned back at her. "You saw all that in one brief meeting?" he asked. "Even while she was trying to squash you like a bug?"

"I did," she said. "I like her. She cares. But, Harry, what my father thinks of you and my marrying you will be his concern. I do believe, though, that he will be happy to know that I have a man again to support and protect me and guide me through all the dangers of life."

They smiled at each other and rubbed noses.

"Well, you know," he said, "you must allow me if ever you are attacked by bears or wolves to do the manly thing and come roaring to your rescue and tear them limb from limb with my bare hands."

"Or force them to their knees and then to attention before apologizing for frightening me," she said. "You do that awfully well, Harry."

"You made me redundant when I tried it, though," he told her. "You tore young Piper limb from limb without even raising your voice, Lydia. I do not believe, alas, that you are ever going to need me to ride into the lists to your defense."

"Thank you anyway," she said, settling her head against his shoulder again, "for forcing him to his knees."

"I will be leaving you to face the gossips alone for two whole days," he said.

"So you will," she said. "How dreadful. I shall be quite without male protection. I might crumble. I might—"

He stopped her by settling his mouth over hers.

"I must go," he said with a sigh a minute or so later.

"Yes, you must," she agreed.

And he did indeed leave less than twenty minutes later.

Dinner at Hinsford was half an hour early that evening and ended with the men leaving the dining room with the women rather than remaining to enjoy their port and their male conversation. Everyone headed for the music room rather than the drawing room.

The children were to perform a show for their entertainment, organized by Winifred, Elizabeth, and Joel. Sarah and Alice Cunningham, Josephine Archer, and Eve Handrich, dressed in flowing white with floral wreaths in their hair and floral streamers in their hands, danced to accompaniment provided by Elizabeth; Jacob Cunningham and George Handrich in black, and Jonah Archer and Nathan Westcott in white, engaged in a ferocious fencing match with wooden swords to rescue a wilting Rebecca Archer, who was bound with pink silk ribbons and jealously guarded by Robbie Cunningham, who was dressed all in black with matching fingernails that were hooked into claws as he hovered, hissing and panting, over his intended prey. Winifred played a gentle

rhythm on the lower keys of the pianoforte while her brother
Samuel plonked out an almost-accurate tune on the upper
keys. All the children, with the exception of the babies and
Andrew, who was deaf, had been conscripted into a choir
and sang a few folk songs with lusty good cheer and ques-
tionable musicality, to Elizabeth's accompaniment.

Andrew disappeared with Joel during the singing and
came back afterward carrying a large rock—*"which came
with us all the way from Bath,"* Joel explained with a grimace that turned to a grin when he saw Camille toss a
glance at the ceiling. The rock was set carefully down on a
small table Colin had placed in front of the pianoforte, and
Andrew, smiling broadly at his audience, indicated it with
one hand and beckoned with the other. When they all came
for a closer look, they could see that the stone enclosed on
three sides the chiseled form of a cat—a domestic cat,
surely—curled up and contentedly asleep with its head
turned to rest on its paws. Yes, contentedly. One could almost hear the cat purr.

"I have a talented boy here," Joel said, ruffling his son's
hair while everyone exclaimed with wonder and smiled at
the boy or hugged him. "I could not get him interested in
drawing or painting. Then I found him one day doing this
sort of thing, with a knife he had borrowed—and ruined—
from the kitchen."

There was more singing and dancing. The show ended
with the littlest children—except those who could not yet
walk—playing three rounds of ring a ring o' roses, shrieking with glee every time they all fell down, and looking to
parents and aunts and uncles and grandparents for approval.

Despite the early dinner, the children were late to bed.

"And very much too overexcited to settle easily," Anna

said when she came into the drawing room after helping settle her own four. "Jonah wants to do it all again tomorrow. I suspect he wants Avery to show him how to be a bit flashier with his swordplay."

"But I cannot have my son outshining me," Avery protested. "Not when he is only five years old."

"Come back to the music room with me, Anna?" Harry said, getting to his feet. "I want to have a closer look at Andrew's cat if it is still there."

"It is," Joel said while Anna looked at Harry in some surprise. "It is on the pianoforte. It is a lazy cat and not likely to have moved from there."

Anna preceded Harry from the room while he held the door open, and then took his arm as they made their way back down to the music room. Fortunately it was empty. Harry took a candle in with him from one of the wall sconces outside and lit the candles on the mantel.

"I can remember the concerts we used to put on as children," he said. "Some of them right here. We were always *so* proud of ourselves."

He wished he had not said it then, when he turned to look at her. She had not been there to be part of those concerts. She had been at the orphanage in Bath.

"All children love to perform," she said. "We did too when I was growing up at the orphanage. This concert tonight was a lovely idea. I believe it was Winifred's. She has changed so much in the ten years since I taught her in the orphanage school. In what seems like another lifetime. She has grown up, of course. But more than that—she is becoming the person she was always meant to be. And I have to give *so* much credit to Camille and Joel, who took her from the orphanage, adopted her, and just loved her."

The door clicked open, and Harry turned his head in

some annoyance to see who it was. Avery stepped inside
and closed the door behind him. He looked with raised eyebrows from Harry by the fireplace to Anna closer to the
pianoforte and strolled toward the chairs, which were still
in rows. He sat down on one at the back.

"Do not mind me," he said, and waved one beringed
hand as though permitting them to proceed.

It was too late *not* to proceed now, Harry thought.

"Anna," he said, "I have not been kind to you in the past
ten years."

She ran one hand along the top of the pianoforte before
lifting her head to look at him. "You have not been unkind,
Harry," she said. "I have tried to imagine what it must have
felt like for you and Camille and Abigail and Aunt Viola
when the whole family—and I—were sitting in that salon at
Archer House listening to your solicitor telling us what he
had discovered from the inquiries he had made in Bath about
the supposedly bastard daughter our father had supported at
the orphanage there. I am not sure I have ever succeeded. My
life was turned upside down and inside out as a result. But
yours was . . . shattered. It was not to be expected that any of
you would welcome me with open arms."

"I did," Avery said.

"Oh, not at first, Avery," she said crossly, turning her
head toward him. "You were horrid."

"Was I, my love?" he asked her. "But it was your shoes,
you see. They were so . . ." He circled one beringed hand in
the air.

"Ugly?" she suggested.

"The very word," he said. "Thank you."

"They were my Sunday best," she protested.

He smiled at her. One did not often see Avery smile.

"I think," Harry said, "you were hurt when none of us would accept your offer to share your fortune four ways."

"Ah," she said, returning her attention to him. "I was. But I approached the matter far too soon and without any tact at all. I was so *happy* at the thought of our all sharing the great bounty our father had left that it did not occur to me that I would appear condescending, even insulting. And quite insensitive."

"No," Harry said. "You must not take any of the blame upon yourself, Anna. You did absolutely no wrong. Neither did we except to lash out in our pain at a living target rather than a dead one. We could no longer hurt our father. So we hurt you instead. And felt not one whit the better for it. At least I did not. And never have. Will you forgive me?"

"Harry," she said, "there is nothing to forgive. Except that your continued stubbornness sometimes drives me to distraction."

"Hinsford?" he said.

"It will be yours eventually," she said. "Or your children's, if you should happen to predecease me. Just as the one quarter of our father's fortune will be yours—*with* the interest it is gathering."

"Will it please you if I take the money now?" he asked.

Her eyes brightened. "*Will* you, Harry?" she asked. "Oh, please. *Will* you?"

"I will," he said. "And with it I will purchase Hinsford."

"But—"

He held up a hand. "I must," he said. "There are four of us, Anna. There would be no fairness about my ending up with more than anyone else just because I am male."

"But it is—"

"Harry is right," Avery said, getting to his feet and strolling toward Anna. "It is you, my love, who have always talked of fairness."

"But I do not—"

"I think you must demand a hundred pounds for the property," he said.

"One hundred pounds?" Harry said. "That is a *joke*, Avery."

"Too much?" Avery said. "Seventy-five pounds, then. No, make that guineas."

"I am *serious* about this," Harry protested. "I wish you had stayed—"

"Sixty guineas," Anna said loudly and distinctly. "And that is my final word."

"Anna—"

"My *final word*," she said.

Avery tapped her cheek with one finger and strolled back to sit on the same chair in the back row.

"Anna." Harry drew a deep breath and let it go on a sigh. "This is really not about money at all, you know. I live very well as I am and can continue to do so even wh— Even if I marry. It is just that I want to set things right with you. You are my sister. Just as Cam is and Abby. I want to be your brother. I mean . . . I always have been. But . . ."

She came hurrying across the distance between them then and walked into the arms he held open. They closed about her, and he shut his eyes.

They stood thus for a silent minute or two.

"If only Cam and Abby would—" he began, but she raised her head from his shoulder and pressed two fingers to his lips.

"They both have," she said. "They came to me separately. And now you. And Aunt Viola has had her dowry back with all the interest that would have accrued on it in the years of her supposed marriage to our father."

Harry had not known any of that.

"And now I am complete," Anna said, her head still tipped back to look into his face. It beamed with what looked to Harry like real happiness. "My family is whole. And is about . . ." She turned her head to look back at Avery. "May I tell him?"

"I would imagine, my love," he said, "that soon the whole world will know without having to be told."

"We are expecting another child," she told Harry. "Perhaps *this* time Avery will get his spare to go with Jonah."

Avery was strolling toward them.

"I already have a trio of girls to torment my every waking moment," he said with a sigh. "If I have to suffer a quartet, I shall probably do it with my usual cheerful acceptance of what cannot be changed."

Harry hugged his sister with one arm and laughed as he held out a hand to shake his brother-in-law's. "Congratulations," he said. "I shall hope for another nephew, then, but be prepared to welcome another niece if I must."

"Must you really go to London tomorrow, Harry?" Anna asked. He had mentioned at dinner that he was going, to a great deal of puzzled protest. His grandmother Westcott had commented rather caustically that it was deliberately contrary of him to go there now when they were all *here*— and all for the sake of buying a new *shirt*. He had merely smiled and assured her that he would be back before dinner on Wednesday evening.

Avery was looking keenly at him from beneath his usual lazy eyelids. "You cannot find any decent shirts in Eastend, Harry?" he asked.

"Oh, good Lord, no," Harry said. "Not for evening wear, anyway. Not for my birthday ball, perish the thought, with all the family present and other guests too."

"Quite so," Avery said. "And I suppose there are one or two other items you need that can be purchased only in London."

"Yes," Harry said. "It is a bit of a nuisance to have to dash up there when the house is full of guests. But it should not take me long. I will leave early in the morning and be away just one night."

"Well, I wish you did not have to go," Anna said. "I daresay you have several shirts right here that would be perfectly suitable for your ball."

"But, my love," Avery said, sounding pained, "a man cannot be expected to wear a shirt he has worn before when he is celebrating a birthday as significant in the grand scheme of things as his thirtieth. Or a shirt of possibly inferior workmanship, which is all one might expect to find in a provincial town. It is perfectly understandable that Harry would wish to toddle up to London to see his tailor."

"How absurd you both are," Anna said.

Avery knows, Harry thought. Was there anything in this world he did *not* know?

Twenty-two

Lydia had expected the days between Monday and Friday to be quiet ones. They were not to be, however.

On Tuesday morning, when she was out of bed but only just—she had let Snowball outside and was getting the stove heated up in the kitchen to make her morning porridge and tea, but she was still in her nightgown, with bare feet and her hair in a braid down her back—the yapping of her dog preceded a knock upon her front door.

"I am on my way," Harry said when she opened the door a crack and peered about it. "I thought you must be up when I saw Snowball outside. Just listen to her, Lydia. She is putting the fear of God into my poor horse." Lydia opened the door wider. "And I hoped you would be up. I forgot to ask you for the loan of a ring, if you have one. You look rather gorgeous." He grinned appreciatively.

She looked dubiously at her wedding ring, which she was planning to take off today and put away.

"No," he said. "Not that one."

"There is my mother's ring," she said, "which I rarely wear."

"Does it fit your ring finger?" he asked.

"Yes," she said. "I will go and fetch it."

She handed it to him a few moments later in its leather box.

"I will guard it with my life," he said in all seriousness, "and return it tomorrow."

"I trust you," she said.

"Thank you." He put the box into an inner pocket of his long drab riding coat. "I also wanted an excuse to give you an early morning kiss."

She stepped right into the doorway and set her hands on his shoulders. He grasped her waist and kissed her.

"Ride carefully, Harry," she said.

"I will," he promised, grinning at her again. "I have much to return for."

"Your birthday party?"

He laughed. "That too. Stay safe."

"I will," she said.

She stood in the doorway without even a dressing gown to lend decency to her appearance until he had ridden out of sight; then she waited for Snowball to trot inside, and she shut the door with a sigh. The next few days were going to seem endless.

The Earl and Countess of Riverdale and Baron and Lady Hodges called upon her before the morning was out. At least by then she was dressed, with her hair coiled neatly at her neck and her apron on. She had a batch of fruit scones almost ready to come out of the oven.

"Do come in," she said. "I hope I do not have flour on the end of my nose or something embarrassing like that to see in the mirror after you have gone."

"Not a speck," Lord Hodges said. "Let me have a closer look, though. A dab on your left cheek, actually."

"Oh." She dashed a hand across her cheek.

"Got it," he said. "Something smells good."

"Scones," Lydia said. "They will be ready in five minutes. Will you have some with a cup of coffee?"

"Oh, we will not bother you, Mrs. Tavernor," the countess said. "We came—"

"Speak for yourself, Wren," Lord Hodges said. "Coffee and a scone sound lovely to me."

"Agreed," the earl said. "Thank you, Mrs. Tavernor."

"All we came for," the countess said, laughing as Lydia directed them all to seats in the living room, "was to see that you had recovered from that nasty incident yesterday. The way you handled that boy was quite admirable, by the way."

"Thank you," Lydia said. "Jeremy Piper has caused a great deal of trouble in his short life, poor boy."

"Poor boy?" The earl raised his eyebrows.

"I cannot help but feel a bit sorry for him, you see," Lydia said.

"Even though he was responsible for your husband's death?" he asked.

Lydia had to excuse herself to take the scones out of the oven and brew a pot of coffee.

"Those scones really do smell heavenly. May I butter them for you while you make the coffee?" Lady Hodges had followed her to the kitchen. She had an open, kindly face and a warm manner seemingly designed to set other people at their ease. And she was the "Cousin Elizabeth" Harry had spoken of, the one who had once escaped a violently abusive marriage.

"That would be good of you," Lydia said.

"Harry went to London this morning—at some deadly

hour, before anyone else was up," Lady Hodges told her. "To buy a shirt suitable to wear at his birthday ball, if you please. Have you ever heard of anything more absurd? He is abandoning his house guests for two whole days for the sake of a shirt."

"Oh," Lydia said.

"Alexander suspects a less trivial reason for his going," Lady Hodges added as she sliced a few scones and set a pat of butter on each to melt into them.

"Oh?" Lydia said again.

"But Harry was not saying, and we—the four of us—are not going to spread any unfounded rumors," Lady Hodges said, a thread of laughter in her voice. "There. Two scones each for the men and one each for the women."

"The coffee is ready," Lydia said.

Her visitors sat with her for half an hour before taking their leave. Lydia walked with them to the gate. The earl turned back to her as the others walked away.

"It is of some importance to my wife and the other ladies of the family who have been diligently planning a party for Harry since Christmastime that as many people as possible from the neighborhood attend," he said. "Will you come, Mrs. Tavernor?"

He must *know*, Lydia thought, or at least suspect. His sister's words earlier had suggested it.

"I will," she said. "I am honored to have been invited."

He smiled—a very handsome man indeed—and held her gaze for a moment before turning to catch up with the others.

And that was just the beginning. Denise called and helped her eat a few more scones. "Are you going to the ball?" she asked. "You really must. I shall come and drag you there myself if necessary."

Hannah called a little later, and both Mrs. Bartlett and Mrs. Bailey came while she was still there. Mirabel Hill and her cousin Miss Ardreigh arrived on her doorstep a mere five minutes after they had all left, claiming to be feeling footsore after an outing during which they had been talking so much they had not realized how far they had walked.

All of them wanted to know if Lydia was going to the ball.

And no sooner had they taken their leave than the Reverend and Mrs. Kingsley came from Hinsford to introduce themselves since they understood Mrs. Tavernor was the widow of the former vicar of Fairfield. The Reverend Kingsley was the Marchioness of Dorchester's brother and therefore Harry's uncle. They stayed for half an hour, though they would not take refreshments, a pleasant couple who were easy to talk with. The whole time she was there, Mrs. Kingsley had Snowball on her lap, patting and petting her and threatening to kidnap her and take her back to Dorsetshire.

On Wednesday afternoon, the Dowager Countess of Riverdale came in person with Viscount and Viscountess Dirkson and accepted the offer of tea and cake.

"You have a pretty place here, Mrs. Tavernor," the dowager said as she looked around from her chair to one side of the fireplace. "But if you were *my* granddaughter, I would scold you for disdaining to have even as much as a maid to lend you respectability here."

"But Mrs. Tavernor is *not* your granddaughter, Mother," Lady Dirkson pointed out.

"You have scolded her anyway," the viscount said, looking at Lydia with twinkling eyes.

"And the only way she ever could be," his wife added,

pursuing her point, "would be if she were Harry's wife. Or Peter's or Ivan's, though they are far too young for her. And she has already refused Harry."

"But do not let that fact deter you from attending Harry's birthday ball, Mrs. Tavernor," the dowager countess said, glaring very directly at her. "I can assure you that none of his family will make any reference at all to his ill-advised proposal and your very proper refusal."

"But she has already accepted her invitation, Mother," the viscountess said. "She told Alexander so. We look forward to seeing you on Friday evening, Mrs. Tavernor."

They left soon afterward. She had the stamp of approval from the family, then, did she? Lydia thought as she watched until the carriage had moved away from her gate. And the head of the family—*both* heads, the Earl of Riverdale and the dowager countess—had made a point of coming to tell her, if not in so many words. She smiled, though the smile faded when she thought of the trick that was to be played on them on Friday morning. They were trying to ensure that she would attend the ball—with their blessing—but had no idea that by then she and Harry would be married. Somehow it was a bit of an uncomfortable thought.

And finally—finally!—Harry returned late on Wednesday afternoon, looking weary and travel worn and cheerful. Lydia had been watching for him since before he possibly could be expected. She flung open the door and dashed out to the gate as he drew rein beyond it. She did not even stop to wrap a shawl about her shoulders, though it was a chilly day.

He swung down from the saddle, leaned across the fence, and kissed her. "Mission completed," he said. "Two new shirts. Oh, and—" He reached inside his coat and drew out the leather box with her mother's ring. "Returned safe and sound, as promised, though I had to fight off three sets of highwaymen to guard it."

"Thank you." She laughed as she took it from him and held it for a moment to her lips.

"Lydia." His own smile faded. "You have had two days to do nothing but think. Any second thoughts?"

She laughed. "I have had nothing but visitors," she said. "I have had scarcely a moment to think at all. But no, Harry. No second thoughts. You?"

"Yes, actually. I ought to have taken you with me and married you in London." He grinned ruefully at her. "Dash it all, I will not be able to see you tomorrow much either. There is to be a family picnic, weather permitting, in honor of my cousin Boris's betrothal to Miss Leeson. I will come tomorrow evening, though, to make final plans for Friday. I had better get back to the house and get bathed and changed for dinner."

"Yes," she said. "Do not make yourself late."

He kissed her again, mounted his horse, and rode off up the drive, turning to wave before he rode out of sight.

Perhaps tomorrow she would have a quiet day, Lydia thought. To think at last. To prepare herself.

She was not to have it, however, for it was on Thursday that her father and two elder brothers arrived on her doorstep.

Harry was feeling unaccountably melancholy. He was out on the lawn south of the house, surrounded by his family and other house guests, celebrating Boris and Audrey's betrothal. A happy occasion. Chairs had been set out for the older people, while blankets had been spread for everyone else. The sun was shining again. The wind that had gusted this morning had died down. They had just feasted upon sumptuous picnic fare. Alexander in his role as head of the Westcott family had toasted the couple with champagne. It was a dizzying thought that Boris, who seemingly just yesterday had been giving Aunt Mildred and Uncle Thomas fits of alarm and outrage with one mischievous boyish prank after another, along with brothers Peter and Ivan, was now twenty-five years old and a mature, responsible young man and obviously deeply in love with his bride-to-be.

They would all be together again tomorrow—along with numerous outside guests—to celebrate his birthday. It would be the culmination of this house party, which had been arranged for him by his family out of the depths of their love for him.

None of them would be at his wedding.

Except for Gil, that was, who had agreed to come as a witness and as Harry's best man, though he had been a bit long-faced when Harry had made it clear that he did not want Abby to come too and would be obliged if Gil did not even tell her.

"I say, Harry," he had said. "It is not so easy to keep secrets from one's spouse, you know. And not terribly honorable either."

Gil and Abby's wedding at the village church four years ago with only the vicar and his wife and Harry present had seemed perfect. His and Lydia's wedding tomorrow morning would be equally so, Harry told himself.

Except that the circumstances would be different.

His family—the whole of it—would be here, busily preparing for the party in the evening, perhaps wondering where he had gone, unaware that he was at the church nearby marrying Lydia.

He should be over the moon with excitement today. He was getting married tomorrow.

But he could not shake off the feeling that it was somehow not *right*. He looked at his mother, whose arm was drawn through Marcel's as they talked with Aunt Matilda and Dirkson. And at Camille, who was sitting on one of the blankets repairing Alice's braid while Joel beside her had one twin standing and bouncing on fat little legs between his thighs while the other twin was against his shoulder, having her back patted. And at Abby, who was almost forehead to forehead with Jessica on another blanket, the two of them giggling like girls. And at Anna, who was holding Beatrice, her youngest, and smiling while she conversed with Adrian Sawyer and Sally Underwood and Gordon Monteith.

The inner circle of his family.

Who did not know that tomorrow was his wedding day.

Dash it all, it did not feel right.

"Harry." Alexander, still holding his champagne glass, set a hand on his shoulder. "Is this all a bit much for you, as it was four years ago, as I recall? Are you wishing us all a thousand miles away, as you were then?"

"No," Harry said. "Quite the contrary, in fact. I am so extraordinarily well blessed, Alex, that I will make an idiot of myself if I try to put it into words."

Alexander squeezed his shoulder. "None of us felt well blessed ten years ago," he said. "Or six years ago after Waterloo. Or four years ago, when Avery and Gil and I brought you home from Paris."

"Do you feel well blessed now?" Harry asked.

His cousin hesitated. "Yes," he said. "I must confess I do, Harry. Though you must know that I really did not want—"

"I do know," Harry said. "You need not be apologetic about being happy. I am a happy man too."

"You did not look happy a moment ago," Alexander said.

"The natural expression of my face in repose," Harry said with a grin.

Ah, they were about to be disturbed. Someone had come up the drive—two people, actually, two men—and paused to look at the crowd gathered on the lawn. They were not any of the neighbors. They were strangers, in fact. Harry hoped they would proceed to the main doors so that Brown could deal with whatever their business was.

They were not proceeding to the door, however. They were striding across the grass, two men on some important mission and apparently unembarrassed at intruding upon a private event.

Most of the children were still roaring about the grass and among the trees, intent upon their noisy games. Almost everyone else turned to watch the men. The taller of the two, who walked slightly ahead of the other, stopped when he was close enough to be heard—most conversation had died away anyway.

"Which one of you is Westcott?" he asked.

"A large number of us are," Harry said, stepping forward with a smile on his face. "Which Westcott were you looking for in particular?"

"Major Harry Westcott," the man said.

"That would be me," Harry said, taking another step toward his visitor. "What may I—"

His visitor had taken more than one step toward him. He put an abrupt end to the sentence with a fist that collided with Harry's chin and mouth with such force that Harry, taken completely by surprise, found himself measuring his length on the grass, gazing up at stars in the middle of the afternoon.

He became fuzzily aware of uproar. Voices, both male and female, all talking at once. A few screams. A demand to be let go. A command to stop struggling before an arm got broken. A contemptuous demand to get up and fight like a man. That one got Harry's attention. Since he was probably the only one down, the invitation to get up was probably being directed at him.

No teeth—Harry did a quick check with his tongue— appeared to be missing or broken. His chin felt as if it might have been punched all the way through to the back of his head, but when he moved his jaw the chin seemed still to be attached to it. He shook his head—big mistake— and sat up. He shook his head more gently at the hand that was being offered him—Boris's—and got to his feet.

Everyone was standing, including the elderly ladies. The children had abandoned their games for the greater excitement of seeing what was about to happen. The first man had Alexander's hand clamped on his shoulder. The second man had his arms behind him, held there by Gil. Both men were frowning ferociously and breathing fire and brimstone—or so it seemed to Harry's still-fuzzy brain.

"Fight, you coward," the first man said from between his teeth. "Put your fists up, or are you going to hide behind all the skirts here and allow other *men* to protect you?"

Harry had a horrid premonition. And good God, yes. This was *just* how he would expect them to behave.

"I am *not* going to fight either one of you," he said. "Alex, you can step aside. Gil, you would probably be sorry if you really did break his arm. Let go, there's a good fellow. Is either one of you by any chance a Winterbourne? Or both of you?"

"You will name your time and place, Westcott," man number one said curtly. "Your weapons too if you wish. And you *will* fight or be exposed to the world as a debaucher and a coward. I am James Winterbourne."

"Oh, I say," Uncle Thomas said above the swell of sound that succeeded Winterbourne's words.

Harry held up a staying hand. "Have you spoken with your sister?" he asked.

"My sister's name will not pass your lips," Winterbourne said. "We will take care of her from this moment on, you may be assured. She will come home, where she belongs, and where we can keep her safe from the likes of you."

"Well," Harry said. "She may have something to say about that, you know. And if you have *not* had a word with her, perhaps you ought. In fact, maybe the three of us should. This is your brother, I assume?"

How the devil had they found out? Gossip had wings indeed, it seemed.

"William Winterbourne," the brother confirmed, narrowing his eyes at Harry. "And you will get within a mile of our sister again over my dead body."

"A rather suicidal threat," Avery said, his voice languid, as he strolled into sight from somewhere to Harry's left. "I believe Mrs. Tavernor's cottage is within half a mile of where we stand. In my experience, it is always a mistake of colossal proportions for men to flex their muscles instead of recognizing that women have voices—and often surprisingly sensible minds behind those voices."

"I shall go and have a word with Mrs. Tavernor," Harry's mother said, stepping up beside him and within range of the iron fist that had collided with Harry's chin not so long ago. "She is very fortunate to have two brothers who care so deeply for her. I am the Marchioness of Dorchester,

Harry's mother. I am pleased to make your acquaintance, Mr. Winterbourne." And she extended her right hand to the elder brother, who still looked as though fumes might blow out his ears at any moment.

Bizarrely, he took her hand and even bowed over it, murmuring something unintelligible.

"Harry will accompany me," his mother continued. "I shall certainly see to it that he offers no sort of insult to Mrs. Tavernor, whom I have found to be a woman of dignity and integrity. Will you accompany us, Mr. Winterbourne? And your brother?"

The Westcott family, Harry thought, might never have been more silent. Even the children were unnaturally quiet.

The brothers exchanged glances.

"I will not allow my sister to be bullied, ma'am," William Winterbourne said.

"Good gracious," Harry's mother said. "Nor will I. More to the point, from what I know of Mrs. Tavernor, nor will she. Harry? Your arm, please."

Two minutes later they were making their way down the drive, the four of them, Harry's mother—bonnetless—on his arm, the two Winterbourne men coming along behind. Harry did not turn his head to look at them, but he would wager they both looked pretty sheepish.

"The power of women," Harry's mother murmured.

Twenty-three

❦

Lydia was feeling a bit melancholy and was trying desperately to shake off the feeling. Tomorrow was her wedding day! And she was excited about it. She loved Harry. She could not be happier.

So why did happiness feel so . . . *flat*?

She had decided to spend the day at home alone. She wanted to rest after what had been a busy week. She wanted to get ready for tomorrow. Though there was precious little to do. She had chosen an old dress she had not worn for several years, though she had worn it precisely once. It was too frivolous and too pale a green for a vicar's wife, Isaiah had said. Lydia had chosen it because it reminded her of springtime and lifted her mood. There were pink rosebuds embroidered about the hem and smaller ones about the edges of the sleeves. It must be woefully out of fashion by now, though Lydia had no idea quite how much.

It was going to be her wedding dress notwithstanding.

She had washed it and hung it to dry and ironed it and . . . there was no other way to get ready.

At least today she did not have to fear any visits from the Westcotts. They were having a picnic to celebrate the betrothal of Harry's cousin. If the weather was kind, Harry had said. The weather was very kind.

She did not have to fear any visits from her friends either. Mrs. Bailey had invited them and a few other ladies to tea at the vicarage. She had invited Lydia too but had understood when Lydia had refused. Mrs. Bailey knew about the wedding, of course. She was to be one of the witnesses, and the Reverend Bailey was to conduct the service. She was not really happy about it. She had not said so to Lydia, but she had looked troubled when she had agreed to be a witness.

Since Monday, Lydia thought early in the afternoon as she sat idle on her chair by the fireplace, her heels resting inelegantly on the edge of the seat cushion while her arms hugged her legs to her bosom and she rested her chin on her knees, she had seen Harry precisely twice—for a few minutes when he was leaving for London on Tuesday morning, and for a few minutes yesterday afternoon as he was coming home. She would not see him all day today and would see him probably only briefly this evening while they made final arrangements for tomorrow.

Had they been unwise to decide upon such a rushed wedding?

Had they been mad to decide to marry at all?

And were these last-minute, second-thought wedding nerves she was having?

She felt so very alone.

There was only one thing she was sure of. No, two. And

they did help calm her as she pulled in her chin and rested her forehead on her knees. She loved Harry Westcott with all her being. More important—oh, by far—she *trusted* him. Their marriage would be a partnership, a companionship, a friendship, a . . . *romance* of equals. It would be, despite what both civil and church law might say to the contrary. Tomorrow she would promise to obey, but Harry would never hold her to that. Not that she could know for absolute certain, of course. One never could of the future. But one could trust, and she trusted Harry. With her life. For that was exactly what she would be doing tomorrow.

Oh, tomorrow was her wedding day. Why oh why did she feel so flat today? Why did it all seem somehow wrong? Or if not wrong precisely, then not quite right? She had no wish for a grand wedding or crowds of guests. She had no wish—

Oh, *who* was coming now? She had heard horses and carriage wheels and had assumed it was someone on the way to Hinsford. There had been much coming and going all week. But the conveyance was unmistakably drawing to a halt outside her gate. She straightened up in some annoyance to see who it was.

And then she was hurtling out the door, leaving it open behind her, Snowball bouncing along at her side, yipping in a frenzy of excitement. And she was throwing open the garden gate and hurling herself into her father's arms as he descended from the carriage. And bursting into tears.

"Papa. Papa!"

"Lydie. Lydie!"

That was almost the full extent of the conversation for the next minute or two, though there was a great deal of hugging and kissing and back patting and hiccuping and barking.

"James. Oh, James."

"Lydie. Lydie, Lydie."

"William. Oh."

"Lydie."

"It is all over now, Lydie," her father said as everyone crowded into the house and seemed to fill it to overflowing. "Lady Hill wrote to me on Sunday as soon as she heard and sent the letter by special messenger. You have a true friend there. As for all the rest of it, it is nonsense and I would like nothing better than to crack a few heads together. But it is all over now."

"It is just what we warned you about, Lydie," William said. "But we have not come to scold. You must have been suffering enough."

"Will and I will go get rooms at the village inn in a short while," James said. "We cannot stay here with just the one bedchamber. But early tomorrow we will be on our way back home with you, and you can shake the dust of Fairfield off your shoes forever, Lydie."

"We will look after you," her father said. "And if any gossip should follow you home, well, we will know how to deal with it. You will not have to worry about a thing."

It was hard to get a word in edgewise, but Lydia did eventually after drying her eyes and blowing her nose and smiling fondly from one to the other of them. "But I am not leaving here," she said. "I—"

"Now, Lydie," James said

And they were off again, and all she had to do for the rest of her life, Lydia understood, was relax into their love and strength and protection. They were precious indeed. She was almost overflowing with love for them. And for a while there was no point in arguing. She had no wish to argue. She had not fully realized until she had seen whose carriage was drawn up outside her gate how very much she wanted to see them all. She went into the kitchen, filled the kettle, and put it on to boil.

"Now, Lydie," James said, coming to stand in the archway. "This is not right, you being in the kitchen making the tea yourself. But today will be the last day. From tomorrow on you will be properly looked after. We will see to it."

"How is Esther?" she asked, and he beamed as he told her how his wife was remaining so sweet and cheerful even though he was insisting that she spend most of her days on the chaise in her room or the long couch in the drawing room, with her feet up.

"Though I have insisted that while I am away she remain in her room," he said. "Until I return to carry her down to the drawing room, that is."

Lydia smiled and took the leftover scones and cake out of the pantry. Her mind was beginning to race. She and Harry had agreed to keep their betrothal and wedding plans strictly secret from everyone except the vicar and the two witnesses. Their reason had been that it would not seem fair to involve his family when her own was far away. Now suddenly most of her family was here. Only Esther and Anthony were missing. But she could not say anything. Not without consulting Harry first.

James and William would not stay for a cup of tea even though they must be hungry and thirsty after their journey. They insisted upon going without delay to reserve rooms and find stabling for the horses.

So Lydia settled down to a visit with her father while her mind kept on churning over what she could say. It was unlikely Harry would come until much later, and it was important to her that any decision to be made be made together.

She had less time to wait than she had expected. Within an hour after her brothers left, there was a knock upon her door and she opened it to discover on her doorstep two scowling brothers, a smiling, bonnetless, gloveless Marchioness of Dorchester, and a hatless Harry with a bright red chin and an upper lip that looked considerably fatter than it normally did.

What—?

"Lydie, you are not to worry—"

"We will have you away from here, Lydie—"

"Good afternoon, Mrs. Tavernor."

"Hello, Lydia."

They all spoke at the same time.

"What in *thunder*?" Her father had come up behind her. "Is *this* the villain? Get him away from here. He is not coming inside this house. I forbid it. Lydie has her father to look after her now."

"Papa," Lydia said, "this is *my* house. Please come in, all of you. Lady Dorchester, this is my father. The Marchioness of Dorchester, Papa. Major Westcott's mother."

What on *earth* had happened? But it was a rhetorical question. Clearly the need to go to the inn in such a hurry to reserve rooms had been merely an excuse on her brothers' part to go and confront Harry.

"How do you do, Mr. Winterbourne?" the marchioness said. "How reassuring it must be for Mrs. Tavernor to have relatives who care so much for her that they have come a long distance in support of her. You will be returning home with your father, Mrs. Tavernor?"

"I will *not*," Lydia said. "Oh, this cottage was not built for so many people *looming*. Will you all please *sit down*?"

Amazingly they all did except for Harry, who stood just inside her living room, his hands clasped at his back.

"And I suppose," Lydia continued, "one of you—James, at a guess—felt that you must defend my honor by finding Harry and *hitting* him. I suppose Lady Hill in her letter to Papa mentioned the fact that he *kissed* me when he conveyed me home from a village assembly in his carriage. Perhaps she even mentioned that he kissed me *on the forehead*. And thus, of course, he became the grand villain of the piece and you must all rush here to haul me home and punish the man who kissed my brow. I see no marks on either James or William. Was Harry too sensible to fight back? And did either of you even *think* of consulting me first? Of asking me exactly what happened? Of discovering *from me* if Harry did anything that was remotely either disrespectful or villainous? Has either of you even noticed during the past twenty-eight years that I have a *voice*? Has either of you even considered the possibility that perhaps I have a *mind*?"

"Now, Lydie—" her father began.

"And *you*, Papa," she said, turning her glare on him. "Were you a party to this? Did you know that the first thing James and William intended to do after they arrived here was to go and mete out punishment without even asking me for my side of the story and my feelings and preferences? No, do not answer. *Of course* you knew. And you should be ashamed of yourself. All three of you should. You came here to *take me home*. Can't you understand I *am* home? This is where I belong and where I choose to stay. I love you all very dearly, but I want to hear your apology to Harry."

Oh dear. Where had all that come from?

"Lydia." Harry's hands had come to her shoulders from behind. "Perhaps we should tell your father and brothers? And my mother too?"

"You are not worthy to shine Lydie's shoes," her father

said. "I do not like to see your hands on her. Or to hear you make free with her name."

"Yes," Lydia said, speaking to Harry.

"Lydia and I are betrothed," Harry said.

His mother got to her feet.

"Because we love each other," Harry said. "*Not* because of the very foolish gossip concocted by a Peeping Tom of a boy and his hysterical mother. We will be getting married."

"Oh," his mother said, clasping her hands to her bosom and looking at Lydia with glowing eyes.

"May I?" Harry asked Lydia.

"Yes," she said.

"Tomorrow morning," he said. "In the church here in the village. It was to have been a very private ceremony, even though all my family is currently staying at Hinsford Manor to celebrate my birthday, also tomorrow. We did not want a family wedding without any of Lydia's family in attendance. But we also did not want to wait. Now it can be a family wedding after all."

"Oh," the marchioness said again.

Lydia's father and brothers could not seem to find even that much to say.

Harry squeezed Lydia's shoulders almost hard enough to hurt. She raised a hand and covered one of his own.

And suddenly the prospect of tomorrow morning no longer seemed flat. Suddenly there was nothing but joy.

The village of Fairfield was already in a state of suppressed excitement the following day when word began to spread from house to house, from business to business, as news and rumor and gossip always did in any community, that *something was going on* at the church. It was Major Harry

Westcott's birthday, and the illustrious Westcott family, not to mention the Kingsleys and other guests, had been causing a stir all week as they paid calls in the village upon the favored ones among them. Almost everyone had been invited to the ball tonight. It was many years since there had been any such entertainment at the manor.

But now, when it was still only morning, something was happening at the church. Carriage after carriage was rolling up to it, and it looked as though everyone from the manor was descending from those carriages and going inside. Which seemed odd as this was *Friday*, not Sunday. Perhaps, someone suggested, the vicar was going to do a special thanksgiving service for the thirty years Major Westcott had spent on this earth—against the odds, it might be added, while he was still a military man.

Doors opened on houses that were within sight of the church and remained open. Some people strolled up to the church, as though they just happened by pure chance to be in this place at this time. Yet others came hurrying up lest they miss something and made no pretense of being anything other than curious. Soon there was an impressive crowd gathered about the church gates, though they kept a respectful distance from it so they would not block the path being followed by each new arrival.

And then Major Westcott himself arrived and descended from his carriage before waiting for his brother-in-law Mr. Gilbert Bennington to step out after him. Both men were dressed very smartly. But it was Major Westcott's carriage upon which much of the attention was focused. For it was lavishly decorated with flowers and greenery and could only be—

"God love him," someone said loudly before having her

voice drowned out by a swell of murmurings. "Our Lord
Harry is getting himself married."

As the two men disappeared inside the church and the
carriage moved off, at least temporarily, speculation was
rife about the identity of the bride. There were a few very
pretty young ladies staying at the manor, though there had
been no indication all week that any one of them was affi-
anced to Major Westcott.

"Lydia?" Denise Franks whispered to Hannah Corning
after moving through the crowd to stand beside her friend.
"Is it possible?"

"She has not said a word to me," Hannah said. "And
Harry has not said a word to Tom."

And then they turned to watch with everyone else. Two
large men, both strangers, were striding up the street toward them, looking a bit ferocious. The crowd instinctively
parted to let them through, though they were not arriving
by carriage, and there was no real indication that their destination was the inside of the church.

Behind them came another formidable-looking man,
just as large as the other two, but a bit more portly, and
older. He did not attract as much attention as the first ones,
however, for as soon as the two in front began to move past
the crowd, everyone had a clear view of the woman who
was holding his arm.

Mrs. Tavernor!

She was simply dressed in green, with a straw bonnet
that had been trimmed with fresh pink flowers—to match
those that had been embroidered upon the hem of her dress.
It struck a few of the observers that she had never appeared
this dainty or this youthful and pretty when she had been
the vicar's wife.

When they looked more closely, a few people could remember seeing the older man before, and maybe the taller of the other two. They had been here for the Reverend Tavernor's funeral, had they not? The older man was Mrs. Tavernor's *father*? A man of wealth and property and influence, it was said.

The group of four made its way up the church path and into the church, and the crowd, buzzing with excitement and opinion, set itself to wait.

"Oh, Denise," Hannah said. "I am going to *cry*."

"Better not, Han," Tom said. "I have only one handkerchief with me, and I may need that myself. My best friend is getting married."

His wife dug him fondly in the ribs with her elbow.

Twenty-four

The church would have looked distinctly lopsided if those connected with Harry had sat on one side and those with Lydia on the other. They had therefore been redistributed. Those guests from the manor who were not related by blood to Harry or were not *married* to a blood relative would sit on the bride's side with Mr. Winterbourne and his two sons. Those people included Estelle and Bertrand Lamarr, Adrian Sawyer, Sally Underwood, Miranda and Gordon Monteith, and Mrs. Leeson and her daughters. Boris joined the elder Miss Leeson there.

Harry half noticed the arrangement as he entered the church with Gil. It was something he would not have thought of himself. He would not have thought either of any decorations for the church, though he could recall that Mrs. Jenkins had made a floral garden of it for Abby and Gil's wedding four years ago. The appearance of the church this morning more than matched it. The sweet scents of flowers competed with the usual smells of candles and old prayer books.

Grandmama Kingsley had threatened a heart attack yesterday when he returned from Lydia's cottage and announced his wedding by special license—*tomorrow morning*.

Grandmama Westcott had displayed more fortitude. "And I suppose, Harry," she had said, fixing him with a severe eye, "you have not given a single thought to flowers. Or wedding breakfasts. Or speeches. *Matilda?*"

"I suppose," Avery had said sotto voce to Harry, "you did also purchase a shirt or two, Harry? Just in case someone asked?"

"I did," Harry had assured him. "Also a wedding ring. Someone is bound to ask at any moment now."

"Harry," Aunt Louise had said, "I suppose you have given no thought to a ring?"

Gil had the wedding ring in his pocket now.

Harry's legs felt as though they did not quite belong to him, and if he had eaten any breakfast at all—he had not—he would swear that a large portion of it had lodged somewhere just below his throat and was refusing to be dislodged. He was *not* having second or twenty-second thoughts or any doubts at all, in fact. But the possibility that Lydia was having them had kept him awake half the night.

She had been so adamant until just a few days ago that freedom and independence meant more to her than anything else and that she would never give them up to any man. She had been happy in her little cottage, cooking and doing for herself. Had she acted too impulsively in the last few days? She did occasionally *speak* impulsively, after all. Would she live to regret today—if she turned up today, that was?

But then, after he had been sitting on the front pew for endless minutes, gazing ahead and trying not to think at all—and thinking more than he had ever thought in his life, one thought teeming upon another without even waiting politely for the one before it to move out of the way—she came.

At least, her brothers did—large, menacing, scowling. No, unfair. Harry had not even turned his head to look at them as they appeared at the edge of his vision and took their seats in the pew across from him. He did glance their way after they were seated. They were both looking straight ahead, no discernible expression on their faces. Harry touched his tongue to his upper lip. Not as much damage had been done as he had thought yesterday. It was still a bit tender, but not swollen enough to mar his wedding day.

Good Lord, those two were about to be his brothers-in-law. But suddenly Harry was glad Lydia had such fierce defenders. She was much loved, even if that love was sometimes a bit overpossessive and provoked the sort of scold she had given them yesterday.

The Reverend Bailey appeared before them, clad in his clerical vestments, and invited the congregation to stand. Harry turned to watch Lydia come along the very short nave on the arm of her father. Looking calm and beautiful. And meeting his eyes and smiling at him and bringing all the sunshine of the outdoors inside with her.

His legs were suddenly back, and the blockage in his throat had magically cleared. His restless sleep was forgotten, and all his anxieties had dissipated.

For there was not only sunshine in her face. There was also love. And . . . trust.

And it was their wedding day.

* * *

Lydia had surprised herself by sleeping soundly all night.
She might indeed have slept longer if Snowball had not
been huffing beside her bed, begging to be let out.

She had thrown back the curtains from the windows and
left the front door open as her dog bounced outside. The
sun was shining. The tree branches were still. The air was
already warm.

She had stood in the doorway, waiting for the onslaught
of doubt. She had raised her eyes to the sky. Pure blue except for a few small fluffy white clouds.

She had felt only blessings.

Today was her wedding day. To Harry.

All doubts over their decision not to wait but to marry
now, today, on Harry's birthday, before his party, had been
lifted by the arrival of her father and brothers—who would
be here later to walk to church with her.

She had eaten breakfast, having discovered none of the
expected loss of appetite. She had donned the green dress and
felt no impulse to pull it off in favor of something more sober.
She had styled her hair in a simple knot at her neck to accom-
modate her bonnet—the straw one she had owned before her
first marriage and scarcely worn during it for the usual reason, though she had never understood what was frivolous
about plain, unadorned straw. It was *very* unadorned. That
thought had sent her outside to pick some blooms from her
garden—all of them pink—and some greenery. She had wo-
ven them into the straw about the crown.

Even the arrival of her father and brothers had not put a
dent in her happiness, although they had all looked as if
they were about to attend a funeral. But after she had
laughed at the sight of them and hugged them all in turn

and told them this was the happiest day of her life and their being here made it absolutely perfect, they had all cheered up and hugged her again and assured her that all they wanted for her—all they had ever wanted—was that she be happy.

"And with a good man to look after you, Lydie," James had not been able to resist adding.

"I think it may just be possible," her father had conceded, "that Westcott *is* a good man, James. Good breeding. He must get it from his mother. His father was a scoundrel."

"The Westcotts do not seem to hold it against him that he is a bas—that his birth was irregular," William had said. "So why should we?"

"Why indeed?" Lydia had asked, bending over his chair to kiss the top of his head.

They had walked to church, something that turned into a bit of an ordeal when it became obvious that a small crowd had gathered outside the gate. The arrival of carriages from Hinsford must have alerted everyone. They had come down the drive in a steady stream and with a great deal of noise and pomp while Lydia was still at home.

But the crowd parted before James and William, who were walking side by side ahead of Lydia and her father, and watched them proceed through the gate and up the path to the church.

And oh, she was so, *so* glad Harry's whole family was here for their wedding after all. And that her father and two of her brothers were here too. She watched James and William stride on into the church and down to the front pew and then turned to her father.

He had tears in his eyes.

"Lydie." He bent his head and kissed her cheek. "Be

happy. It is all I have ever wanted for you. It is all your mother would have wanted."

She swallowed and took his arm. And then she was walking with him to meet her bridegroom. What was that line from surely the loveliest of all the psalms?

My cup runneth over, she thought as she smiled at Harry and watched the tension and anxiety fade from his face before he smiled back.

They turned together to face the Reverend Bailey. Her father released her arm and took her hand in his instead— ready to give it to the man who was about to become her husband.

"Happy birthday," Lydia whispered.

"Dearly beloved," the vicar said.

By the time they came out of the vestry after signing the register, with Mrs. Bailey and Gil signing as witnesses, the members of the congregation were no longer sitting in their pews, speaking in hushed, reverential whispers, but were on their feet, talking and moving about.

His mother, Harry saw, was hugging Mr. Winterbourne, while Marcel and Joel were shaking the hands of his sons. But there was little chance to notice details, for as soon as he appeared, his bride on his arm, the church erupted in a most indecorous, irreverent burst of applause.

Lydia laughed.

Harry grinned.

Almost immediately they were engulfed in hugs and kisses and handshakes and backslappings and . . . And really everything was very much as Harry remembered Jessica and Gabriel's wedding to have been two years ago in a small London church. Except that it felt different when one was the bridegroom instead of just a family member, and when it was one's bride—one's *wife*—who was being enfolded in the arms of Aunt Matilda and then sobbed over by her father. And when one was oneself being hugged and laughed over by two sisters who had once upon a time thought him lower on the scale of living beings than a toad, and then by a third sister who told him she loved him more than she could possibly say. And then clutched to the bosom of first one grandmother and then the other. And having his arm squeezed by a radiantly smiling Winifred.

He bent down to allow Josephine to wrap her arms about his neck and kiss his cheek and noticed that Lydia was doing the same for Alice and Sarah.

By the time Harry was able to reclaim his bride and take her arm through his to lead her from the church, he was aware that a number of the younger people, including all the children, had disappeared, and he knew what was awaiting them outside. But how absolutely *splendid* it felt to be the bridegroom and about to be the victim instead of the perpetrator—which he had been numerous times.

"Well, Mrs. Westcott," he said as they approached the doors. "Are you ready to face the ordeal?"

"Oh, Harry," she said, turning her head to smile at him—and all the sunshine was *still* there inside her and beaming out from her eyes and her whole face. Had she left any outside, or was it all dark and gloomy out there? "I am, am I not? I am Lydia Westcott."

The crowd beyond the gate had surely swelled since his arrival with Gil, Harry noticed. There was a crowd inside the gate too. The church path was lined with them on both sides —all the children over the age of about five, Cousins Peter and Ivan, Adrian Sawyer, Sally Underwood. And—a grinning Tom Corning.

All of them, of course, had fistfuls of flower petals. Some of the older ones had bags bulging with extra supplies.

And there was plenty of sunshine too.

"Oh," Lydia said, and laughed.

Harry released her arm and took her hand in his instead. He laced their fingers tightly. "They will all be horribly disappointed if we do not run for it," he said. "Ready?"

And they dashed along the path, pelted from all sides, Harry laughing, Lydia shrieking and laughing until they were through the gate, which someone had been kind enough to open for them. But Lydia stopped abruptly.

"Oh," she said. "Oh, Harry, *look*."

Her eyes were wide with wonder as she beheld the flower-bedecked carriage. It had been decorated early this morning. Harry had come to church in it. He would wager the fortune that was about to be his, however, that since then it had been further decorated—on its underside.

And then they were inside it and the door had been shut upon them. The congregation was spilling out of the church, the church bell began to ring, and the carriage moved away from the gate—to an unholy din from all the debris that had been fastened below it.

"Oh," Lydia said again. At least, her mouth formed the word, though Harry could not hear the sound of it. He set an arm about her shoulders, cupped the side of her face with his other hand, and kissed her.

It was only as he did so and her arm came about him that he realized that had been a cheering, *friendly* crowd. Those who were hostile to Lydia and perhaps him too had maybe not come to watch the show, of course. Or maybe some of them were realizing that there had been no scandal at all. Only a blossoming romance.

He drew back his head and gazed into Lydia's eyes. "I love you," he said.

She laughed and cupped a hand about her ear. *"What?"*

There was obviously no point in trying to hold any sort of conversation. Harry kissed his bride again. And if they were not both stone-deaf by the time they reached the house, it would be some sort of miracle.

Snowball welcomed Lydia back to her cottage in the middle of the afternoon with ecstatic yips and barks and bounced about Harry with only slightly less enthusiasm.

There had been a grand wedding breakfast at Hinsford, despite Harry's plea yesterday that there be no such thing because his staff would be quite busy enough with preparations for the ball this evening. He might as well have saved his breath and accepted the fact that his authority had counted for precisely nothing since the arrival of his family one week ago. He was assured, though, that this evening's banquet, planned to take place early, before outside guests began arriving for the ball, had been merely moved forward, with a few modifications, and they would all just peck at the leftovers before the evening's celebrations.

Harry could not imagine the Westcotts *pecking* at any meal, but he would not be there to witness what exactly that would mean. After a sumptuous feast, followed by wedding cake—yes, his intrepid cook had doubtless remained up all night to produce one, as Harry remembered she had for Abby and Gil's wedding—and champagne, toasts, and speeches, everyone needed to prepare for the ball, even if preparing consisted only of resting for an hour or so. Harry could only imagine the frenzy of activity going on belowstairs.

He and Lydia had headed for her cottage—on foot. His valet was going to come there later with his evening clothes—including one of his new London shirts—and all the rest of the paraphernalia necessary to make him presentable for the ball.

"But not for at least three hours yet," he said, turning to Lydia after the dog had returned from a leisurely frolic in the garden and was noisily lapping water in the kitchen. "That is a wicked smile, Lydia."

"And is that a *leer* I see on your face?" she asked him.

"It is," he said.

They were in each other's arms then, laughing and kissing—until they were doing neither, but were simply gazing into each other's eyes, their foreheads touching.

"Mrs. Westcott," he murmured.

"Yes."

"I like the sound of it," he said.

"Because you now own me?" she asked.

"I positively refuse to quarrel on my wedding day," he said. "Ask me again tomorrow."

They both laughed.

"Lydia." He rubbed his nose against hers. "I did not rush you too much?"

"Rush?" she said. "Harry. This has been the longest week of my life. Someone must have stopped all the clocks. I thought today would never come."

"I wish someone would stop the clocks for the next three hours," he said. "But since no one is going to, *why* are we standing here? Could we not find something better to do?"

"I will leave you to answer that," she said. "I might blush."

He drew back his head a little. "You are already doing it," he said, smiling slowly at her.

She proved his point.

"Lydia."

But he could find no words to express the feelings that were welling up inside him. He scooped her up in his arms instead and carried her through to her bedchamber—*their* bedchamber for now and tonight and perhaps the next few nights until their house guests had returned to their own homes. He had no idea what would happen to the cottage then. They had not had a chance to discuss it. But that discussion could wait. They had a lifetime in which to decide.

For now—for this moment and the next three hours—there was only one thing that mattered.

"Home," he said, setting her down on her feet beside the bed. "Here. Hinsford. You. Me. Do you wonder I can never remember a whole speech?"

She laughed softly. "And very thankful I am for it at the moment," she said. "Make love with me, Harry."

He did that for the next three hours. Or, rather, they did.

With me, she had said.

Not *to me*, but *with me*.

Twenty-five

※

The morning of Harry's birthday, which was to have been filled with all sorts of frenzied last-minute preparations for the birthday ball, was given over instead to the totally unexpected matter of a wedding to attend. The Westcott ladies might have been forgiven if they had thrown up their hands in despair as they contemplated disaster to their carefully crafted plan B. They were, however, made of sterner stuff and *adapted*.

The cold luncheon that had been planned for the noon hour was replaced by a grand wedding breakfast. Heart palpitations had been averted, however, when Elizabeth had suggested that they simply move the preball banquet forward by a few hours. The champagne that would have been used to toast Harry would now be used to toast the newlyweds *and* Harry.

"Alexander and Avery make speeches in the House of Lords all the time," the dowager countess had reminded them. "They can make speeches at the breakfast. Gil too, since he is to be Harry's best man. And Marcel or Joel might wish to say a few words too."

"Or Viola or Camille or Abigail," Wren had added, a twinkle in her eye. "Or Anna."

The wedding cake, magnificently iced, had been purely the initiative of Harry's cook and had taken them all by surprise.

Plans for the evening had been changed too. Harry was to have stood in the receiving line with his mother and his three sisters, greeting the outside guests as they arrived and allowing them all a moment to wish him a happy birthday. Harry and Camille were to have led off the dancing with a country set. There was to have been another toast to Harry at the late supper and the cutting of the birthday cake.

Harry was no longer to be in the receiving line. He was, in fact, to be nowhere in sight until after everyone else had arrived. The entry of the new Mr. and Mrs. Harry Westcott was to be an Event in itself—Matilda wrote it on her new planning list with a capital letter. And the dancing was to begin not with a country set but with a *waltz*—to be danced for the first few minutes by the bride and groom alone.

"Could there be anything more romantic?" Mary Kingsley had asked with a sigh.

"Nothing in the world, Mary," Viola had said, and looked dreamy-eyed for a moment until Matilda brought them back to order by asking who should announce the arrival of the bridal couple.

Alexander had been appointed in his absence.

And so it was that well before the middle of the evening, the small ballroom at Hinsford Manor, decorated to resemble the most lavish of gardens, was packed with family, house guests, villagers, neighboring gentry, and tenants.

Viola and Marcel and her daughters and Anna and their husbands no longer stood in the receiving line. But the dancing had not yet begun, for everyone still awaited the arrival of the bride and groom. The orchestra, instruments tuned and ready, awaited instructions.

"And so," Estelle Lamarr said to her twin, "the last of our stepsiblings is married. And that leaves only us, Bertrand."

He draped an arm loosely about her shoulders and grinned at her. "Do I detect a wistful note in your voice, Stell?" he asked.

They were in their middle twenties, both still single. They had mingled with society for a number of years, both of them with a great deal of success—they were, after all, the children of the Marquess of Dorchester, and both were darkly handsome. But two years ago they had decided to retire together to the country home where they had grown up with an aunt and uncle; no one lived there now but the two of them and their servants. Both felt the need to do some reflecting before moving on with their lives.

"You must admit," Estelle said, "that there is something very . . . affecting about a romance. And a wedding."

He chuckled. "I admit nothing."

Camille, half hiding behind Joel in order to push back into her elaborate and very elegant coiffure an errant lock—the usual one—that had broken ranks with its fellows to fall down over her shoulder, sighed audibly.

"Can we possibly have been married for *nine years*?" she asked him.

"Does it feel more like ninety some days?" he asked.

She laughed and nudged him with her elbow. "It seems like yesterday," she said. "Bath Abbey. Was it not the most wonderful wedding ever?"

"I could point out a few couples in this very room who might disagree," he said. "But yes, it was. Indisputably. And it is a good thing we *have* been married that long when you stop to count our children."

"Are we not the most fortunate couple in the world?" She beamed at him.

"We are." He smiled at her. "Here, Camille, let me fix your hair for you."

Colin, Lord Hodges, tucked Elizabeth's arm beneath his as she turned away from her mother. "You are happy?" he asked her.

"I am," she said. "I was worried about Harry. We all were. He seemed so . . . lost after he came home from Paris. We would all have given the world to help him, but it is never quite enough, is it? It is sometimes so hard to help other people."

"I think you all did—*we* all did—the only thing we could do," he told her. "We gave him love and we gave him space."

"Space," she said. "Sometimes it is the hardest thing to give. Why are you so wise?"

He chuckled. "Perhaps because I am married to you and have caught it from you?" he suggested, provoking answering laughter from her.

Alexander and Wren were standing close to the orchestra dais so Alexander could hop up onto it as soon as Brown, Harry's butler, appeared in the doorway to give the signal.

"Do you think Harry has finally and fully forgiven you for taking his title?" Wren asked.

"I think he has." He smiled down at her. "I think he did it with his intellect a long time ago. I believe he has done it with his heart more recently. Just as I have forgiven him for loading my life down with such helpless guilt."

"Oh, Alex," she said. "I do love you."

"Exactly as much as I love you," he said.

Winifred, at her first ever ball, dressed all in white with her hair prettily styled by her mother's maid, was wondering if she looked foolish or if it was just that she was feeling very, very self-conscious. She glanced gratefully at young Gordon Monteith, who had come to stand beside her and compliment her on her appearance before turning as red as a beetroot. She was grateful for his blushes and his freckles and the spots that had broken out on his chin. Bertrand Lamarr—the *gorgeous* Bertrand—had complimented her earlier with great kindness and courtliness of manner, and she had almost crumpled into a heap of stammers and terror.

Three plushly upholstered chairs with arms had been placed side by side along the far wall of the ballroom for the comfort of the Dowager Countess of Riverdale in the middle, and Mrs. Monteith and Mrs. Kingsley on either side of her.

"They look a bit like thrones," Thomas, Lord Molenor, commented to his wife and her sisters.

"The queen and her princesses," Charles, Viscount Dirkson, his brother-in-law, agreed.

"That is horribly disrespectful, Charles," Matilda scolded before laughing.

"Well," her husband said, "I was going to call the other two *attendants*, my love, but that seemed definitely disrespectful."

"Mama *does* fancy herself as something of a queen," Mildred said. "She was very hard on Mrs. Tavernor—on *Lydia*—just a few days ago. Is she here on sufferance tonight, do you think?"

"Mildred!" Louise said, all amazement. "Mama *adores* anyone who stands up to her."

"As I know from personal experience," Charles said with a grin.

"Yes." Matilda heaved a heartfelt sigh and then smiled fondly at him.

Mrs. Kingsley was looking toward the doors. The three chairs had been placed with a direct view across to them. "Harry deserves happiness more than anyone else I know," she said. "I am partial, of course, since he is my only grandson. *Will* he be happy with Lydia? I do hope so."

The dowager's tall pink and purple hair plumes nodded as she turned her head. *"Happy?"* she said. "He is over the moon. That was as clear as day this morning. So is she. And so they ought to be. It was extremely naughty of them to meet in that cottage when not a soul lives there with her unless you count that ball of fluff that calls itself a dog. Goodness knows *what* went on in there."

"But we can guess, Eugenia," her sister said. "Harry would have to be a dreadful slowtop for *nothing* to have gone on, and I do not believe he is a slowtop. Just as he was not this afternoon, I daresay."

Mrs. Kingsley looked a mite shocked. The dowager countess merely nodded her head and her plumes slowly.

Abigail and Gil were strolling about the room, stopping to exchange words with some of the guests. But they were between groups at the moment, and he covered her hand on his arm with his own.

"Do you feel any regret," he asked, moving his head closer to hers, "that we did not wait to do something like this four years ago?"

They had married in the village church and returned here for a wedding breakfast. But apart from Harry and the vicar and Mrs. Jenkins, there had been no guests. They had spent their wedding night here at the manor and then gone to London to convince a judge to release Katy from her grandparents' care into theirs.

"This is a lovely wedding," she said. "But it is Harry's, Gil. And Lydia's. Our wedding was ours. And it was perfect. I would not have had a single detail of it different."

"Even though there was no mention of love?" he asked her.

"Even though," she said. "We grew into love. And oh, it was worth every moment of the journey."

"Do you remember how angry you were with me the first time you saw me?" he asked her.

"Well," she said, "you *were* shirtless and chopping wood and looking for all the world like a servant who was taking unpardonable liberties by being so close to the house. And then you allowed Beauty to come galloping around the corner from the stables to attack me, and I saw my life flashing before my eyes."

"I should have called her Lamb," he said, grinning at her.

"Yes, you ought," she said, smiling back. "She *is* a bit of a lamb. She is all beauty, though. Gil, I *loved* our wedding day."

"So did I," he said.

They stopped to talk with Lydia's brothers and Lawrence Hill.

Boris and Audrey were standing in a group with Peter and Ivan and Fanny Leeson.

"And *this* is the family you are going to marry into," Ivan said, addressing his future sister-in-law. "Boris had no choice. Pete and I had no choice. We were *born* into it. You have made the free choice, Audrey. Are you *mad*?" He grinned cheekily at her.

"You can be quiet anytime you wish now, Ivan," Boris informed him cheerfully.

"Or he will plant you a facer," Peter said.

Fanny laughed.

"I cannot think of any family I would *rather* marry into," Audrey said. "Unless it were the Wayne family, your father's side."

"Good answer, my love," Boris said.

"And I really cannot wait for my own wedding day," she added.

Ivan made a gargoyle face and clutched his neck with both hands, threatening ruin to his neckcloth.

"I cannot take him into decent company without him disgracing me," Peter said, shaking his head.

"I am *so* glad we chose to come to London this year," Jessica was saying to Gabriel. "I missed Abby's wedding. *Everyone* did except Harry. I was never more vexed in my life. I would have hated to miss Harry's too. When I was a girl, you know, I thought it was most unfair that one ought not to marry one's first cousin. He was my absolute hero. I thought I would never meet anyone more handsome or more . . . dashing."

"And now, Jessie," Gabriel said, "you have squashed all my self-esteem."

She laughed. "Oh, that was when I was a very young *girl*," she said. "When I became a woman I met an insufferably arrogant man who informed me almost at our first meeting that he intended to marry me. *Informed* me. He did not bother to ask. But then I decided that I would marry him anyway because I discovered that he was . . full of *passion*."

"Hmm," he said. "Self-esteem restored."

She laughed again as Boris and Audrey came up to them and wanted to know what the joke was.

Avery, Duke of Netherby, was standing in what was always his favorite spot in any room—a corner. Gorgeously clad and sparkling with jewels on his fingers and in his elaborately tied neckcloth and embedded in the handle and about the rim of his quizzing glass, he gazed through the glass before lowering it. His posture was indolent, his eyes keen. He turned them upon Anna, who was beside him and sparkling, not so much with jewels as with bright animation.

"Happy, my love?" he asked with a soft fondness in his voice that might have surprised almost everyone else in the room, who saw only his public manner except upon very rare occasions.

Anna turned her eyes upon him, and they brightened with tears, though none spilled over.

"I still sometimes expect to wake up one of these days to find myself back in the classroom at the orphanage in Bath," she said.

"Please do not," he said. "I would miss you."

"Would you?" She smiled softly at him—one of the few people ever to look at him so.

"You would take my heart with you," he said. "And my very life."

"Oh," she said.

"Not to mention my unborn child," he added.

"I looked at you ten years ago," she said, "and hated you on sight."

"I know," he said with a sigh. "And how could I resist the challenge? I could not—despite those shoes. I had to have you."

His eyes gazed lazily into hers until something distracted him.

"Ah," he said, nodding toward the ballroom doors. "I believe the bride and groom must be in the house."

Anna turned her head to see Viola and Marcel slip from the room.

"I *am* happy," she said. "You asked, Avery. The answer is yes."

"I can see it in your eyes, my heart," he said softly.

Viola had deliberately stayed close to the ballroom doors so the butler could give her the nod from beyond them when Harry arrived with Lydia.

"I want to be the first to see them and hug them," she had told Marcel, who had waited with her. "I missed Abby's wedding. I do not want to miss one moment of Harry's."

She did, however, beckon Lydia's father before she left the room. He was talking with the Hills and Elizabeth and Colin.

"And so all your children are happily settled," Marcel said, offering his arm to escort her downstairs. "Now you can relax at last."

"They *will* be happy," Viola said, smiling at him. "I liked Lydia the moment I met her. I knew she was right for Harry as soon as I learned she had refused his marriage offer."

Marcel laughed. "The logic of women," he said.

"And your two," she said. "Estelle and Bertrand. Do you worry about them, Marcel?"

She knew he did, of course, for she knew he had never quite let go of his guilt over the way he had neglected them during their growing years, leaving them almost exclusively in the care of their aunt, his first wife's sister, after his wife's accidental death when the twins were still babies.

"Not at all," he said. "They are amazingly strong people. I am prouder of them than I deserve to be. They will each find their happiness when the time is right. You are *not* to start worrying about them on my behalf, Viola. Or on theirs."

"Do I do that all the time?" she asked him.

"It is one thing I love about you," he said. "You are everything but selfish. I, on the other hand, am unabashedly selfish. I want you all to myself."

"You do not," she said. "You may think I am all that matters to you, but you value family as much as I do. Perhaps more, because you came near to losing your own."

"I love you very much," he said.

"I know." She flashed him another smile. "You told me so last night."

"Ah," he said, "last night . . ."

But they were downstairs, and here were Harry and Lydia, both of them flushed and bright-eyed and dressed very smartly indeed, Lydia in vibrant pink, Harry in a combination of silver, gray, and white and looking both old-fashioned in his knee breeches and quite gorgeous enough to make every other man in the ballroom look at him in envy and wish that fashions could be turned back a decade or two. And to make every woman look at him with envy for his bride.

Viola enfolded Lydia in her arms while Marcel shook Harry warmly by the hand and winked at him and Mr. Winterbourne reached the bottom of the stairs.

He opened his arms to Lydia and gathered her to him even as he reached out one hand to shake Harry's.

"I believe my Lydie is in good hands after all, my boy," he said. "Sons are a precious gift, but daughters are a treasure beyond price. Look after her."

Harry's eyes twinkled. "I will, sir," he promised. "Though I believe Lydia has plans to look after me."

Lydia slipped her hand through Harry's arm as they ascended the stairs to the ballroom. He held it to his side as he clasped her hand and laced their fingers.

"I am afraid," he said to her, "there is going to be no sneaking inside unnoticed."

"I do not mind," she said. "This is our wedding day. I want to savor every moment of it."

She had savored their wedding, impressing every detail upon her memory. She had done the same with their wedding breakfast. And with the afternoon of lovemaking, which had been wonderful beyond any imagining—and would be repeated tonight, Harry had promised her when it had been imperative that they get up before his valet arrived, bringing unexpectedly with him the marchioness's personal maid to help with her hair. She was going to savor the ball too, thankful that she had had the village assembly as a sort of rehearsal.

The sweet, heady scent of myriad flowers and perfumes met them as they reached the top of the stairs, as well as the sounds of numerous voices raised in conversation and laughter. Lydia's father and the Marquess and Marchioness of Dorchester slipped into the ballroom ahead of them, and Harry's butler—now her own too, Lydia supposed, a bit startled—indicated with one raised hand that the two of them should wait a moment and stepped into the doorway in order to nod regally in the direction of some unseen person.

A moment later there was a decisive chord from the orchestra, and the sound of conversation almost immediately faded away to silence. A single voice replaced it: the Earl of Riverdale's.

"Ladies and gentlemen," he said, "welcome to Hinsford and to the ball that is celebrating two events. Harry West-cott has arrived at his thirtieth birthday today. And he and Mrs. Lydia Tavernor were married this morning in the vil-lage church. Welcome Mr. and Mrs. Westcott now, if you please, and join me in wishing Harry a happy birthday."

The orchestra struck another chord while Lydia stepped with Harry into the doorway and through it into the ball-room, to be met with a chorus of birthday greetings and applause.

Just a week ago, Lydia thought, she had come close to being made a pariah. There was no sign of it tonight. And perhaps the danger had always been far less than it had seemed at the time, and confined to just one element of the village. But she would not think of that again tonight—or ever again if she could help it.

She smiled about her while Harry's hand gripped hers and her hand gripped Harry's, and saw her brothers across the room with Hannah and Tom Corning. She saw Denise Franks with her husband, and the Reverend and Mrs. Bai-ley, and all of Harry's family, most of whom she could now name without having to stop too long to connect a name with a face. She saw her father standing with Harry's aunt Louise, the Dowager Duchess of Netherby.

She had never been happier in her life.

The orchestra played another chord and silence fell again.

"The ball will begin with a waltz," the Earl of Riverdale announced, "to be danced by Mr. and Mrs. Westcott. Step forward onto the floor, please, Lydia and Harry. It is all yours."

"Oh dear," Lydia said.

Harry had turned his head and was grinning down at her. "I will try my very best," he said, raising his voice so almost everyone would hear, "not to tread upon my wife's toes."

Oh.

"And I will very definitely," Lydia said, matching Harry's voice in volume, "keep them from being trodden upon."

"That is telling you, Harry," a voice called out—Tom's— amid general laughter.

And then they were standing on what seemed a vast expanse of empty ballroom floor while the laughter faded and very little conversation took its place. Harry released her hand, and she withdrew her arm from his so they could stand face-to-face. His eyes, smiling, burning, looked steadily into hers as he set one hand behind her waist and took her right hand in the other. She set her left hand on his shoulder.

And the music began.

Oh, brave words that she would keep her feet from beneath his when both her legs felt as though they were made of wood, and if she had ever known how to waltz, all memory of the steps and the rhythm had fled without a trace, and at least a million eyes were riveted upon her.

"My love," Harry said softly, "it is our wedding day. Here and now. Our happily-ever-after is beginning. And you are my someone to cherish every moment for the rest of our lives. My darling."

He had sensed her sudden fright. Oh, how foolish to be afraid. This *was* her wedding day. She was Harry's love, just as he was hers. And he had called her, for the first time ever, his darling. No one had ever called her that before now.

Lydia smiled at him.

And suddenly her legs were her own again, and *of course* she knew the steps of the waltz, and he was the partner of her dreams. Literally. Of her dreams.

Harry twirled her about one corner of the ballroom floor, drawing her closer to him as he did so, and Lydia tilted back her head and laughed.

The waltz was without any doubt the loveliest dance ever invented.

She was Harry's *darling*.

Ah, and she was his cherished *someone* for all the rest of their days.

As he was hers.

READ ON FOR AN EXCERPT FROM THE FIRST BOOK
IN MARY BALOGH'S WESTCOTT SERIES,

Someone to Love

AVAILABLE NOW FROM JOVE

Despite the fact that the late Earl of Riverdale had died without having made a will, Josiah Brumford, his solicitor, had found enough business to discuss with his son and successor to be granted a face-to-face meeting at Westcott House, the earl's London residence on South Audley Street. Having arrived promptly and bowed his way through effusive and obsequious greetings, Brumford proceeded to find a great deal of nothing in particular to impart at tedious length and with pompous verbosity.

Which would have been all very well, Avery Archer, Duke of Netherby, thought a trifle peevishly as he stood before the library window and took snuff in an effort to ward off the urge to yawn, if he had not been compelled to be here too to endure the tedium. If Harry had only been a year older—he had turned twenty just before his father's death— then Avery need not be here at all and Brumford could prose on forever and a day as far as he was concerned.

By some bizarre and thoroughly irritating twist of fate, however, His Grace had found himself joint guardian of the new earl with the countess, the boy's mother.

It was all remarkably ridiculous in light of Avery's notoriety for indolence and the studied avoidance of anything that might be dubbed work or the performance of duty. He had a secretary and numerous other servants to deal with all the tedious business of life for him. And there was also the fact that he was a mere eleven years older than his ward. When one heard the word *guardian*, one conjured a mental image of a gravely dignified graybeard. However, it seemed he had inherited the guardianship to which his father had apparently agreed—in writing—at some time in the dim distant past when the late Riverdale had mistakenly thought himself to be at death's door. By the time he did die a few weeks ago, the old Duke of Netherby had been sleeping peacefully in his own grave for more than two years and was thus unable to be guardian to anyone. Avery might, he supposed, have repudiated the obligation since he was not the Netherby mentioned in that letter of agreement, which had never been made into a legal document anyway. He had not done so, however. He did not dislike Harry, and really it had seemed like too much bother to take a stand and refuse such a slight and temporary inconvenience.

It felt more than slight at the moment. Had he known Brumford was such a crashing bore, he might have made the effort.

"There really was no need for Father to make a will," Harry was saying in the sort of rallying tone one used when repeating oneself in order to wrap up a lengthy discussion that had been moving in unending circles. "I have no brothers. My father trusted that I would provide handsomely for my mother and sisters according to his known wishes, and of course I will not fail that trust. I will certainly see to it too that most of the servants and retainers on all my properties are kept on and that those who leave my employ for whatever reason —Father's valet, for example—are properly compensated. And you may rest assured that my mother and Netherby will see that I do not stray from these obligations before I arrive at my majority."

He was standing by the fireplace beside his mother's chair in a relaxed posture, one shoulder propped against the mantel, his arms crossed over his chest, one booted foot on the hearth. He was a tall lad and a bit gangly, though a few more years would take care of that deficiency. He was fair-haired and blue-eyed, with a good-humored countenance that very young ladies no doubt found impossibly handsome. He was also almost indecently rich. He was amiable and charming and had been running wild during the past several months, first while his father was too ill to take much notice and again during the couple of weeks since the funeral. He had probably never lacked for friends, but now they abounded and would have filled a sizable city, perhaps even a small county, to overflowing. Though perhaps *friends* was too kind a word to use for most of them. *Sycophants* and *hangers-on* would be better.

Avery had not tried intervening, and he doubted he would. The boy seemed of sound enough character and would doubtless settle to a bland and blameless adulthood if left to his own devices. And if in the meanwhile he sowed a wide swath of wild oats and squandered a small fortune, well, there were probably oats to spare in the world and there would still be a vast fortune remaining for the bland adulthood. It would take just too much effort to intervene, anyway, and the Duke of Netherby rarely made the effort to do what was inessential or what was not conducive to his personal comfort.

"I do not doubt it for a moment, my lord." Brumford bowed from his chair in a manner that suggested he might at last be conceding that everything he had come to say had been said and perhaps it was time to take his leave. "I trust Brumford, Brumford & Sons may continue to represent your interests as we did your dear departed father's and his father's before him. I trust His Grace and Her Ladyship will so advise you."

Avery wondered idly what the other Brumford was like and just how many young Brumfords were included in the "& Sons." The mind boggled.

Harry pushed himself away from the mantel, looking hopeful. "I see no reason why I would not," he said. "But I will not keep you any longer. You are a very busy man, I daresay."

"I will, however, beg for a few minutes more of your time, Mr. Brumford," the countess said unexpectedly. "But it is a matter that does not concern you, Harry. You may go and join your sisters in the drawing room. They will be eager to hear details of this meeting. Perhaps you would be good enough to remain, Avery."

Harry directed a quick grin Avery's way, and His Grace, opening his snuffbox again before changing his mind and snapping it shut, almost wished that he too were being sent off to report to the countess's two daughters. He must be very bored indeed. Lady Camille Westcott, age twenty-two, was the managing sort, a forthright female who did not suffer fools gladly, though she was handsome enough, it was true. Lady Abigail, at eighteen, was a sweet, smiling, pretty young thing who might or might not possess a personality. To do her justice, Avery had not spent enough time in her company to find out. She was his half sister's favorite cousin and dearest friend in the world, however— her words—and he occasionally heard them talking and giggling together behind closed doors that he was very careful never to open.

Harry, all eager to be gone, bowed to his mother, nodded politely to Brumford, came very close to winking at Avery, and made his escape from the library. Lucky devil. Avery strolled closer to the fireplace, where the countess and Brumford were still seated. What the deuce could be important enough that she had voluntarily prolonged this excruciatingly dreary meeting?

"And how may I be of service to you, my lady?" the solicitor asked.

The countess, Avery noticed, was sitting very upright, her spine arched slightly inward. Were ladies taught to sit that way, as though the backs of chairs had been created merely to be decorative? She was, he estimated, about forty years old. She was also quite perfectly beautiful in a mature, dignified sort of way. She surely could not have been happy with Riverdale—who could?—yet to Avery's knowledge she had never indulged herself with lovers. She was tall, shapely, and blond with no sign yet, as far as he could see, of any gray hairs. She was also one of those rare women who looked striking rather than dowdy in deep mourning.

"There is a girl," she said, "or, rather, a woman. In Bath, I believe. My late husband's . . . daughter."

Avery guessed she had been about to say *bastard*, but had changed her mind for the sake of gentility. He raised both his eyebrows and his quizzing glass.

Brumford for once had been silenced.

"She was at an orphanage there," the countess continued. "I do not know where she is now. She is hardly still there since she must be in her middle twenties. But Riverdale supported her from a very young age and continued to do so until his death. We never discussed the matter. It is altogether probable he did not know I was aware of her existence. I do not know any details, nor have I ever wanted to. I still do not. I assume it was not through you that the support payments were made?"

Brumford's already florid complexion took on a distinctly purplish hue. "It was not, my lady," he assured her. "But might I suggest that since this . . . person is now an adult, you—"

"No," she said, cutting him off. "I am not in need of any suggestion. I have no wish whatsoever to know anything about this woman, even her name. I certainly have no wish for my son to know of her. However, it seems only just that if she has been supported all her life by her . . . father, she be informed of his death if that has not already happened, and be compensated with a final settlement. A handsome one, Mr. Brumford. It would need to be made perfectly clear to her at the same time that there is to be no more— ever, under any circumstances. May I leave the matter in your hands?"

"My lady." Brumford seemed almost to be squirming in his chair. He licked his lips and darted a glance at Avery, of whom—if His Grace was reading him correctly—he stood in considerable awe.

Avery raised his glass all the way to his eye. "Well?" he said. "*May* her ladyship leave the matter in your hands, Brumford? Are you or the other Brumford or one of the sons willing and able to hunt down the bastard daughter, name unknown, of the late earl in order to make her the happiest of orphans by settling a modest fortune upon her?"

"Your Grace." Brumford's chest puffed out. "My lady. It will be a difficult task, but not an insurmountable one, especially for the skilled investigators whose services we engage in the interests of our most valued clients. If the . . . person indeed grew up in Bath, we will identify her. If she is still there, we will find her. If she is no longer there—"

"I believe," Avery said, sounding pained, "her ladyship and I get your meaning. You will report to me when the woman has been found. Is that agreeable to you, Aunt?"

The Countess of Riverdale was not, strictly speaking, his aunt. His stepmother, the duchess, was the late Earl of Riverdale's sister, and thus the countess and all the others were his honorary relatives.

"That will be satisfactory," she said.

Anna Snow had been brought to the orphanage in Bath when she was not quite four years old. She had no real memory of her life before that beyond a few brief and disjointed flashes—of someone always coughing, for example, or of a lych-gate that was dark and a bit frightening inside whenever she was called upon to pass through it alone, and of kneeling on a window ledge and looking down upon a graveyard, and of crying inconsolably inside a carriage while someone with a gruff, impatient voice told her to hush and behave like a big girl.

She had been at the orphanage ever since, though she was now twenty-five. Most of the other children there—there were usually about forty of them—left when they were fourteen or fifteen, after suitable employment had been found for them. But Anna had lingered on, first to help out as housemother to a dormitory of girls and a sort of secretary to Miss Ford, the matron, and then as the schoolteacher when Miss Rutledge, the teacher who had taught her, married a clergyman and moved away to Devonshire. She was even paid a modest salary. However, the expenses of her continued stay at the orphanage, now in a small room of her own, were still provided by the unknown benefactor who had paid them from the start. She had been told that they would continue to be paid as long as she remained.

Anna considered herself fortunate. She had grown up in an orphanage, it was true, with not even a full identity to call her own, since she did not know who her parents were, but in the main it was not a charity institution. Almost all her fellow orphans were supported through their growing years by someone—usually anonymous, though some knew who they were and why they were there. Usually it was because their parents had died and there was no other family member able or willing to take them in. Anna did not dwell upon the loneliness of not knowing her own story. Her material needs were taken care of. Miss Ford and her staff were generally kind. Most of the children were easy enough to get along with, and those who were not could be avoided. A few were close friends, or had been during her growing years. If there had been a lack of love in her life, or of that type of love one associated with a family, then she did not particularly miss it, having never consciously known it.

Or so she always told herself.

She was content with her life and was only occasionally restless with the feeling that surely there ought to be more, that perhaps she should be making a greater effort to *live* her life. She had been offered marriage by three different men—the shopkeeper where she went occasionally, when she could afford it, to buy a book; one of the governors of the orphanage, whose wife had recently died and left him with four young children; and Joel Cunningham, her life-long best friend. She had rejected all three offers for varying reasons and wondered sometimes if it had been foolish to do so, as there were not likely to be many more offers, if any. The prospect of a continuing life of spinsterhood sometimes seemed dreary.

Joel was with her when the letter arrived.

She was tidying the schoolroom after dismissing the children for the day. The monitors for the week—John Davies and Ellen Payne—had collected the slates and chalk and the counting frames. But while John had stacked the slates neatly on the cupboard shelf allotted for them and put all the chalk away in the tin and replaced the lid, Ellen had shoved the counting frames haphazardly on top of paintbrushes and palettes on the bottom shelf instead of arranging them in their appointed place side by side on the shelf above so as not to bend the rods or damage the beads. The reason she had put them in the wrong place was obvious. The second shelf was occupied by the water pots used to swill paint brushes and an untidy heap of paint-stained cleaning rags.

"Joel," Anna said, a note of long suffering in her voice, "could you at least try to get your pupils to put things away where they belong after an art class? And to clean the water pots first? Look! One of them even still has water in it. Very *dirty* water."

Joel was sitting on the corner of the battered teacher's desk, one booted foot braced on the floor, the other swinging free. His arms were crossed over his chest. He grinned at her.

"But the whole point of being an artist," he said, "is to be a free spirit, to cast aside restricting rules and draw inspiration from the universe. My job is to teach my pupils to be true artists."

She straightened up from the cupboard and directed a speaking glance his way. "What utter rot and nonsense," she said.

He laughed outright. "Anna, Anna," he said. "Here, let me take that pot from you before you burst with indignation or spill it down your dress."

But before he could say anything more, the classroom door was flung open without the courtesy of a knock to admit Bertha Reed, a thin, flaxen-haired fourteen-year-old who acted as Miss Ford's helper now that she was old enough. She was bursting with excitement and waving a folded paper in one raised hand.

"There is a letter for you, Miss Snow," she half shrieked. "It was delivered by special messenger from London and Miss Ford would have brought it herself but Tommy is bleeding all over her sitting room and no one can find Nurse Jones. Maddie punched him in the nose."

"It is high time someone did," Joel said, strolling closer to Anna. "I suppose he was pulling one of her braids again."

Anna scarcely heard. A letter? From London? By special messenger? For *her*?

"Whoever can it be from, Miss Snow?" Bertha screeched, apparently not particularly concerned about Tommy and his bleeding nose. "Who do you know in London? No, don't tell me—that ought to have been *whom*. *Whom* do you know in London? I wonder what they are writing about. And it came by *special messenger*, all that way. It must have cost a *fortune*. Oh, do open it."

Her blatant inquisitiveness might have seemed imperti-nent, but really, it was so rare for any of them to receive a letter that word always spread very quickly and everyone wanted to know all about it. Occasionally someone who had left both the orphanage and Bath to work elsewhere would write, and the recipient would almost invariably share the contents with everyone else. Such missives were kept as prized possessions and read over and over until they were virtually threadbare.

Anna did not recognize the handwriting, which was both bold and precise. It was a masculine hand, she felt sure. The paper felt thick and expensive. It did not look like a personal letter.

"Oliver is in London," Bertha said wistfully. "But I don't suppose it can be from him, can it? His writing does not look anything like that, and why would he write to you anyway? The four times he has written since he left here, it was to me. And he is not going to send any letter by special messenger, is he?"

Oliver Jamieson had been apprenticed to a bootmaker in London two years ago at the age of fourteen and had promised to send for Bertha and marry her as soon as he got on his feet. Twice each year since then he had faithfully written a five- or six-line letter in large, careful handwriting. Bertha had shared his sparse news on each occasion and wept over the letters until it was a wonder they were still legible. There were three years left in his apprenticeship before he could hope to be on his feet and able to support a wife. They were both very young, but the separation did seem cruel. Anna always found herself hoping that Oliver would remain faithful to his childhood sweetheart.

"Are you going to turn it over and over in your hands and hope it will divulge its secrets without your having to break the seal?" Joel asked.

Stupidly, Anna's hands were trembling. "Perhaps there is some mistake," she said. "Perhaps it is not for me."

He came up behind her and looked over her shoulder. "Miss Anna Snow," he said. "It certainly sounds like you. I do not know any other Anna Snows. Do you, Bertha?"

"I do not, Mr. Cunningham," she said after pausing to think. "But whatever can it be about?"

Anna slid her thumb beneath the seal and broke it. And yes, indeed, the paper was a thick, costly vellum. It was not a long letter. It was from Somebody Brumford—she could not read the first name, though it began with a J. He was a solicitor. She read through the letter once, swallowed, and then read it again more slowly.

"The day after tomorrow," she murmured.

"In a private chaise," Joel added. He had been reading over her shoulder.

"*What* is the day after tomorrow?" Bertha demanded, her voice an agony of suspense. "*What* chaise?"

Anna looked at her blankly. "I am being summoned to London to discuss my future," she said. There was a faint buzzing in her ears.

"Oh! By who?" Bertha asked, her eyes as wide as saucers. "By *whom*, I mean."

"Mr. J. Brumford, a solicitor," Anna said.

"Josiah, I think that says," Joel said. "Josiah Brumford. He is sending a private chaise to fetch you, and you are to pack a bag for at least a few days."

"To *London*?" Bertha's voice was breathless with awe.

"Whatever am I to do?" Anna's mind seemed to have stopped working. Or, rather, it *was* working, but it was whirring out of control, like the innards of a broken clock.

"What you are to do, Anna," Joel said, pushing a chair up behind her knees and setting his hands on her shoulders to press her gently down onto it, "is pack a bag for a few days and then go to London to discuss your future."

"But what future?" she asked.

"That is what is to be discussed," he pointed out.

The buzzing in her ears grew louder.

READ ON FOR AN EXCERPT FROM THE NEXT BOOK IN
MARY BALOGH'S WESTCOTT SERIES,

Someone Perfect

COMING IN 2021

England was not renowned for long runs of perfect summer days. This year so far even brief runs had been in lamentably short supply. It seemed something of a miracle, then, when the morning had dawned with the promise of being yet another lovely day. The second in a row.

By the middle of the afternoon, the sky was a deep indigo blue and cloudless. The air was hot without being oppressive—the merest hint of a breeze saw to that. It also caused the leaves to flutter on the trees and the water to ripple on the river. The grass on both sides of the river was green and lush after all the rain, and liberally strewn with daisies, buttercups, and clover. Birds trilled from among the thick foliage of the trees, though it was not always easy to see them. Unseen insects whirred and chirped in the grass.

So much life. So much beauty.

Lady Estelle Lamarr had been walking along the riverbank, but she stopped in order to fill all her senses with the perfection of the moment, wild nature at its most profuse and benign. Even the old single-arched stone bridge farther along seemed to be an integral part of the scene rather than a man-made intrusion upon it, just as a bird's nest or an ant-hill or a beaver dam would be. There surely could not possibly be anything to surpass the loveliness of the English countryside on a summer day. How very privileged she was to live here.

Yesterday she had fretted a little at being kept at home on a similar day by the impending departure of her uncle and aunt and cousin, who had all been staying at Elm Court for the past three weeks. Although Aunt Jane had talked of leaving early, by eight o'clock at the latest, it was actually after three in the afternoon by the time their carriage rolled out of sight down the drive and the chance to enjoy the outdoors had been virtually at an end.

First Uncle Charles had lingered over breakfast as though he had all day, deep in conversation with Bertrand, Estelle's twin brother. Then Ellen, their cousin, had decided she really ought to send a quick note to her fiancé to explain that their return home would be delayed because her mama had decided they must call upon friends who lived not far off their intended route, and those friends were bound to invite them to stay for a few days. The conversation finally at an end and Ellen's letter written, Aunt Jane was hopeful of a midmorning start. But that hope was dashed when the vicar arrived from the village and had been positively delighted to find that he had come in time to send the travelers on their way with a blessing.

The Reverend John Mott, a deeply pious man, was a longtime acquaintance of Aunt Jane's and a great favorite of hers. At her urging, the blessing had developed into ex-tended prayers and scripture readings in the sitting room and had been succeeded by a lengthy discussion, initiated by Aunt Jane, about the deteriorating moral fiber of the nation, especially its heedless youth. And since by then noon was fast approaching, Estelle had invited the vicar to join them all for a light luncheon that she had guessed—correctly—their cook was already preparing with feverish haste for six people instead of the two she had been planning for.

After the dishes had been cleared from the table and their second cup of coffee had been poured, the conversation had turned to a discussion of the uncertain future of the monarchy, since King George IV was in perennial ill health and the only heir closely related to him was a young girl, Victoria, daughter of the Duke of Kent. The other royal dukes had been prolific in the production of children, it was true, but not, unfortunately, of the legitimate variety. It was all quite scandalous, in Aunt Jane's opinion.

The carriage had been outside the door at three o'clock, had been fully loaded with its three passengers by quarter past, and had finally rolled on its way at half past, all the last-minute thanks and well wishes and reminders to do *this* and be sure to avoid doing *that* having been called out the window. By Aunt Jane, of course.

"So much for a perfect summer day," Estelle had said, turning to her brother—but with a twinkle in her eye. For of course she was exceedingly fond of her relatives and had actually enjoyed the day as it unfolded.

"All in a good cause," Bertrand had said. "We will miss them. There will be other lovely days to spend outdoors."

And sure enough, along had come the unexpected gift of today.

When she left the house earlier, Estelle had intended on walking all the way to Prospect Hall to call upon Maria

Wiley. The heat was giving her second thoughts by now, however. The hall was a mile or so beyond the bridge, on the other side of the river, and she had already walked more than a mile. She looked down at the wildflowers at her feet and stooped to rub a hand over the grass. It was dry. And blessedly cool to the touch. She changed her mind about going farther and sat down close to the river's edge. She arranged her skirts neatly about her legs and clasped her arms around her raised knees.

Aunt Jane would be horrified at such unladylike behavior, especially in a public place where anyone might come along at any moment and see her. Estelle smiled fondly at the thought. Aunt Jane and Uncle Charles had raised Bertrand and her. Their mother had died in a horrible accident before they were even a year old, and their father, overcome with grief and guilt over his conviction that he had caused their mother's death, had effectively disappeared from their lives except for brief, unsatisfactory visits twice a year or so. He had acquired an unsavory reputation as a rake, though they did not know that, of course, until much later.

He was back in their lives now and had been for the past eight years. Estelle loved him dearly, but that did not change the fact that their formative years, from one to seventeen, had been spent in the care of Aunt Jane, their mother's elder sister, and Uncle Charles. And in the company of Oliver and Ellen, their cousins, both older than they.

It had been a strict upbringing, with much emphasis upon duty and moral rectitude and self-discipline and piety. They had also been loved, though. But there had always been a gaping hole in their lives, partly because their mother was dead, though mainly because their father was not. They had longed and yearned for him, watched for him from the attic room of Elm Court, where they had lived through most of those years and lived again now. Yet whenever he had come, they had held themselves aloof from him, waiting and waiting for him to . . . to open his arms and his heart to them. Or give some other sign. Make the first move. *Stay.*

After he left, usually sooner than he had intended, they had hated him and wept for him—yes, Bertrand had wept too—and resolved to forget all about him, to cut him from their lives. Until, that was, they had found themselves in the attic again, watching for his return. Yearning for him.

Ah. Estelle shook her head. She had not intended to sink into *those* memories today of all days. Today was for simple enjoyment. Tomorrow there might be clouds and blustery winds and chill temperatures and rain again. *Three* days in a row was too much to hope for with any confidence this year. Today she was free to do whatever she wished. Much as she had loved having her aunt and uncle and Ellen to stay, she had, as always, felt constrained by their presence. As though she needed to be on her very best behavior every single moment. And to listen meekly to almost daily harangues—though no, that was unfair. *Harangues* was a negative word. Aunt Jane loved her and wanted the best for her—and *of* her. She gave *suggestions* now, and they were often sound advice.

Her aunt did not approve of Estelle's living at Elm Court alone, though Bertrand lived there too and they had always been extraordinarily close despite the fact that they were not, of course, identical twins. Estelle, in Aunt Jane's opinion, really ought to have a female companion living with her—just as Lady Maria Wiley of Prospect Hall did, and very proper too, though one could wish that her companion was a decade or so older than she was. It was bordering upon scandalous that Estelle did not have one at all. Aunt

Jane could not understand why the marchioness did not insist upon it. *The marchioness* was Estelle's stepmother of eight years, her father's second wife. He was the Marquess of Dorchester.

Estelle did not want a companion. Not a female one, anyway. She had Bertrand, and he was enough for her. For a few years, just before their father's marriage to Viola Kingsley and then afterward, they had lived at Redcliffe Court in Northamptonshire, where they had been taken after their father inherited the title and property. Two years ago, however, they had come back to Elm Court, just the two of them, having found themselves overwhelmed by the life of the *ton* into which they had been thrust—with great success, incidentally, and even some enjoyment, until suddenly it had been enjoyable no longer.

They had been in their twenties when it happened, an age at which Estelle at least ought to have been married, according to conventional wisdom. She had never really been tempted, however, though she liked a number of the eligible men she had met. Instead, she had wanted to . . . to *find* herself, for want of a clearer way to describe how she had felt. And of course it was how Bertrand had felt too. They so often thought alike about the important things.

So they had come back to Elm Court to live. Oh, not to become hermits. Far from it. Just this year, for example, they had gone to London for a few weeks of the Season and had proceeded from there to Hinsford Manor in Hampshire to celebrate the thirtieth birthday of Harry Westcott, their stepmother's son and therefore their stepbrother. It was a large family party that had turned unexpectedly into a celebration of Harry's wedding to Lydia Tavernor.

All of it had been thoroughly enjoyable—for both Estelle and her twin. But they had come back here well before the end of the Season. Sometimes Estelle wondered if they would grow old together here, to be known as *those weird and eccentric twins*. But life was ever changing. It was impossible to predict the future. She did not even want to try.

She sat in the sunshine. The heat felt very good. But . . . Well, it was really *quite* hot, and temptation beckoned in the form of the river. Poor Aunt Jane would have heart palpitations. But Aunt Jane was not here, was she? And there was no one else in sight to be scandalized. It was why Estelle always loved walking beside the river north of their property, in fact. No one else ever came here. The bridge, sturdy and picturesque though it was, was rarely used these days, now that the main road nearby had been widened and resurfaced and was far more convenient to travelers than the narrow, rutted track that crossed the bridge. Most people would naturally choose convenience and comfort over a scenic route.

Temptation was not to be resisted, Estelle decided at last, perhaps because she did not put up any great fight against it. She pulled off her shoes and set them neatly beside her, peeled off her stockings and pressed them into the shoes so they would not go wafting away in the breeze, folded the lower half of her skirt neatly over her knees so that some remnant of modesty would be preserved, and lowered her feet gingerly into the river. She gasped at the coldness of the water, but she lowered her legs farther, wiggling her toes as she did so, and found that they quickly adapted. And oh goodness, it felt delicious.

She swished her feet and laughed when a few splashes spread into dark circles on her dress and doubtless penetrated each fold of it. One droplet landed on the side of her nose. She brushed it away and dried her hand on her skirt. She felt herself relax as she brought the whole of her attention back to the scene around her—and in her. For of course she was part of the scene, right to the very core of her being. It was not a case of *her* and *it*. She actually *was* it, just as the birds were and the insects and the grass and the daisies, and that butterfly fluttering over a cluster of clover. This, she thought, was contentment. Even happiness. Just this. She wished Bertrand had come with her.

Her bonnet was protecting her head from the full force of the sun. The brim was shading her eyes and preventing her from acquiring a red and shiny nose, which her maid would cluck over with disapproval and Bertrand would laugh at. But just for a couple of minutes she wanted to feel it all—the brightness and the warmth. She pulled loose the ribbons beneath her chin and took off her bonnet. One of her hairpins caught in the bottom edge of it, and while she wrestled to free it a whole hank of hair came tumbling down over her shoulder. Bother! But it served her right. She set the bonnet on the grass, pulled out the rest of her hairpins, and dropped them carefully into the hat. She shook her head and combed her fingers through her hair in the hope of achieving something like smoothness. It was impossible, of course, since she did not have a brush with her, but so what? She had already decided that she would not go visiting.

A sense of delicious freedom welled up in her and spilled over in exuberance. She kicked her feet, careful not to splash herself again. She propped herself up with her hands spread on the grass behind her, tipped back her head so she could feel the sun on her face and cool air on the back of her neck, and closed her eyes.

This was pure bliss.

Until, that was, she became aware of someone panting—someone who was not her. And then she heard low, menacing growls. And then angry barking. Her eyes flew open and she whipped her head about to see a huge monster of a dog dashing toward her across the grass, all bared teeth and ferocity and flying spittle and giant paws. If Estelle had not been half paralyzed with terror, she might well have jumped screaming right into the river. Instead she sat up sharply, spread her hands before her face, palms out, fingers spread, and cried out. Something idiotic like "Good doggie," she thought afterward. By then she hoped fervently she had not actually said *doggie*.

"Heel, Captain!" The voice that snapped out the command came from somewhere behind Estelle. It was a harsh masculine voice—and instantly effective. The dog stopped in its tracks, a mere six feet from Estelle and towering over her. It growled menacingly once, tipped its head to one side, one brown ear flopping against its head, the other swinging free, black jowls quivering, black nose twitching, black eyes glaring death and destruction—and turned to trot back to where the voice had come from.

Estelle sucked in a deep breath of air, perhaps the first since she had heard the panting. She turned more fully, drawing her feet from the water at the same time, curling her legs under her, and pulling her skirt down over them. All a bit too late for modesty.

No one ever came this way. Well. *Almost* never.

He was astride a massive horse, an equally massive man, or so he appeared to Estelle from her vantage point close to the ground. Oh dear God, her hair was all about her in a half-tangled, untidy mass. Her dress was soggy and clinging to her bare legs. He, on the other hand, was immaculately clad for riding, a man with wide shoulders and broad chest and powerful-looking thighs. He was dark and dour of countenance, though the fact that his tall hat was pulled low over his brow and cast his face in shadow might account for at least part of that impression. His brown, black-faced bloodhound panted up at him as though awaiting the order to attack and kill.

He was some distance away from Estelle, holding his horse quite still while he regarded her in silence. He made no apology. He asked for no assurance that she was unharmed. He uttered no greeting of any sort. Except that even as she thought it he touched his whip to the brim of his hat and inclined his head perhaps an inch and a half in her direction. Then he rode down the track, across the bridge, in among the trees that lay beyond the bank on the other side, and disappeared.

After that one slight acknowledgment of her existence he had not once looked her way.

Well.

Estelle gaped after him. She was trembling, she realized. Her heart was still beating at what felt like double time. It pounded in her chest and sounded like a drumbeat in her ears. Her hands were tingling with pins and needles. Her teeth were chattering, though certainly not with cold despite the fact that her skirt was definitely wet and uncomfortable about her legs. Her hair felt like a jungle and probably looked like one. She felt foolish and humiliated despite the fact that he was a stranger and it was unlikely she would ever see him again. She also felt indignant and ruffled. Downright angry, in fact. How dared he have a vicious dog like that on the loose where it might attack any unwary person walking alone—or sitting with her feet dangling in the water—and tear her to shreds?

Her heart speeded up again if it was possible and made her feel quite faint for a moment. And how dared he not dismount from that monster of a horse and hurry to her assistance, all gentlemanly concern for her well-being? For all he knew, she might have swooned as soon as his back was turned and toppled into the water and drowned and floated away like Ophelia and eventually sunk, never to be seen or heard of again. At the very least he ought to have been abject in his apologies for frightening her. Instead, his silent stare had somehow put *her* at fault, as though she had upset his poor dog—had she *really* called him a doggie? *Captain!* Whoever had heard of calling a dog Captain?

So much for a perfect summer day.

It was ruined.

She wondered if she would tell Bertrand. She could narrate the encounter amusingly. He would laugh—*after* ascertaining that she had taken no real harm. But she would have nightmares for a *week*. Perhaps longer. Perhaps for the rest of her life. She was *still* breathless. She was almost whimpering. A butterfly fluttering past her face made her jump.

She pulled on her stockings, tried unsuccessfully again to comb her fingers all the way through her hair, gave up the struggle, and got to her feet. She pushed them into her shoes and made her way home, her bonnet dangling from the fingers of one hand, her hairpins tinkling around inside it.

Aunt Jane would need to be revived if she could see her now. Not, now that Estelle came to think of it, that she had ever seen her aunt swoon.

Justin Wiley, Earl of Brandon, was *not* in a good mood, and that was putting it mildly. He had no wish to go where he was going, was not looking forward to getting there, and was wondering even now if he should simply turn around and go back even though he had come a long way and was almost at his destination. He did *not*, then, appreciate a distraction on top of everything else, especially when it came in the form of a woman whom he had mistaken at first for a farm wench playing truant from her chores before realizing that she was far too finely clad to be anything but a lady. But a lady out *alone* in the middle of nowhere? With her hair in a dark, unruly cloud down her back and skirts up over her knees while her bare legs and feet dangled in the river?

The very sight of her had irritated him because of course he had reacted as any vigorous male would have in the circumstances—with a surge of sheer startled lust. *After* he had called off Captain, that was, and watched the woman try to contain her terror and at the same time make herself look more respectable. Her efforts had done the opposite by drawing attention to a heaving bosom and bare, shapely legs. And that wanton hair.

It had been a brief distraction, over in a matter of minutes as he rode across the stone bridge that spanned the river and in among the trees on the other side. But his already dark mood had been further ruffled, and he did not appreciate it one little bit. He had frightened a helpless woman—or at least Captain had, which was really the same thing since the dog was his. And he had reacted to her in an undisciplined, quite despicable way, even if he had not acted upon his baser instincts.

Prospect Hall must be close, within a mile or so anyway. That probably meant that the lady who was behaving with such scandalous disregard for propriety back there probably lived somewhere close. It was a fact that accused him, and he did not need more guilt heaped upon him.

For longer than a year now he had had the sole charge of his sister. He was her guardian, but had procrastinated in fulfilling his duty to her simply because she wanted nothing to do with him. He had respected her wishes while she was in mourning for her mother and had stayed away. And so he had perhaps exposed her to the bad influence of neighbors who did not know how to behave. Yet even now, when he had come at last to take charge, he was reluctant to complete his journey and was even tempted not to do so.

Good God, they might be acquaintances, that woman and his sister. *Half* sister, to be more precise. Perhaps they were even friends. It was true that Maria had Miss Vane as a companion for respectability and some protection. But he had never met Miss Vane and knew little about her except that she had once been Maria's governess. He really had been unpardonably derelict in his duty. Even while Maria's mother was still alive he had been his sister's official guardian after his father's death six years ago.

He had just this moment been deficient also in his duty as a gentleman, he realized with a sudden grimace. He had not apologized to that woman for frightening her or explained to her that Captain was far too well trained to attack anyone or any creature, in fact, without his master's say-so—which had never yet been given. Or that Cap was far too good-natured a dog to *want* to attack anyone. Doubtless he had been galloping up on the woman in the hope that she would allow him to slobber and pant all over her in exchange for a belly rub. It was distinctly to the dog's disadvantage that he was so large and fierce-looking with his giant paws and black face and wobbling jowls. And that his bark was deep and loud enough to wake the dead.

Justin had not even stopped long enough to assure himself that the woman had recovered from her fright. His dog had not gone within eight feet of her, but she might well be a vaporish sort. She might even now be stretched senseless upon the riverbank getting fried by the sun.

It was extremely unlikely.

But he resented the distraction and the way the incident had somehow put him in the wrong. He needed to concentrate his mind upon the coming encounter with his sister. Soon. A mile or so beyond the bridge, he had been told at the village he had passed through twenty minutes or so ago. A couple of miles all told. About three miles if he continued along the road, as he would have done if he had been traveling with his carriage. He had sent that by the road with his valet and his baggage and had taken the shorter route himself. Something he now regretted. So. Less than a mile to go.

Maria was the daughter of his father and his father's second wife, now deceased. She was fourteen years younger than Justin. He had not seen her for twelve years. She had been a child then, eight years old, thin and pale, with fine blond hair and big blue eyes, and he had adored her. And she him. But he had left home abruptly and been gone for six years before he inherited the title and properties and fortune upon the death of his father. One of his first acts as Earl of Brandon, before he went home to Everleigh Park, was to have the countess, his stepmother, and therefore her daughter too, sent here to Prospect Hall to live. It was one of his smaller properties, though the house was said to be a comfortable, attractive manor set in pretty grounds and run by a small but competent staff, most of whom had been here forever. Justin had never come in person.

His stepmother's health had broken down a year or two after the move and had deteriorated steadily over the following years. Her illness had become more and more debilitating, until by the end she could neither rise from her bed nor move her limbs nor speak. Even swallowing apparently had become well nigh impossible, according to the brief, very factual reports Miss Vane sent him twice a month. He had sent a physician from London and a few female nurses who had come highly recommended. Each of the nurses had been dismissed within a week. Maria had nursed her mother herself right up to the end. The countess had died a little more than a year ago, and Maria had been left alone with her companion. She would remain under Justin's guardianship until her twenty-fifth birthday or until she married—with his permission. Whichever came first.

His sister had been here, then, since she was fourteen, with a sick mother for three or four of those years. She had been in mourning during the year since her mother's death. One could only imagine the sort of hell she had lived through. Yet she had refused his summons, couched very carefully as an invitation, to return to Everleigh Park after the funeral and again a year later. On the latter occasion, just a couple of months ago, she had dictated her answer to Miss Vane, who had written it in her small, distinct handwriting.

Lady Maria Wiley must confess to a certain degree of puzzlement over the Earl of Brandon's invitation to return home. She is already at home. Unless, that is, his lordship should choose to assert his sole ownership of Prospect Hall and require her removal, in which case she will purchase a home of her own with the inheritance left her by her mother and thus free him of an inconvenience and herself of any future harassment.

He had read and reread the extraordinary letter with amazed incredulity. *Harassment?* Could she hate him so much? It was obvious she could and did.

Did she realize, though, that the money her mother had left her was in trust with him for another five years? Did she understand that he was her legal guardian?

He had thought himself hardened against everything life could possibly hurl his way. He had had long practice, after all. But Maria had found a small chink in his armor. She was all that was left of what he had once valued, of what he had once loved.

A long, long time ago.

A lifetime or two ago.

There was a cluster of cottages up ahead on one side of the track. A picturesque stone manor stood alone on the other side, set back some distance from the road within a large garden of lawns and trellises and roses and myriad other flowers. This must be Prospect Hall.

Even now he considered turning back or simply riding on by. Being hated wore upon one. He was, however, long inured to such pain. He turned onto the wide graveled pathway that led through an open gate and along beside the manor to a stable block behind and to one side of it.

He wondered if in her wildest nightmares Maria had expected him to come here in person to fetch her home. But she had given him no choice.

New York Times Bestselling Author

MARY
BALOGH

"One of the best!"

—#1 *New York Times* Bestselling Author
Julia Quinn

For a complete list of titles,
please visit prh.com/marybalogh